fushigi yûgi™

The Mysterious Play
VOL. 8: FRIEND

Story & Art By
YUU WATASE

FUSHIGI YÛGI
THE MYSTERIOUS PLAY
VOL. 8: FRIEND
SHÔJO EDITION

This volume contains the FUSHIGI YÛGI installments from Animerica Extra
Vol. 5, No. 7, through Vol. 6, No. 1, in their entirety.

STORY AND ART BY YUU WATASE

Editor's Note: At the author's request, the spelling of Ms. Watase's first name has been
changed from "Yû," as it has appeared on previous VIZ publications, to "Yuu."

English Adaptation/Yuji Oniki
Translation Assist/Kaori Kawakubo Inoue
Touch-up Art & Lettering/Andy Ristaino
Design/Hidemi Sahara
Editor (1st Edition)/William Flanagan
Editor (Shôjo Edition)/Yuki Takagaki

Managing Editor/Annette Roman
Director of Production/Noboru Watanabe
Vice President of Publishing/Alvin Lu
Sr. Director of Acquisitions/Rika Inouye
Vice President of Sales & Marketing/Liza Coppola
Publisher/Hyoe Narita

Printed in Canada.

Published by VIZ Media, LLC
P.O. Box 77010
San Francisco, CA 94107

First edition published April 2003

Shôjo Edition
10 9 8 7 6 5 4 3 2 1
First printing, September 2005

www.viz.com
store.viz.com

PARENTAL ADVISORY
FUSHIGI YÛGI is rated T+ for Older Teen and is
recommended for ages 16 and up. This volume
contains sexual situations and realistic violence.

CONTENTS

STORY THUS FAR

Fifteen-year-old Miaka and her best friend Yui are physically drawn into the world of a strange book—*THE UNIVERSE OF THE FOUR GODS*. Miaka is offered the role of the lead character, the Priestess of the god Suzaku, and is charged with a mission to save the nation of Hong-Nan, one that will ultimately grant her any wish. Yui, however, suffers rape and manipulation, which drive her to attempt suicide. Now, Yui has become the Priestess of the god Seiryu, the bitter enemy of Suzaku and Miaka.

The only way for Miaka to gain back the trust of her former best friend is to summon the god Suzaku and wish to be reconciled with Yui, so Miaka reenters the world of the book. The Seiryu Warriors ruined Miaka's first attempt to summon Suzaku, but the oracle Tai Yi-Jun has a new quest for Miaka and her Celestial Warriors—to obtain the treasures that will allow them to summon the god. On the way, a storm created by the Seiryu Warrior Soi forces Miaka's ship to be beached on a mysterious and dangerous island.

THE UNIVERSE OF THE FOUR GODS *is based on ancient Chinese legend, but Japanese pronunciation of Chinese names differs slightly from their Chinese equivalents. Here is a short glossary of the Japanese pronunciation of the Chinese names in this graphic novel:*

CHINESE	JAPANESE	PERSON OR PLACE	MEANING
Hong-Nan	Kônan	Southern Kingdom	Crimson South
Qu-Dong	Kutô	Eastern Kingdom	Gathered East
Bei-Jia	Hokkan	Northern Kingdom	Armored North
Tai Yi-Jun	Tai Itsukun	An Oracle	Preeminent Person
Shentso-Pao	Shinzahô	A Treasure	God's Seat Jewel
Nucheng-Kuo	Nyosei-koku	An Island Kingdom	Woman Fort Country
Hua-Wan	Kaen	A Woman	Flowery Grace
Dou	To	A Tribe	A Measure
Tomolu	Tomoru	An Elder	Earth Silent Duty
Teniao-Lan	Touran	A City	Unique Crow Orchid

No da: An emphatic. A verbal exclamation point placed at the end of a sentence or phrase.

CHAPTER FORTY-THREE
THE SEALED CASTLE WALL

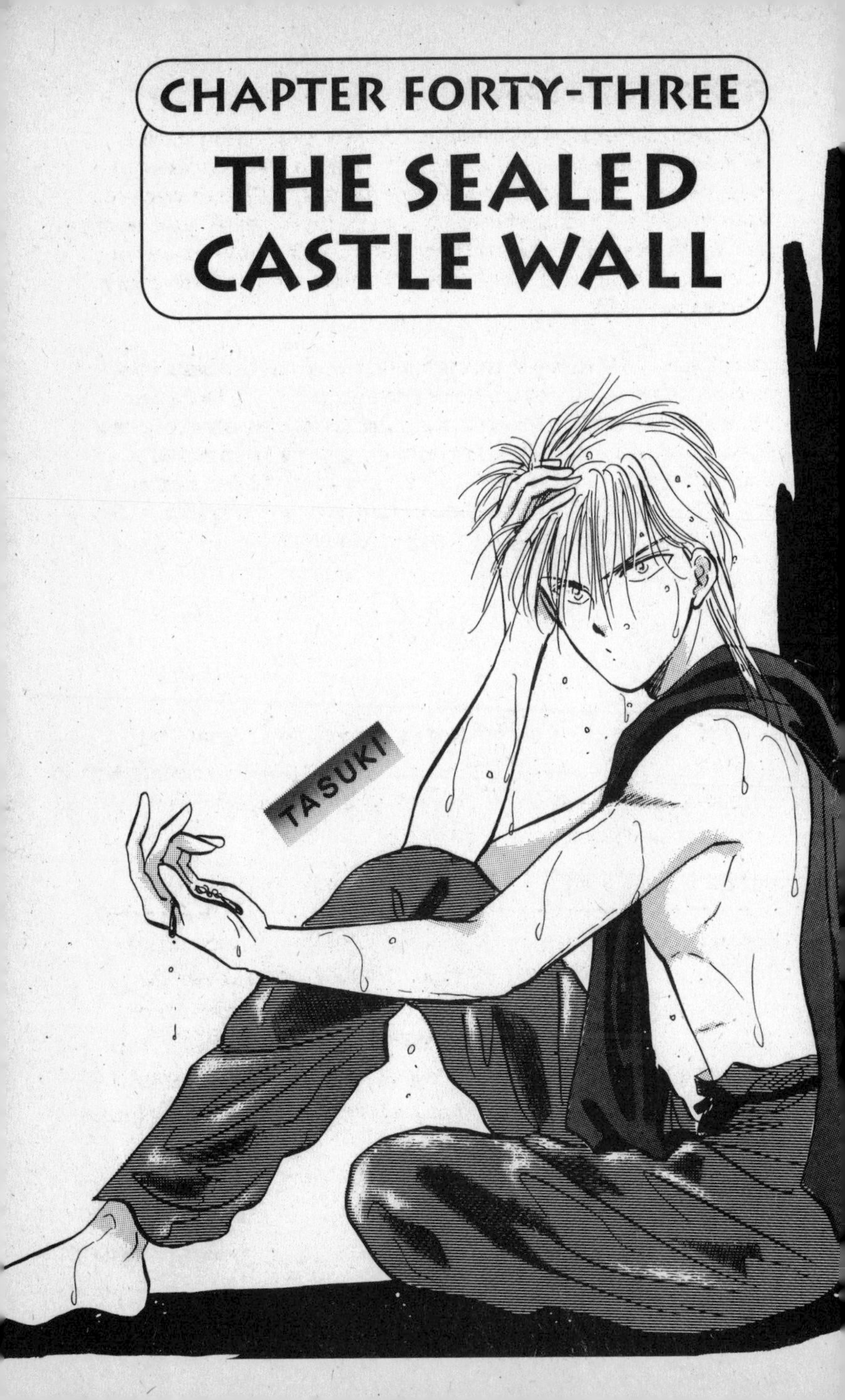
TASUKI

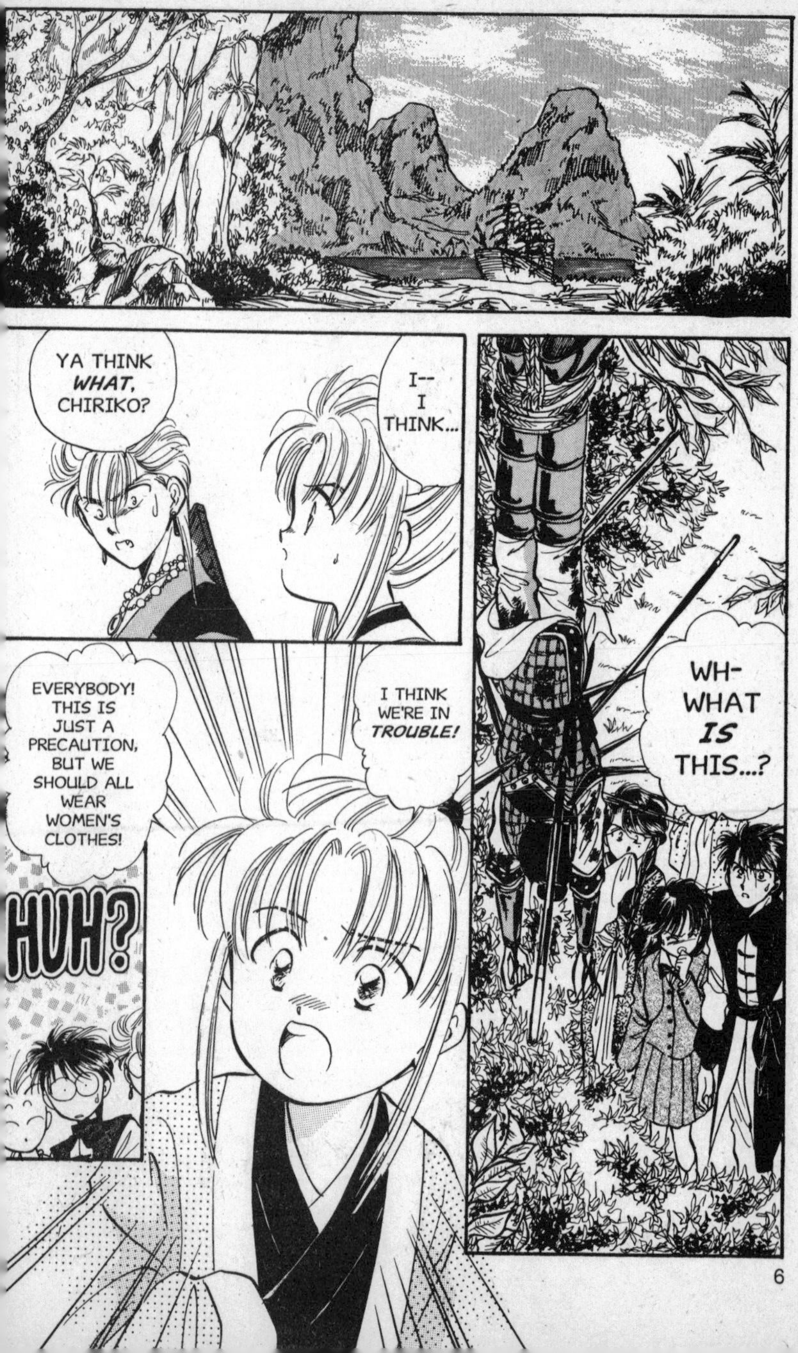
WH- WHAT *IS* THIS...?
I-- I THINK...
YA THINK *WHAT*, CHIRIKO?
I THINK WE'RE IN *TROUBLE!*
EVERYBODY! THIS IS JUST A PRECAUTION, BUT WE SHOULD ALL WEAR WOMEN'S CLOTHES!
HUH?

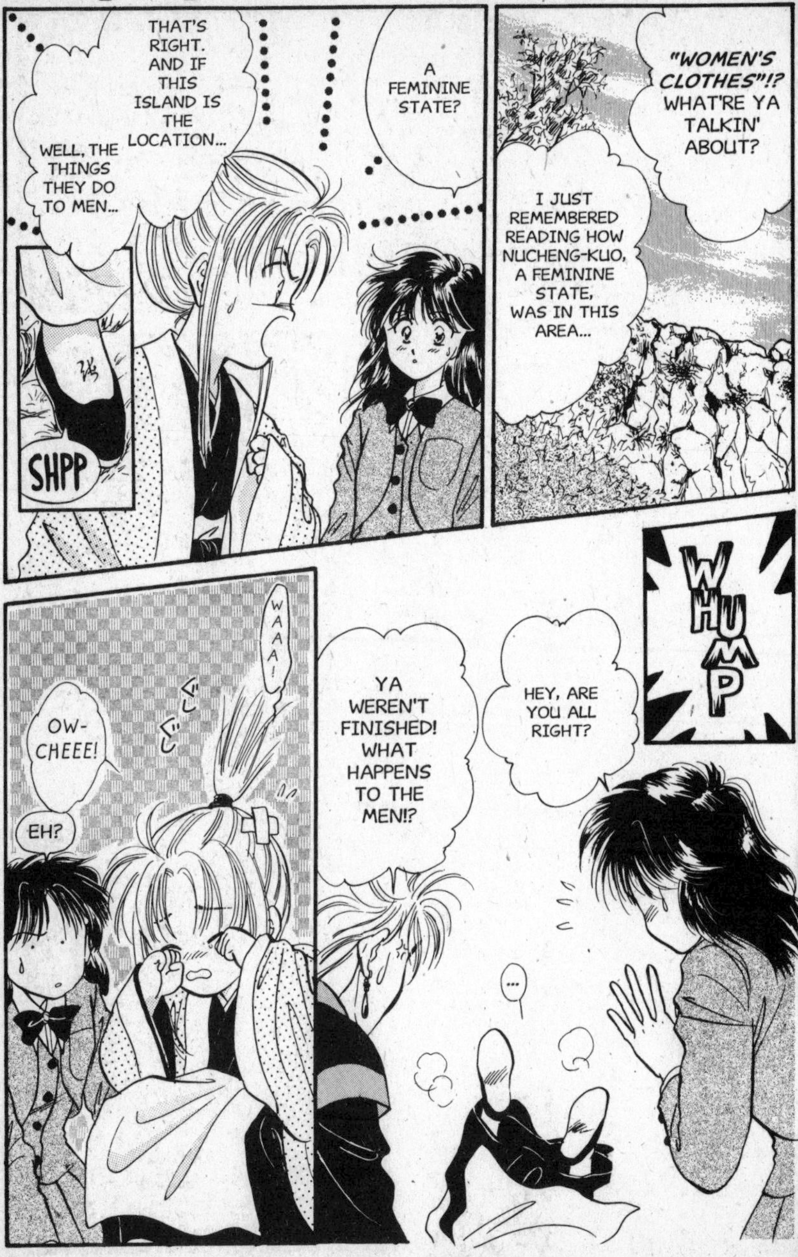
"WOMEN'S CLOTHES"!? WHAT'RE YA TALKIN' ABOUT?
I JUST REMEMBERED READING HOW NUCHENG-KUO, A FEMININE STATE, WAS IN THIS AREA...
A FEMININE STATE?
THAT'S RIGHT. AND IF THIS ISLAND IS THE LOCATION...
WELL, THE THINGS THEY DO TO MEN...
SHPP
WHUMP
HEY, ARE YOU ALL RIGHT?
YA WEREN'T FINISHED! WHAT HAPPENS TO THE MEN!?
WAAA!
OW-CHEEE!
EH?
...

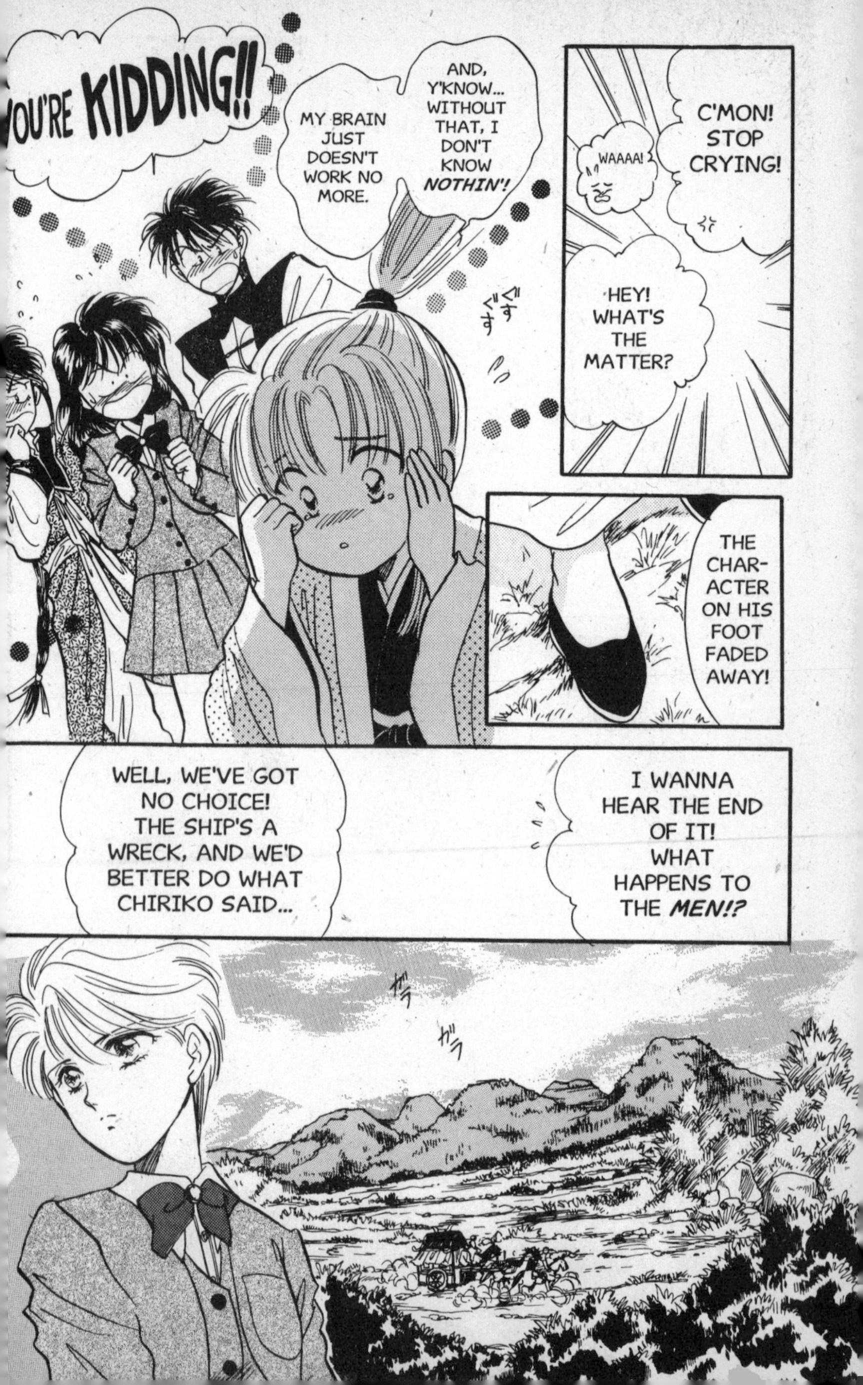
C'MON! STOP CRYING!
WAAAA!
HEY! WHAT'S THE MATTER?
THE CHARACTER ON HIS FOOT FADED AWAY!
ぐすぐす
AND, Y'KNOW... WITHOUT THAT, I DON'T KNOW *NOTHIN'!*
MY BRAIN JUST DOESN'T WORK NO MORE.
OU'RE KIDDING!!
I WANNA HEAR THE END OF IT! WHAT HAPPENS TO THE *MEN!?*
WELL, WE'VE GOT NO CHOICE! THE SHIP'S A WRECK, AND WE'D BETTER DO WHAT CHIRIKO SAID...
ガラ
ガラ

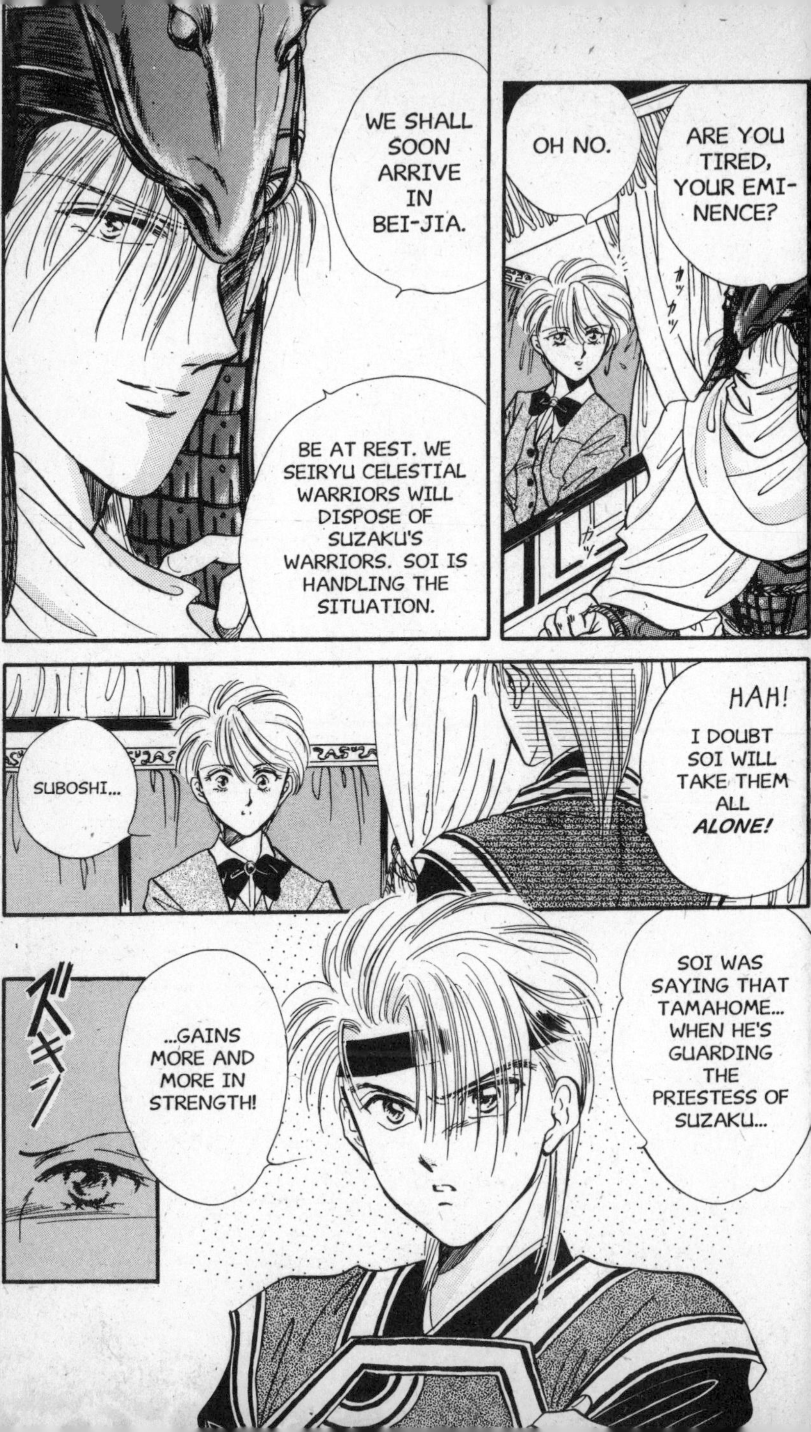
ARE YOU TIRED, YOUR EMI-NENCE?
OH NO.
WE SHALL SOON ARRIVE IN BEI-JIA.
BE AT REST. WE SEIRYU CELESTIAL WARRIORS WILL DISPOSE OF SUZAKU'S WARRIORS. SOI IS HANDLING THE SITUATION.
HAH!
I DOUBT SOI WILL TAKE THEM ALL *ALONE!*
SUBOSHI...
SOI WAS SAYING THAT TAMAHOME... WHEN HE'S GUARDING THE PRIESTESS OF SUZAKU...
...GAINS MORE AND MORE IN STRENGTH!
ズキン

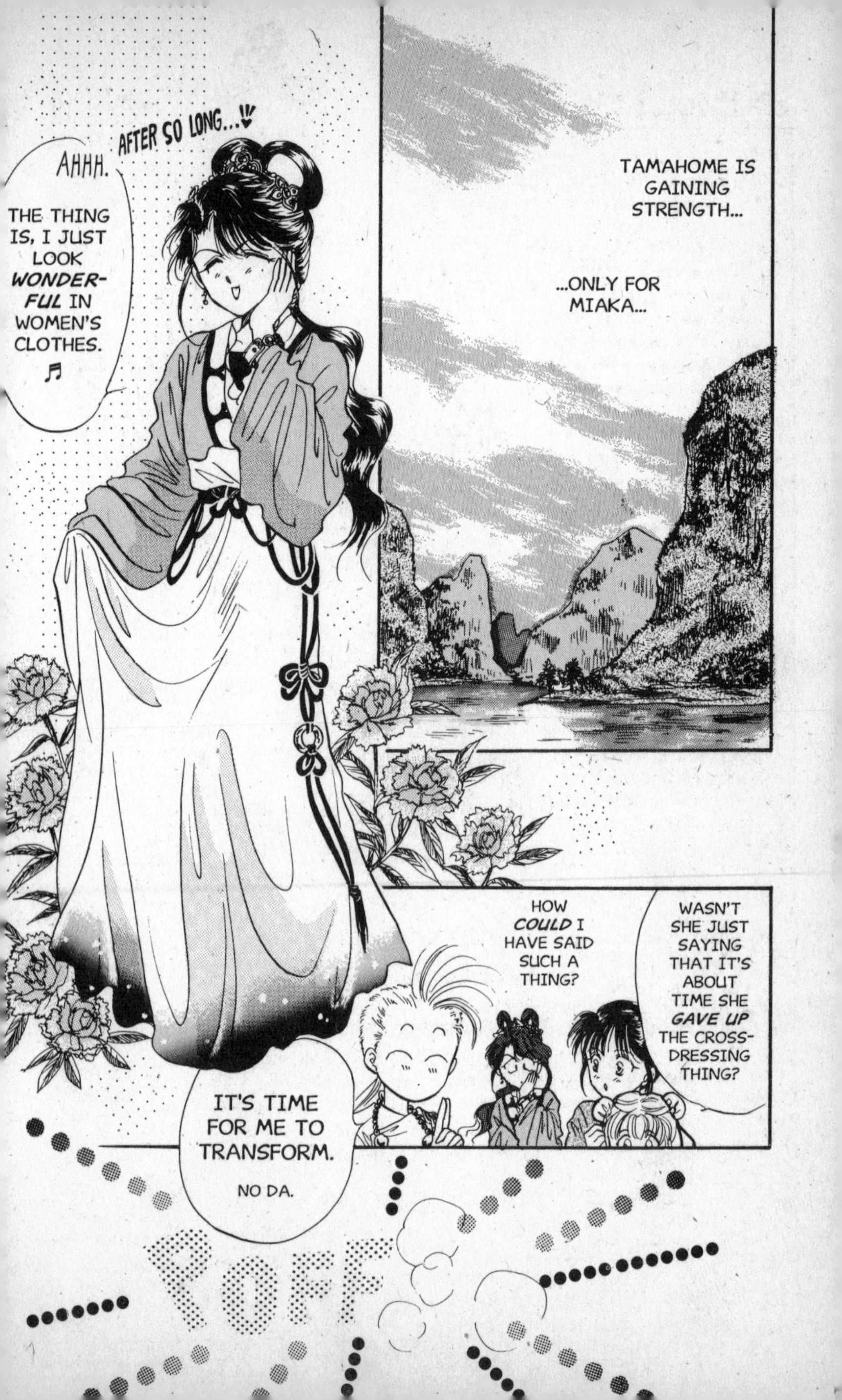

TAMAHOME IS GAINING STRENGTH...
...ONLY FOR MIAKA...
WASN'T SHE JUST SAYING THAT IT'S ABOUT TIME SHE GAVE UP THE CROSS-DRESSING THING?
HOW COULD I HAVE SAID SUCH A THING?
IT'S TIME FOR ME TO TRANSFORM.
NO DA.
AFTER SO LONG...!!
AHHH.
THE THING IS, I JUST LOOK WONDERFUL IN WOMEN'S CLOTHES. ♬
POFF

Friend

Hello. This is Yuu Watase. I want to wish you all a "Happy New Year." My new year is off to a great start.
At the end of October, my stress level began to take its toll on my body. I was in such poor shape I couldn't even let my assistants into the office! So I went to see a doctor. I'm all right now. Stress can be scary! In November, while working on manga, I started wondering why I was putting myself through this... And that's when I realized I was in trouble.
The sight of my office was enough to make me feel nauseous. My right hand ached, and I kept on dropping my pen. But I worked when I could, and I managed to finish my installments on my own. So I can calm my stress all by myself. (Although when I work alone, I do end up putting a little too much detail in each frame. ☺ My assistants did help me out on volume 8. I'm such a delicate creature. (Are you callin' me a liar?) I put up a tough front, but I really need to be bolder and more self confident.

• And so this volume was written by a woman under stress. ☺ Please take that into consideration when you read it.

• Last volume, I ran on and on with talk about my dog, and in this one, I think I'll tell you about my trip to China.
Well, let's see what I come up with as we move through "Fushigi Yūgi."

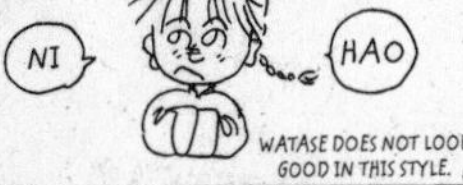
NI
HAO
WATASE DOES NOT LOOK GOOD IN THIS STYLE.

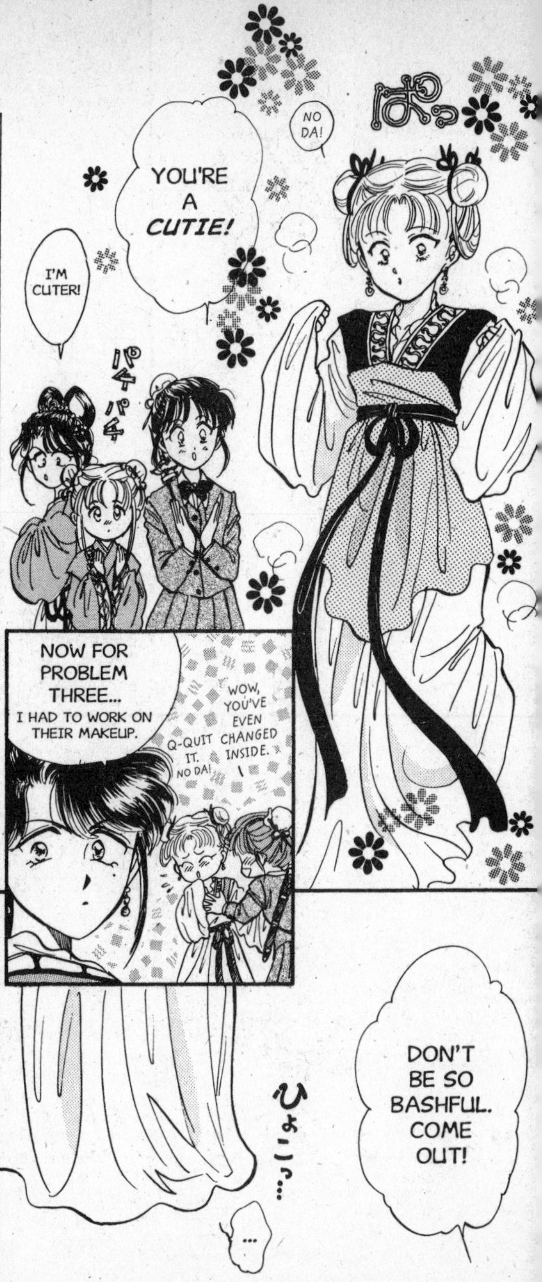
ぱっ
NO DA!
YOU'RE A CUTIE!
I'M CUTER!
NOW FOR PROBLEM THREE...
I HAD TO WORK ON THEIR MAKEUP.
WOW, YOU'VE EVEN CHANGED INSIDE.
Q-QUIT IT. NO DA!
DON'T BE SO BASHFUL. COME OUT!
ひょこっ...
...

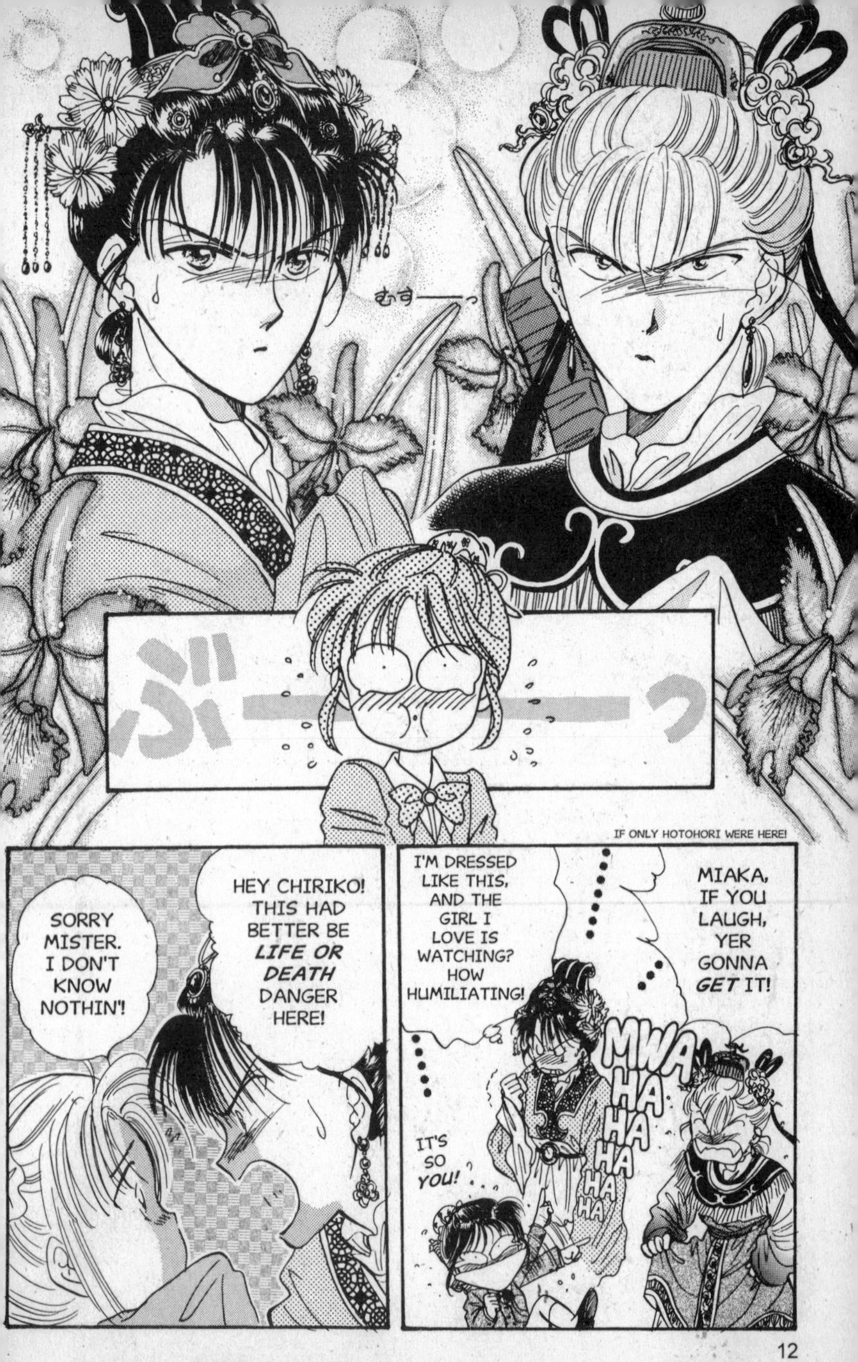
むす——っ
ぶ——っ
IF ONLY HOTOHORI WERE HERE!
MIAKA, IF YOU LAUGH, YER GONNA *GET* IT!
I'M DRESSED LIKE THIS, AND THE GIRL I LOVE IS WATCHING? HOW HUMILIATING!
MWA HA HA HA HA HA
IT'S SO *YOU!*
HEY CHIRIKO! THIS HAD BETTER BE *LIFE OR DEATH* DANGER HERE!
SORRY MISTER. I DON'T KNOW NOTHIN'!

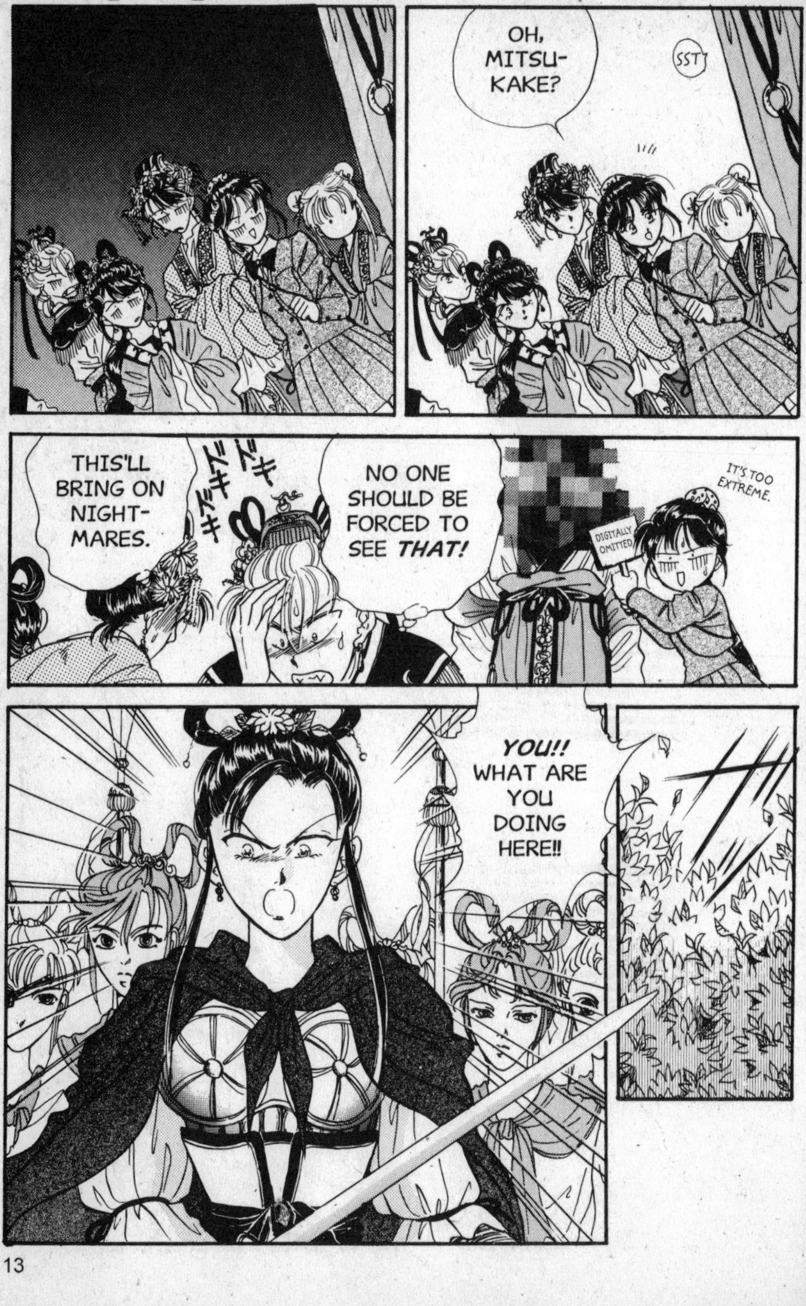
OH, MITSU-KAKE?
SST
IT'S TOO EXTREME.
DIGITALLY OMITTED
NO ONE SHOULD BE FORCED TO SEE THAT!
ドキ
ドキドキ
THIS'LL BRING ON NIGHT-MARES.
YOU!! WHAT ARE YOU DOING HERE!!

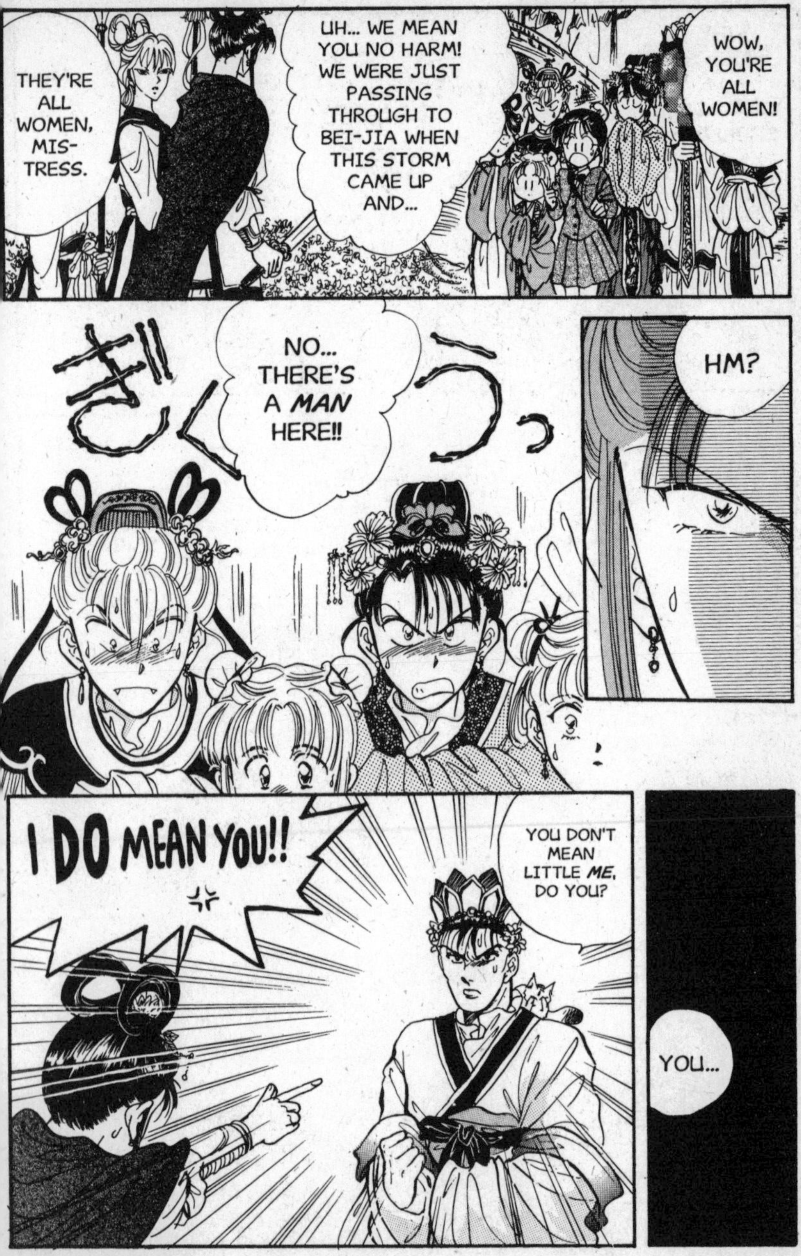
WOW, YOU'RE ALL WOMEN!
UH... WE MEAN YOU NO HARM! WE WERE JUST PASSING THROUGH TO BEI-JIA WHEN THIS STORM CAME UP AND...
THEY'RE ALL WOMEN, MIS-TRESS.
HM?
うっ
NO... THERE'S A *MAN* HERE!!
ぎく
YOU...
YOU DON'T MEAN LITTLE *ME*, DO YOU?
I DO MEAN YOU!!

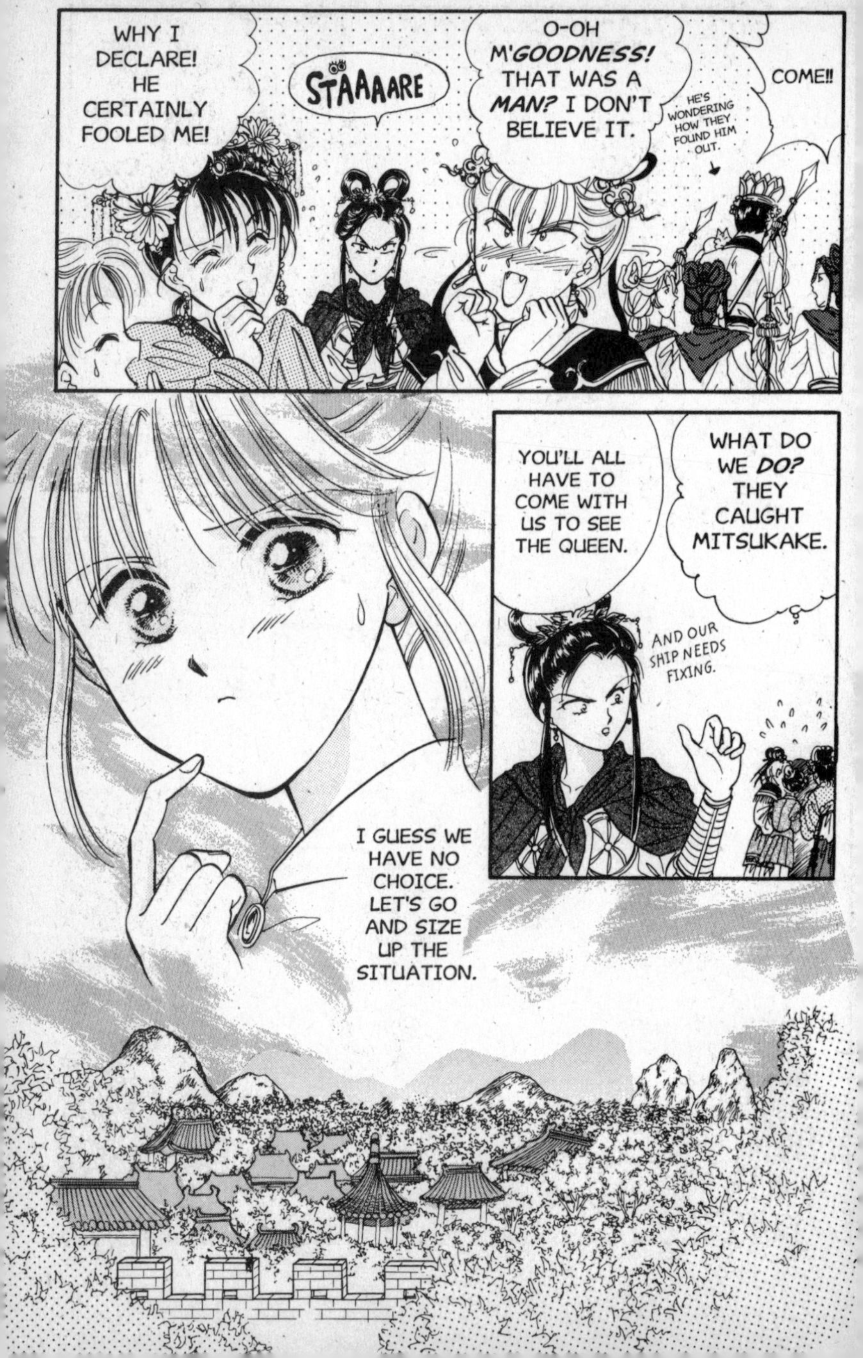
COME!!
HE'S WONDERING HOW THEY FOUND HIM OUT.
O-OH M'GOODNESS! THAT WAS A MAN? I DON'T BELIEVE IT.
STAAAARE
WHY I DECLARE! HE CERTAINLY FOOLED ME!
WHAT DO WE DO? THEY CAUGHT MITSUKAKE.
YOU'LL ALL HAVE TO COME WITH US TO SEE THE QUEEN.
AND OUR SHIP NEEDS FIXING.
I GUESS WE HAVE NO CHOICE. LET'S GO AND SIZE UP THE SITUATION.

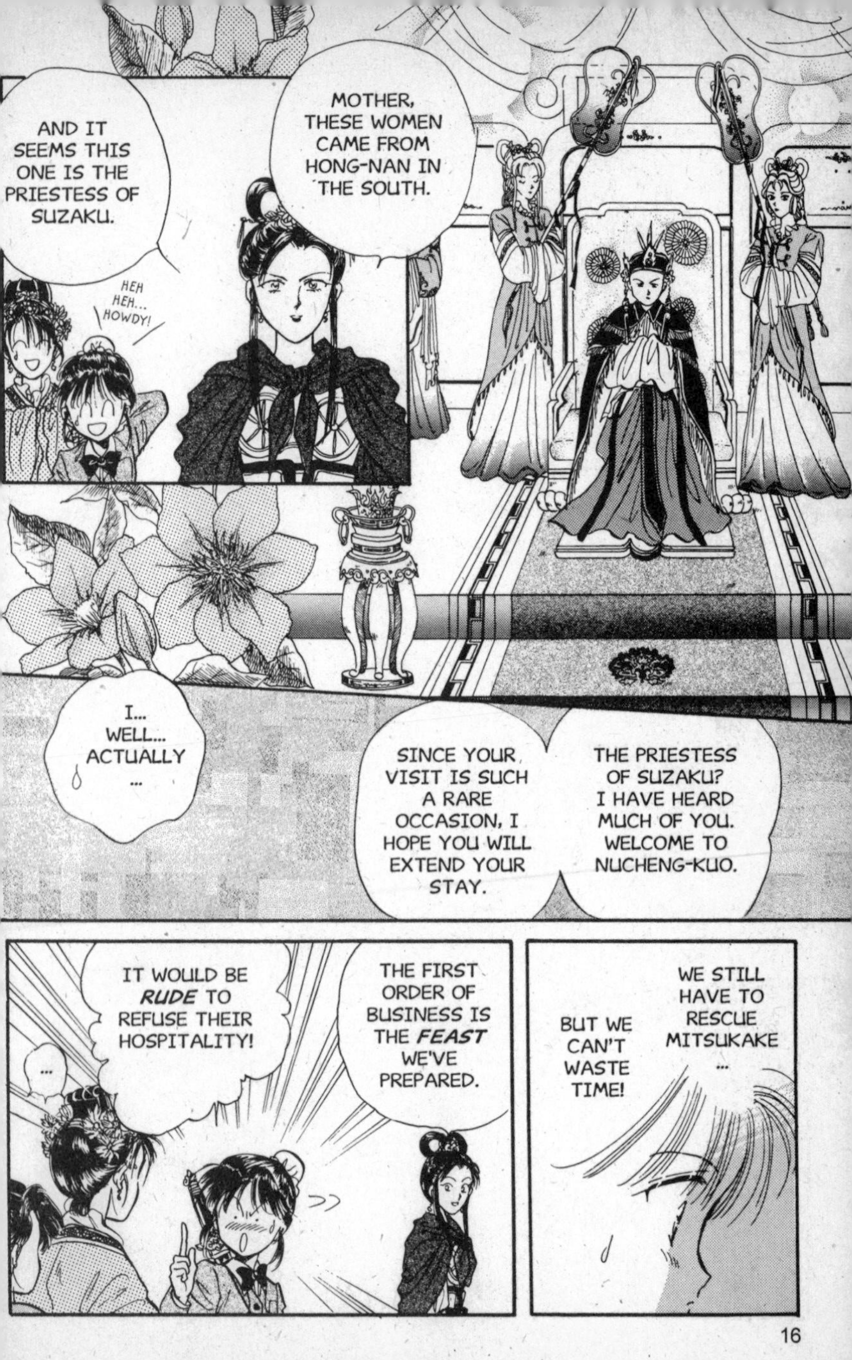
MOTHER, THESE WOMEN CAME FROM HONG-NAN IN THE SOUTH.
AND IT SEEMS THIS ONE IS THE PRIESTESS OF SUZAKU.
HEH HEH... HOWDY!
THE PRIESTESS OF SUZAKU? I HAVE HEARD MUCH OF YOU. WELCOME TO NUCHENG-KUO.
SINCE YOUR VISIT IS SUCH A RARE OCCASION, I HOPE YOU WILL EXTEND YOUR STAY.
I... WELL... ACTUALLY ...
WE STILL HAVE TO RESCUE MITSUKAKE ...
BUT WE CAN'T WASTE TIME!
THE FIRST ORDER OF BUSINESS IS THE *FEAST* WE'VE PREPARED.
IT WOULD BE *RUDE* TO REFUSE THEIR HOSPITALITY!
...

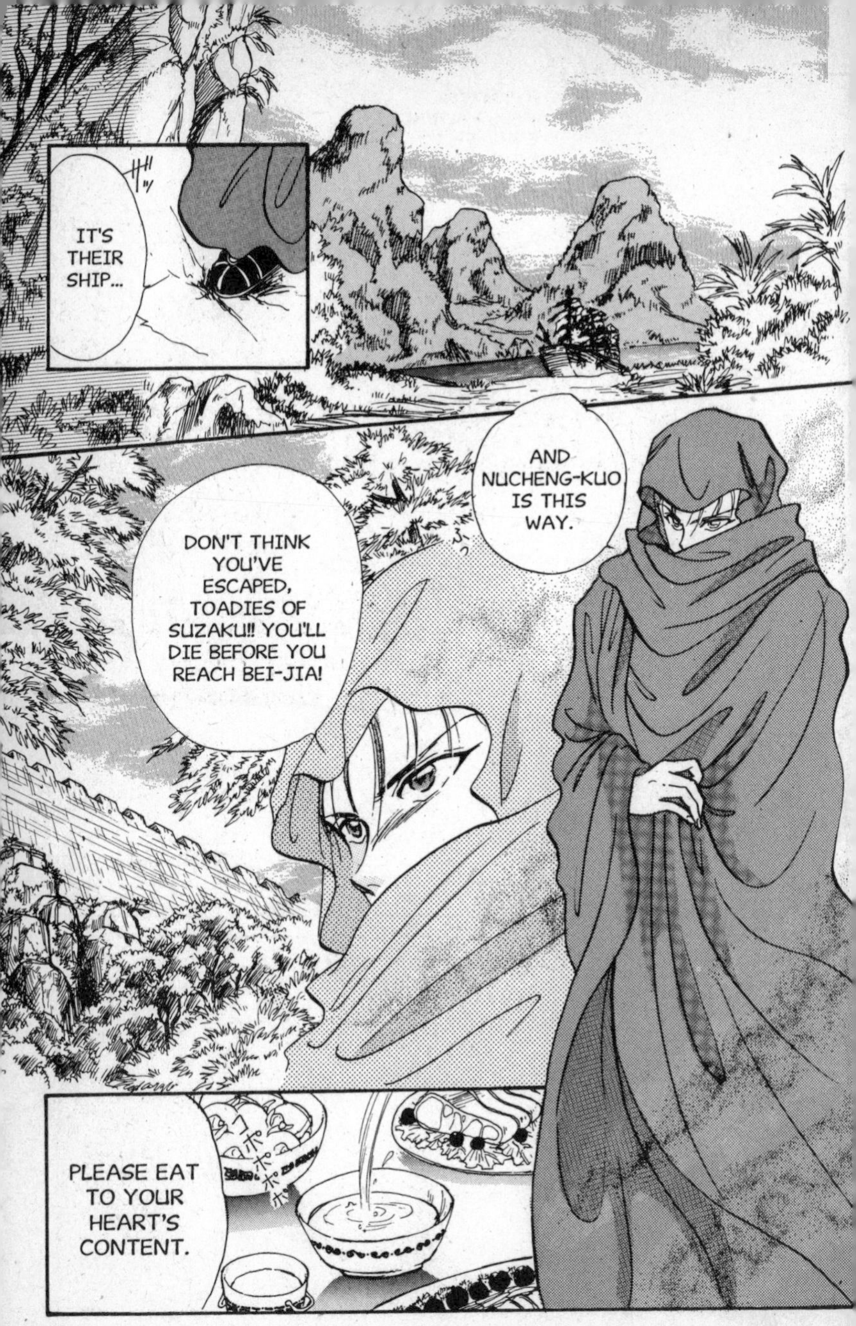
IT'S THEIR SHIP...
AND NUCHENG-KUO IS THIS WAY.
DON'T THINK YOU'VE ESCAPED, TOADIES OF SUZAKU!! YOU'LL DIE BEFORE YOU REACH BEI-JIA!
コポポポ
PLEASE EAT TO YOUR HEART'S CONTENT.

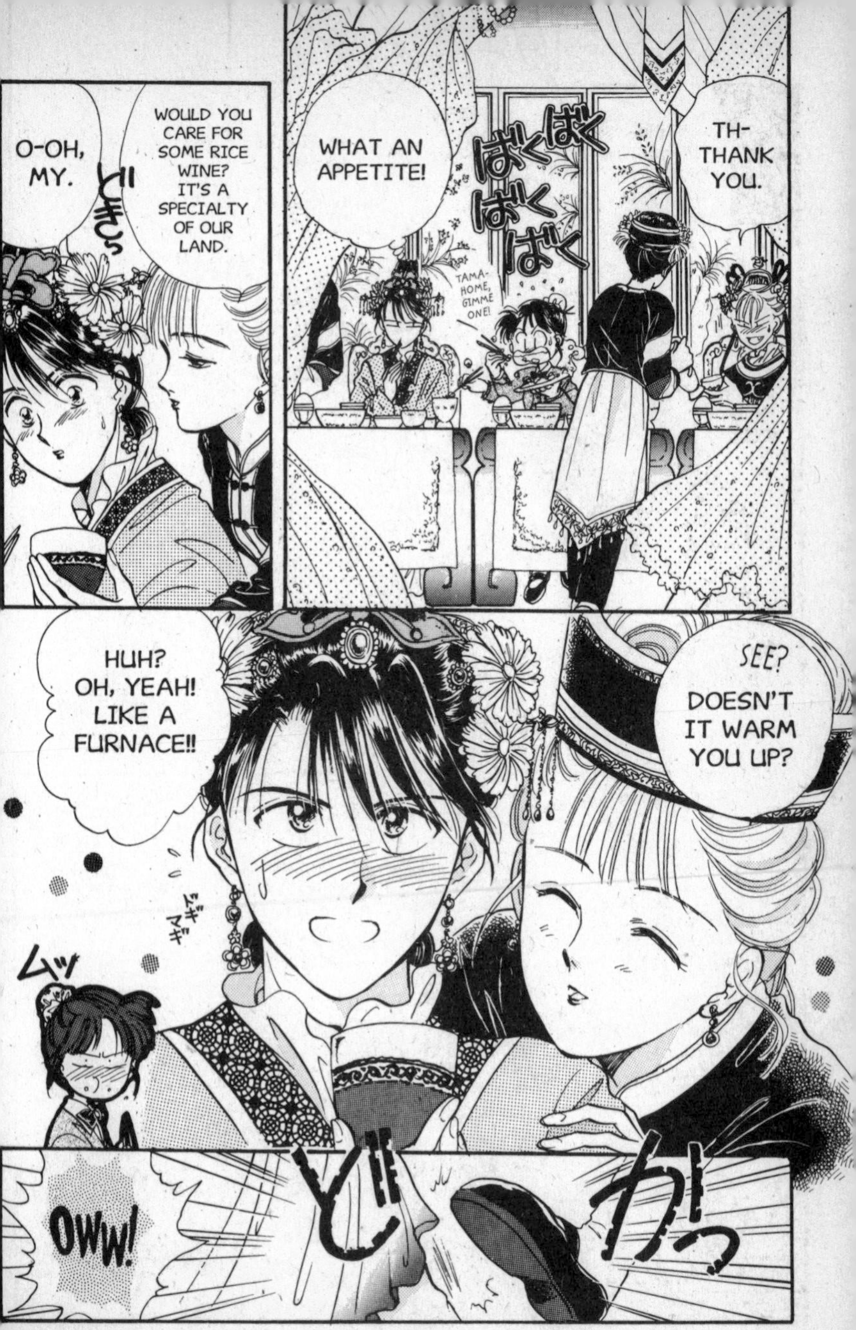
TH-THANK YOU.
ばくばくばくばく
WHAT AN APPETITE!
TAMA-HOME, GIMME ONE!
WOULD YOU CARE FOR SOME RICE WINE? IT'S A SPECIALTY OF OUR LAND.
どきっ
O-OH, MY.
SEE? DOESN'T IT WARM YOU UP?
HUH? OH, YEAH! LIKE A FURNACE!!
ドギマギ
ムッ
どかっ
OWW!

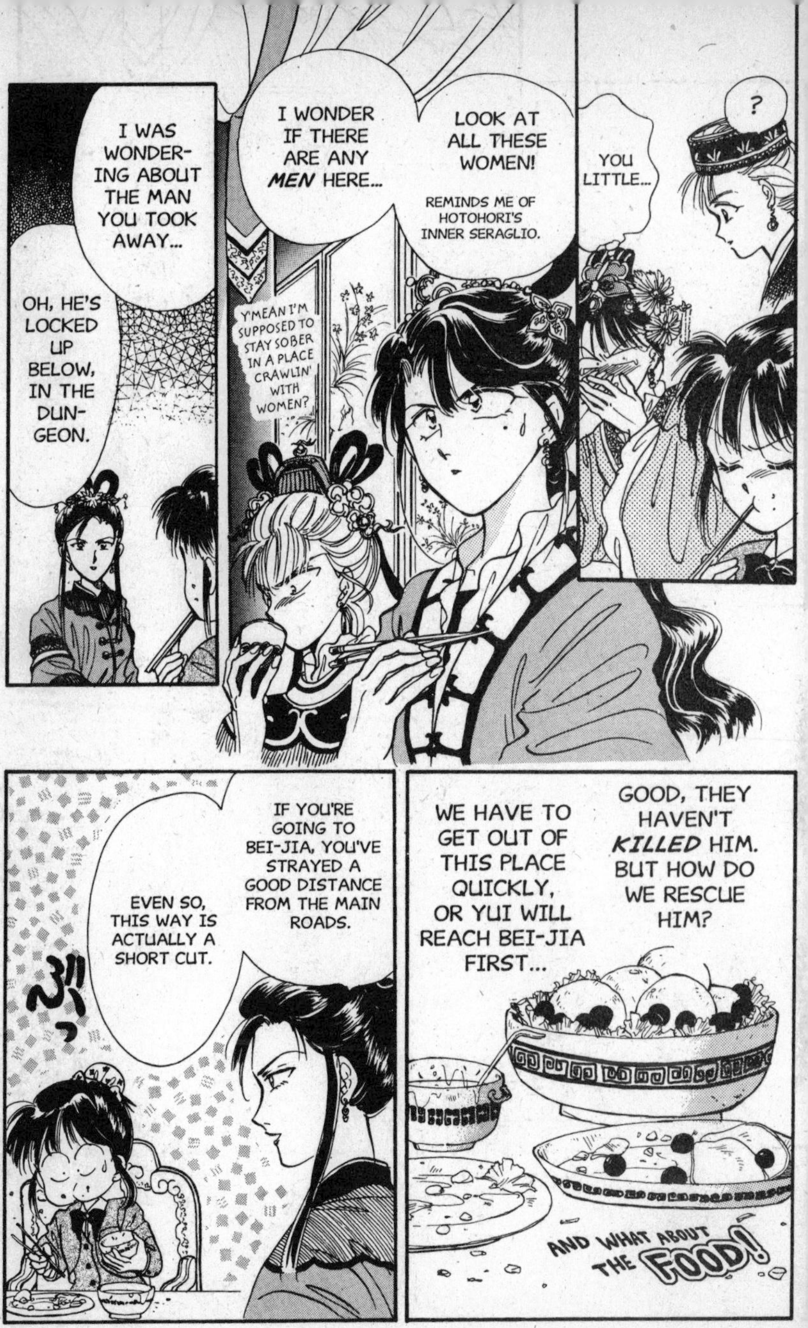
?
YOU LITTLE...
LOOK AT ALL THESE WOMEN!
REMINDS ME OF HOTOHORI'S INNER SERAGLIO.
I WONDER IF THERE ARE ANY MEN HERE...
Y'MEAN I'M SUPPOSED TO STAY SOBER IN A PLACE CRAWLIN' WITH WOMEN?
I WAS WONDER-ING ABOUT THE MAN YOU TOOK AWAY...
OH, HE'S LOCKED UP BELOW, IN THE DUN-GEON.
GOOD, THEY HAVEN'T KILLED HIM. BUT HOW DO WE RESCUE HIM?
WE HAVE TO GET OUT OF THIS PLACE QUICKLY, OR YUI WILL REACH BEI-JIA FIRST...
AND WHAT ABOUT THE FOOD!
IF YOU'RE GOING TO BEI-JIA, YOU'VE STRAYED A GOOD DISTANCE FROM THE MAIN ROADS.
EVEN SO, THIS WAY IS ACTUALLY A SHORT CUT.
ぷいっ

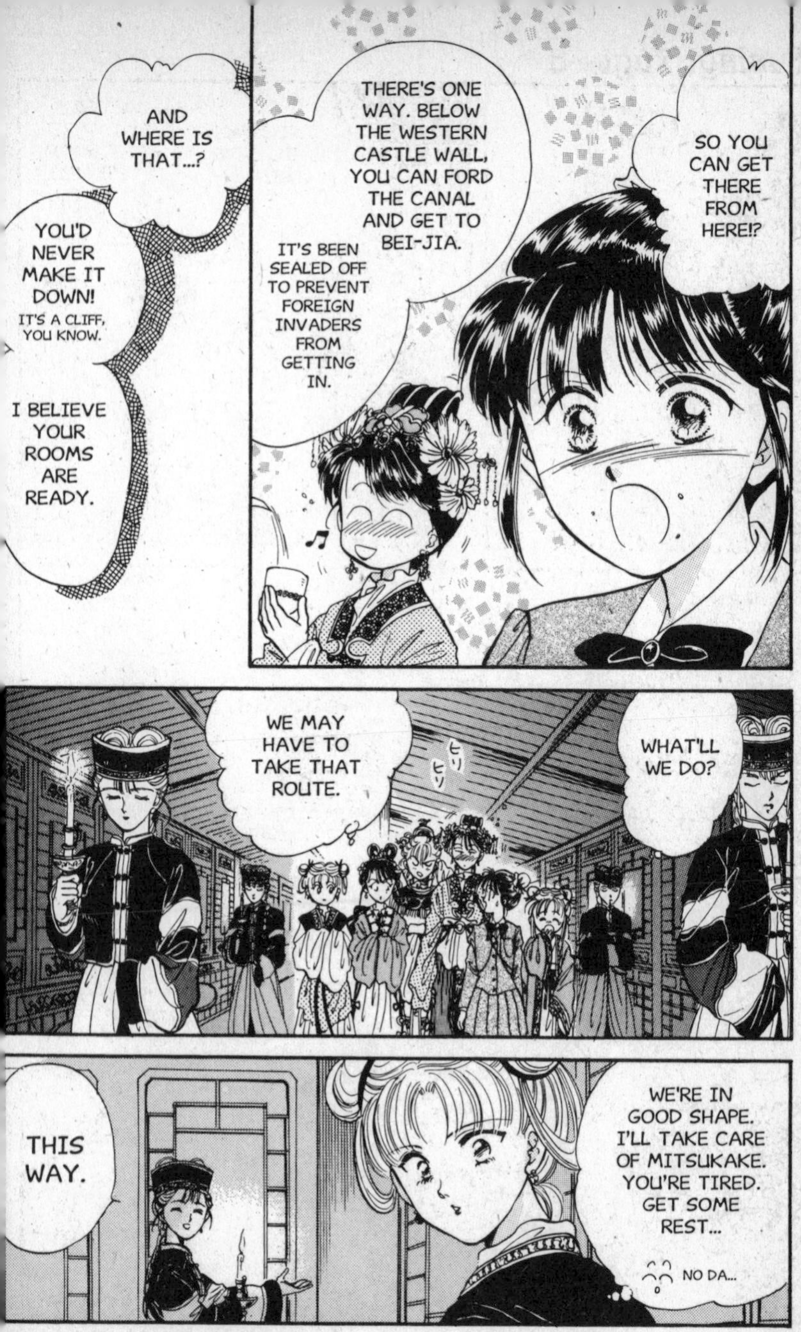
SO YOU CAN GET THERE FROM HERE!?
THERE'S ONE WAY. BELOW THE WESTERN CASTLE WALL, YOU CAN FORD THE CANAL AND GET TO BEI-JIA.
IT'S BEEN SEALED OFF TO PREVENT FOREIGN INVADERS FROM GETTING IN.
AND WHERE IS THAT...?
YOU'D NEVER MAKE IT DOWN!
IT'S A CLIFF, YOU KNOW.
I BELIEVE YOUR ROOMS ARE READY.
WHAT'LL WE DO?
ヒリ ヒリ
WE MAY HAVE TO TAKE THAT ROUTE.
WE'RE IN GOOD SHAPE. I'LL TAKE CARE OF MITSUKAKE. YOU'RE TIRED. GET SOME REST...
NO DA...
THIS WAY.

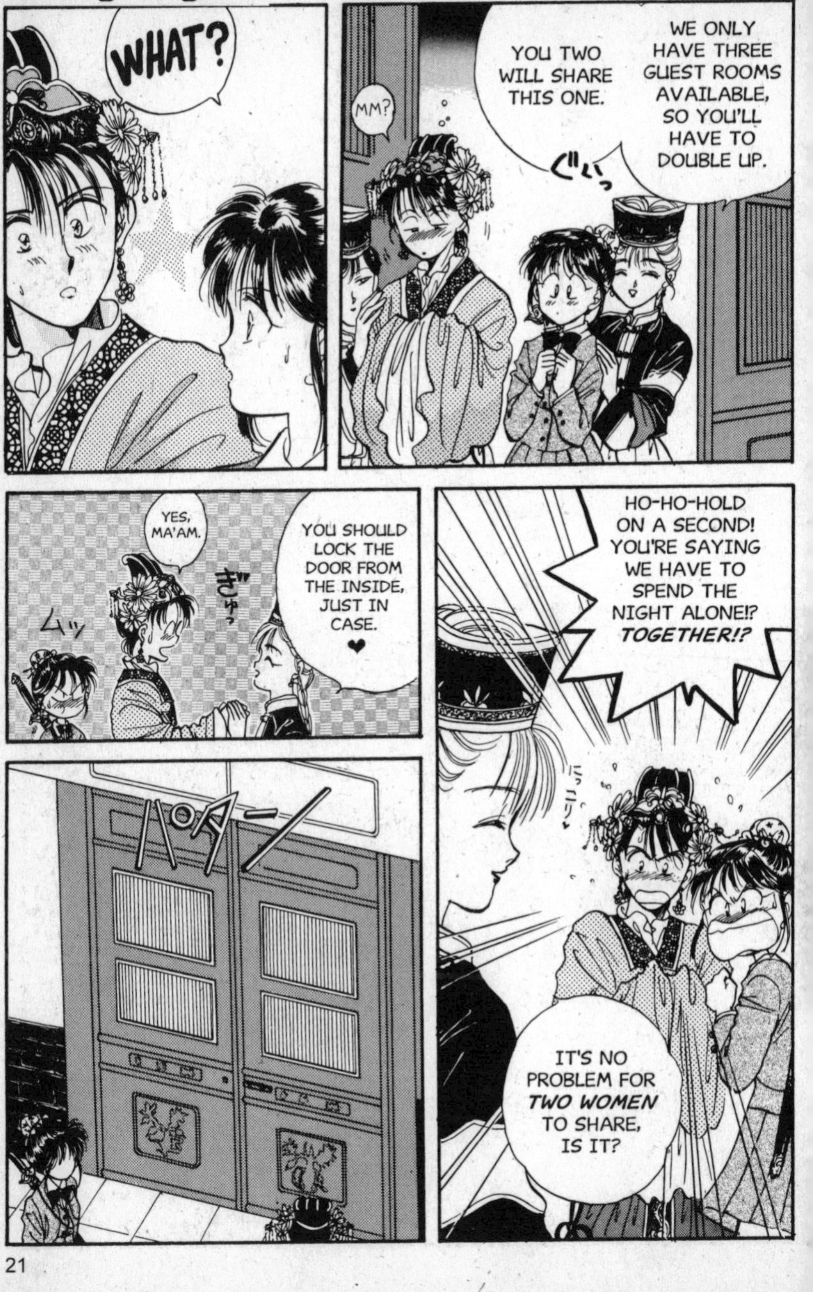
WE ONLY HAVE THREE GUEST ROOMS AVAILABLE, SO YOU'LL HAVE TO DOUBLE UP.
YOU TWO WILL SHARE THIS ONE.
ぐいっ
MM?
WHAT?
HO-HO-HOLD ON A SECOND! YOU'RE SAYING WE HAVE TO SPEND THE NIGHT ALONE!? *TOGETHER!?*
ニッコリ
IT'S NO PROBLEM FOR *TWO WOMEN* TO SHARE, IS IT?
YOU SHOULD LOCK THE DOOR FROM THE INSIDE, JUST IN CASE. ❤
ぎゅっ
YES, MA'AM.
ムッ
パターン

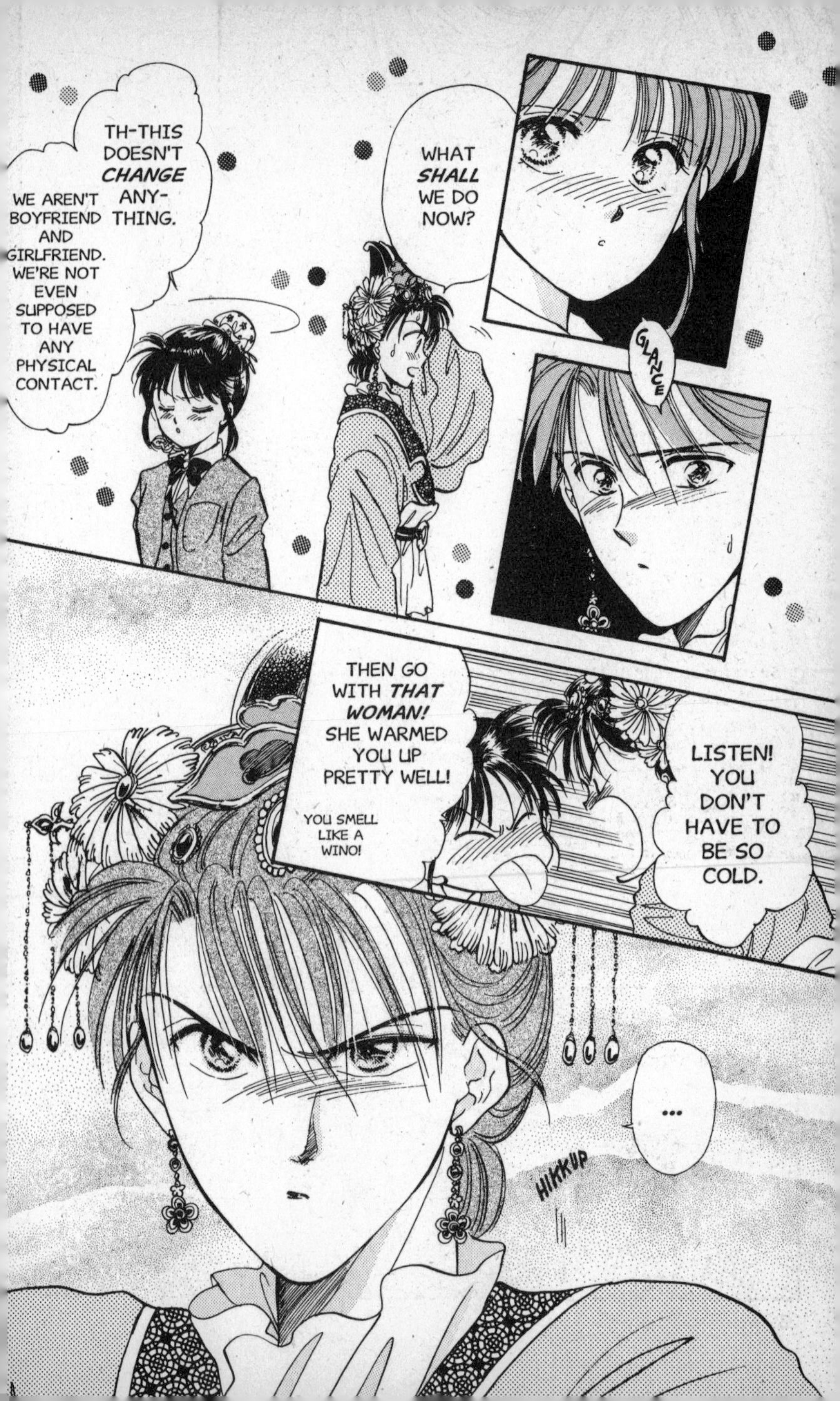
GLANCE
WHAT SHALL WE DO NOW?
TH-THIS DOESN'T CHANGE ANYTHING.
WE AREN'T BOYFRIEND AND GIRLFRIEND. WE'RE NOT EVEN SUPPOSED TO HAVE ANY PHYSICAL CONTACT.
LISTEN! YOU DON'T HAVE TO BE SO COLD.
THEN GO WITH THAT WOMAN! SHE WARMED YOU UP PRETTY WELL!
YOU SMELL LIKE A WINO!
...
HIKKUP

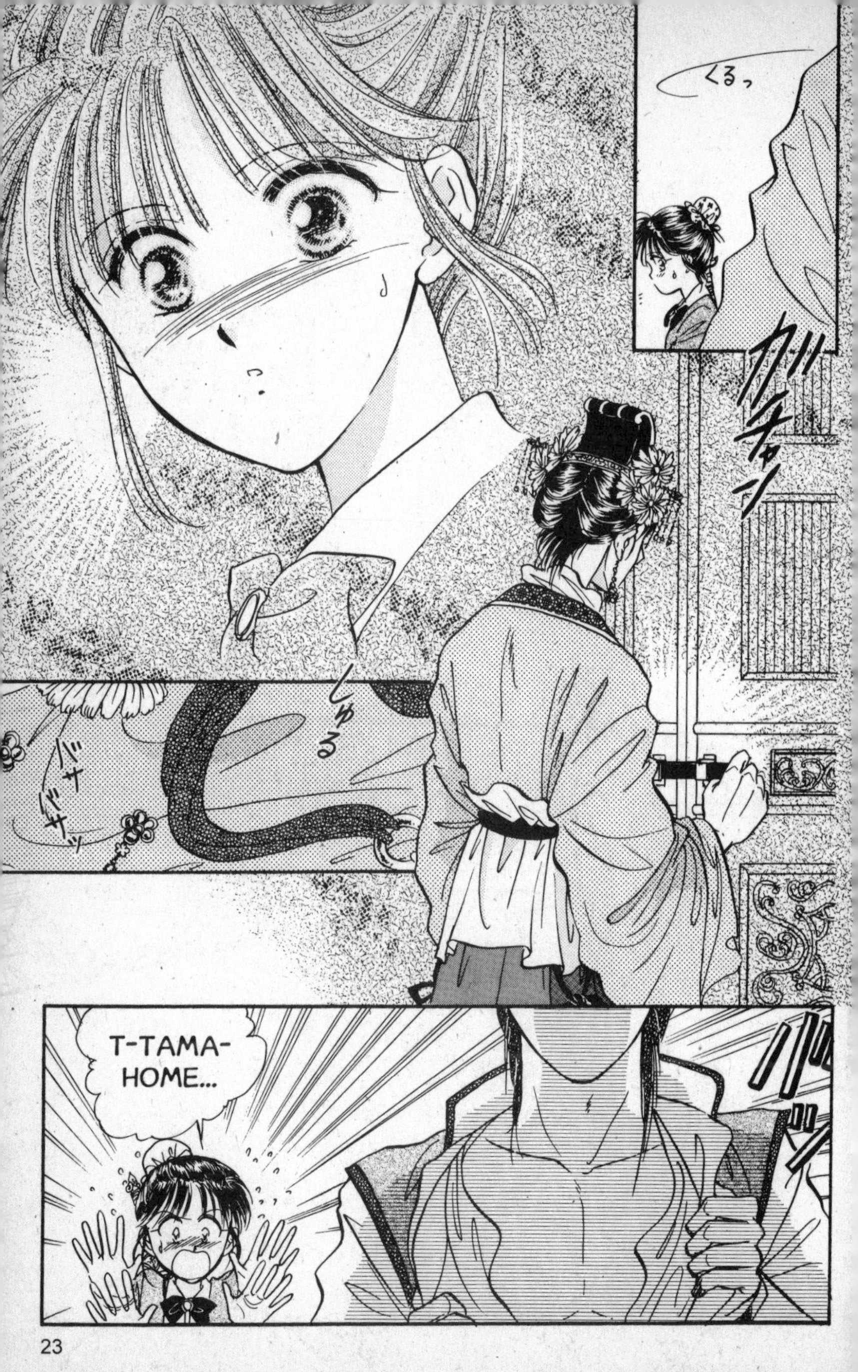
くるっ
ガチャン
しゅる
バサバサッ
T-TAMA-HOME...

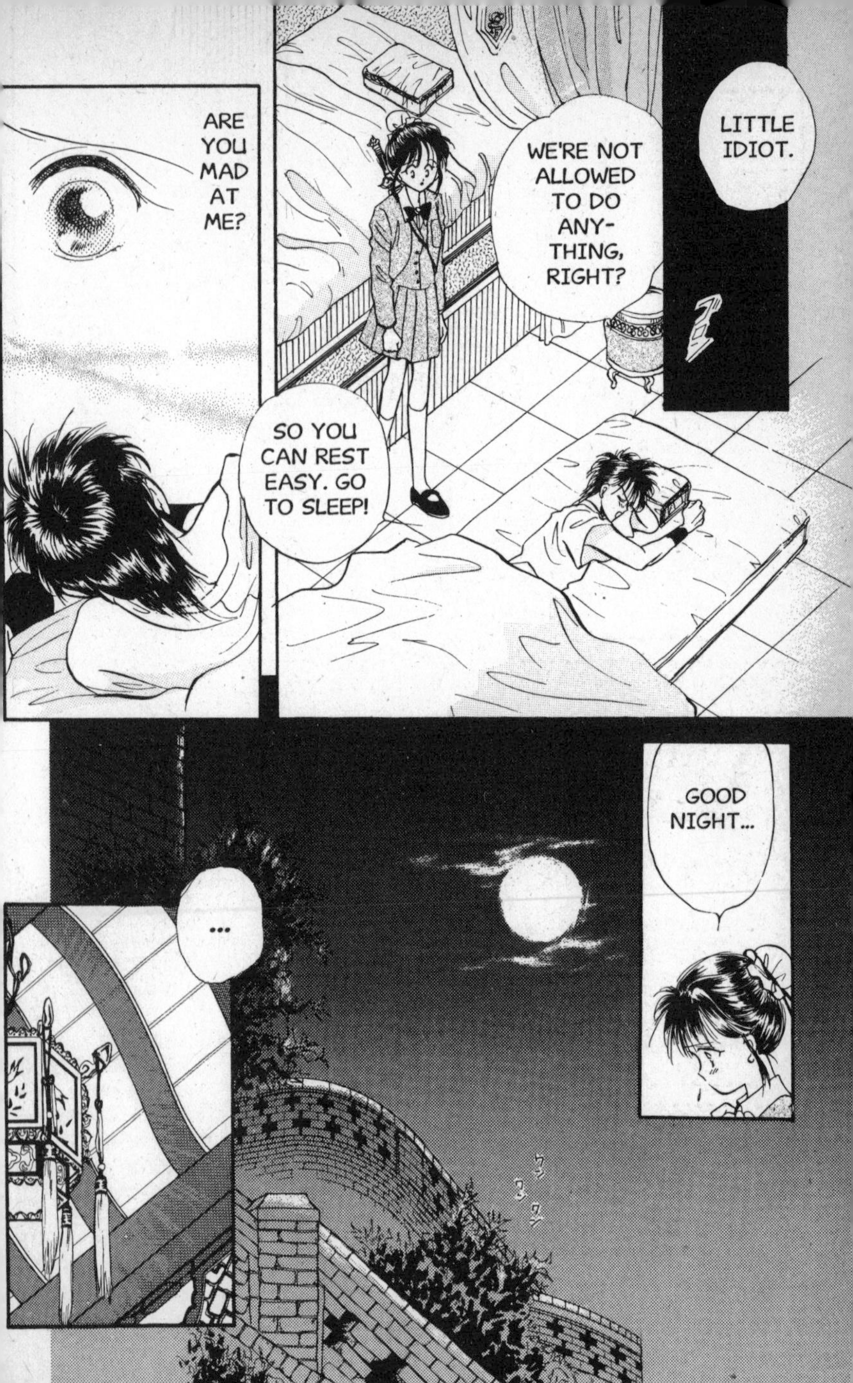
LITTLE IDIOT.
WE'RE NOT ALLOWED TO DO ANY-THING, RIGHT?
SO YOU CAN REST EASY. GO TO SLEEP!
ARE YOU MAD AT ME?
GOOD NIGHT...
...

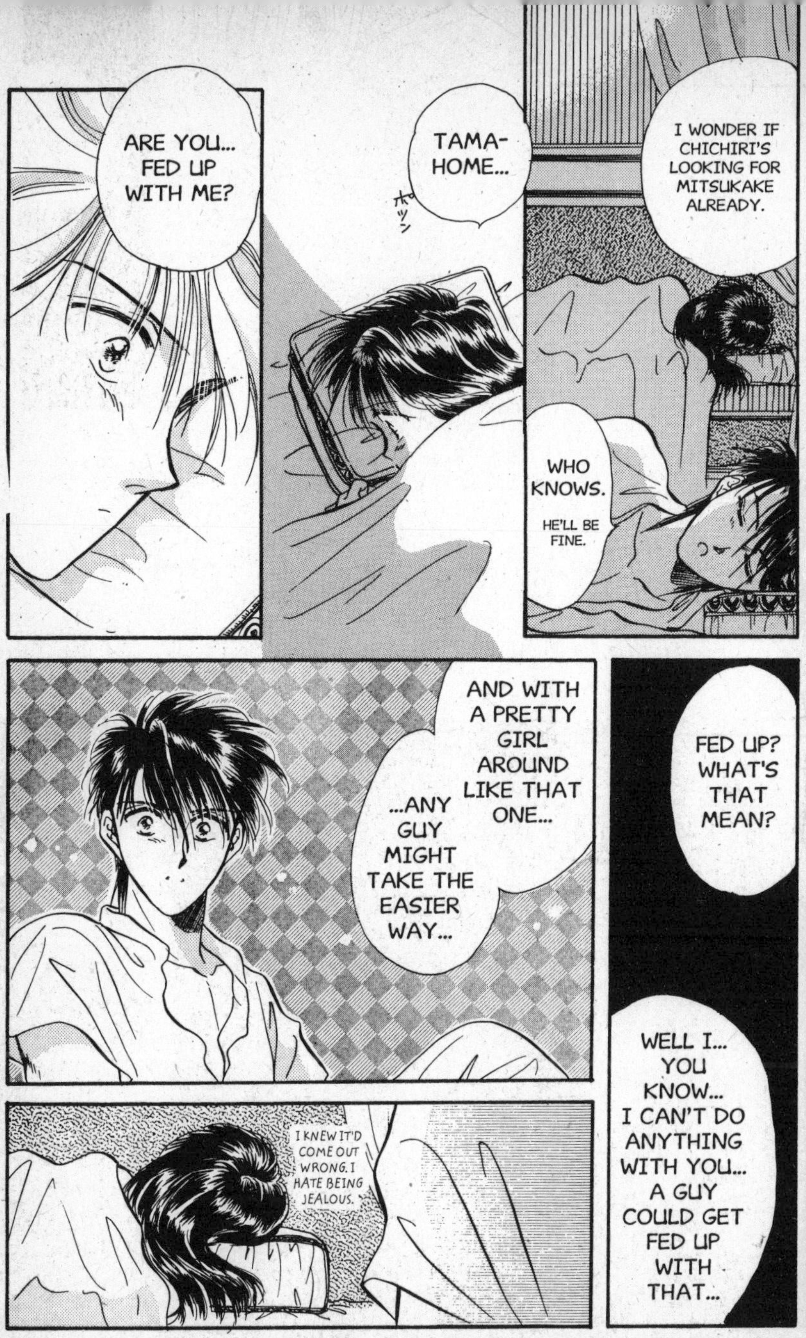
I WONDER IF CHICHIRI'S LOOKING FOR MITSUKAKE ALREADY.
WHO KNOWS.
HE'LL BE FINE.
TAMA-HOME...
ポツン
ARE YOU... FED UP WITH ME?
FED UP? WHAT'S THAT MEAN?
WELL I... YOU KNOW... I CAN'T DO ANYTHING WITH YOU... A GUY COULD GET FED UP WITH THAT...
AND WITH A PRETTY GIRL AROUND LIKE THAT ONE...
...ANY GUY MIGHT TAKE THE EASIER WAY...
I KNEW IT'D COME OUT WRONG. I HATE BEING JEALOUS.

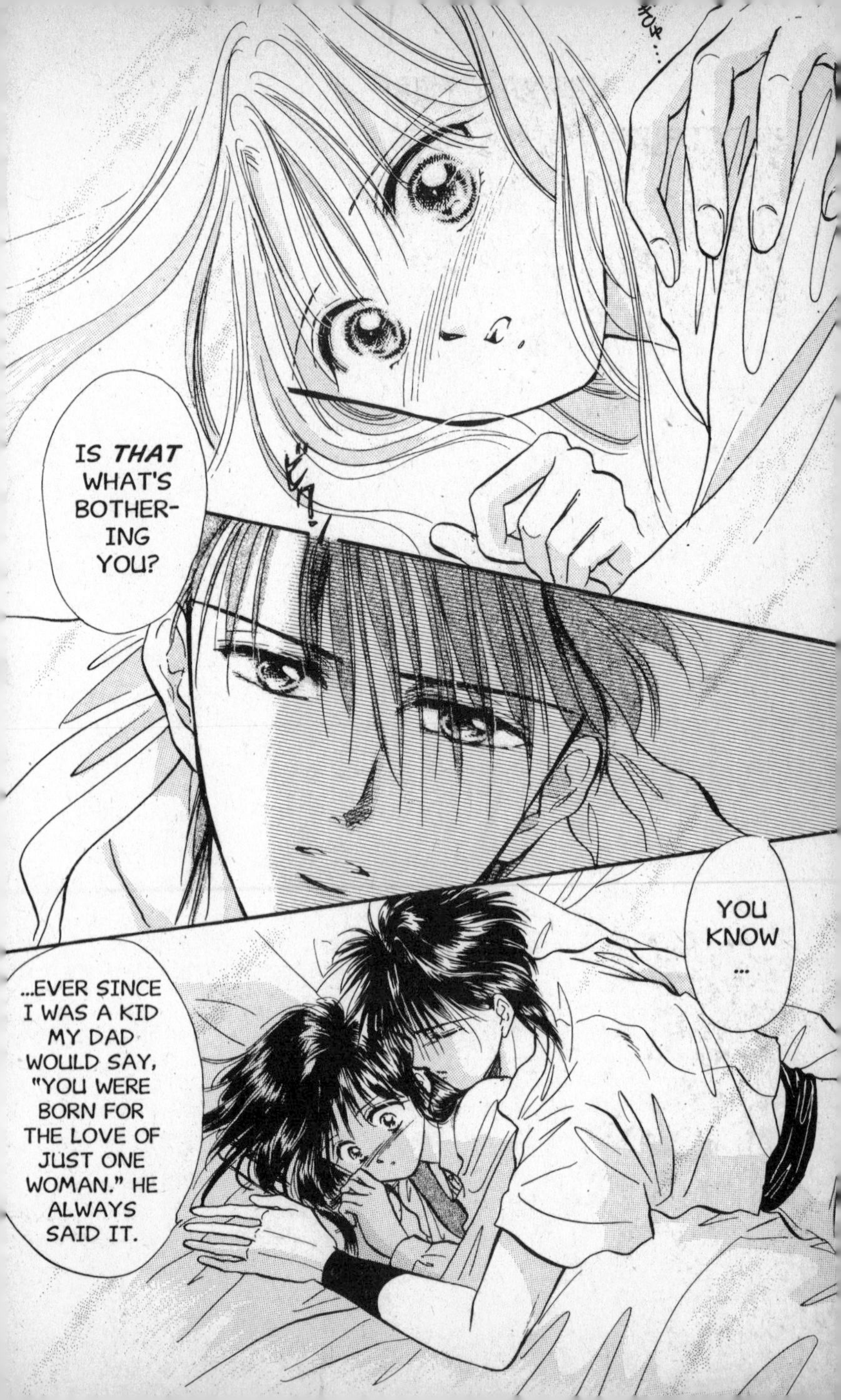
IS *THAT* WHAT'S BOTHER-ING YOU?
YOU KNOW ...
...EVER SINCE I WAS A KID MY DAD WOULD SAY, "YOU WERE BORN FOR THE LOVE OF JUST ONE WOMAN." HE ALWAYS SAID IT.

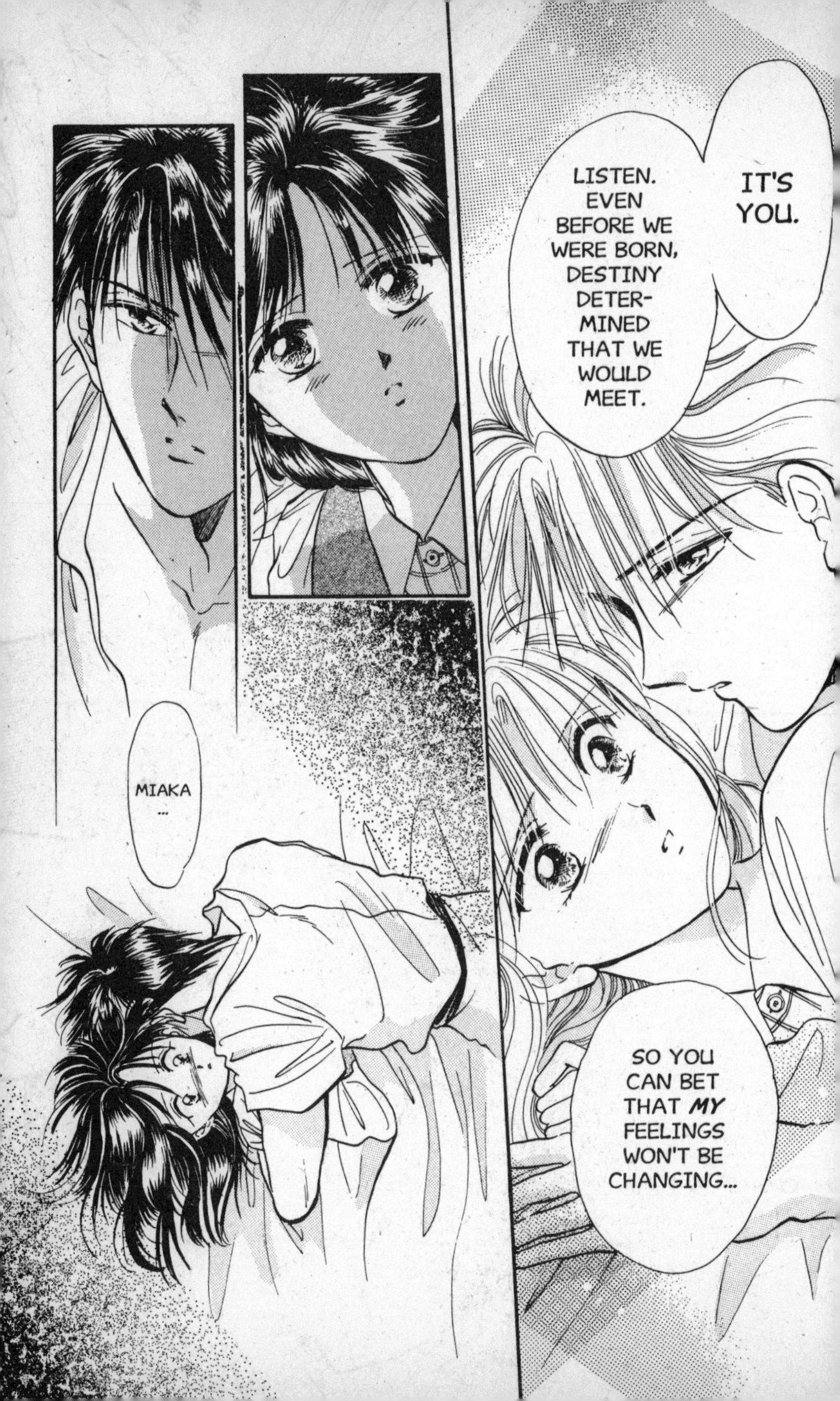
IT'S YOU.
LISTEN. EVEN BEFORE WE WERE BORN, DESTINY DETER-MINED THAT WE WOULD MEET.
SO YOU CAN BET THAT *MY* FEELINGS WON'T BE CHANGING...
MIAKA ...

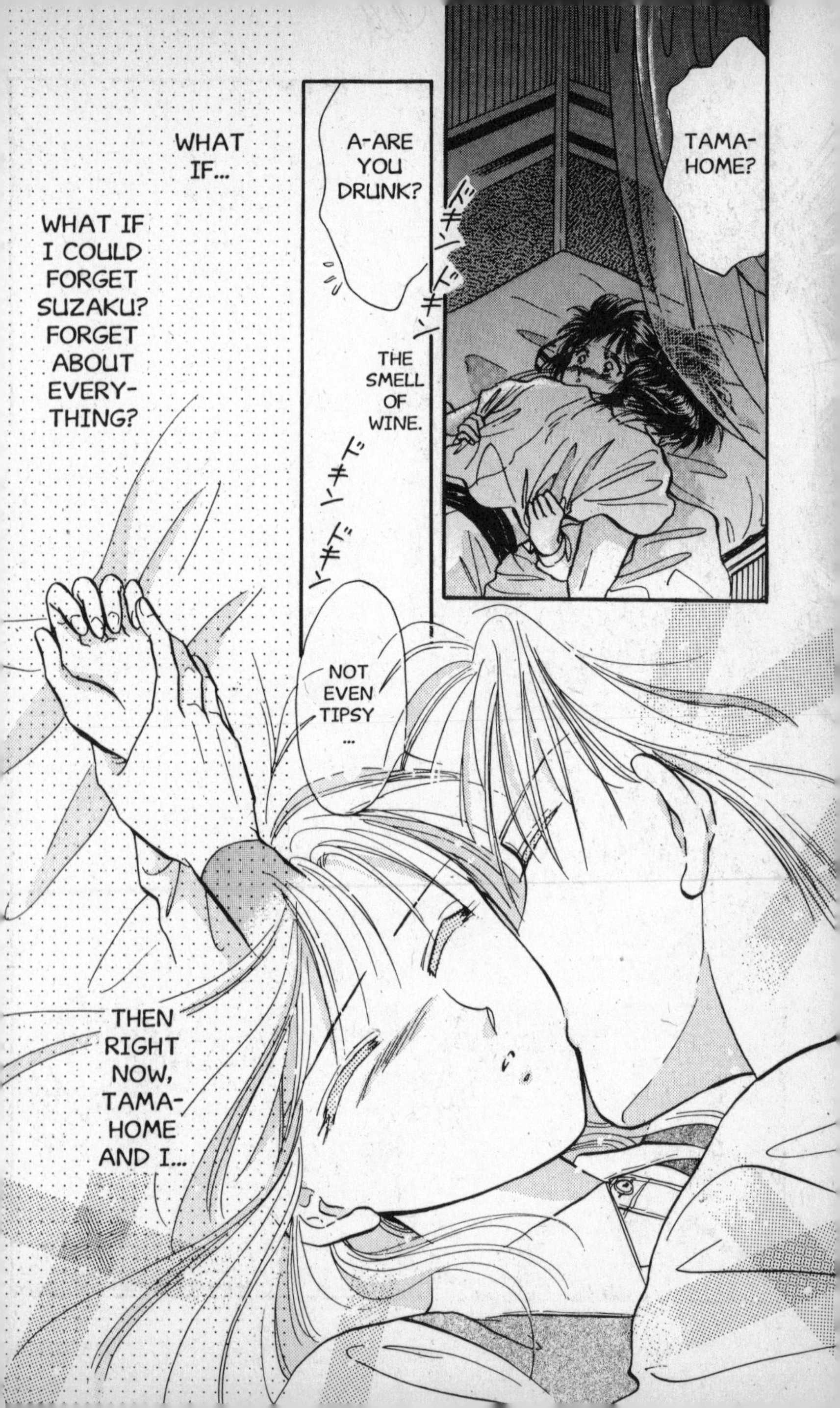
TAMA-HOME?
ドキン ドキン
A-ARE YOU DRUNK?
THE SMELL OF WINE.
ドキン ドキン
WHAT IF...
WHAT IF I COULD FORGET SUZAKU? FORGET ABOUT EVERYTHING?
NOT EVEN TIPSY ...
THEN RIGHT NOW, TAMA-HOME AND I...

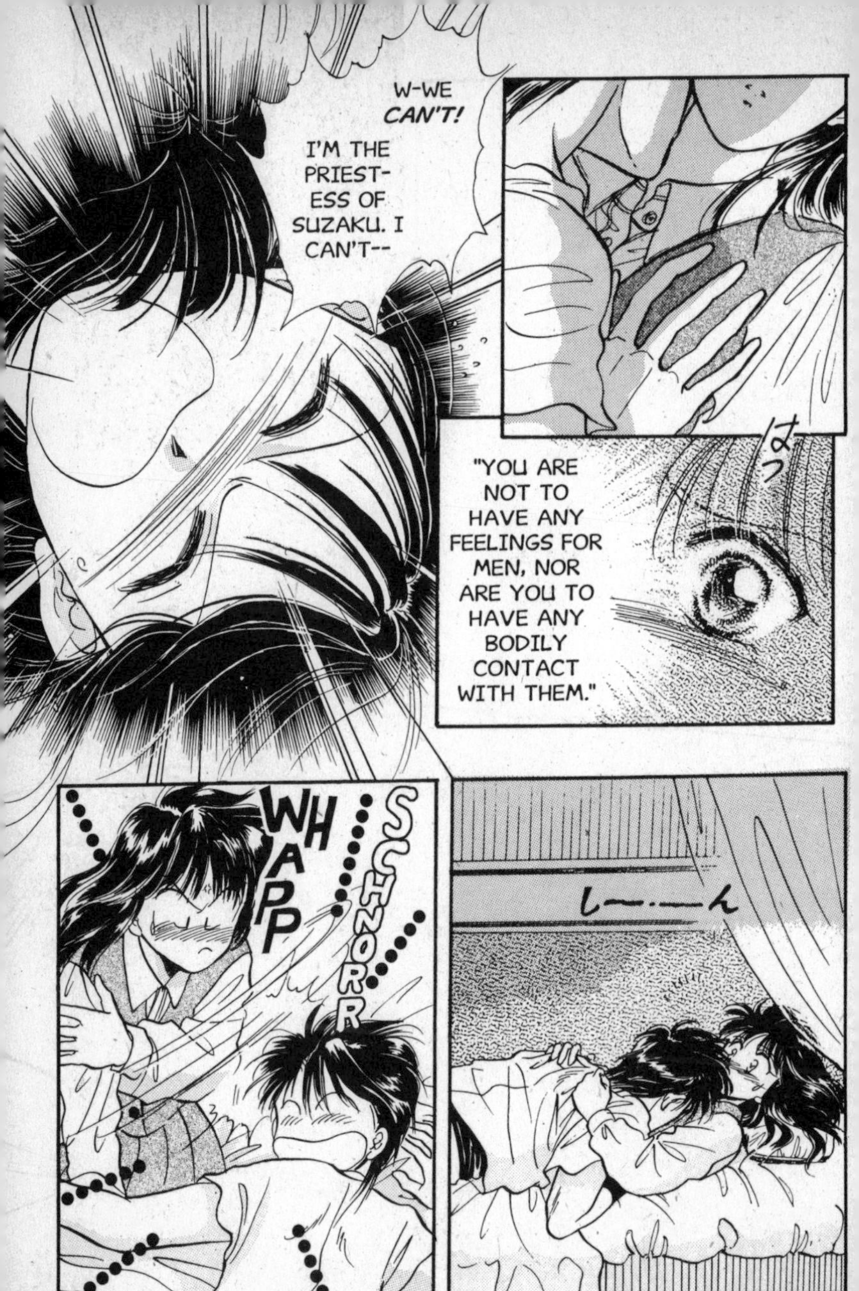
W-WE CAN'T!
I'M THE PRIEST- ESS OF SUZAKU. I CAN'T--
はっ
"YOU ARE NOT TO HAVE ANY FEELINGS FOR MEN, NOR ARE YOU TO HAVE ANY BODILY CONTACT WITH THEM."
しーーん
WHAPP
SCHNORRR

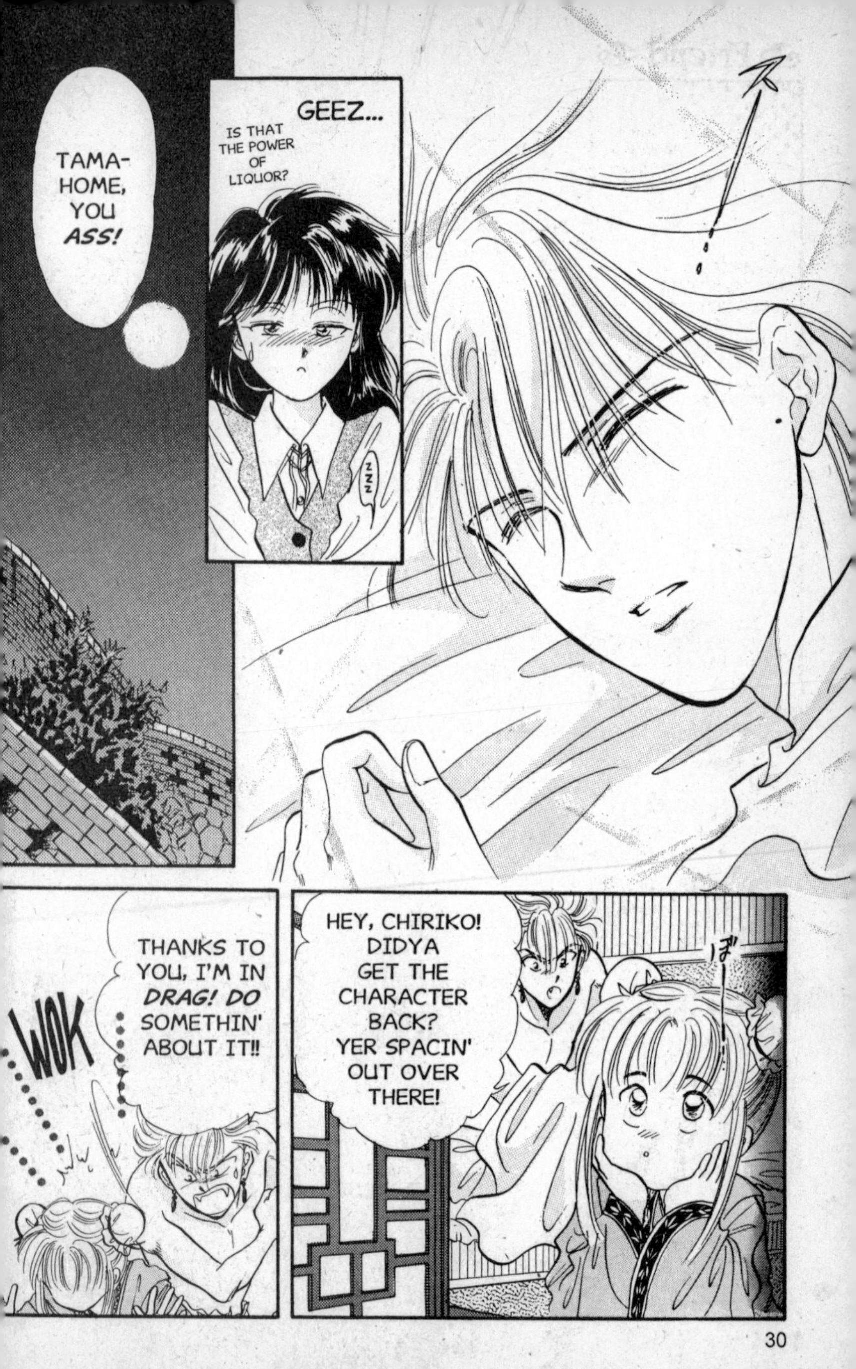
GEEZ...
IS THAT THE POWER OF LIQUOR?
ZZZ
TAMA-HOME, YOU ASS!
HEY, CHIRIKO! DIDYA GET THE CHARACTER BACK? YER SPACIN' OUT OVER THERE!
THANKS TO YOU, I'M IN DRAG! DO SOMETHIN' ABOUT IT!!
WOK

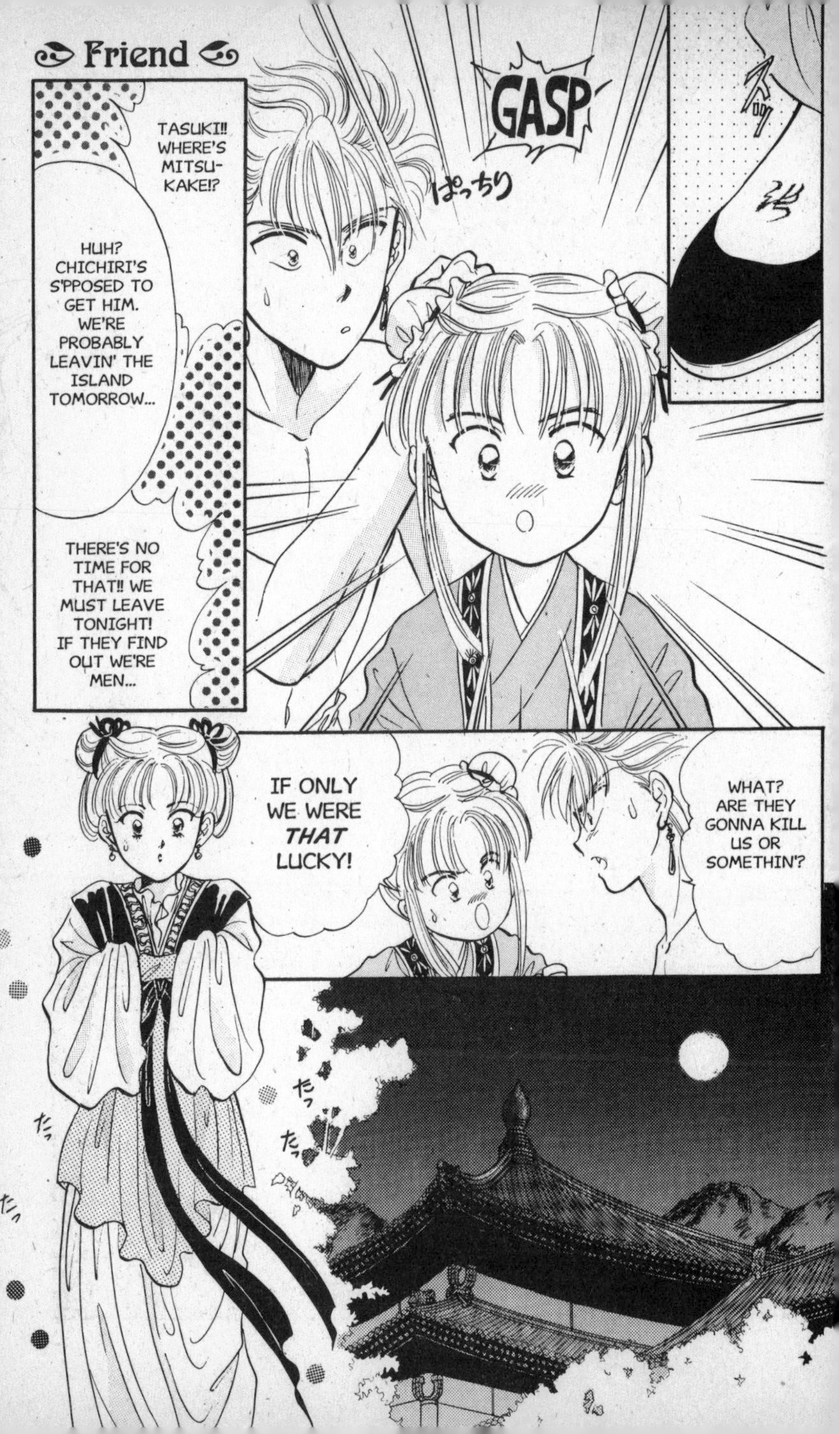
GASP
ぱっちり
TASUKI!! WHERE'S MITSU-KAKE!?
HUH? CHICHIRI'S S'PPOSED TO GET HIM. WE'RE PROBABLY LEAVIN' THE ISLAND TOMORROW...
THERE'S NO TIME FOR THAT!! WE MUST LEAVE TONIGHT! IF THEY FIND OUT WE'RE MEN...
WHAT? ARE THEY GONNA KILL US OR SOMETHIN'?
IF ONLY WE WERE *THAT* LUCKY!
たっ
たっ
たっ
たっ

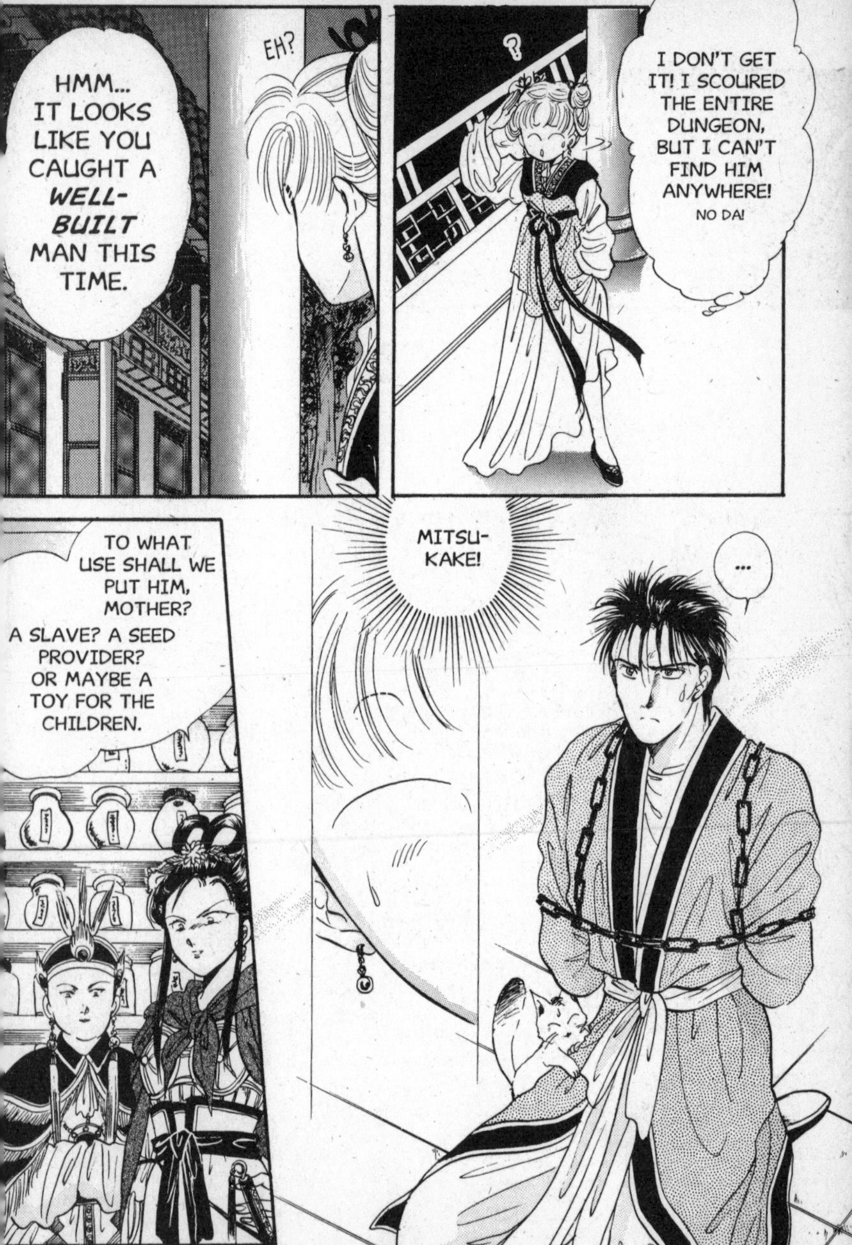
?
I DON'T GET IT! I SCOURED THE ENTIRE DUNGEON, BUT I CAN'T FIND HIM ANYWHERE! NO DA!
EH?
HMM... IT LOOKS LIKE YOU CAUGHT A *WELL-BUILT* MAN THIS TIME.
MITSU-KAKE!
...
TO WHAT USE SHALL WE PUT HIM, MOTHER? A SLAVE? A SEED PROVIDER? OR MAYBE A TOY FOR THE CHILDREN.

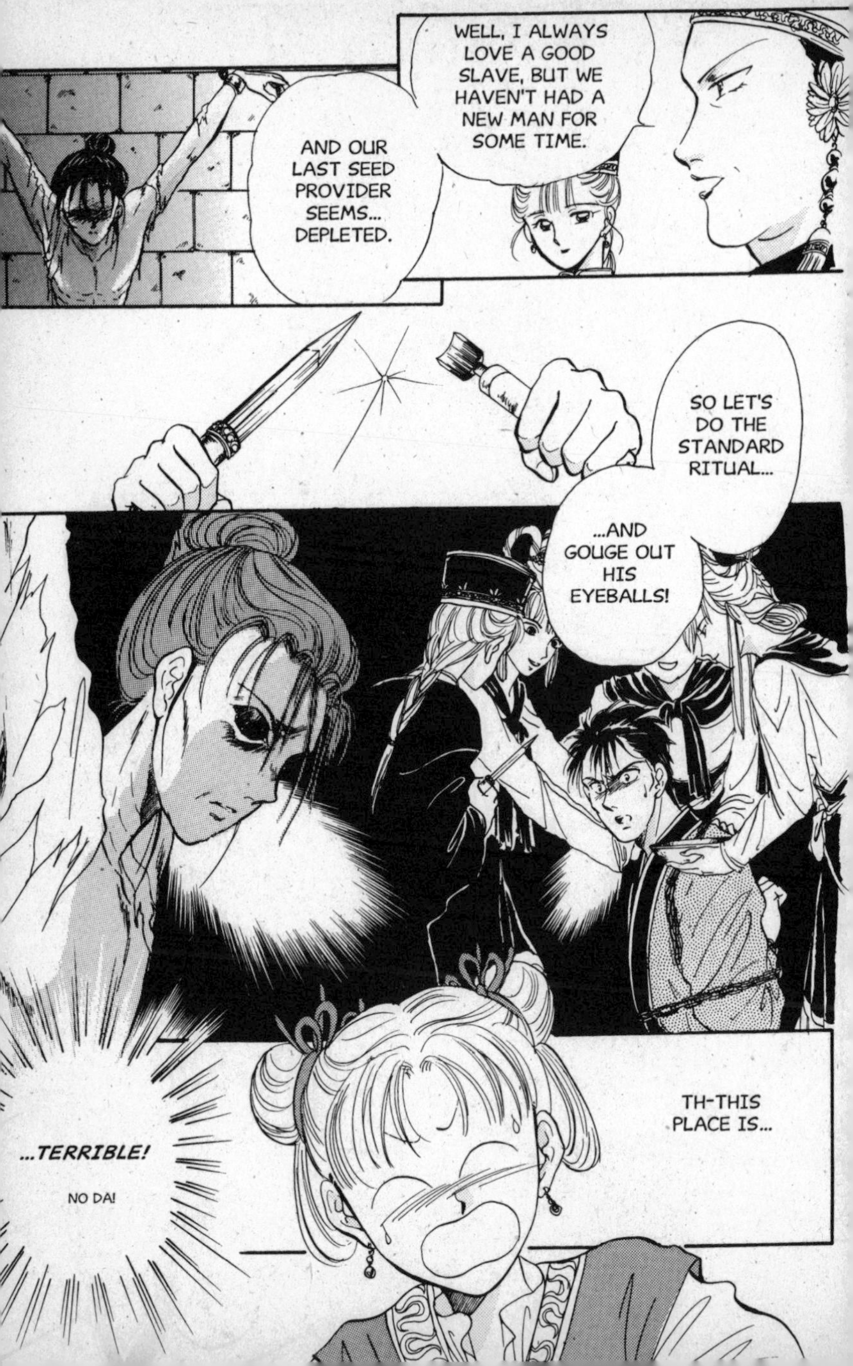
WELL, I ALWAYS LOVE A GOOD SLAVE, BUT WE HAVEN'T HAD A NEW MAN FOR SOME TIME.
AND OUR LAST SEED PROVIDER SEEMS... DEPLETED.
SO LET'S DO THE STANDARD RITUAL...
...AND GOUGE OUT HIS EYEBALLS!
TH-THIS PLACE IS...
...TERRIBLE!
NO DA!

CHAPTER FORTY-FOUR

THE SPARK OF COMBAT

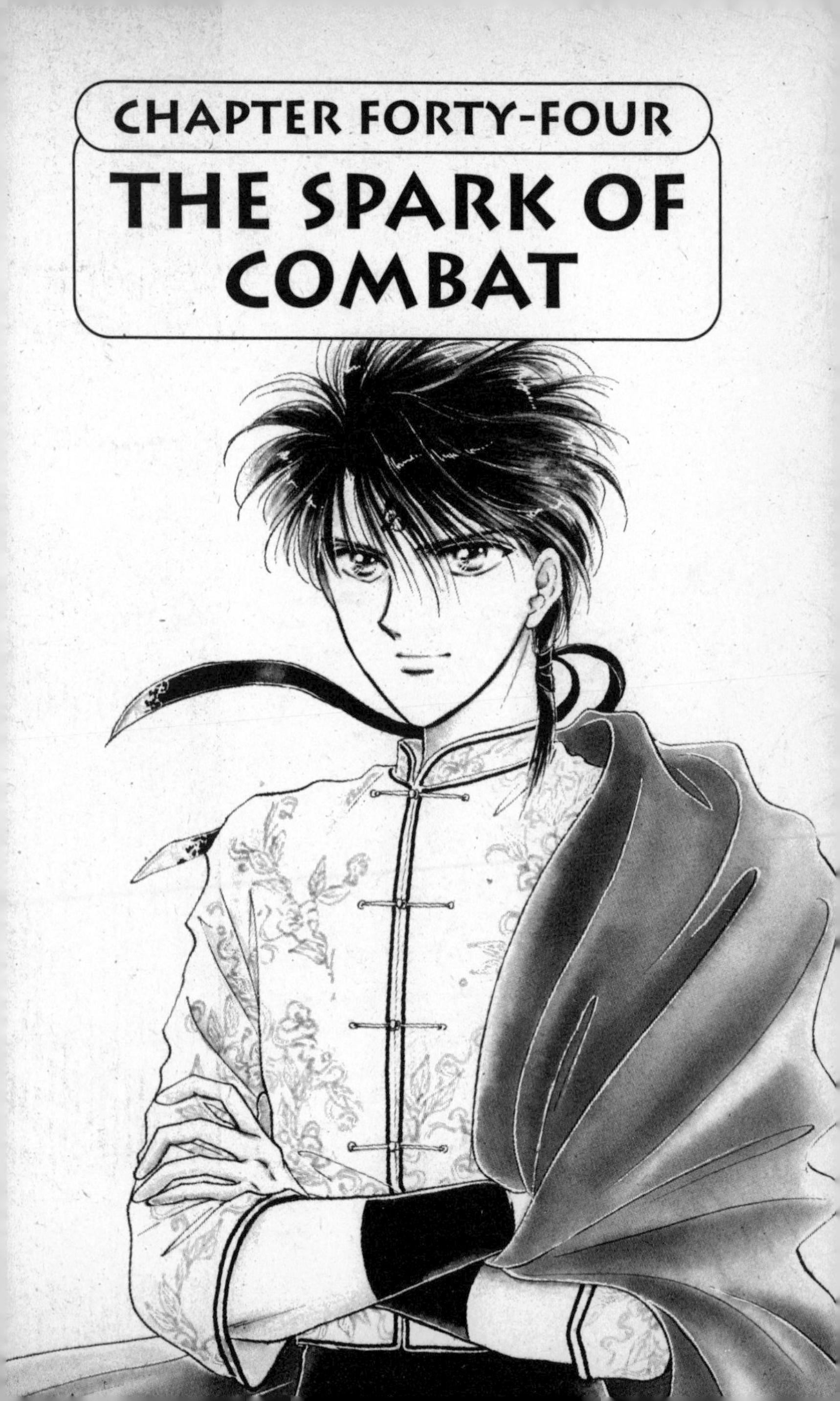

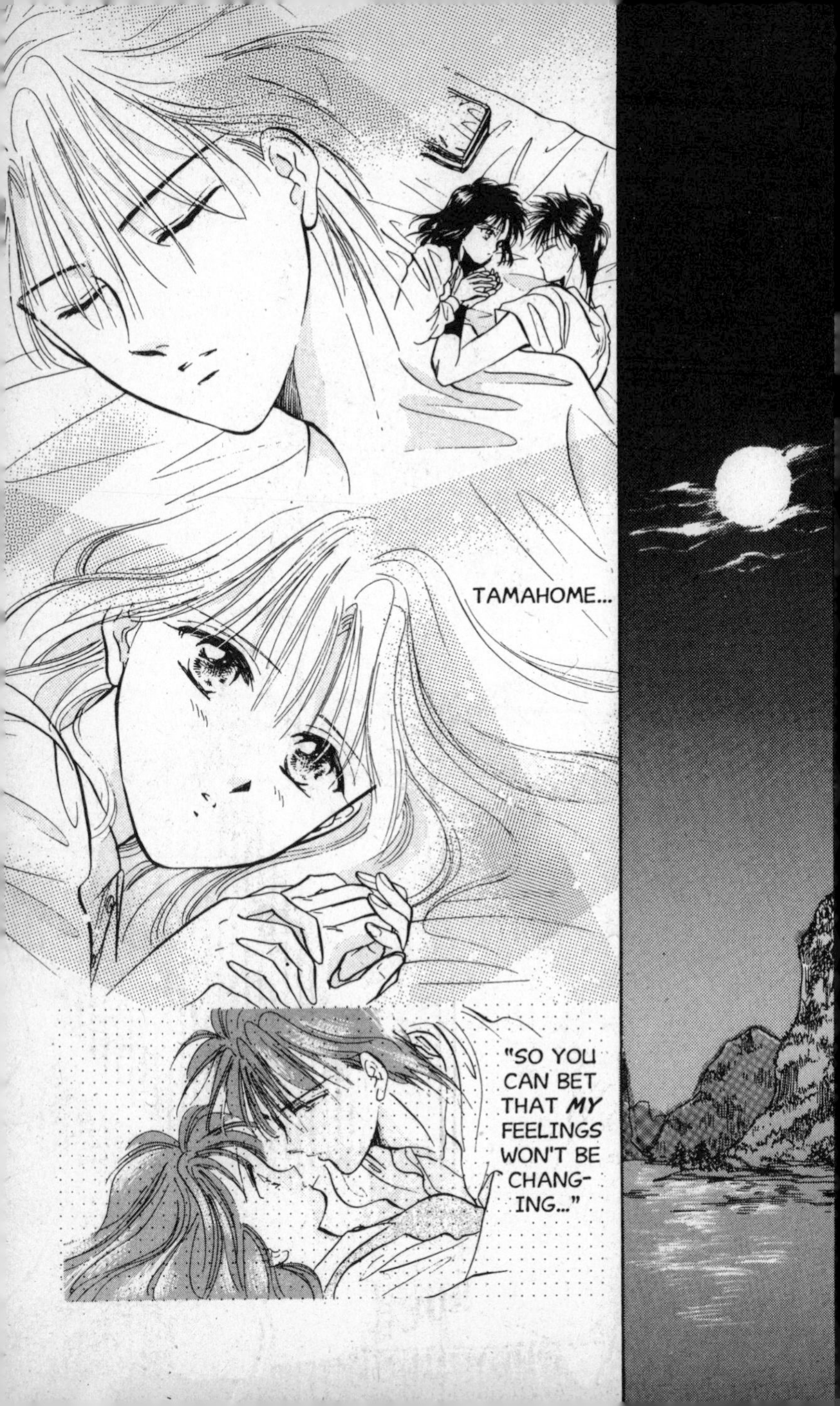
TAMAHOME...
"SO YOU CAN BET THAT *MY* FEELINGS WON'T BE CHANG-ING..."

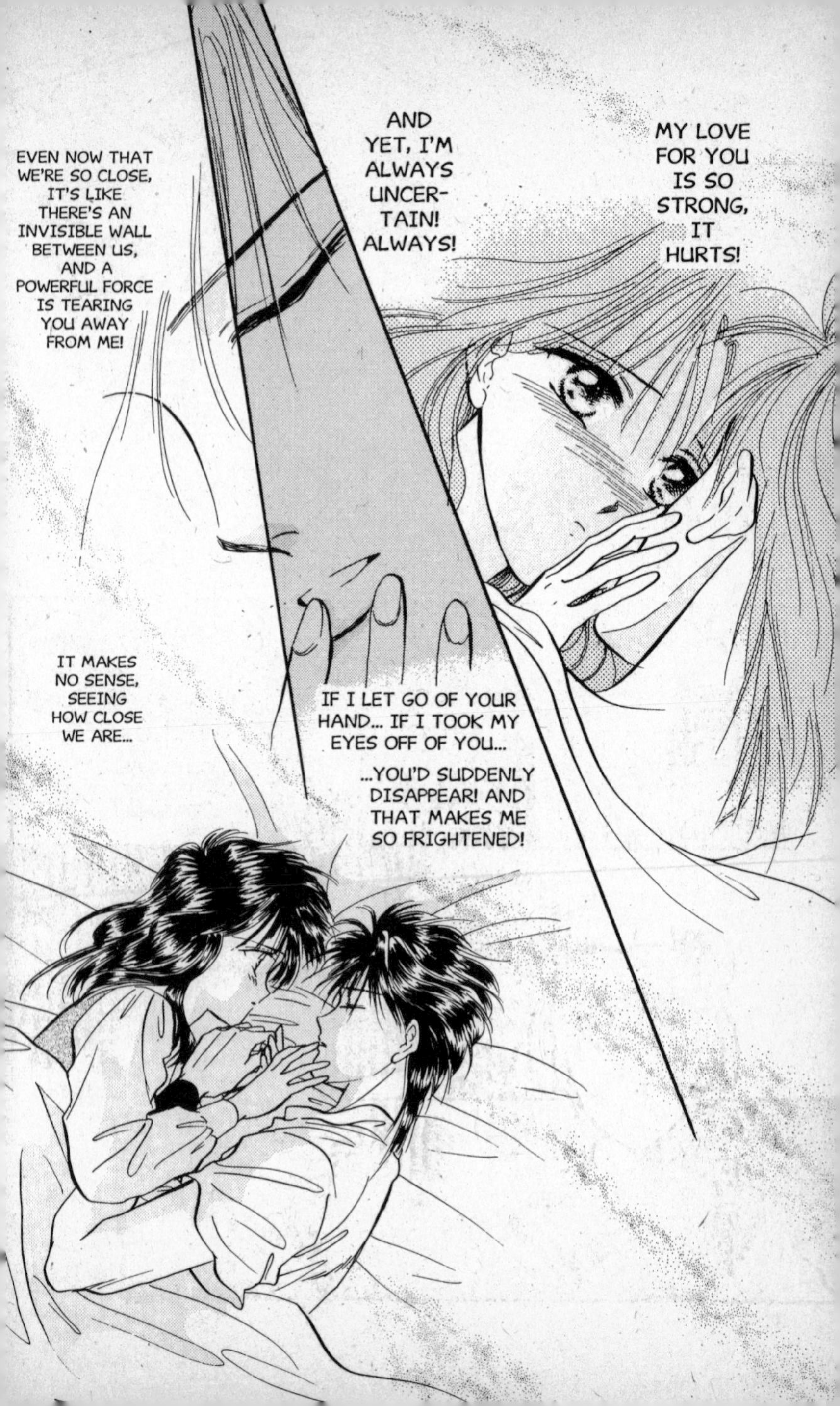
MY LOVE FOR YOU IS SO STRONG, IT HURTS!
AND YET, I'M ALWAYS UNCER-TAIN! ALWAYS!
EVEN NOW THAT WE'RE SO CLOSE, IT'S LIKE THERE'S AN INVISIBLE WALL BETWEEN US, AND A POWERFUL FORCE IS TEARING YOU AWAY FROM ME!
IF I LET GO OF YOUR HAND... IF I TOOK MY EYES OFF OF YOU...
...YOU'D SUDDENLY DISAPPEAR! AND THAT MAKES ME SO FRIGHTENED!
IT MAKES NO SENSE, SEEING HOW CLOSE WE ARE...

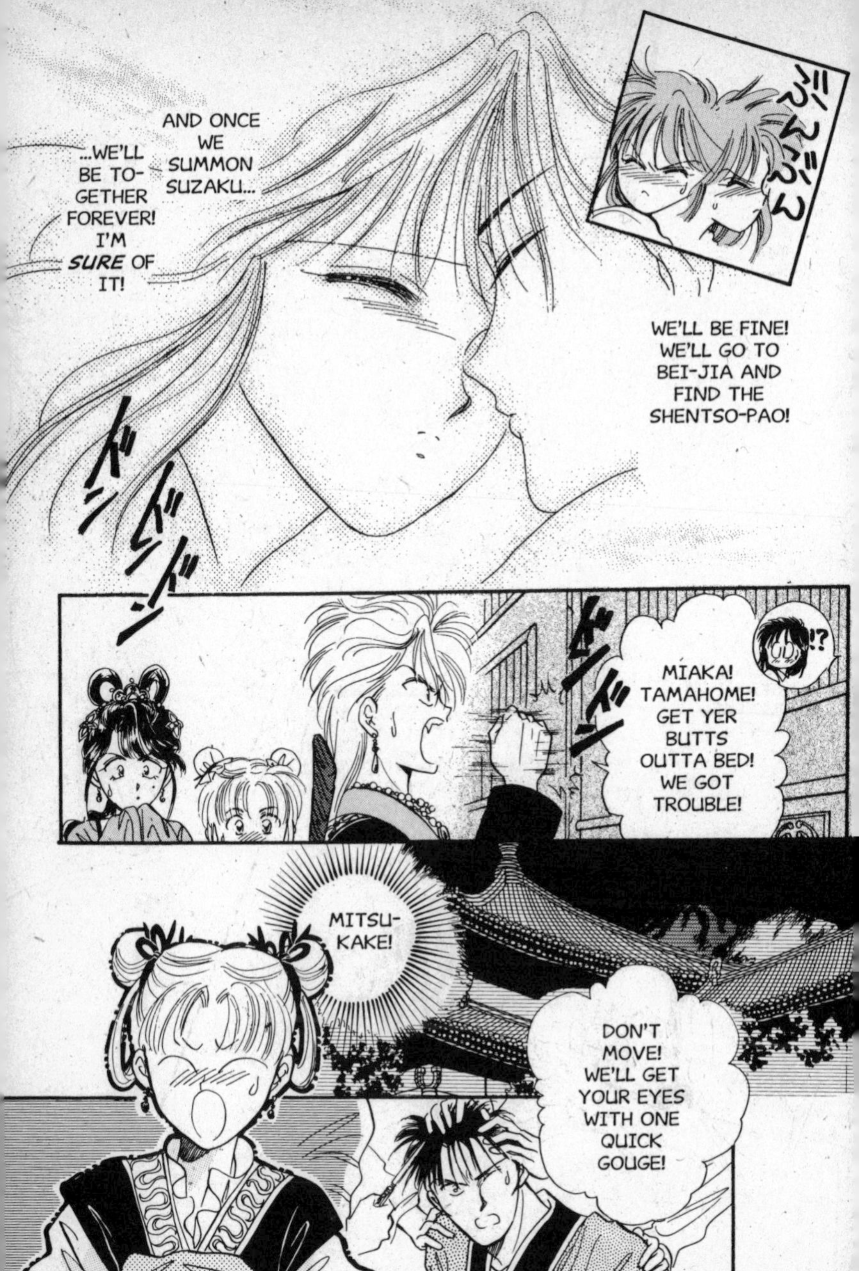

ぶんぶん
WE'LL BE FINE! WE'LL GO TO BEI-JIA AND FIND THE SHENTSO-PAO!
AND ONCE WE SUMMON SUZAKU...
...WE'LL BE TO-GETHER FOREVER! I'M *SURE* OF IT!
ドンドンドン
!?
MIAKA! TAMAHOME! GET YER BUTTS OUTTA BED! WE GOT TROUBLE!
ドンドン
MITSU-KAKE!
DON'T MOVE! WE'LL GET YOUR EYES WITH ONE QUICK GOUGE!

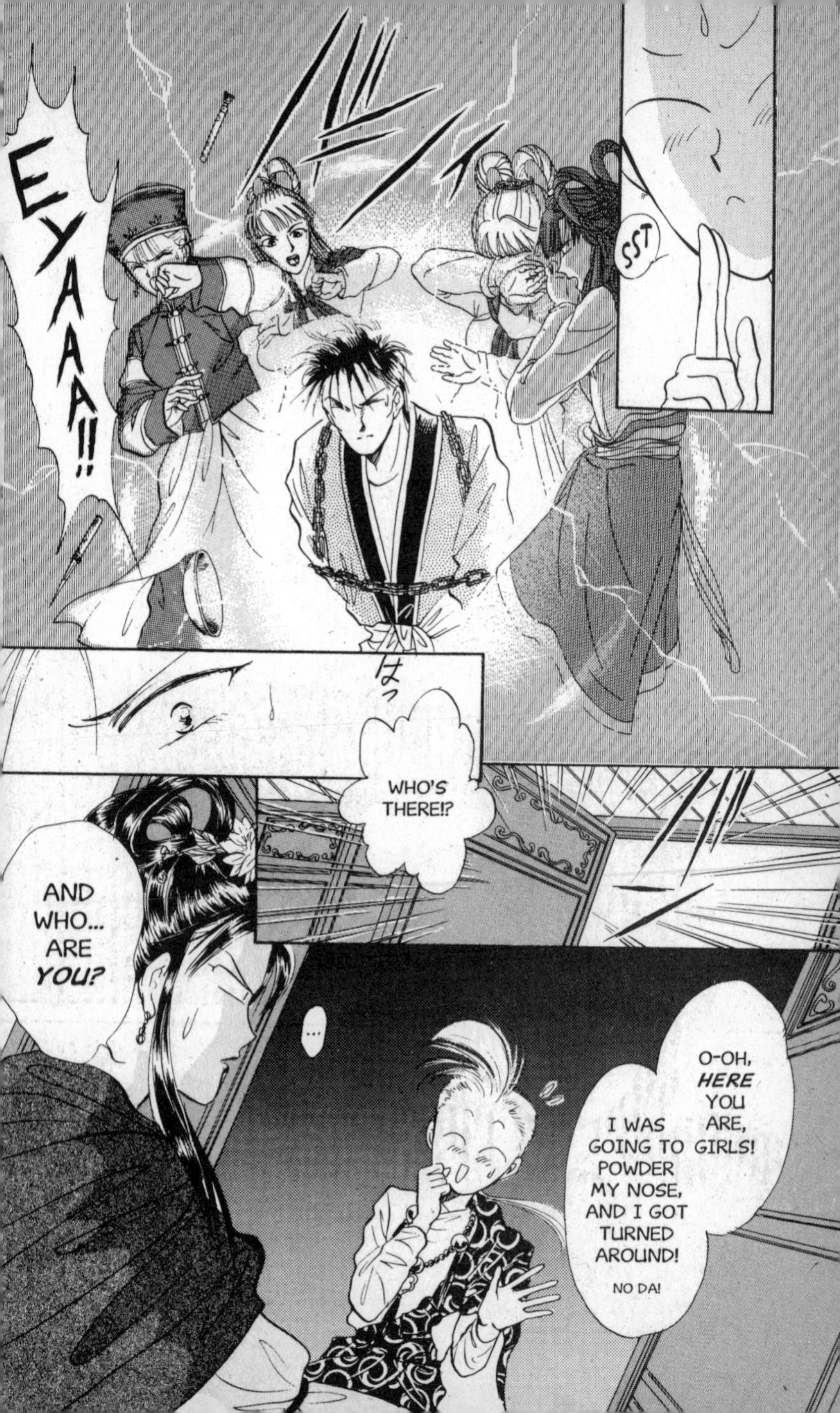

SST
EYAAA!!
はっ
WHO'S THERE!?
O-OH, *HERE* YOU ARE, GIRLS!
I WAS GOING TO POWDER MY NOSE, AND I GOT TURNED AROUND!
NO DA!
...
AND WHO... ARE *YOU?*

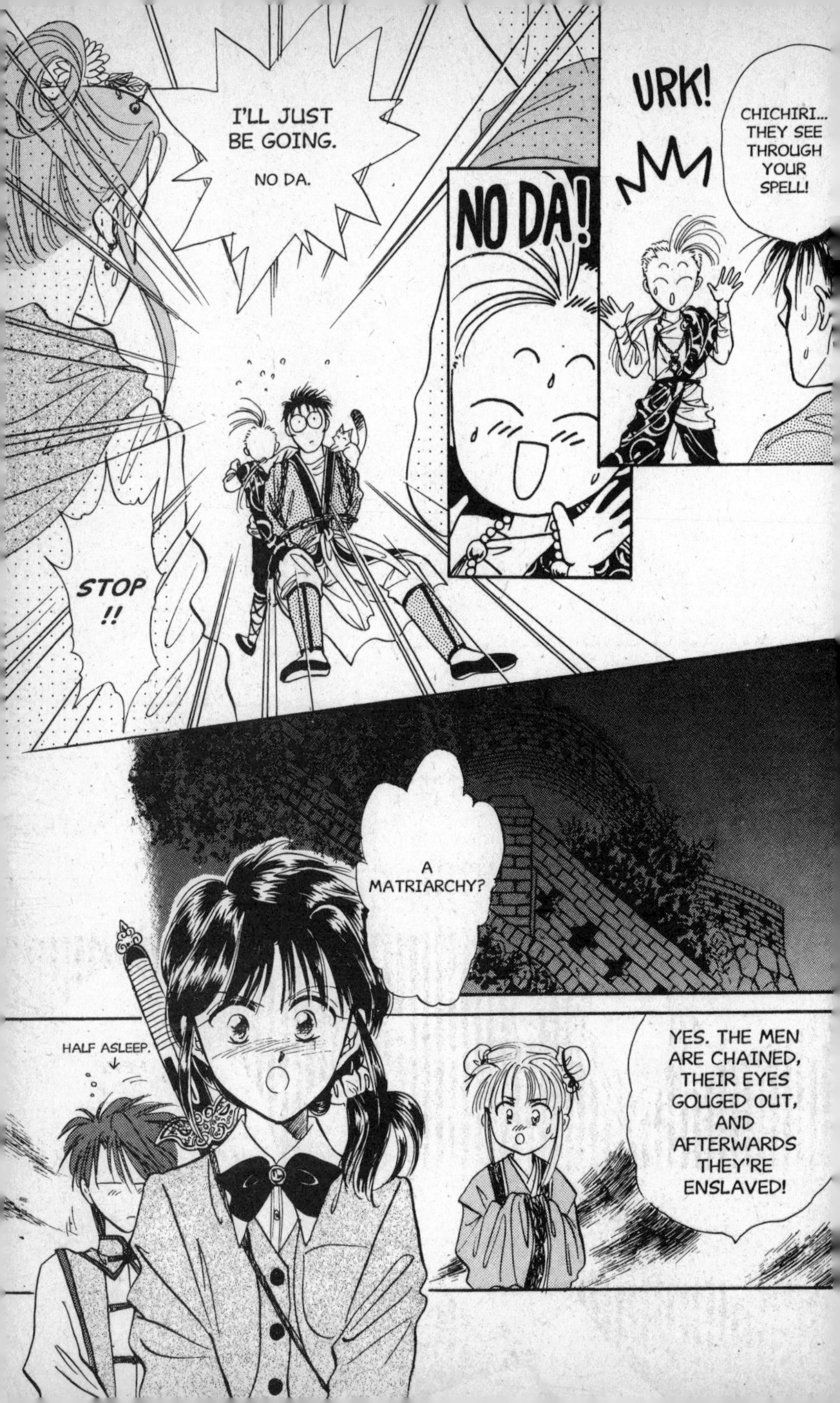
CHICHIRI... THEY SEE THROUGH YOUR SPELL!
URK!
NO DA!
I'LL JUST BE GOING.
NO DA.
STOP !!
A MATRIARCHY?
YES. THE MEN ARE CHAINED, THEIR EYES GOUGED OUT, AND AFTERWARDS THEY'RE ENSLAVED!
HALF ASLEEP.

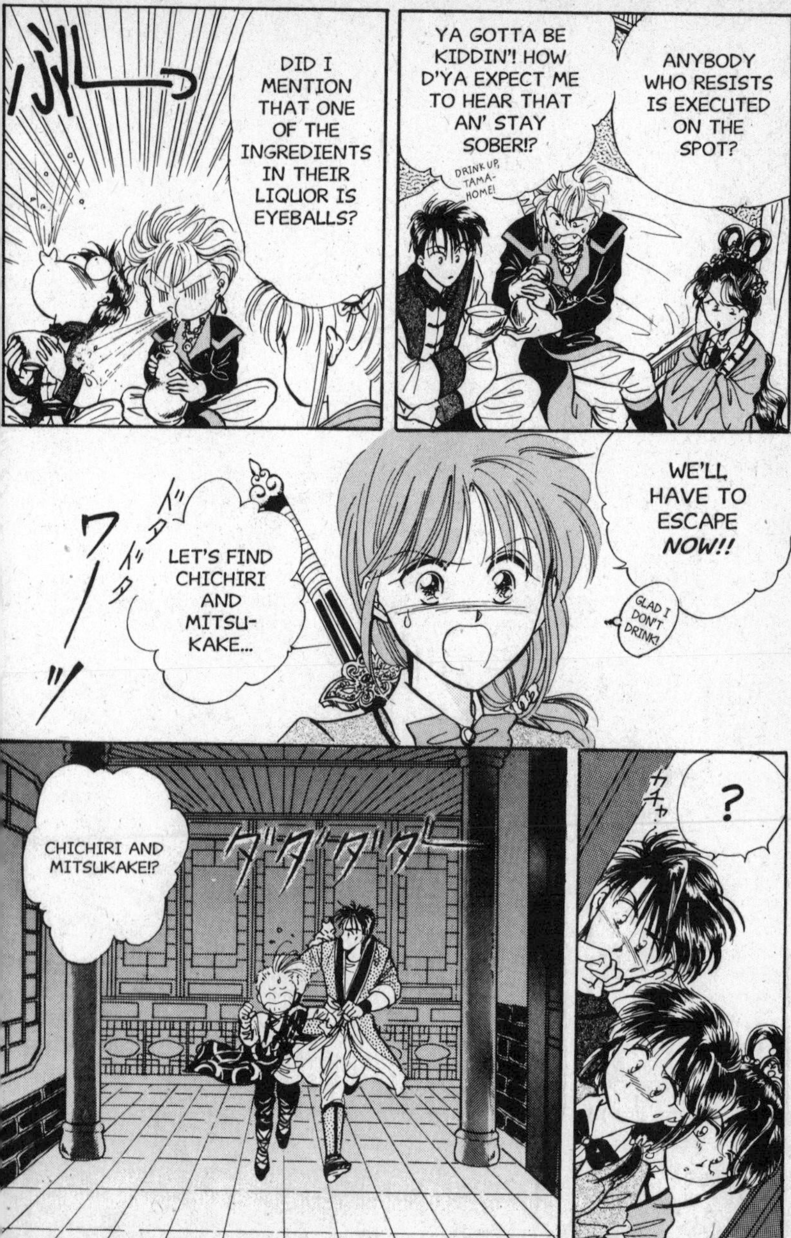
ANYBODY WHO RESISTS IS EXECUTED ON THE SPOT?
YA GOTTA BE KIDDIN'! HOW D'YA EXPECT ME TO HEAR THAT AN' STAY SOBER!?
DRINK UP, TAMA-HOME!
DID I MENTION THAT ONE OF THE INGREDIENTS IN THEIR LIQUOR IS EYEBALLS?
WE'LL HAVE TO ESCAPE *NOW!!*
GLAD I DON'T DRINK!
LET'S FIND CHICHIRI AND MITSU-KAKE...
?
CHICHIRI AND MITSUKAKE!?

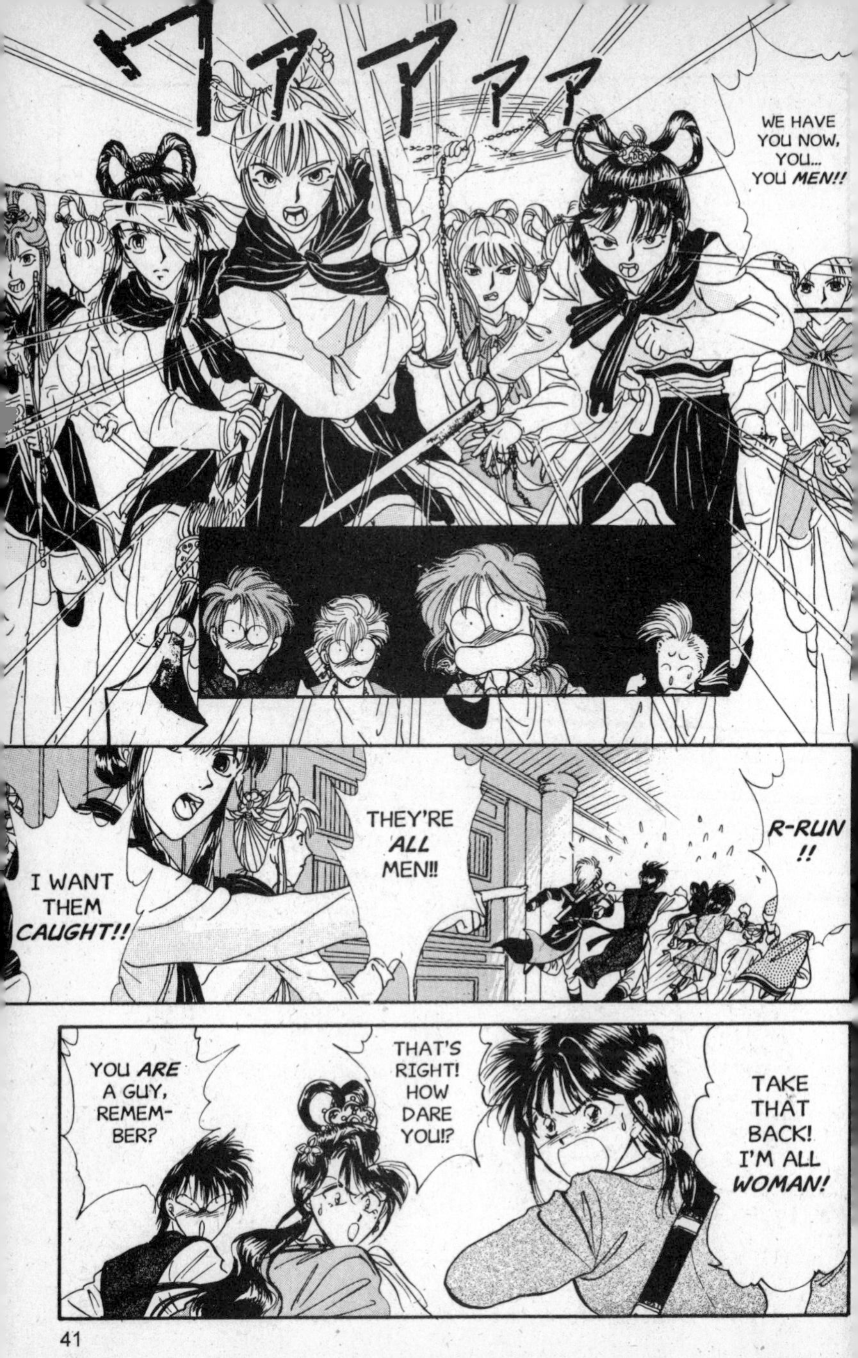

ワアアァァ
WE HAVE YOU NOW, YOU... YOU *MEN!!*
R-RUN !!
THEY'RE *ALL* MEN!!
I WANT THEM *CAUGHT!!*
TAKE THAT BACK! I'M ALL *WOMAN!*
THAT'S RIGHT! HOW DARE YOU!?
YOU *ARE* A GUY, REMEM-BER?

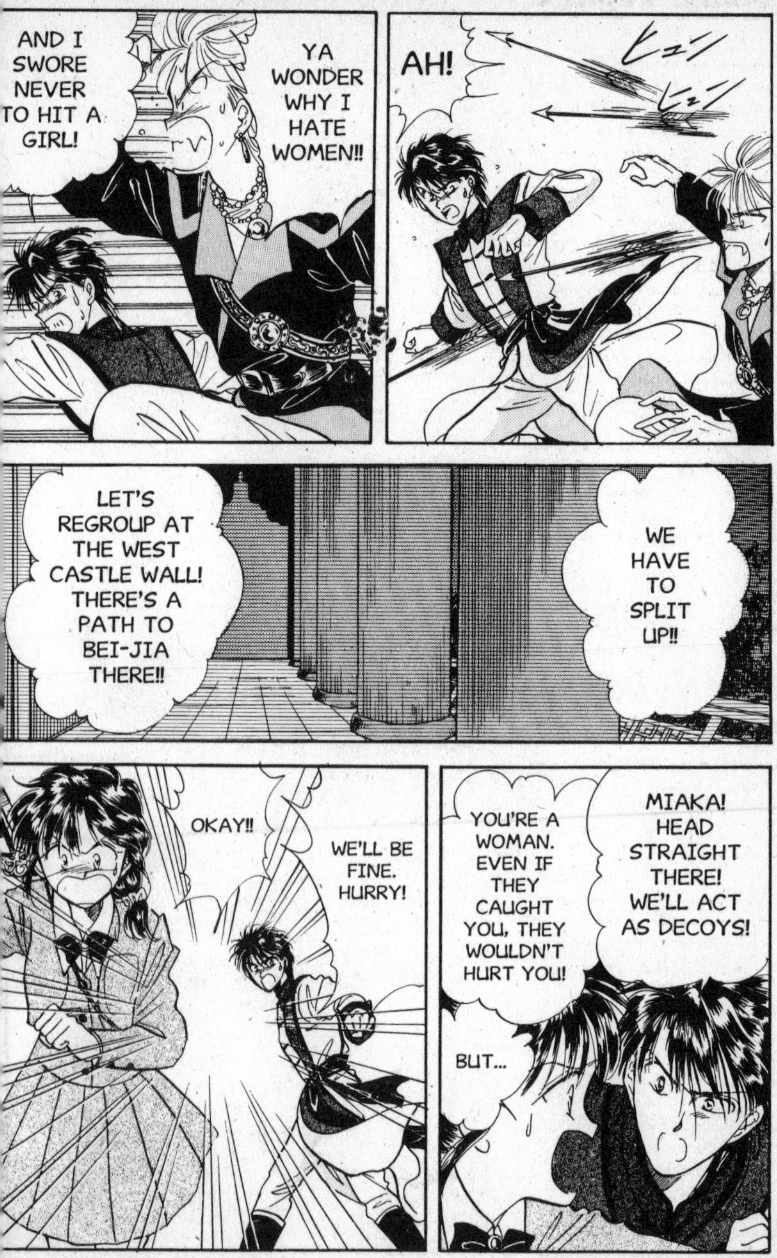
AH!
YA WONDER WHY I HATE WOMEN!!
AND I SWORE NEVER TO HIT A GIRL!
WE HAVE TO SPLIT UP!!
LET'S REGROUP AT THE WEST CASTLE WALL! THERE'S A PATH TO BEI-JIA THERE!!
MIAKA! HEAD STRAIGHT THERE! WE'LL ACT AS DECOYS!
YOU'RE A WOMAN. EVEN IF THEY CAUGHT YOU, THEY WOULDN'T HURT YOU!
BUT...
WE'LL BE FINE. HURRY!
OKAY!!

From July 26 through August 3, I went to China (from Beijing to Xian to Guilin and finally to Shanghai) with my editor K for nine days. We had trouble from the very beginning--our JAL flight was blocked at Beijing Airport by a Chinese airplane. It just wouldn't get out of our way! So we waited for half an hour and finally managed to get off the plane. We took the bus to the famous Tiananmen Square. It was so huge, with so many people, that I wondered what they were all there for! There were even people flying kites.

I was in search of the palaces I've been drawing all this time, and I took loads of photos. The gates are so big. My drawings were based on travel brochures, but the real thing was awesome!!

The meals, of course, were Chinese! They were really tasty (at least for a while...).

Of course, in Beijing the ultimate place is the Forbidden City (the old Imperial Palace) where the events of "The Last Emperor" took place. On our first day there, we had a view of the entire palace (it was really huge!!). Wow! Then the next day, we visited the inside of the building! I was so excited! I mean, it's a real palace (duh). Apparently, it takes a week to view the entire palace, so we went straight to the middle portion. The ceilings were incredibly high, the columns really wide, and the interior decoration and designs of the walls and ceilings were wonderful!! I got it all on film, but it'd be impossible to capture it in a drawing. India was the same! It was in the realm of art!! The border between reality and manga became blurred.

BE CAREFUL, MIAKA!

I WISH YOU THE BEST OF LUCK!

YEAH, THANKS A BUNCH, TAMA MY MAN!

THERE HE IS!!

WHAT!? YOU'RE LEAVING ME *ALONE!?*

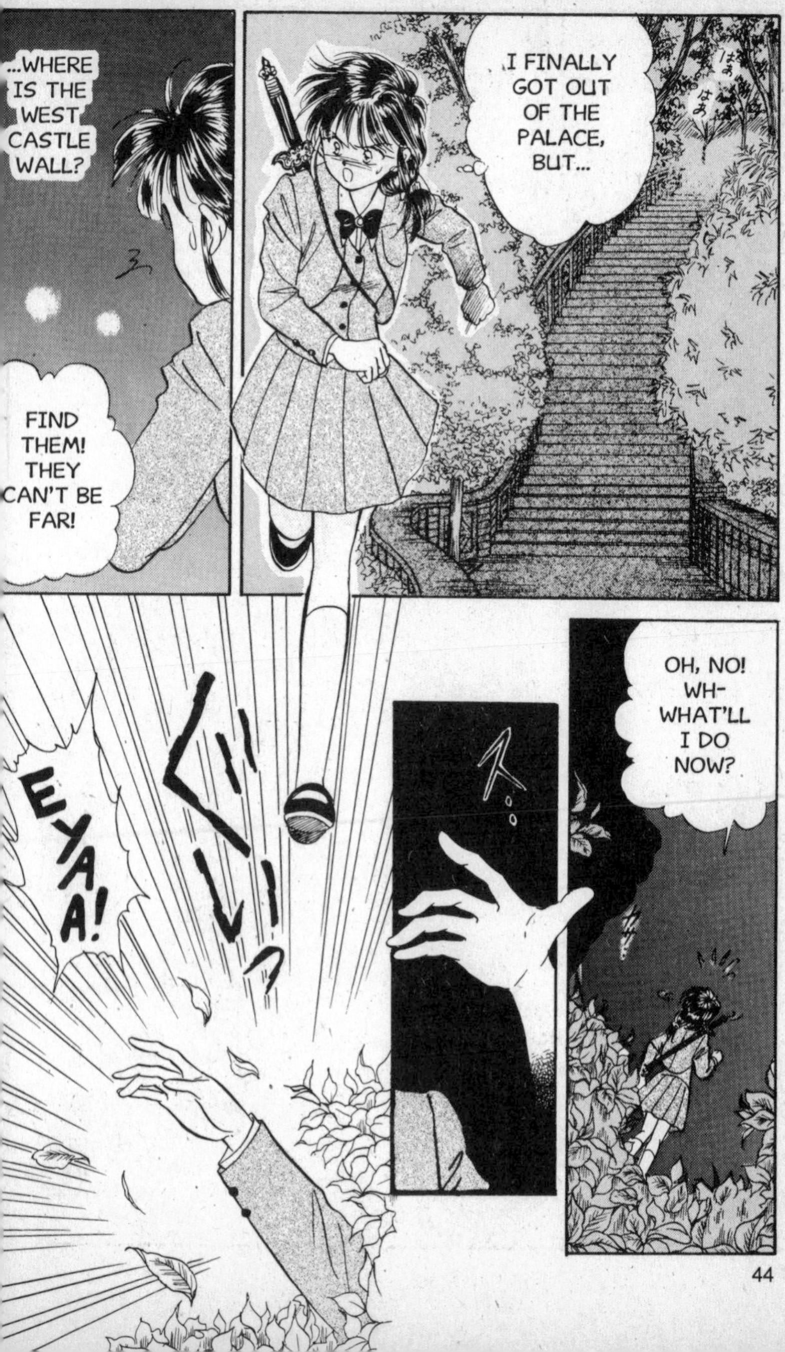
I FINALLY GOT OUT OF THE PALACE, BUT...
はぁ はぁ
...WHERE IS THE WEST CASTLE WALL?
FIND THEM! THEY CAN'T BE FAR!
OH, NO! WH-WHAT'LL I DO NOW?
EYAA!

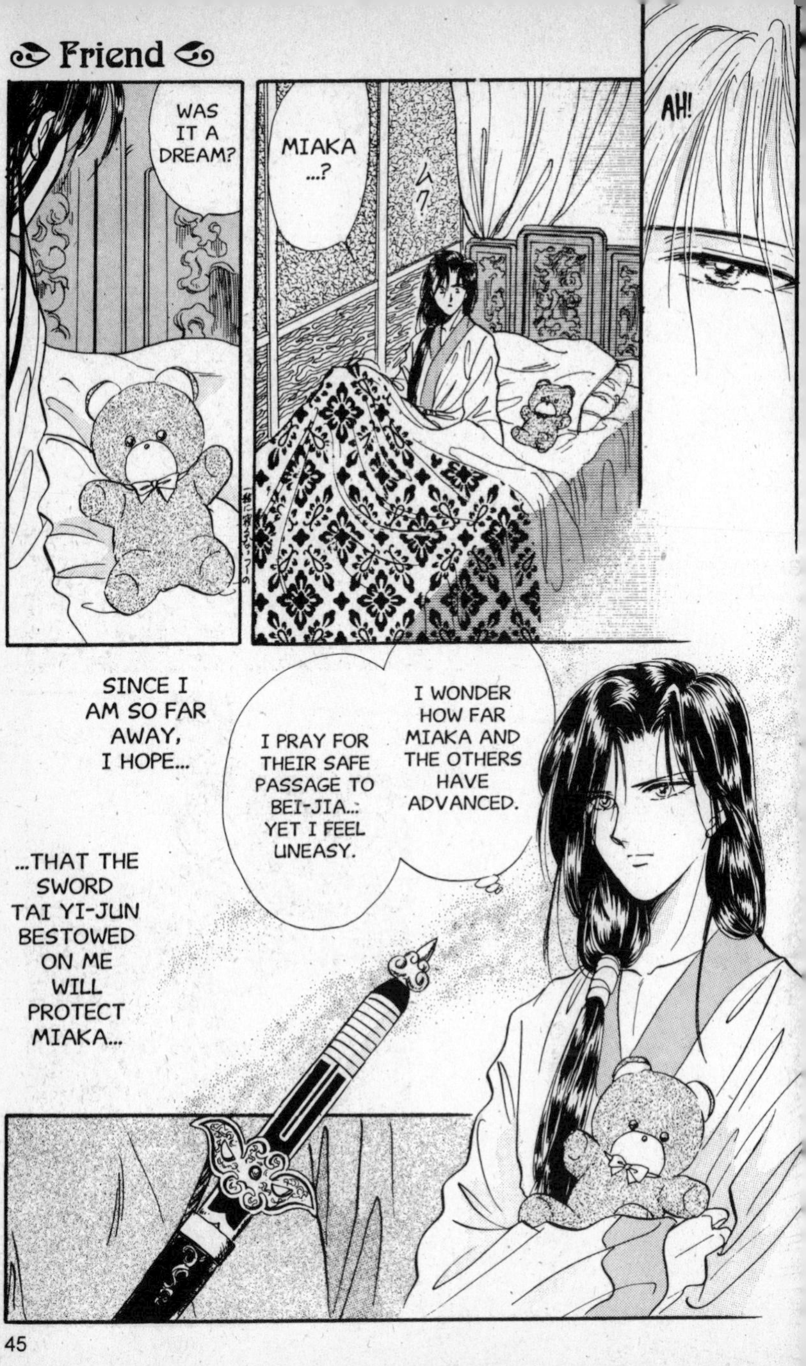
AH!
MIAKA ...?
ムク
WAS IT A DREAM?
I WONDER HOW FAR MIAKA AND THE OTHERS HAVE ADVANCED.
I PRAY FOR THEIR SAFE PASSAGE TO BEI-JIA... YET I FEEL UNEASY.
SINCE I AM SO FAR AWAY, I HOPE...
...THAT THE SWORD TAI YI-JUN BESTOWED ON ME WILL PROTECT MIAKA...

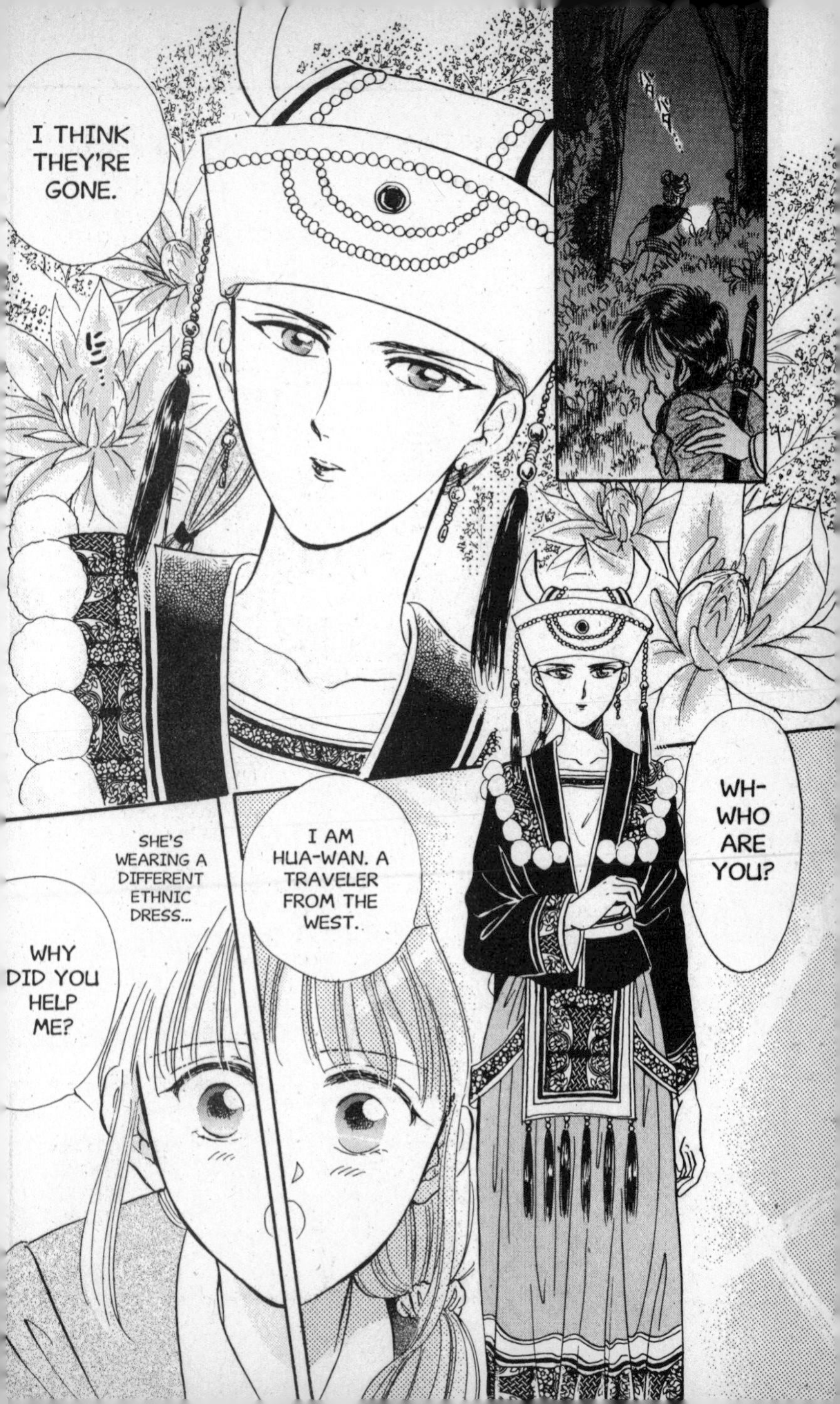
I THINK THEY'RE GONE.
WH-WHO ARE YOU?
I AM HUA-WAN. A TRAVELER FROM THE WEST.
SHE'S WEARING A DIFFERENT ETHNIC DRESS...
WHY DID YOU HELP ME?

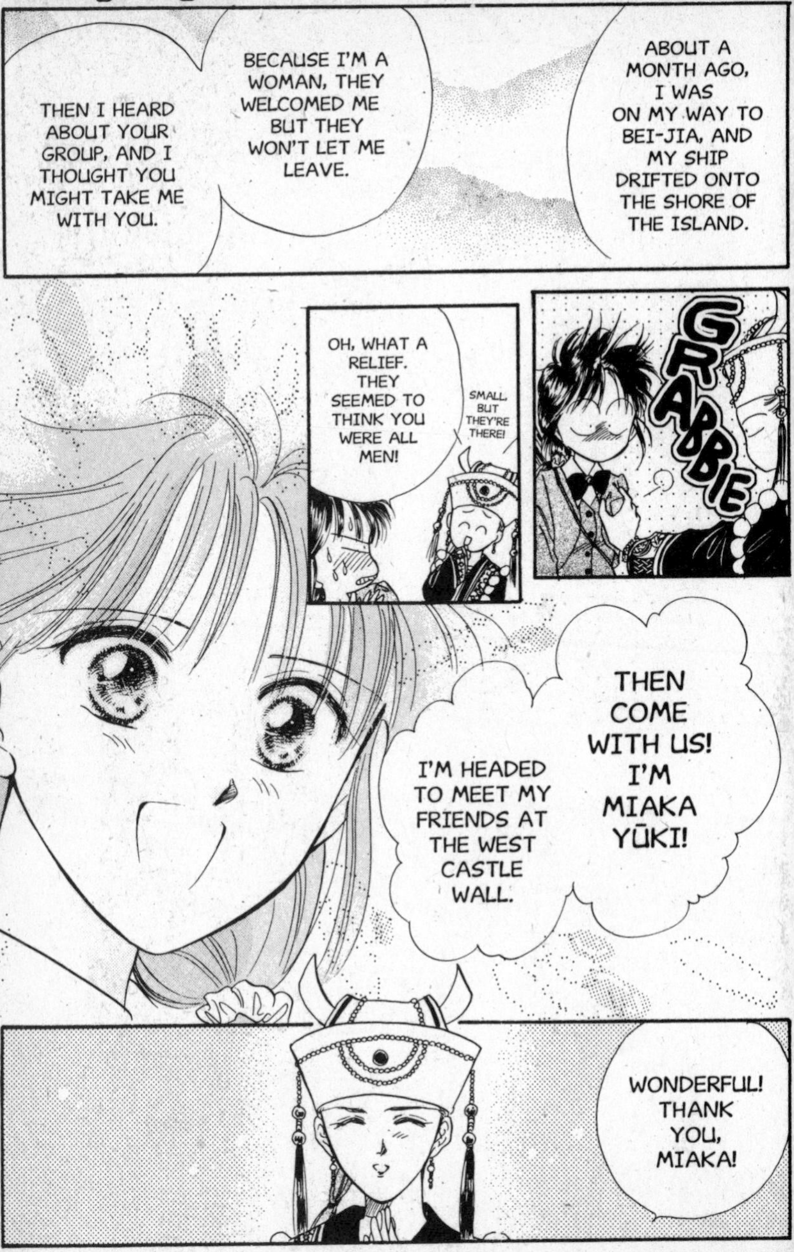
ABOUT A MONTH AGO, I WAS ON MY WAY TO BEI-JIA, AND MY SHIP DRIFTED ONTO THE SHORE OF THE ISLAND.
BECAUSE I'M A WOMAN, THEY WELCOMED ME BUT THEY WON'T LET ME LEAVE.
THEN I HEARD ABOUT YOUR GROUP, AND I THOUGHT YOU MIGHT TAKE ME WITH YOU.
GRABBIE
OH, WHAT A RELIEF. THEY SEEMED TO THINK YOU WERE ALL MEN!
SMALL, BUT THEY'RE THERE!
THEN COME WITH US! I'M MIAKA YŪKI!
I'M HEADED TO MEET MY FRIENDS AT THE WEST CASTLE WALL.
WONDERFUL! THANK YOU, MIAKA!

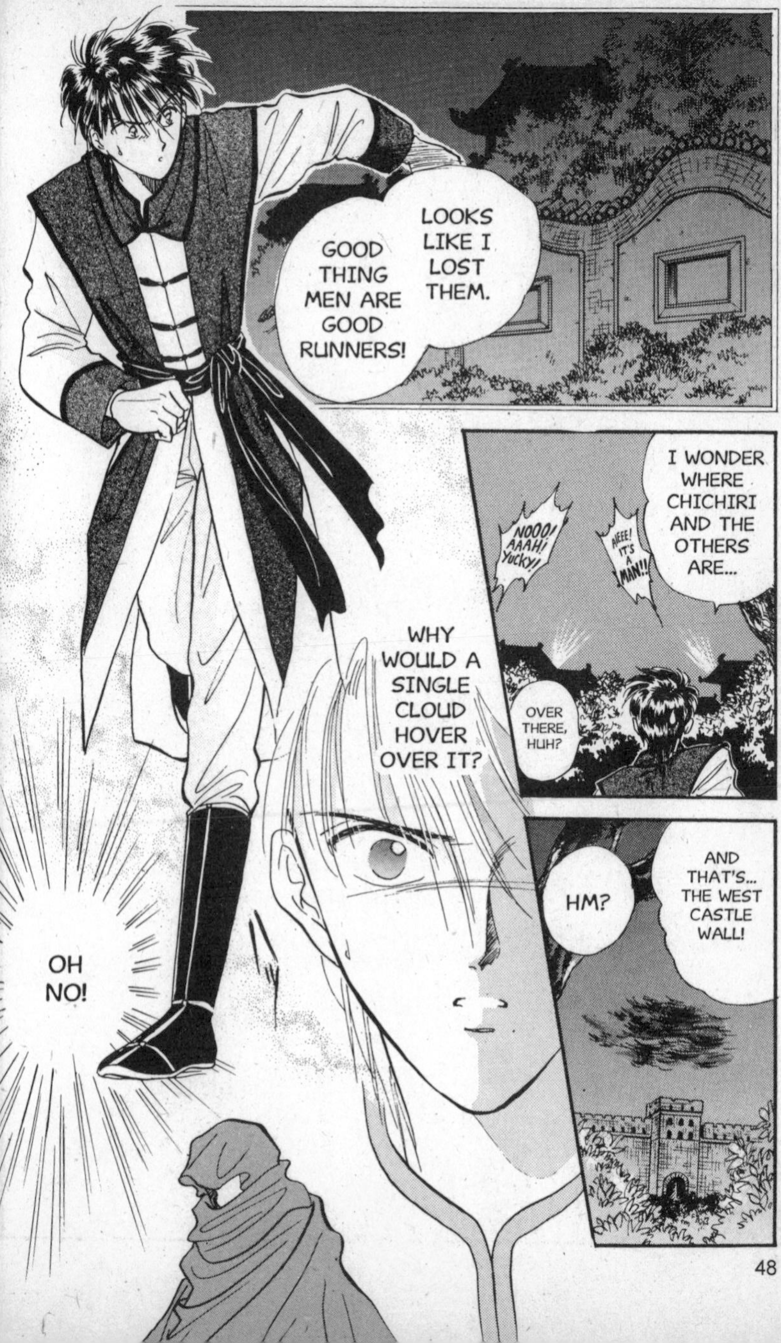
LOOKS LIKE I LOST THEM.
GOOD THING MEN ARE GOOD RUNNERS!
I WONDER WHERE CHICHIRI AND THE OTHERS ARE...
AIEEE! IT'S A MAN!!
NOOO! AAAH! YUCKY!
OVER THERE, HUH?
AND THAT'S... THE WEST CASTLE WALL!
HM?
WHY WOULD A SINGLE CLOUD HOVER OVER IT?
OH NO!

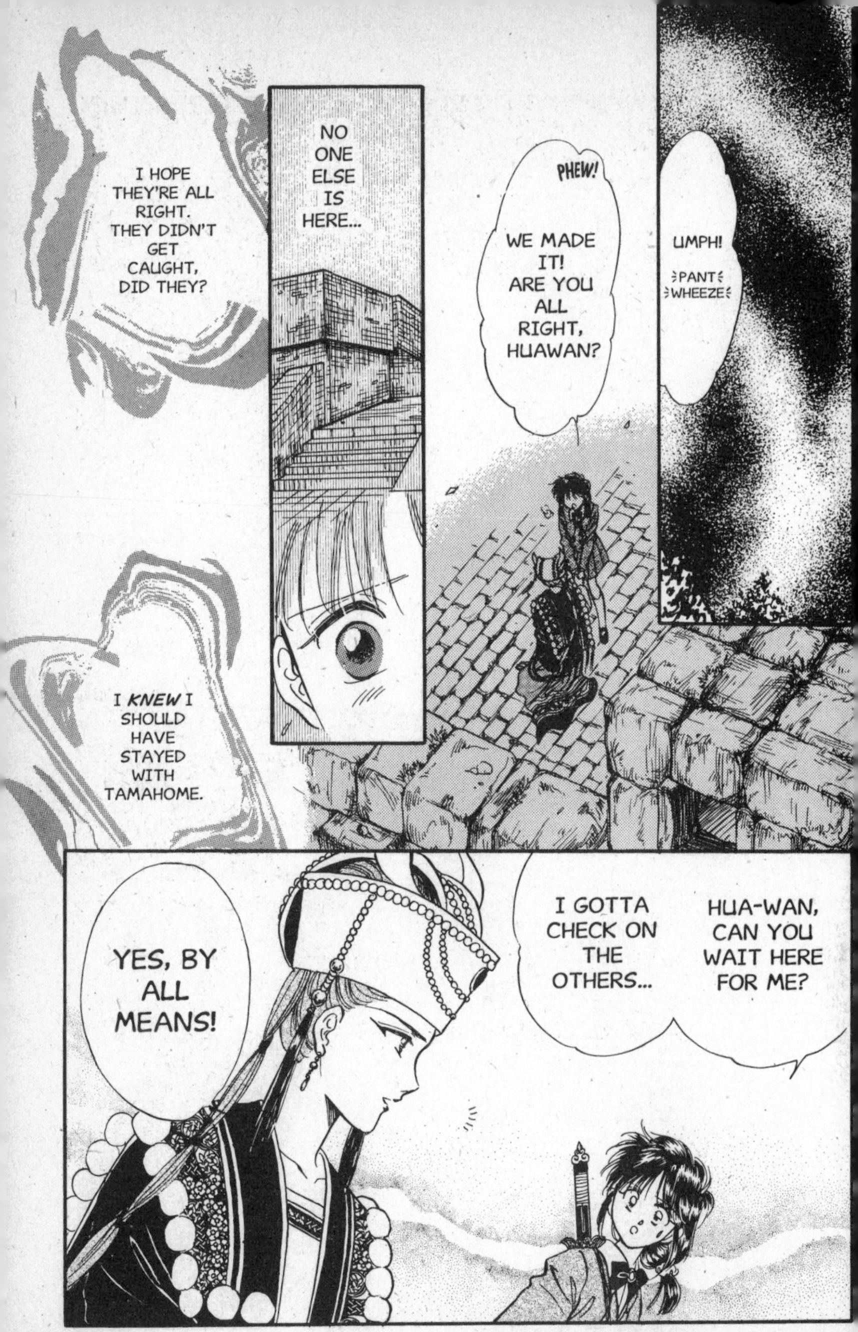
UMPH!
PANT WHEEZE
PHEW!
WE MADE IT! ARE YOU ALL RIGHT, HUAWAN?
NO ONE ELSE IS HERE...
I HOPE THEY'RE ALL RIGHT. THEY DIDN'T GET CAUGHT, DID THEY?
I KNEW I SHOULD HAVE STAYED WITH TAMAHOME.
HUA-WAN, CAN YOU WAIT HERE FOR ME?
I GOTTA CHECK ON THE OTHERS...
YES, BY ALL MEANS!

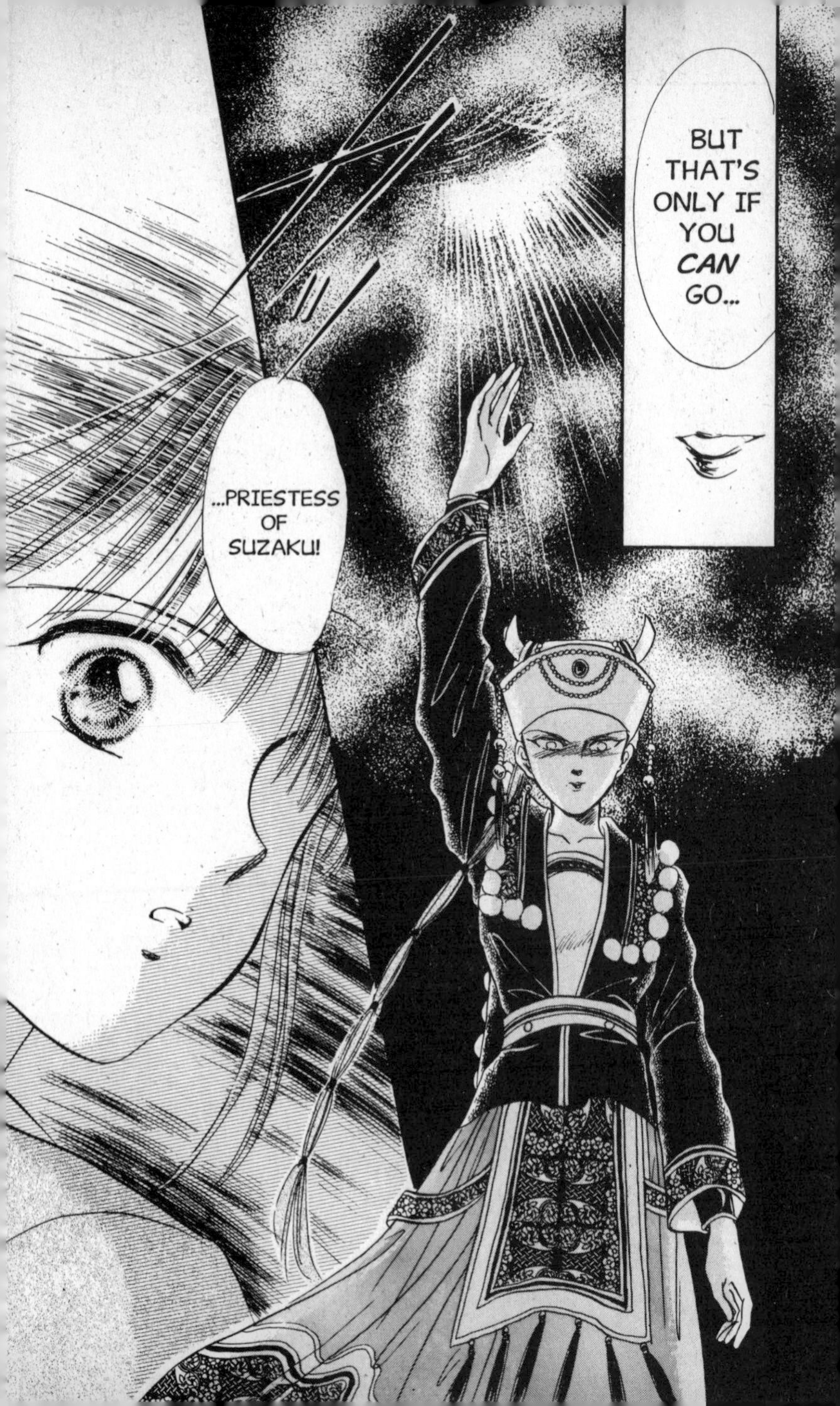
BUT THAT'S ONLY IF YOU *CAN* GO...
...PRIESTESS OF SUZAKU!

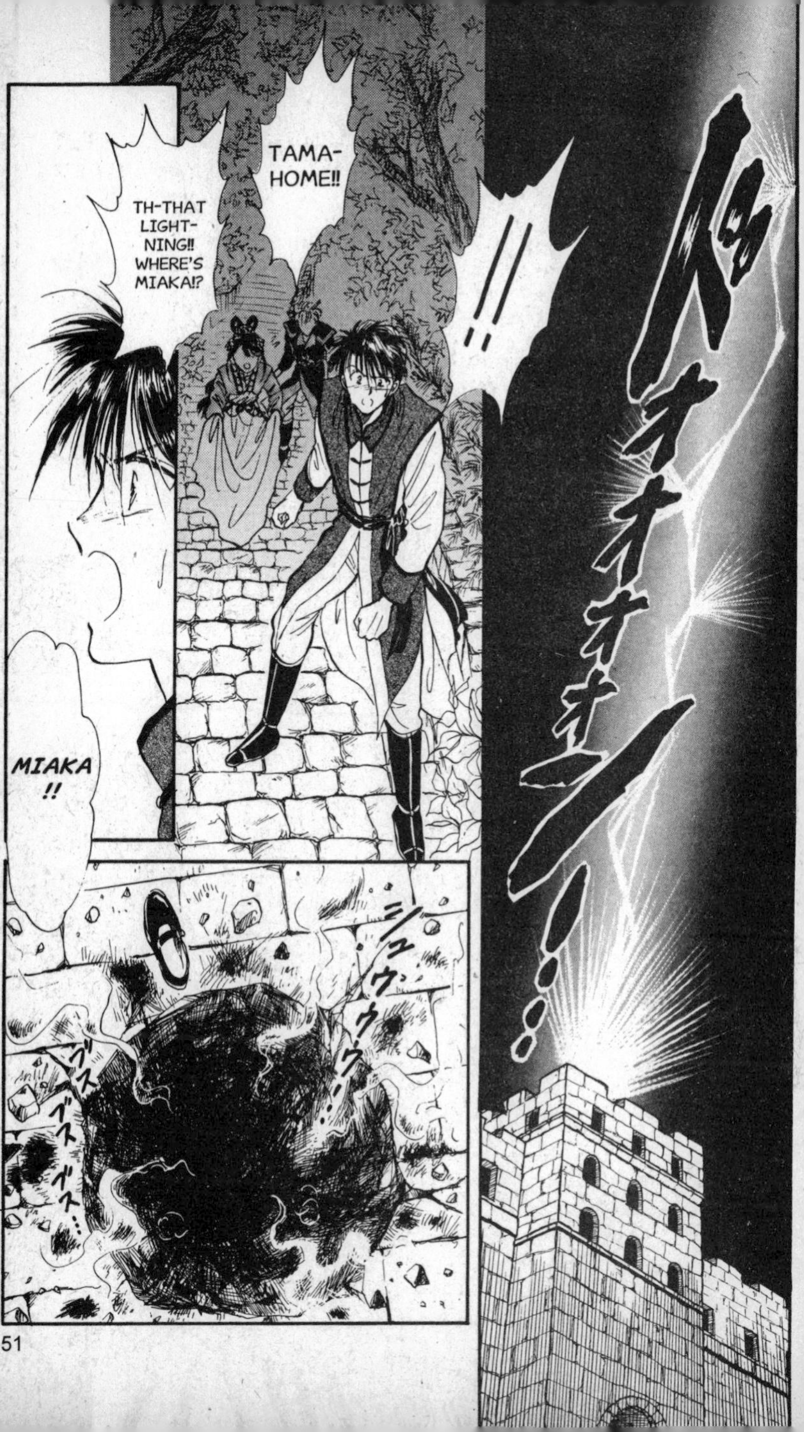
ドォオオオオン…
!!
TAMA-HOME!!
TH-THAT LIGHTNING!! WHERE'S MIAKA!?
MIAKA !!
シュウウウ…
ブスブスブス…

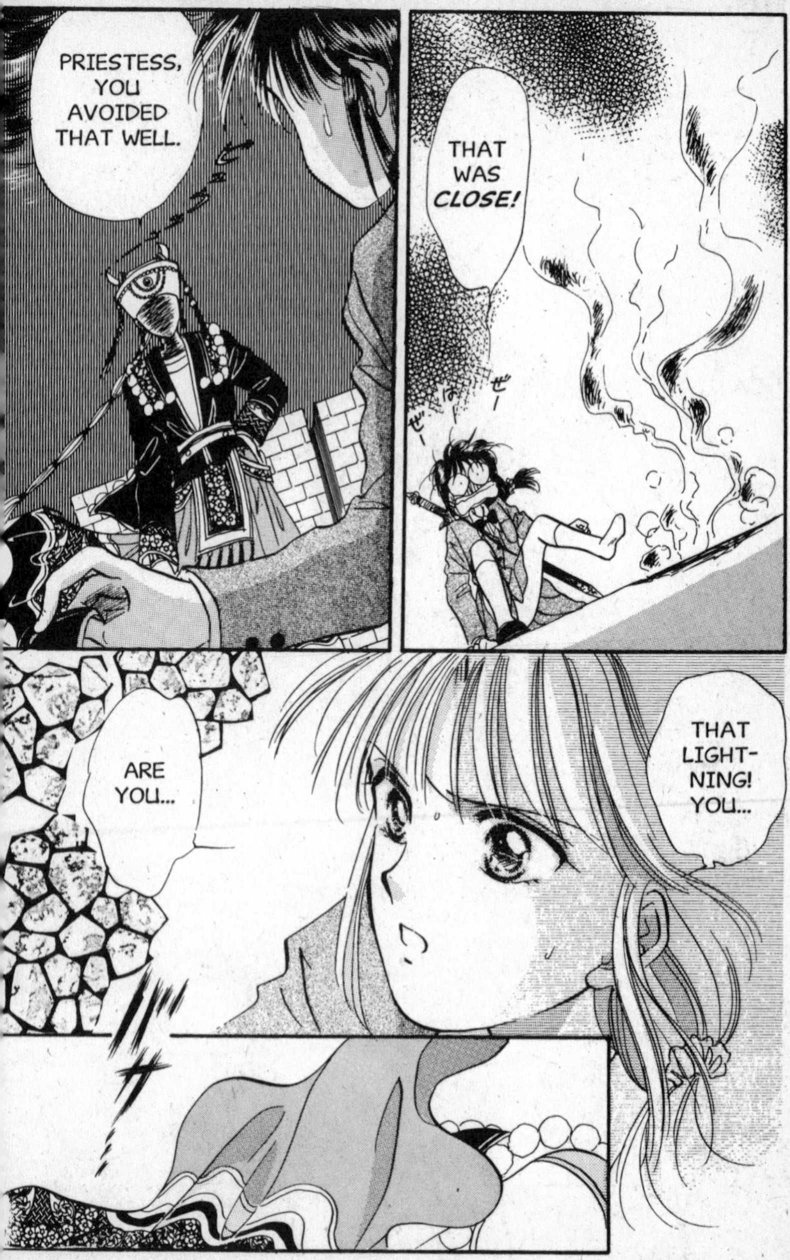
THAT WAS CLOSE!
PRIESTESS, YOU AVOIDED THAT WELL.
THAT LIGHTNING! YOU...
ARE YOU...

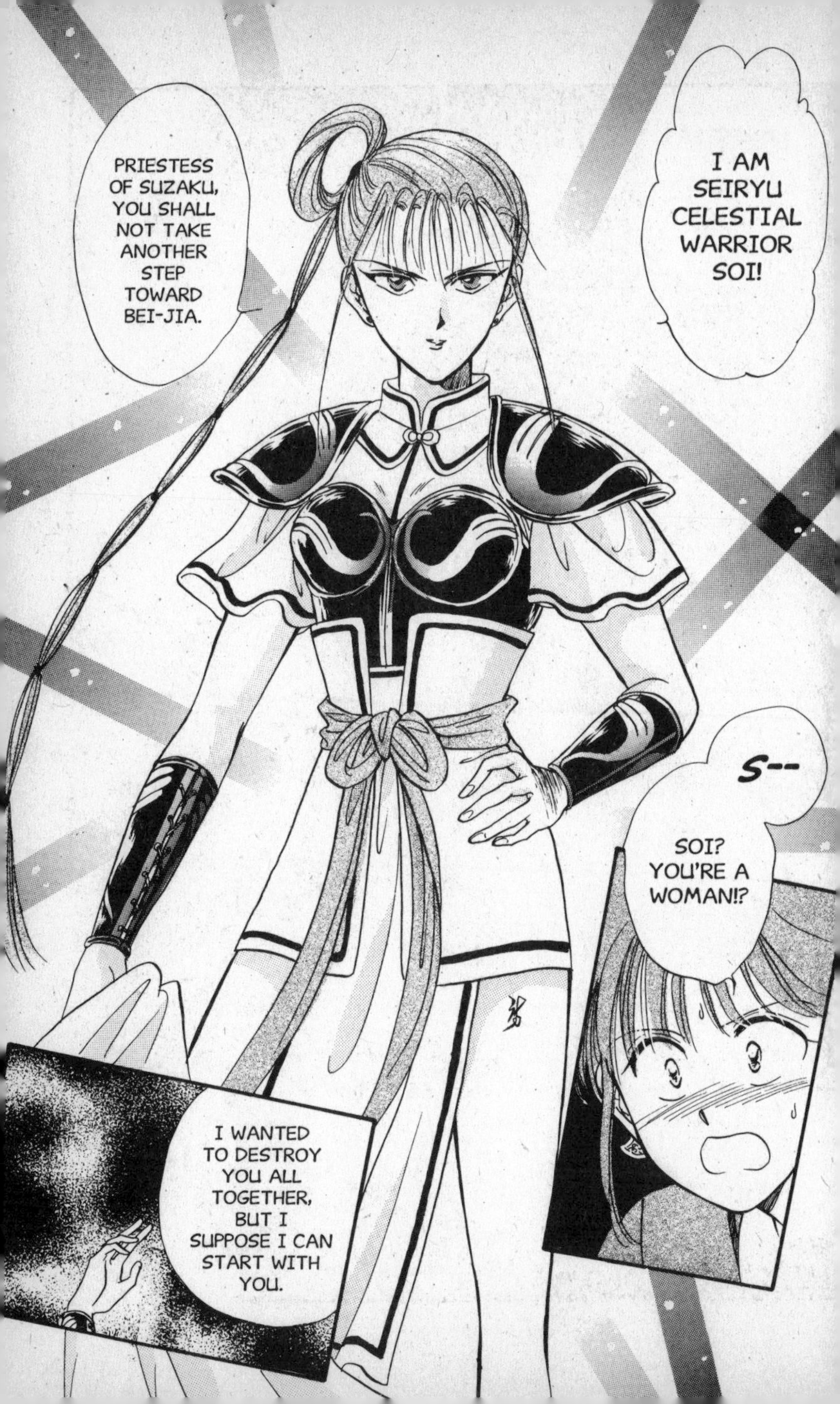
I AM SEIRYU CELESTIAL WARRIOR SOI!
PRIESTESS OF SUZAKU, YOU SHALL NOT TAKE ANOTHER STEP TOWARD BEI-JIA.
S--
SOI? YOU'RE A WOMAN!?
I WANTED TO DESTROY YOU ALL TOGETHER, BUT I SUPPOSE I CAN START WITH YOU.

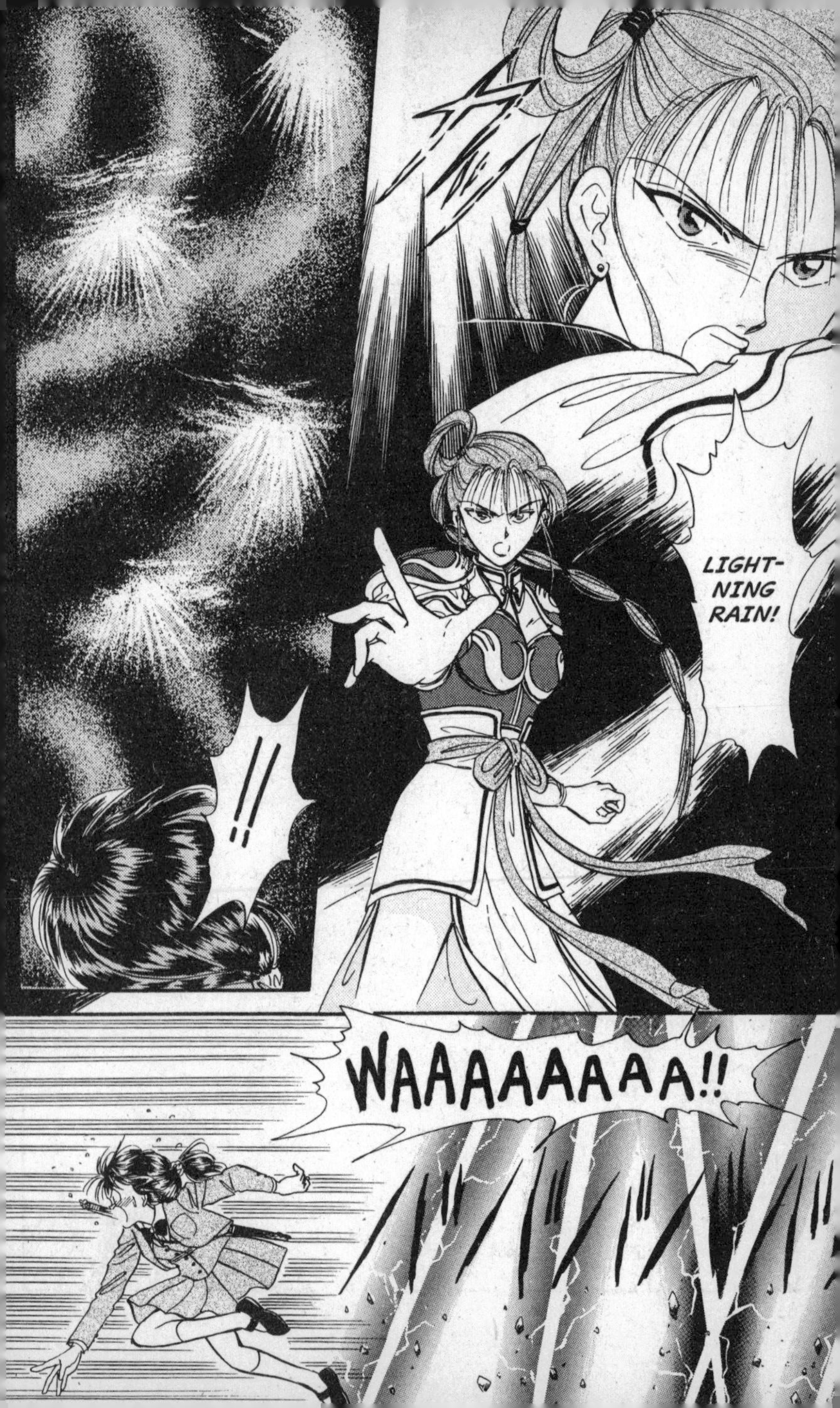
LIGHT-
NING
RAIN!
!!
WAAAAAAAA!!

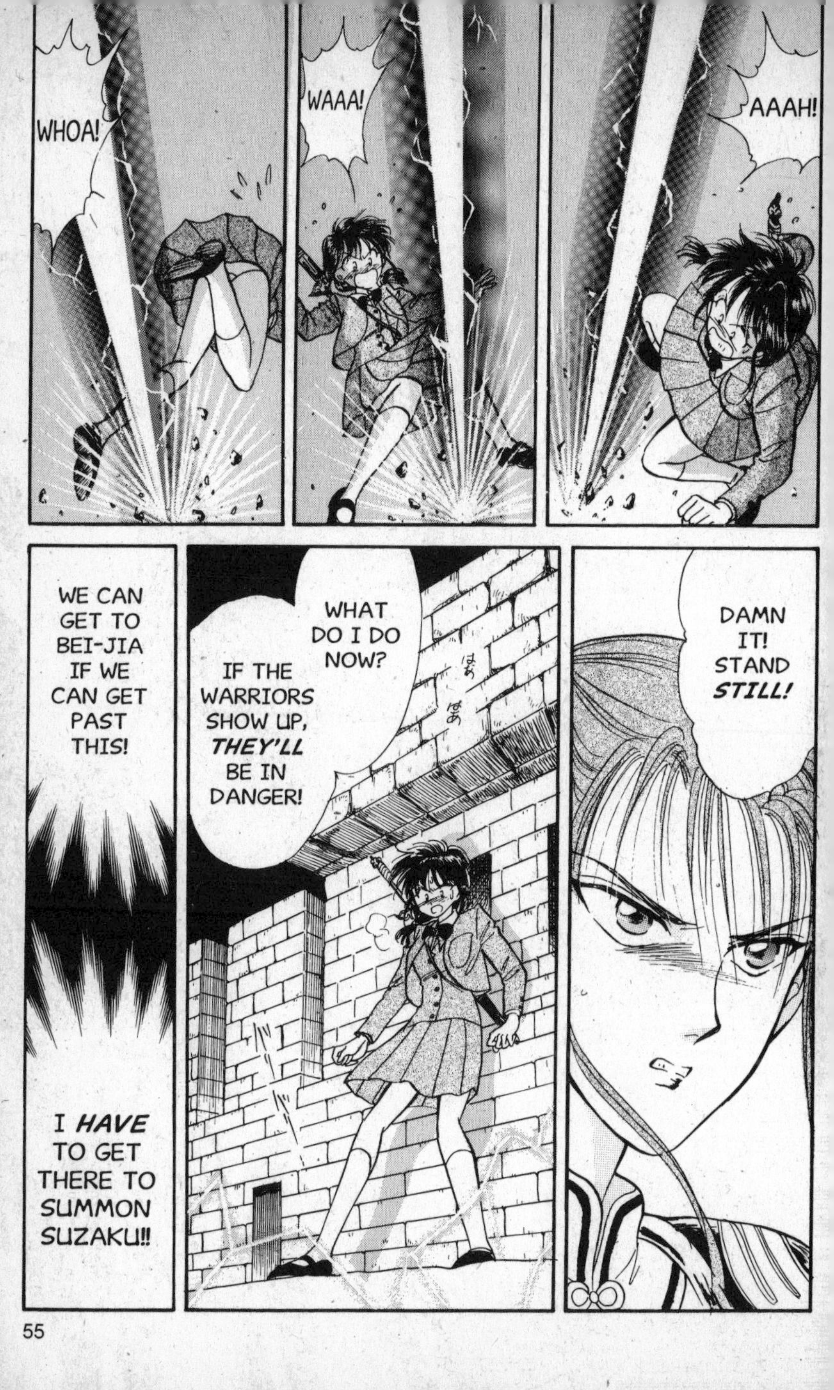
WHOA!
WAAA!
AAAH!
WE CAN GET TO BEI-JIA IF WE CAN GET PAST THIS!
I *HAVE* TO GET THERE TO SUMMON SUZAKU!!
WHAT DO I DO NOW?
IF THE WARRIORS SHOW UP, *THEY'LL* BE IN DANGER!
DAMN IT! STAND *STILL!*

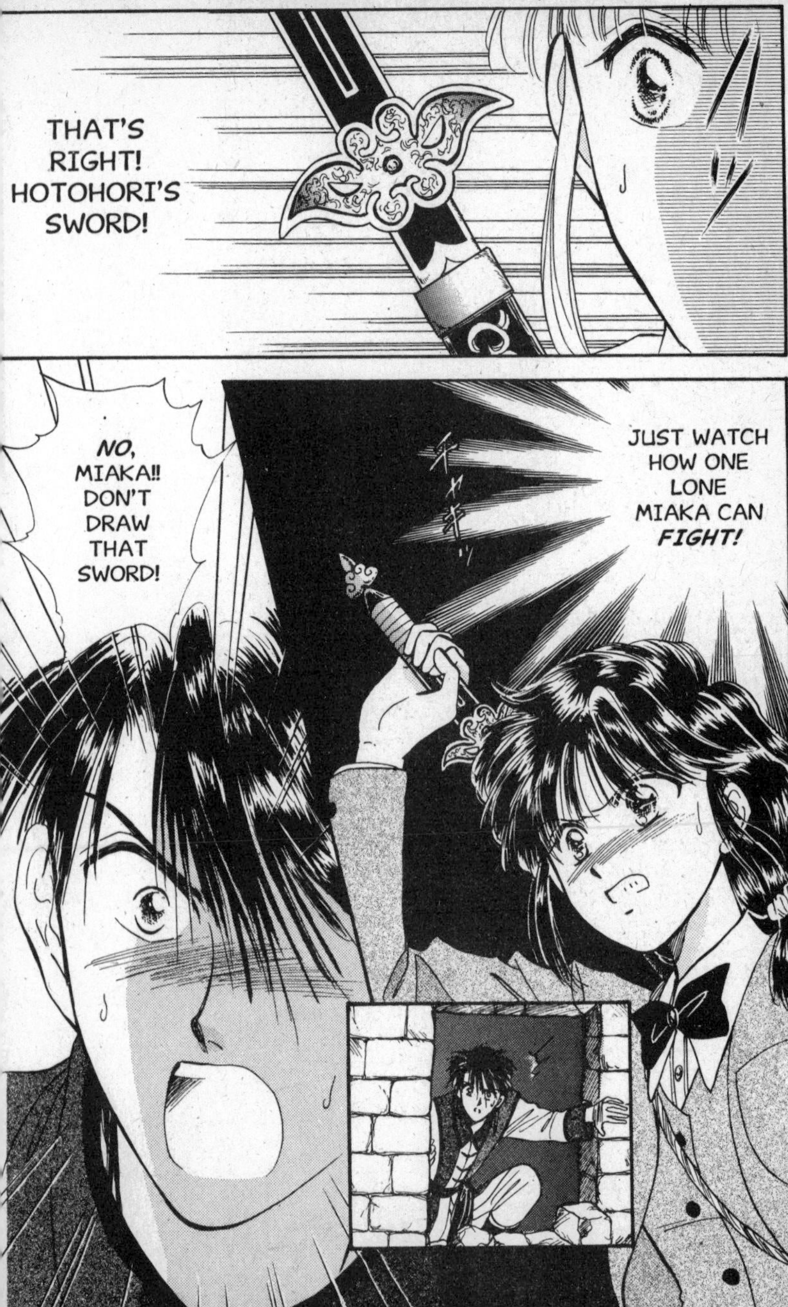
THAT'S RIGHT! HOTOHORI'S SWORD!
JUST WATCH HOW ONE LONE MIAKA CAN *FIGHT!*
NO, MIAKA!! DON'T DRAW THAT SWORD!

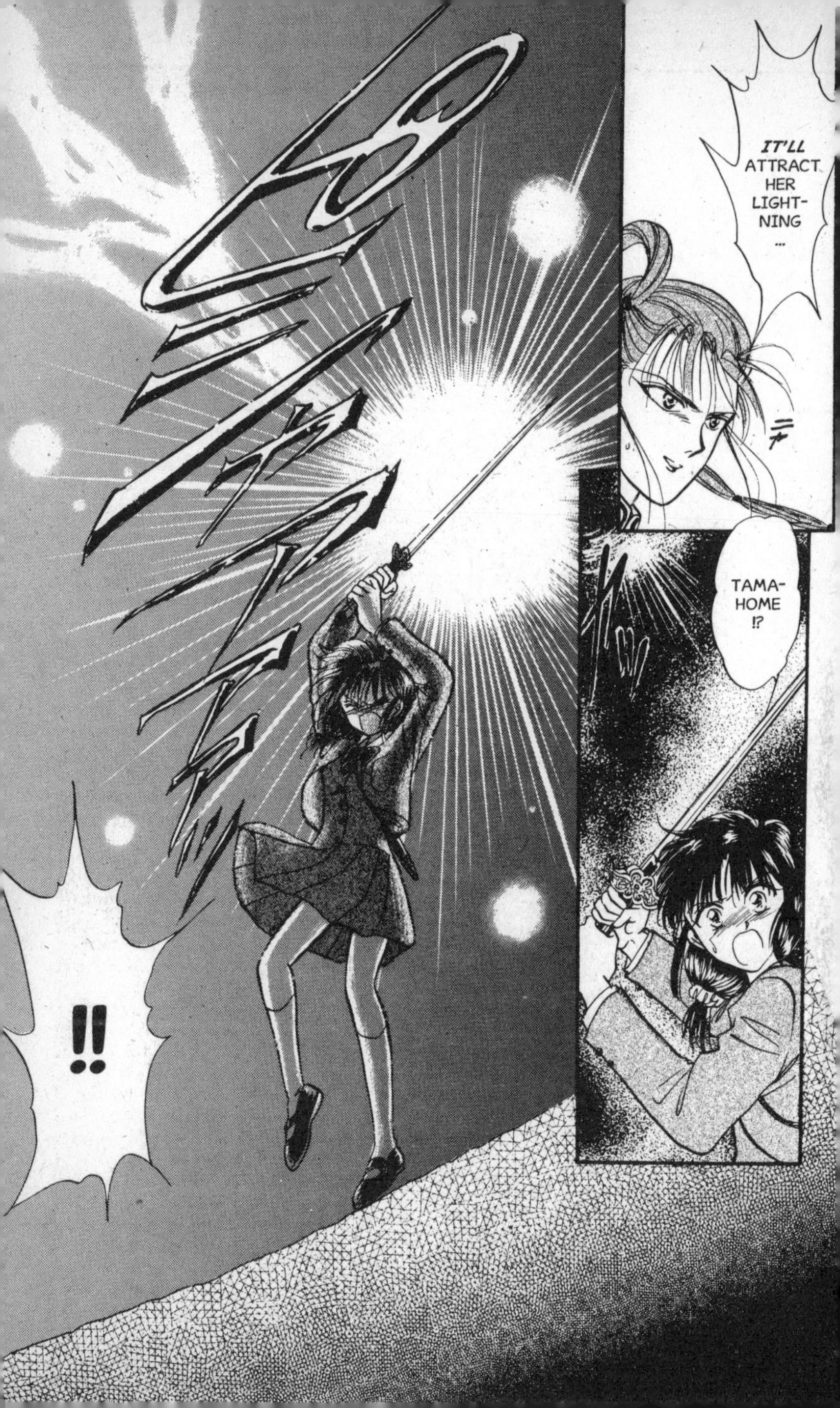
IT'LL ATTRACT HER LIGHTNING ...
TAMA-HOME !?
!!

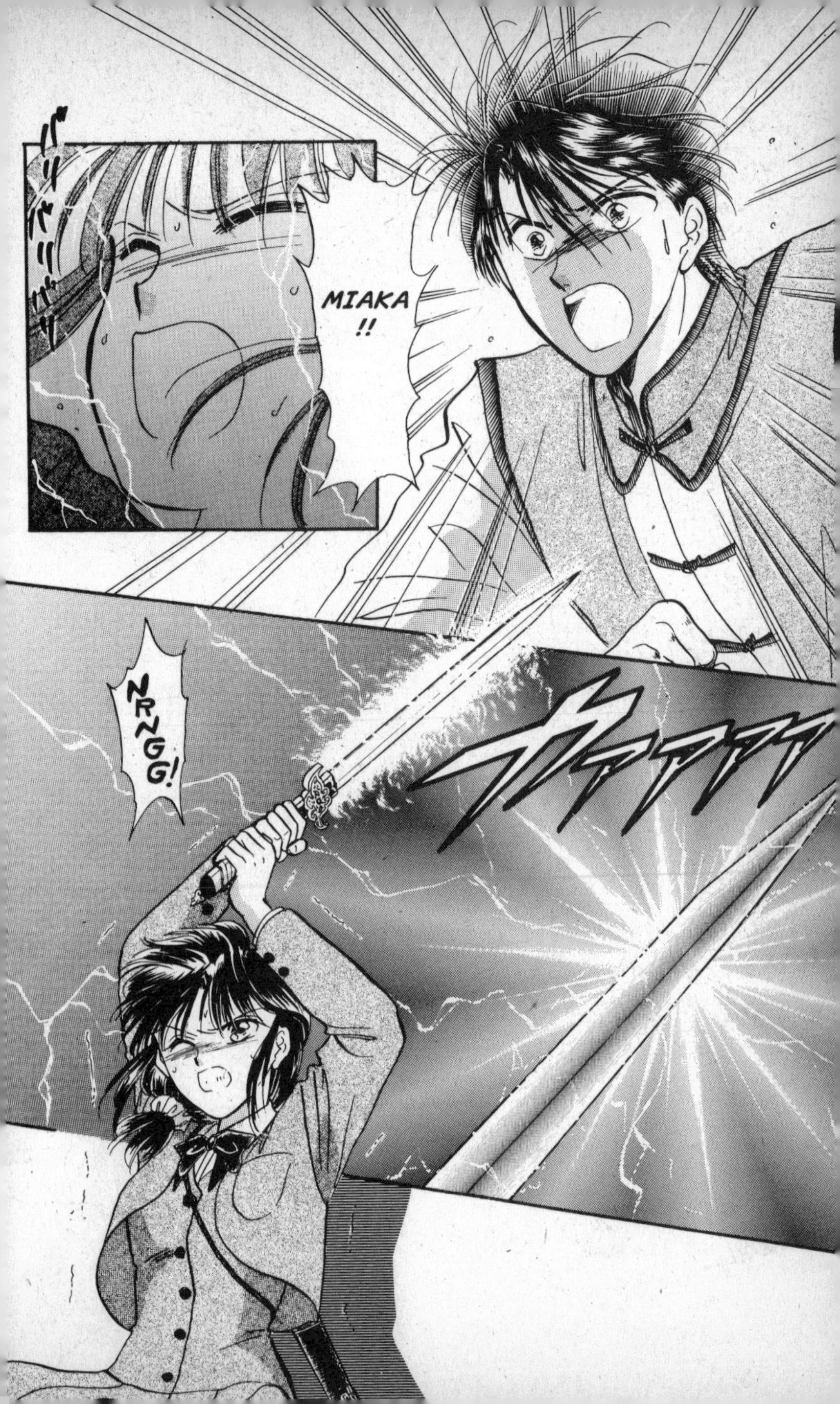
MIAKA !!
NRNGG!

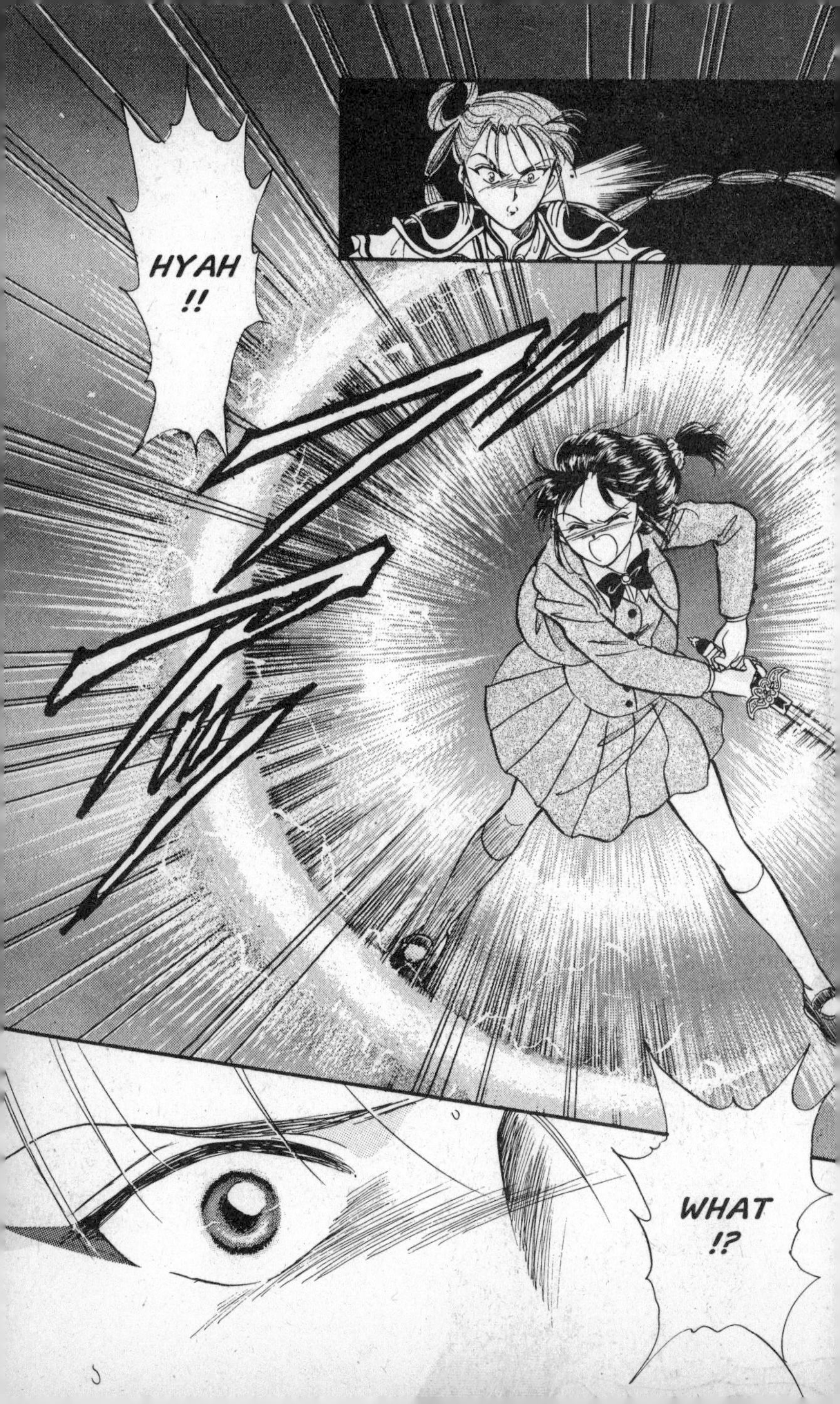
HYAH !!
WHAT !?

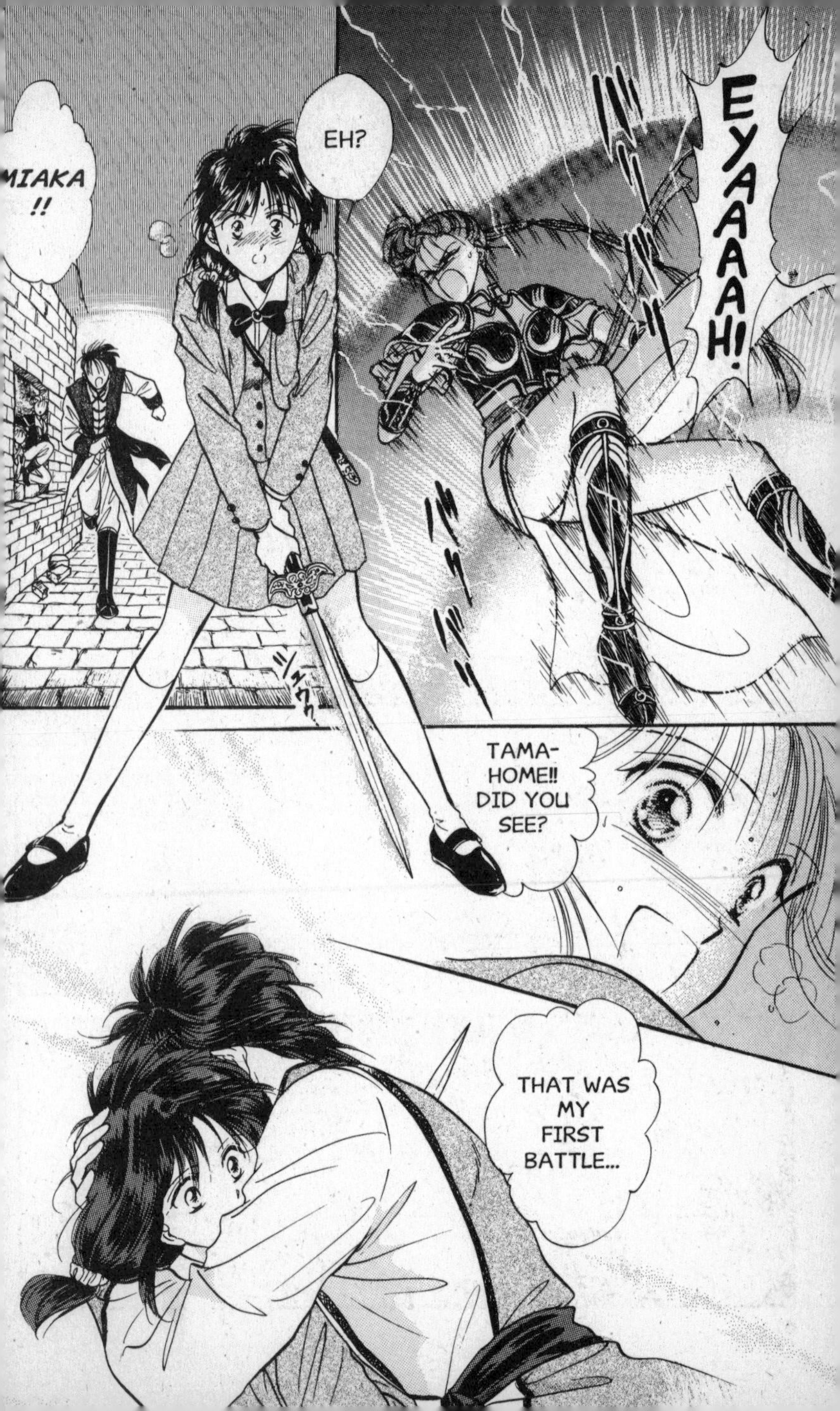
EYAAAAAH!
EH?
MIAKA !!
TAMA-HOME!! DID YOU SEE?
THAT WAS MY FIRST BATTLE...

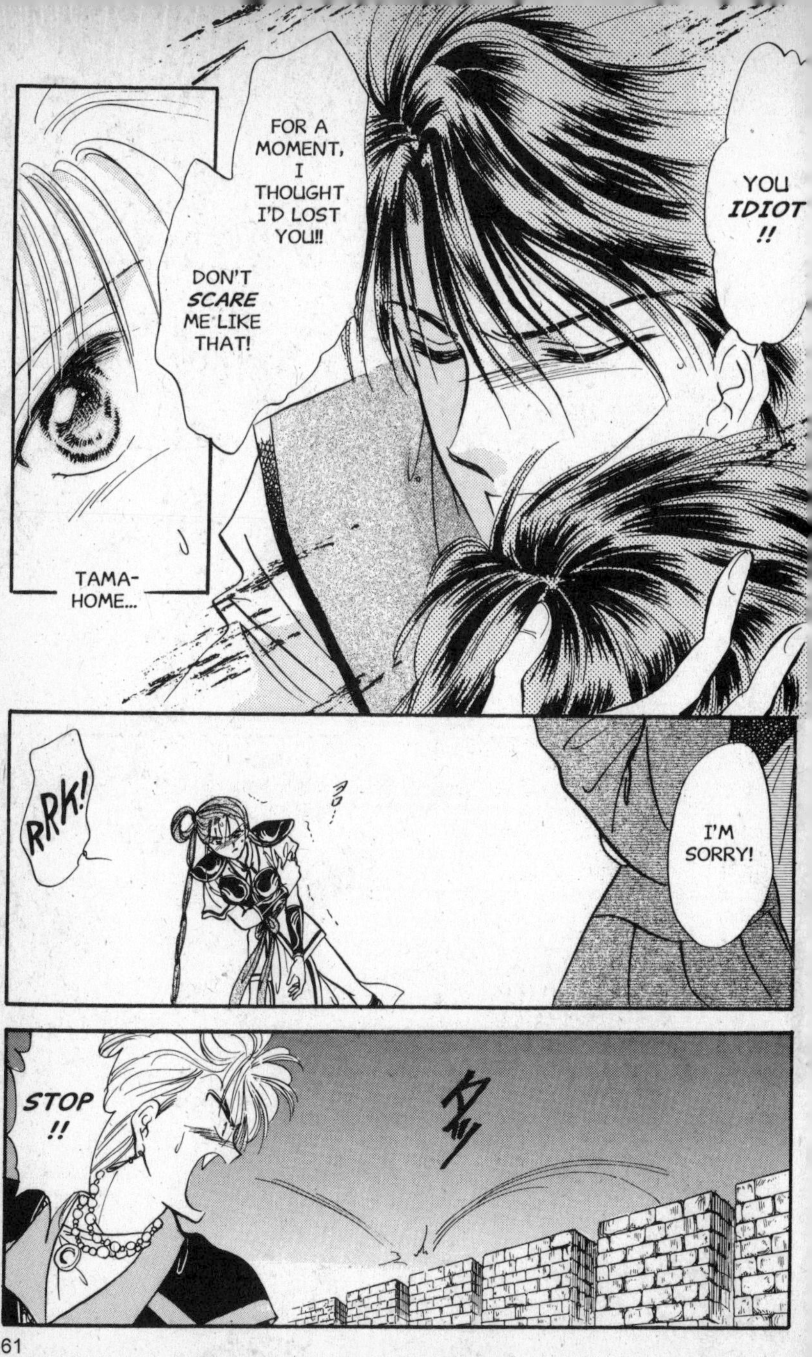
YOU IDIOT!!
FOR A MOMENT, I THOUGHT I'D LOST YOU!!
DON'T SCARE ME LIKE THAT!
TAMA-HOME...
I'M SORRY!
RRK!
STOP!!

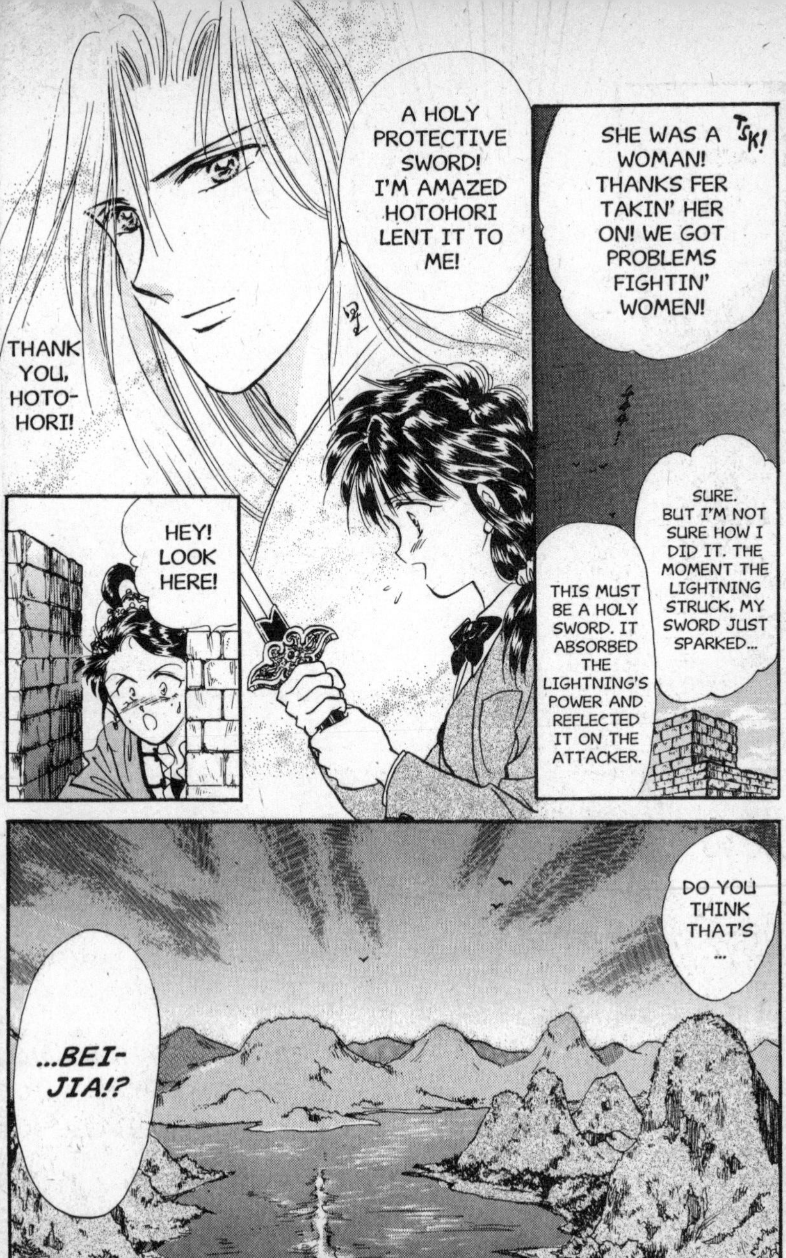
SHE WAS A WOMAN! THANKS FER TAKIN' HER ON! WE GOT PROBLEMS FIGHTIN' WOMEN!
TSK!
SURE. BUT I'M NOT SURE HOW I DID IT. THE MOMENT THE LIGHTNING STRUCK, MY SWORD JUST SPARKED...
THIS MUST BE A HOLY SWORD. IT ABSORBED THE LIGHTNING'S POWER AND REFLECTED IT ON THE ATTACKER.
A HOLY PROTECTIVE SWORD! I'M AMAZED HOTOHORI LENT IT TO ME!
THANK YOU, HOTO-HORI!
HEY! LOOK HERE!
DO YOU THINK THAT'S ...
...BEI-JIA!?

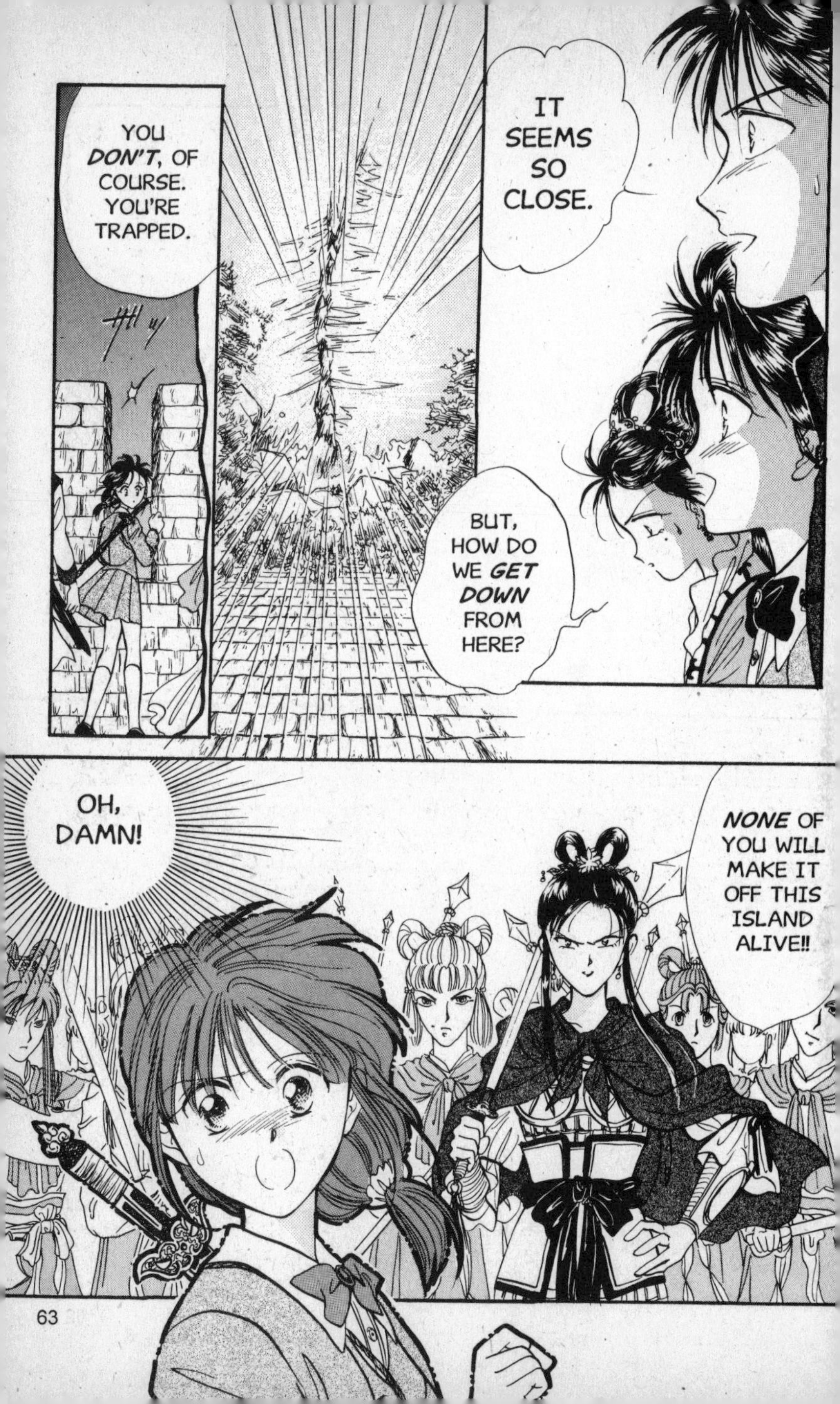

IT SEEMS SO CLOSE.
BUT, HOW DO WE *GET DOWN* FROM HERE?
YOU *DON'T*, OF COURSE. YOU'RE TRAPPED.
NONE OF YOU WILL MAKE IT OFF THIS ISLAND ALIVE!!
OH, DAMN!

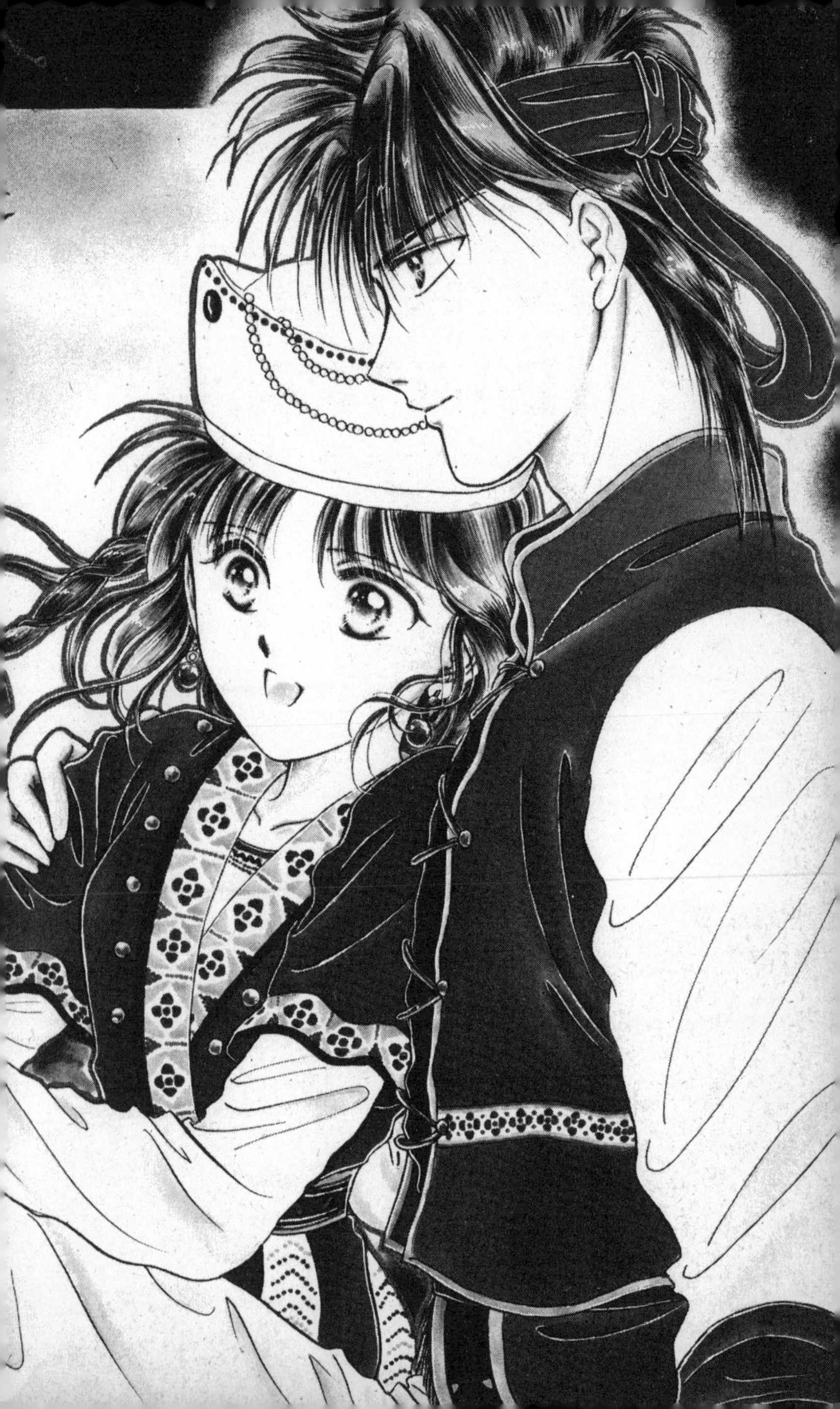

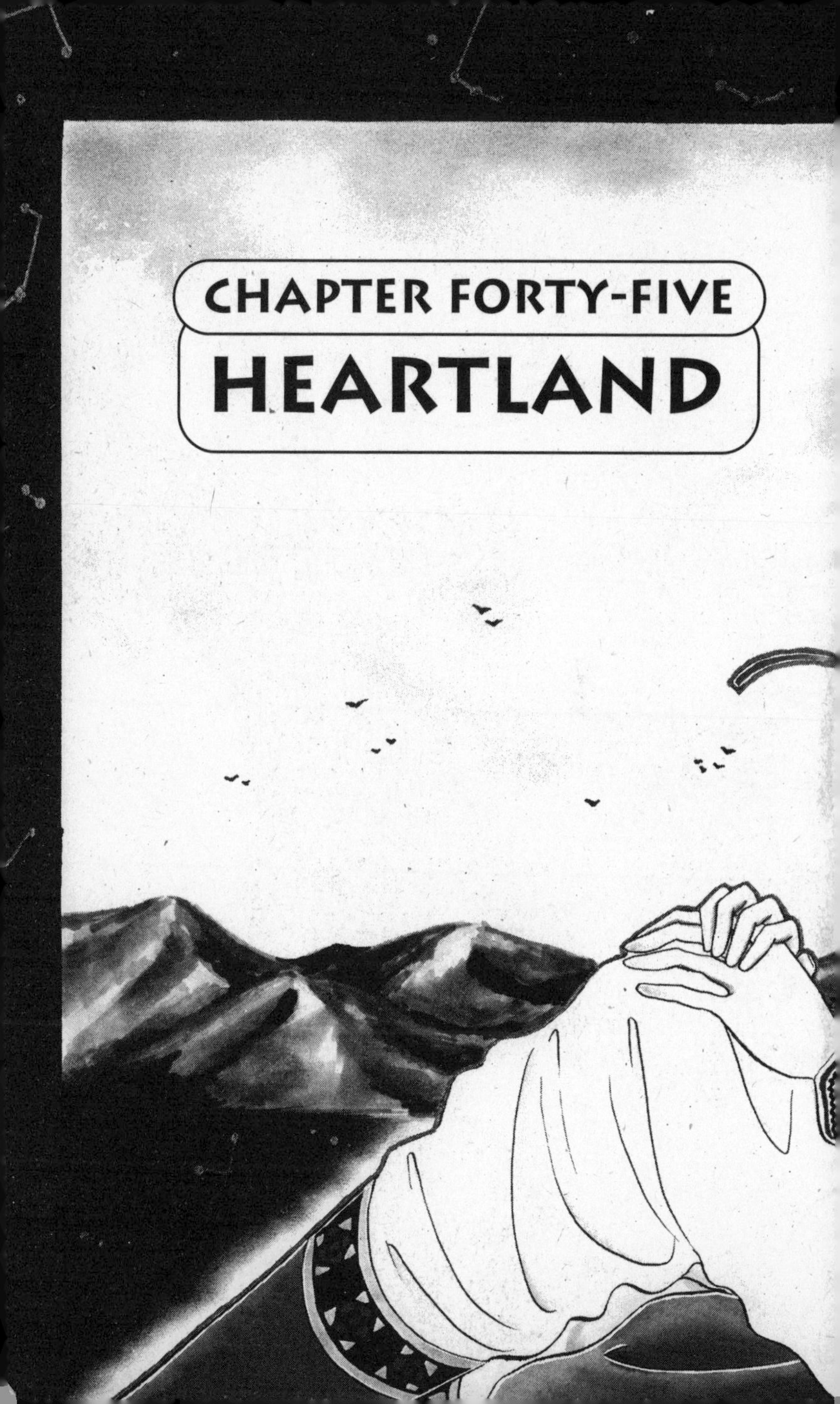
CHAPTER FORTY-FIVE
HEARTLAND

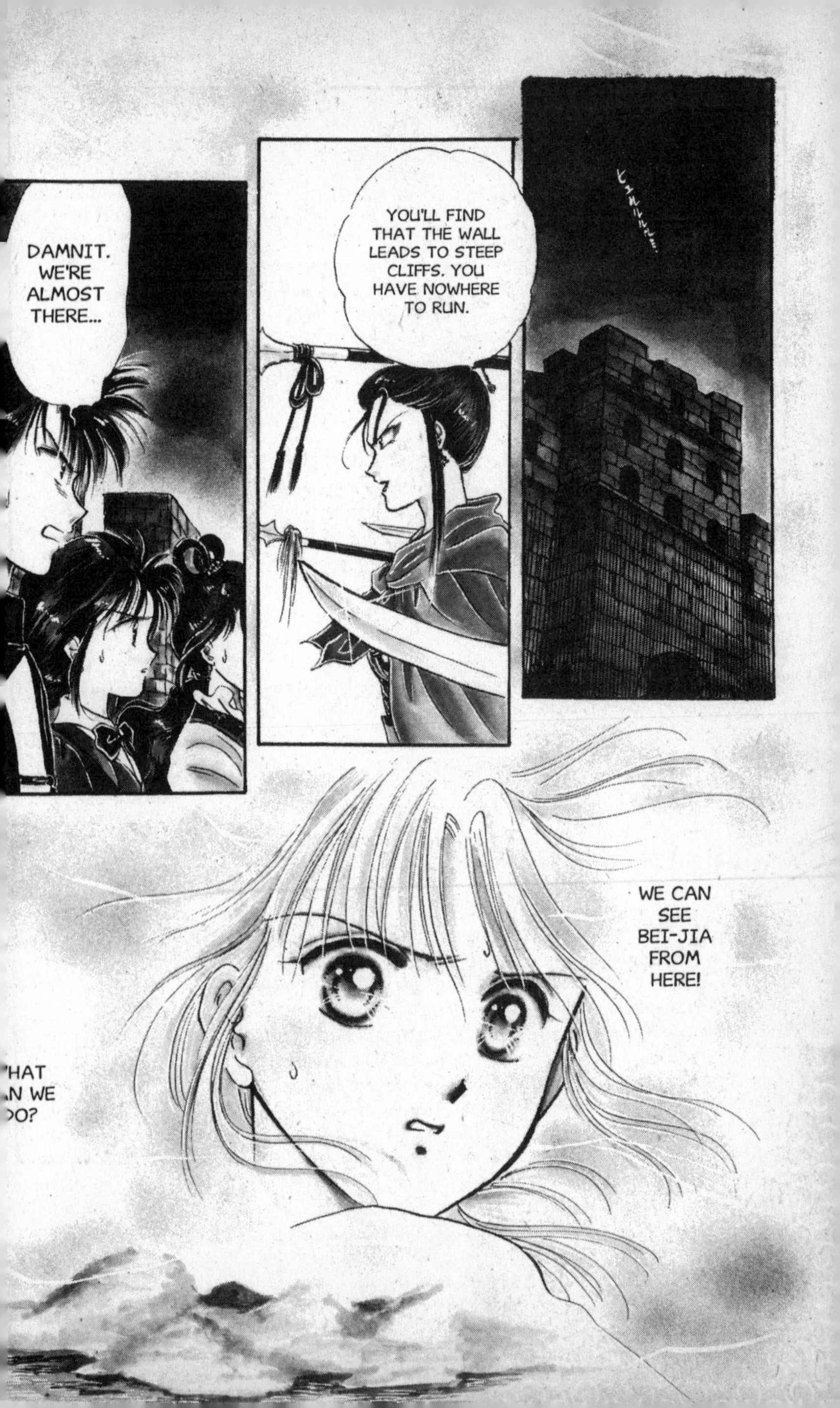

YOU'LL FIND THAT THE WALL LEADS TO STEEP CLIFFS. YOU HAVE NOWHERE TO RUN.
DAMNIT. WE'RE ALMOST THERE...
WE CAN SEE BEI-JIA FROM HERE!

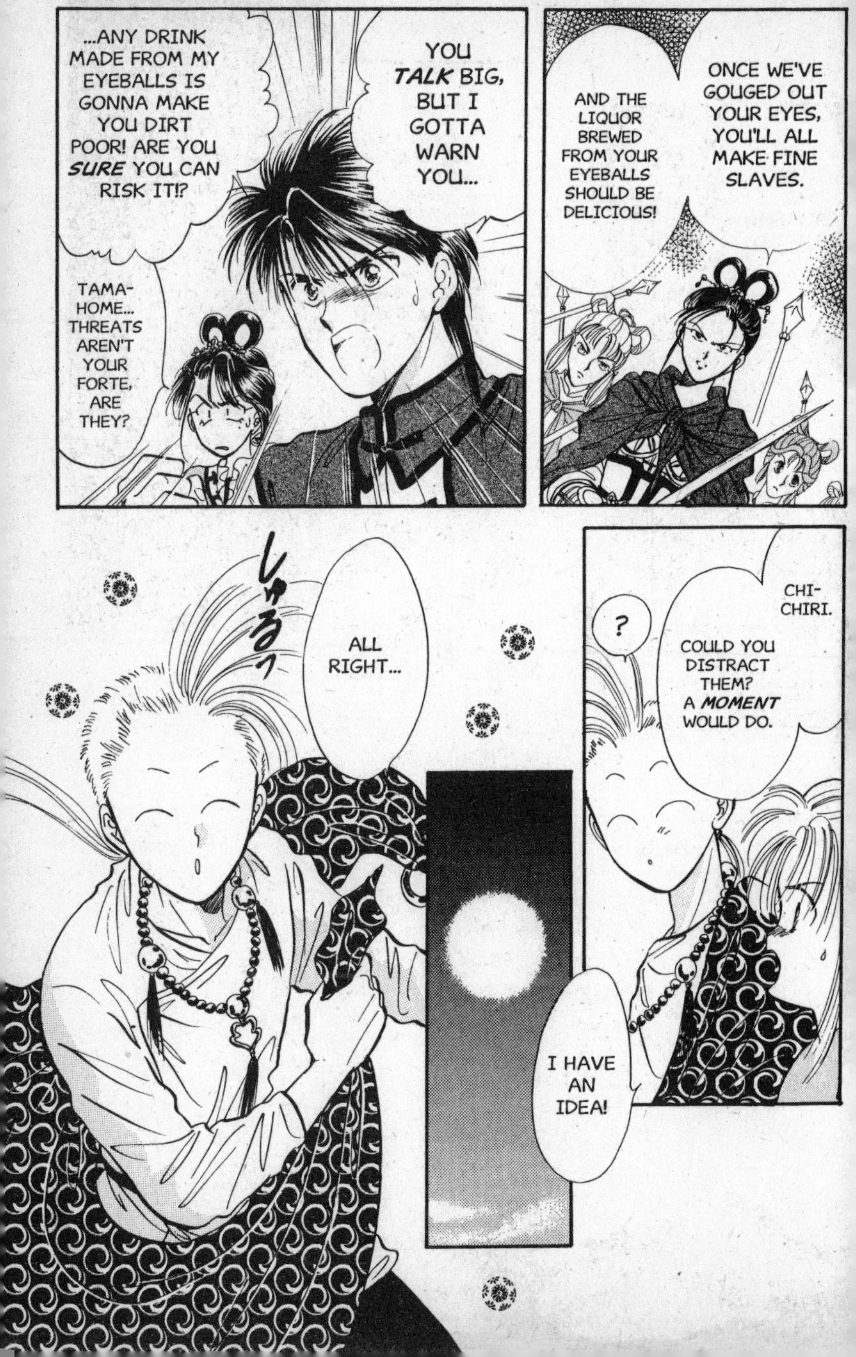
ONCE WE'VE GOUGED OUT YOUR EYES, YOU'LL ALL MAKE FINE SLAVES.
AND THE LIQUOR BREWED FROM YOUR EYEBALLS SHOULD BE DELICIOUS!
YOU TALK BIG, BUT I GOTTA WARN YOU...
...ANY DRINK MADE FROM MY EYEBALLS IS GONNA MAKE YOU DIRT POOR! ARE YOU SURE YOU CAN RISK IT!?
TAMA-HOME... THREATS AREN'T YOUR FORTE, ARE THEY?
CHI-CHIRI. COULD YOU DISTRACT THEM? A MOMENT WOULD DO.
?
I HAVE AN IDEA!
ALL RIGHT...
しゅるっ

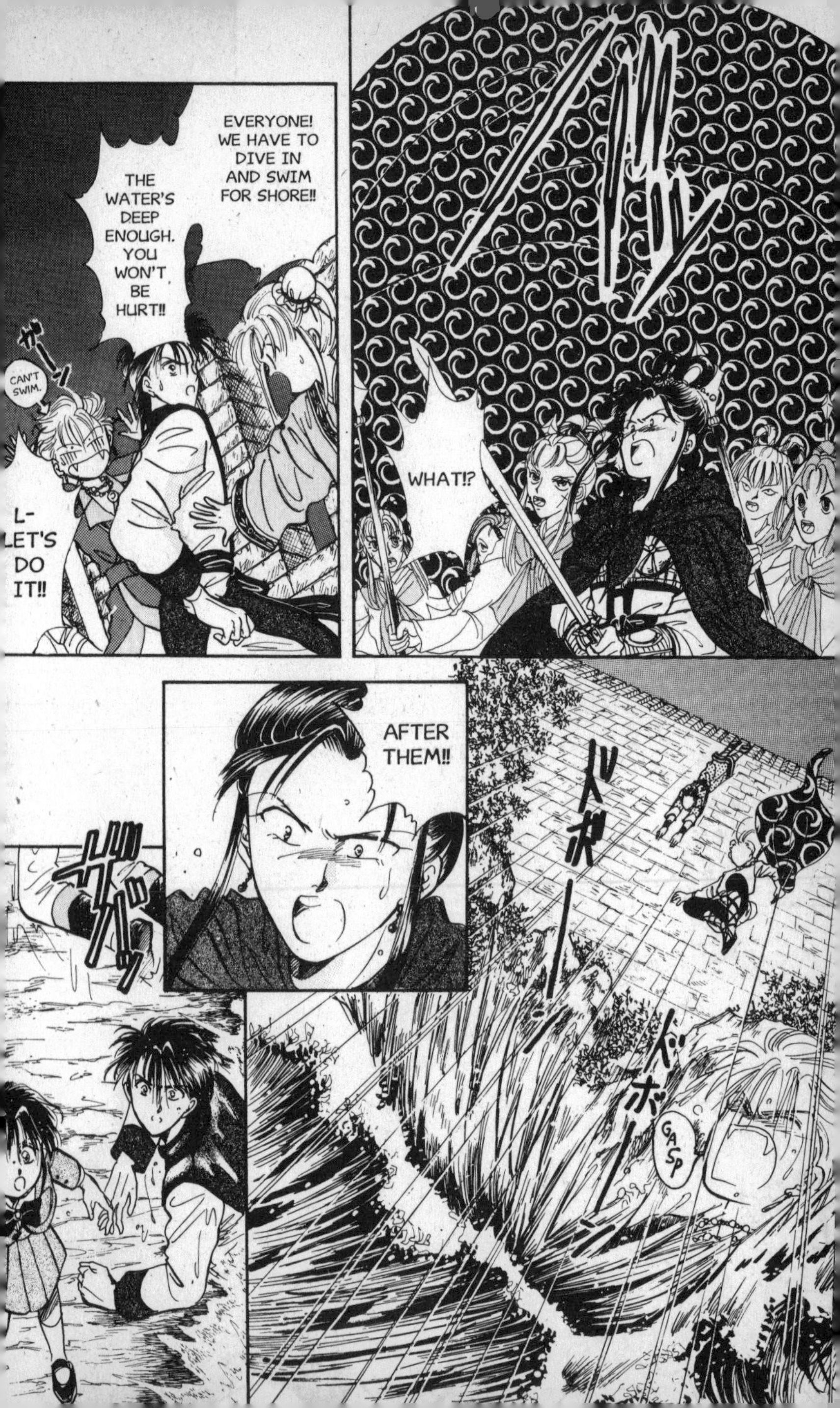
WHAT!?
EVERYONE! WE HAVE TO DIVE IN AND SWIM FOR SHORE!!
THE WATER'S DEEP ENOUGH. YOU WON'T BE HURT!!
CAN'T SWIM.
L-LET'S DO IT!!
GASP
AFTER THEM!!

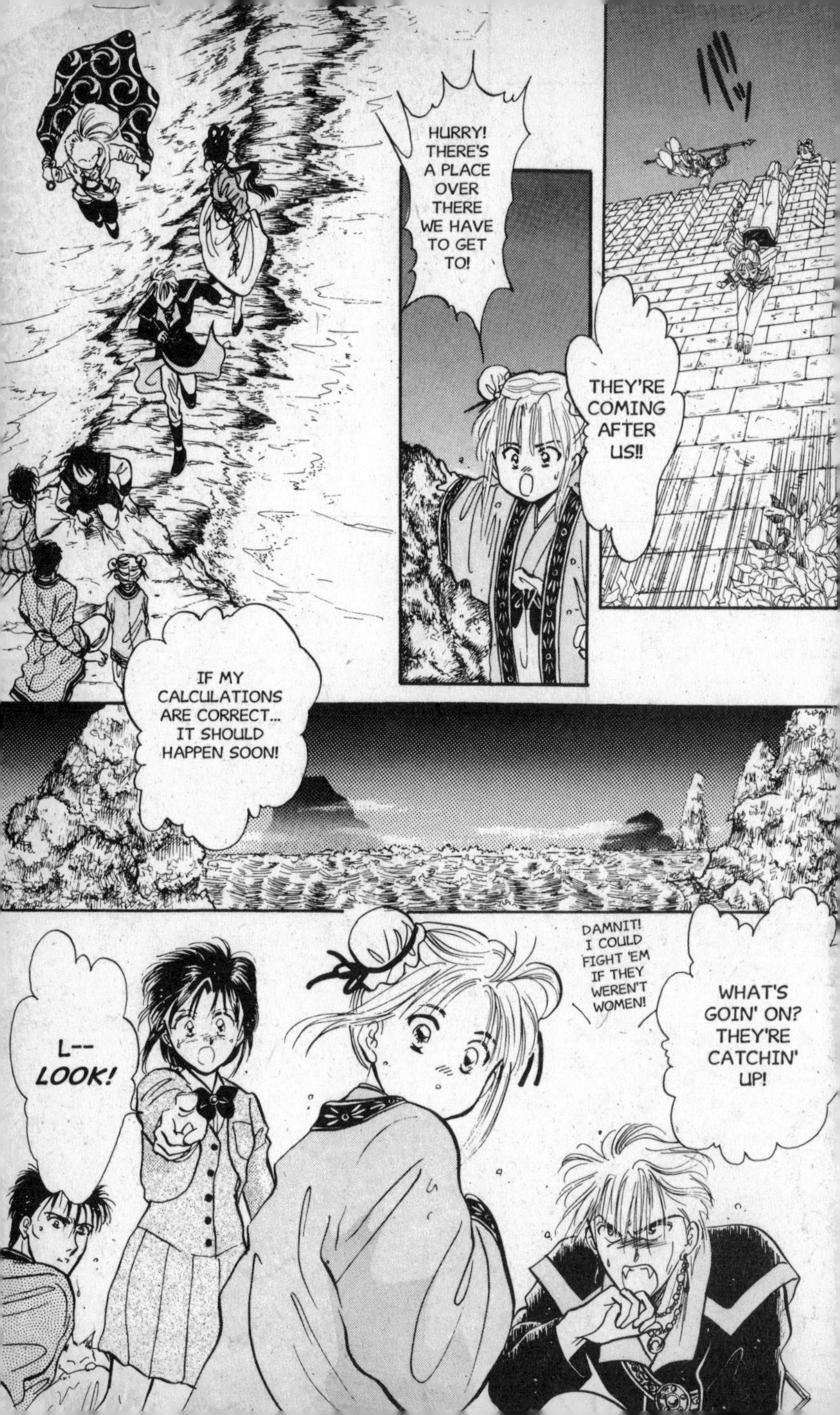
THEY'RE COMING AFTER US!!
HURRY! THERE'S A PLACE OVER THERE WE HAVE TO GET TO!
IF MY CALCULATIONS ARE CORRECT... IT SHOULD HAPPEN SOON!
WHAT'S GOIN' ON? THEY'RE CATCHIN' UP!
DAMNIT! I COULD FIGHT 'EM IF THEY WEREN'T WOMEN!
L-- LOOK!

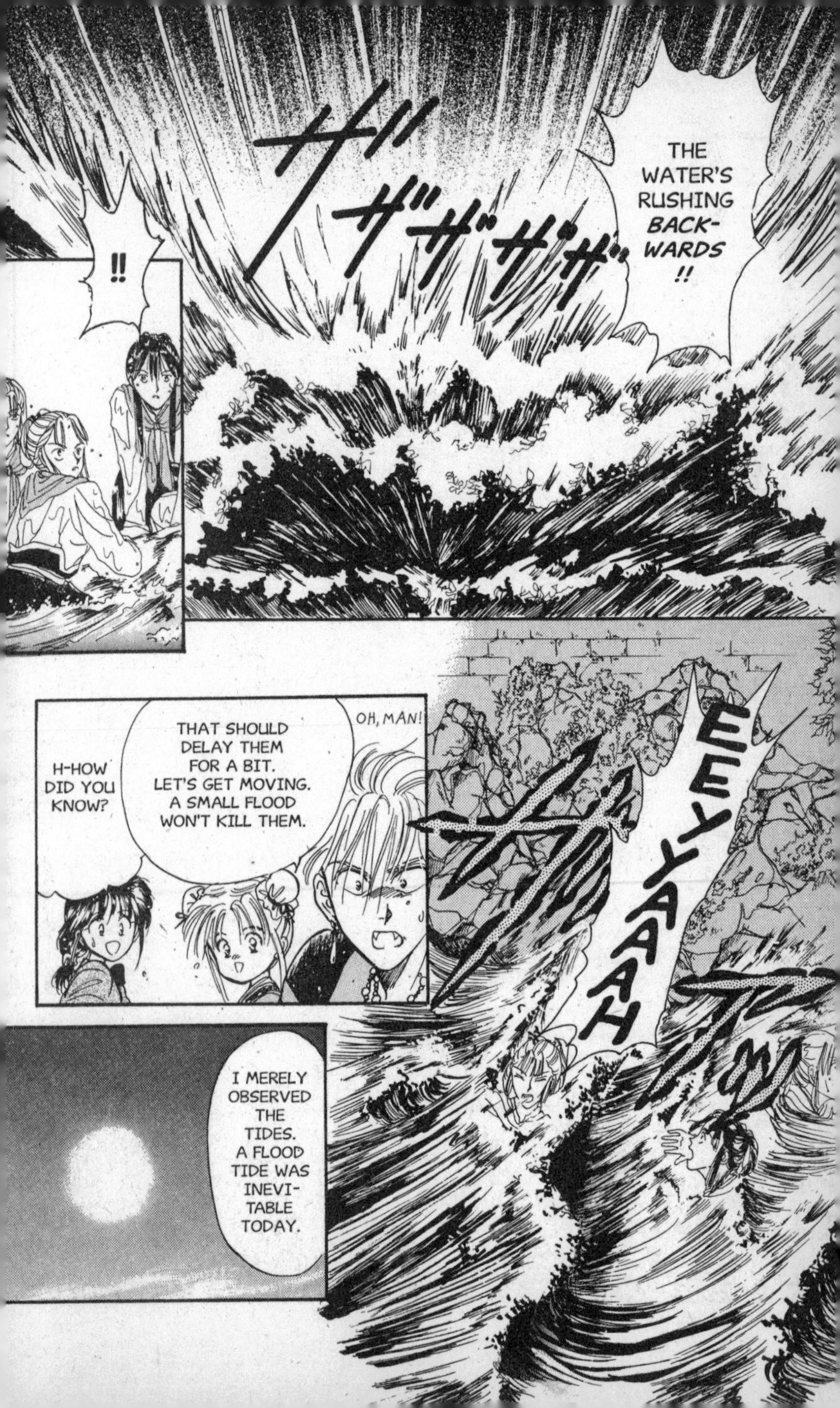
THE WATER'S RUSHING *BACK-WARDS* !!
ザザザザ
!!
EEYAAAAH
OH, MAN!
THAT SHOULD DELAY THEM FOR A BIT. LET'S GET MOVING. A SMALL FLOOD WON'T KILL THEM.
H-HOW DID YOU KNOW?
I MERELY OBSERVED THE TIDES. A FLOOD TIDE WAS INEVI-TABLE TODAY.

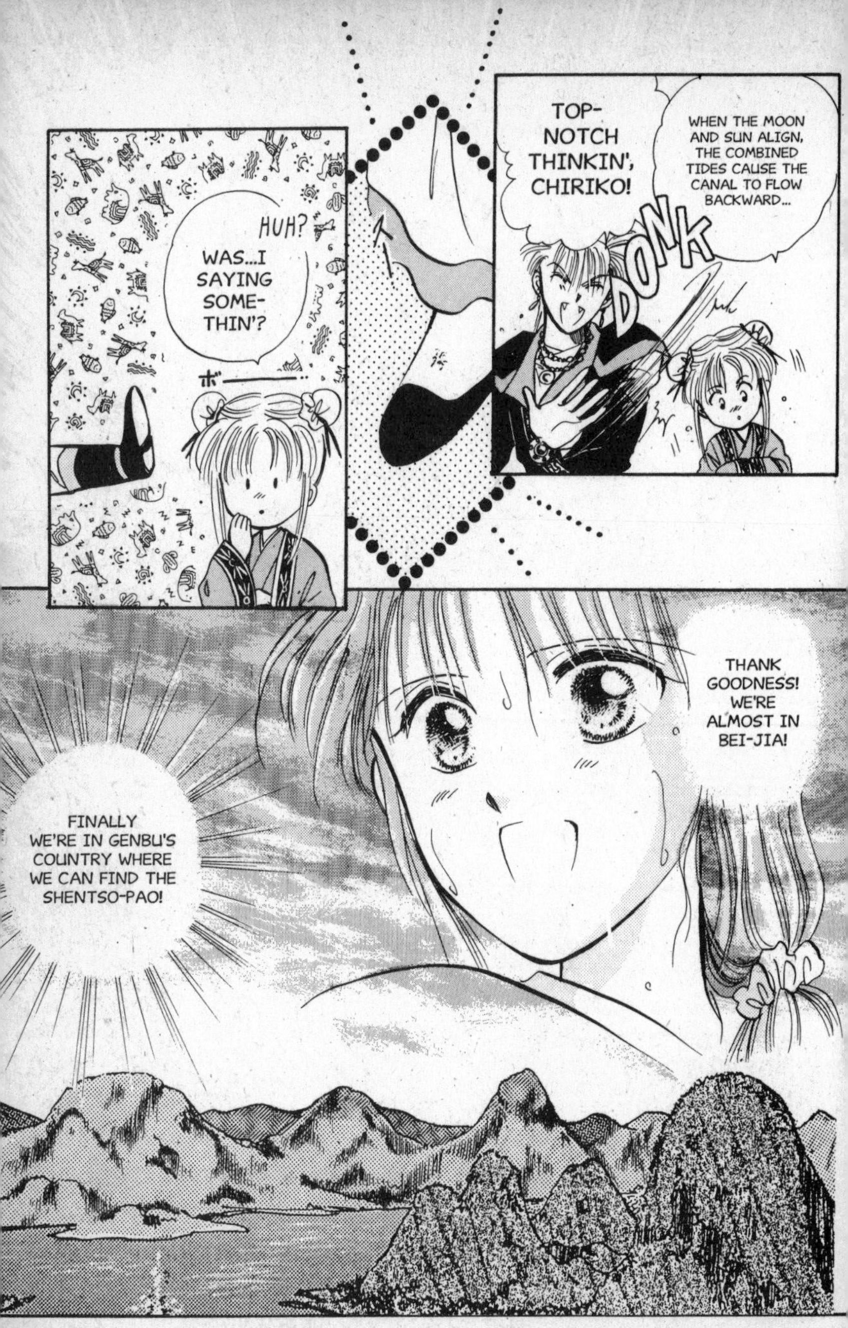
WHEN THE MOON AND SUN ALIGN, THE COMBINED TIDES CAUSE THE CANAL TO FLOW BACKWARD...
TOP-NOTCH THINKIN', CHIRIKO!
DONK
HUH?
WAS...I SAYING SOME-THIN'?
ボー
THANK GOODNESS! WE'RE ALMOST IN BEI-JIA!
FINALLY WE'RE IN GENBU'S COUNTRY WHERE WE CAN FIND THE SHENTSO-PAO!

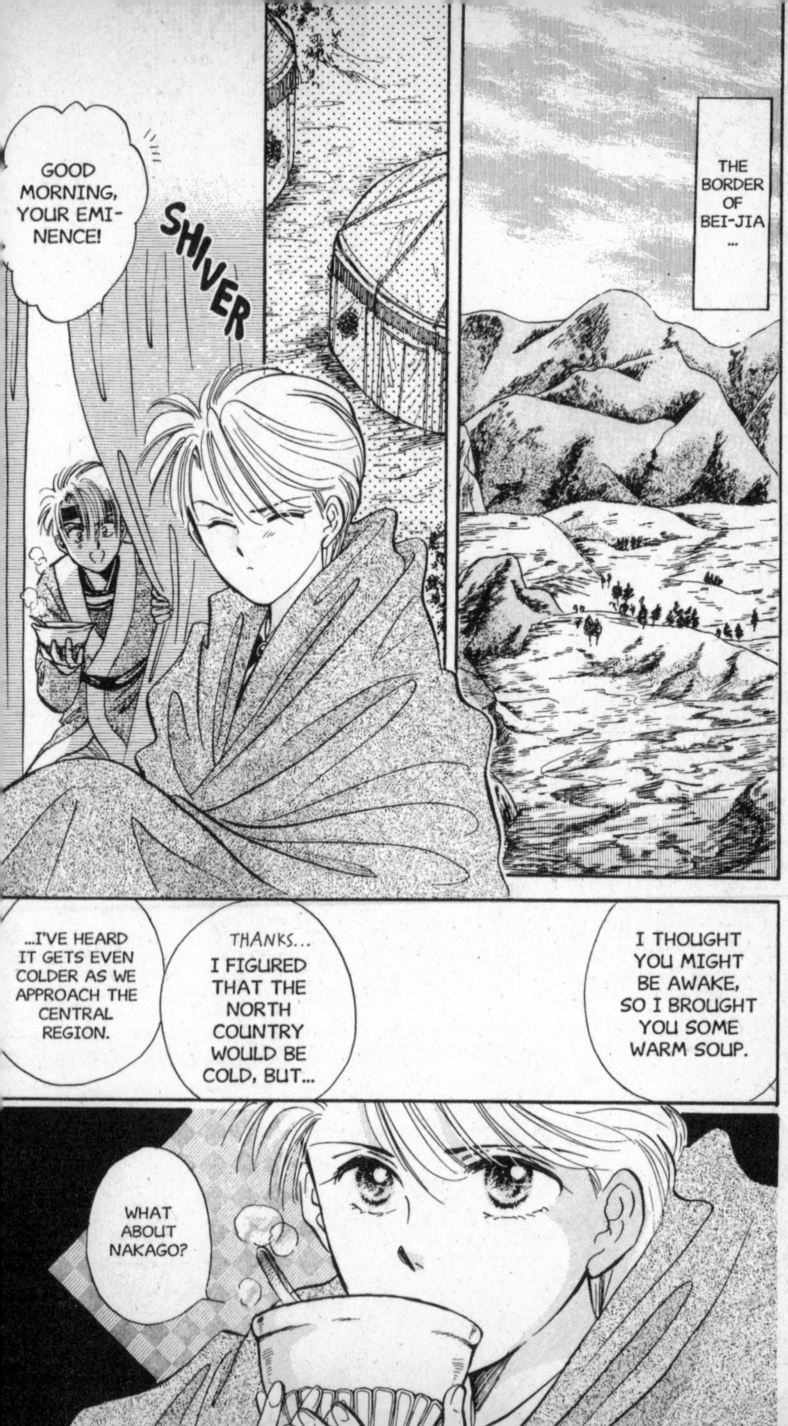
THE BORDER OF BEI-JIA ...
GOOD MORNING, YOUR EMI- NENCE!
SHIVER
I THOUGHT YOU MIGHT BE AWAKE, SO I BROUGHT YOU SOME WARM SOUP.
THANKS...
I FIGURED THAT THE NORTH COUNTRY WOULD BE COLD, BUT...
...I'VE HEARD IT GETS EVEN COLDER AS WE APPROACH THE CENTRAL REGION.
WHAT ABOUT NAKAGO?

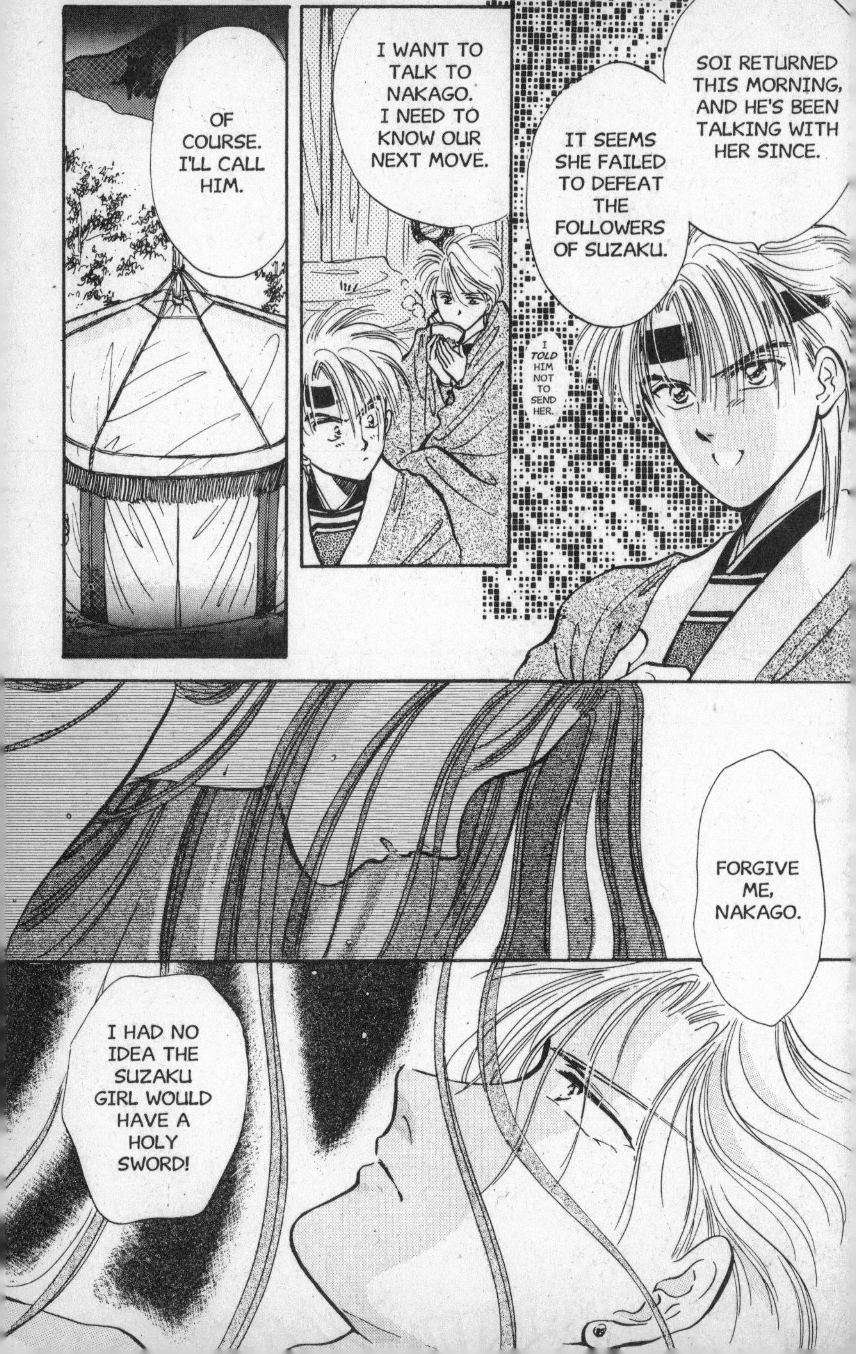
SOI RETURNED THIS MORNING, AND HE'S BEEN TALKING WITH HER SINCE.
IT SEEMS SHE FAILED TO DEFEAT THE FOLLOWERS OF SUZAKU.
I *TOLD* HIM NOT TO SEND HER.
I WANT TO TALK TO NAKAGO. I NEED TO KNOW OUR NEXT MOVE.
OF COURSE. I'LL CALL HIM.
FORGIVE ME, NAKAGO.
I HAD NO IDEA THE SUZAKU GIRL WOULD HAVE A HOLY SWORD!

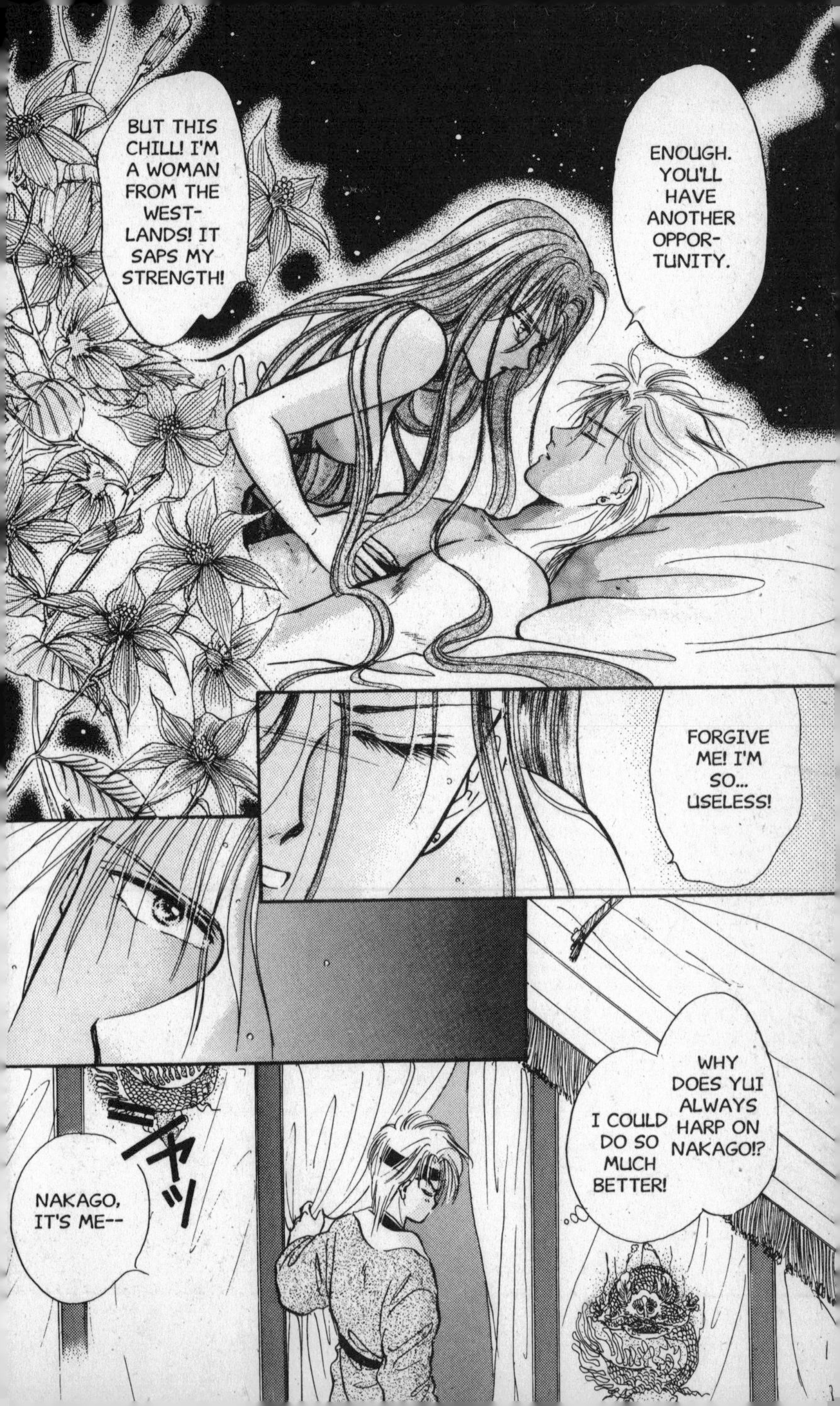

BUT THIS CHILL! I'M A WOMAN FROM THE WEST-LANDS! IT SAPS MY STRENGTH!
ENOUGH. YOU'LL HAVE ANOTHER OPPOR-TUNITY.
FORGIVE ME! I'M SO... USELESS!
NAKAGO, IT'S ME--
WHY DOES YUI ALWAYS HARP ON NAKAGO!?
I COULD DO SO MUCH BETTER!

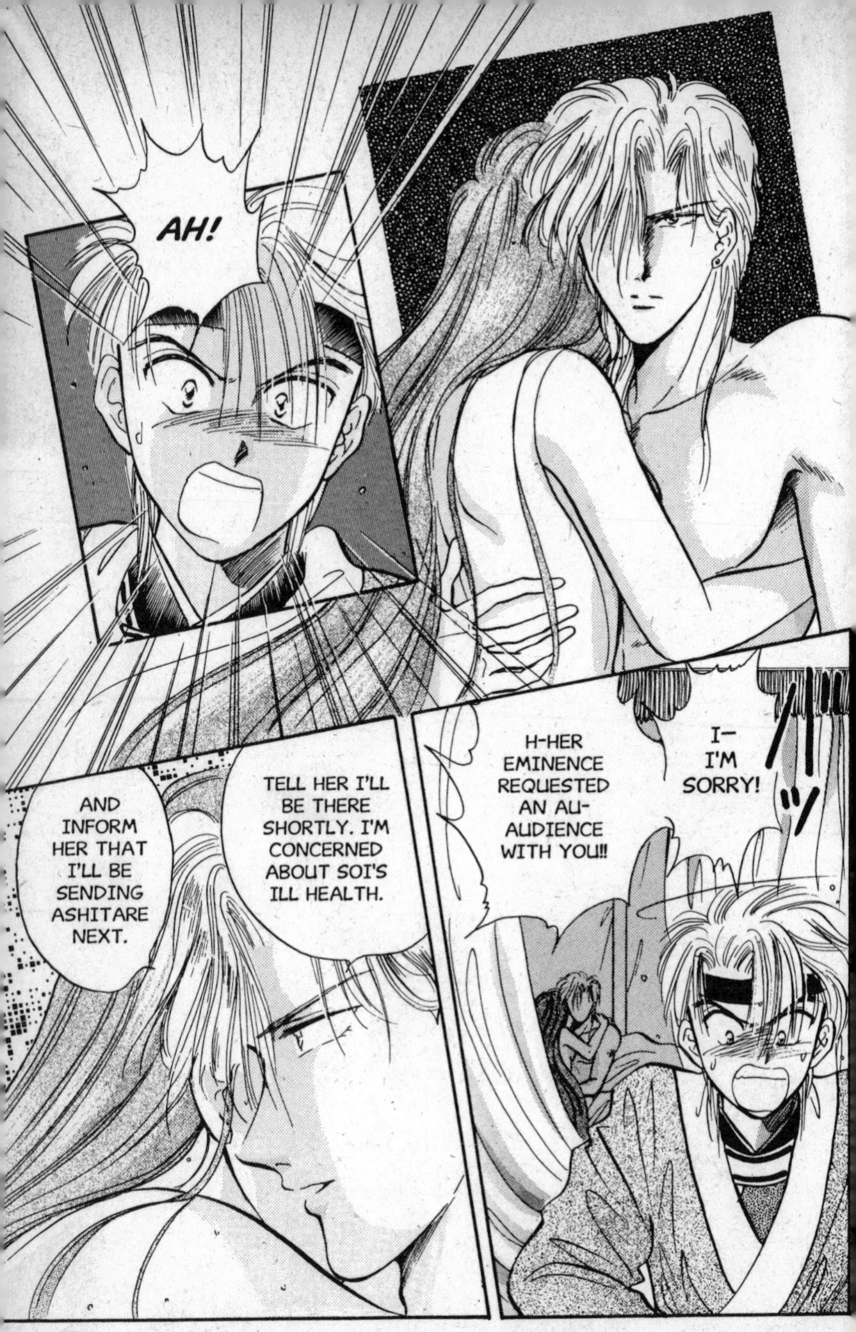
AH!
I— I'M SORRY!
H-HER EMINENCE REQUESTED AN AU- AUDIENCE WITH YOU!!
TELL HER I'LL BE THERE SHORTLY. I'M CONCERNED ABOUT SOI'S ILL HEALTH.
AND INFORM HER THAT I'LL BE SENDING ASHITARE NEXT.

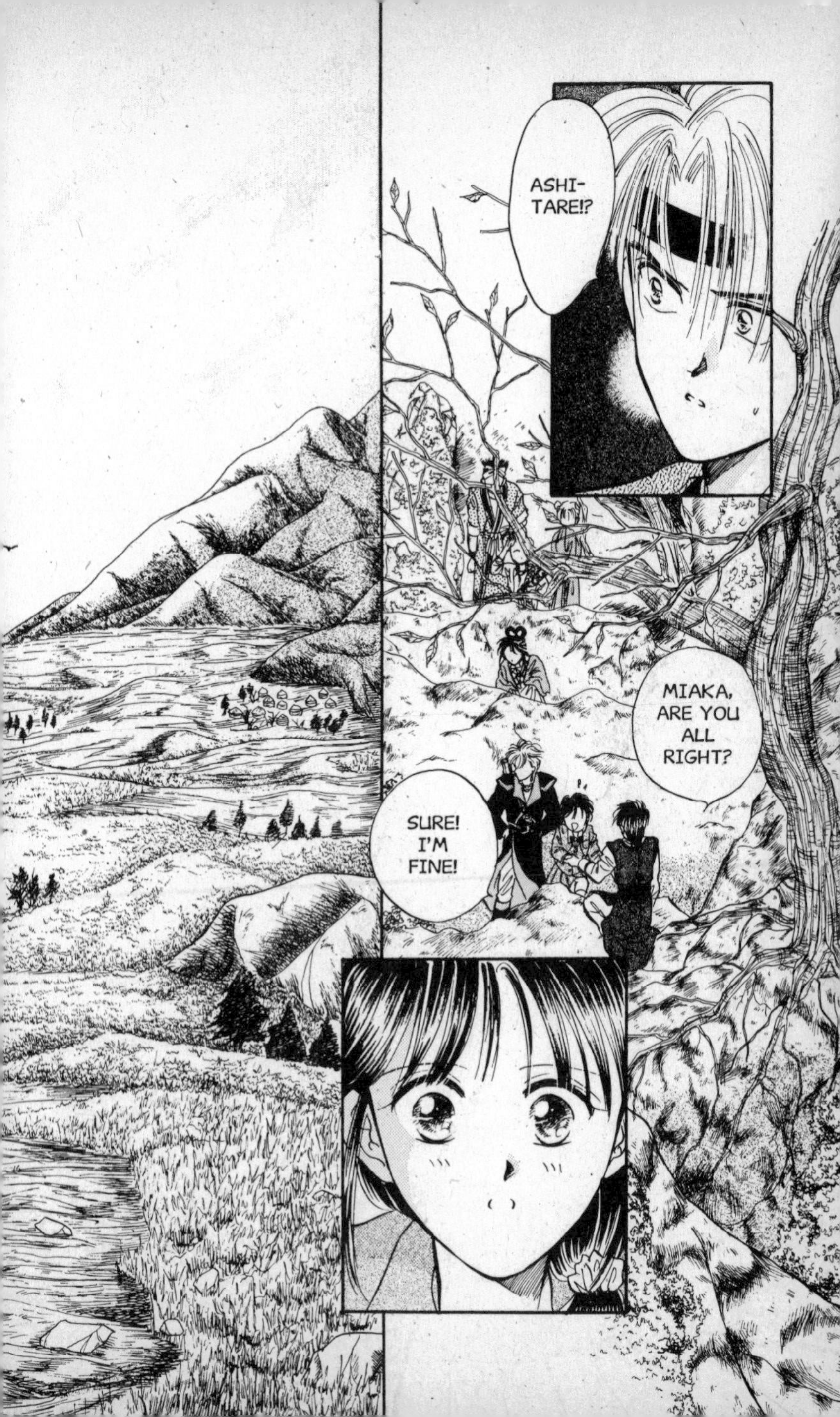
ASHI-TARE!?
MIAKA, ARE YOU ALL RIGHT?
SURE! I'M FINE!

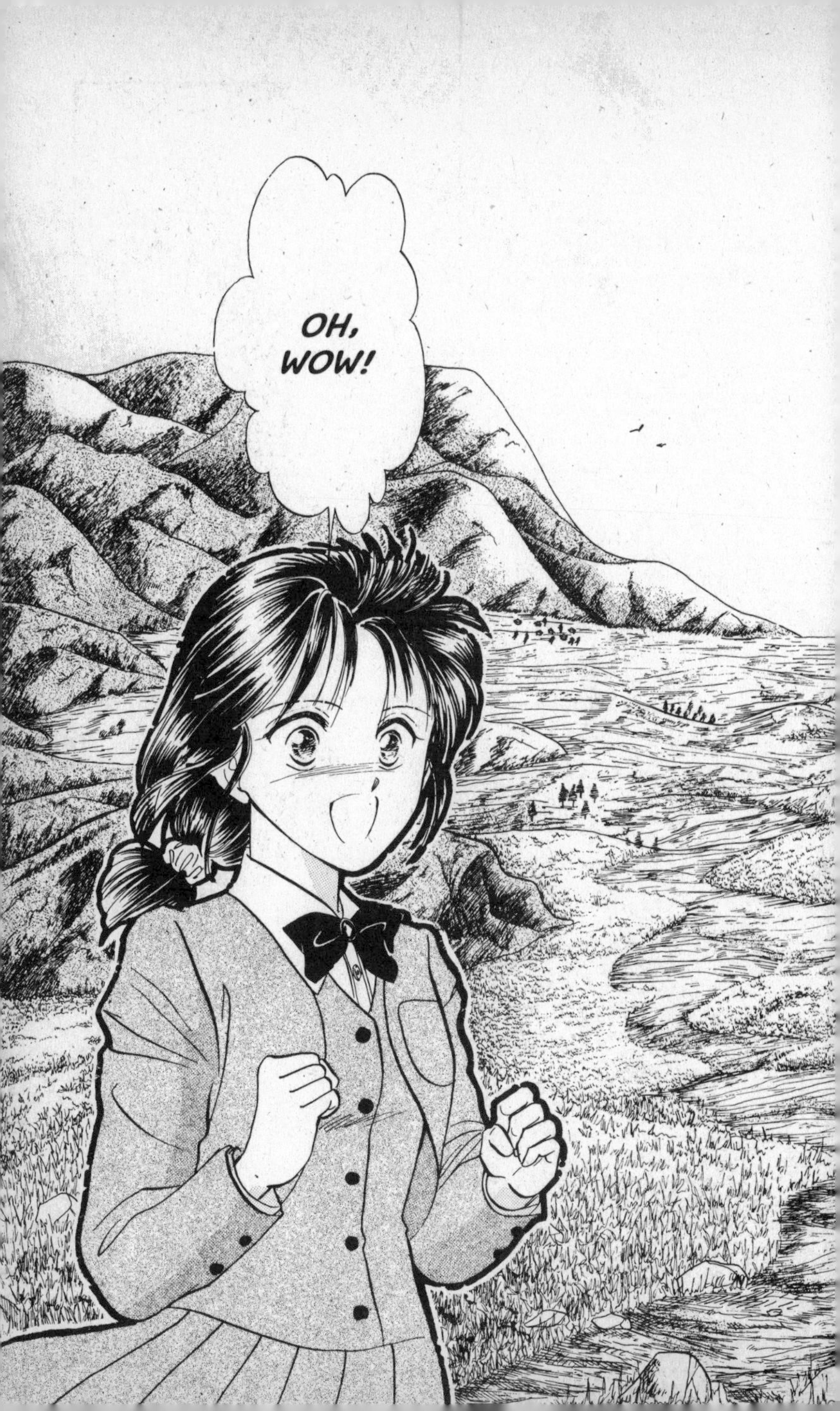
OH, WOW!

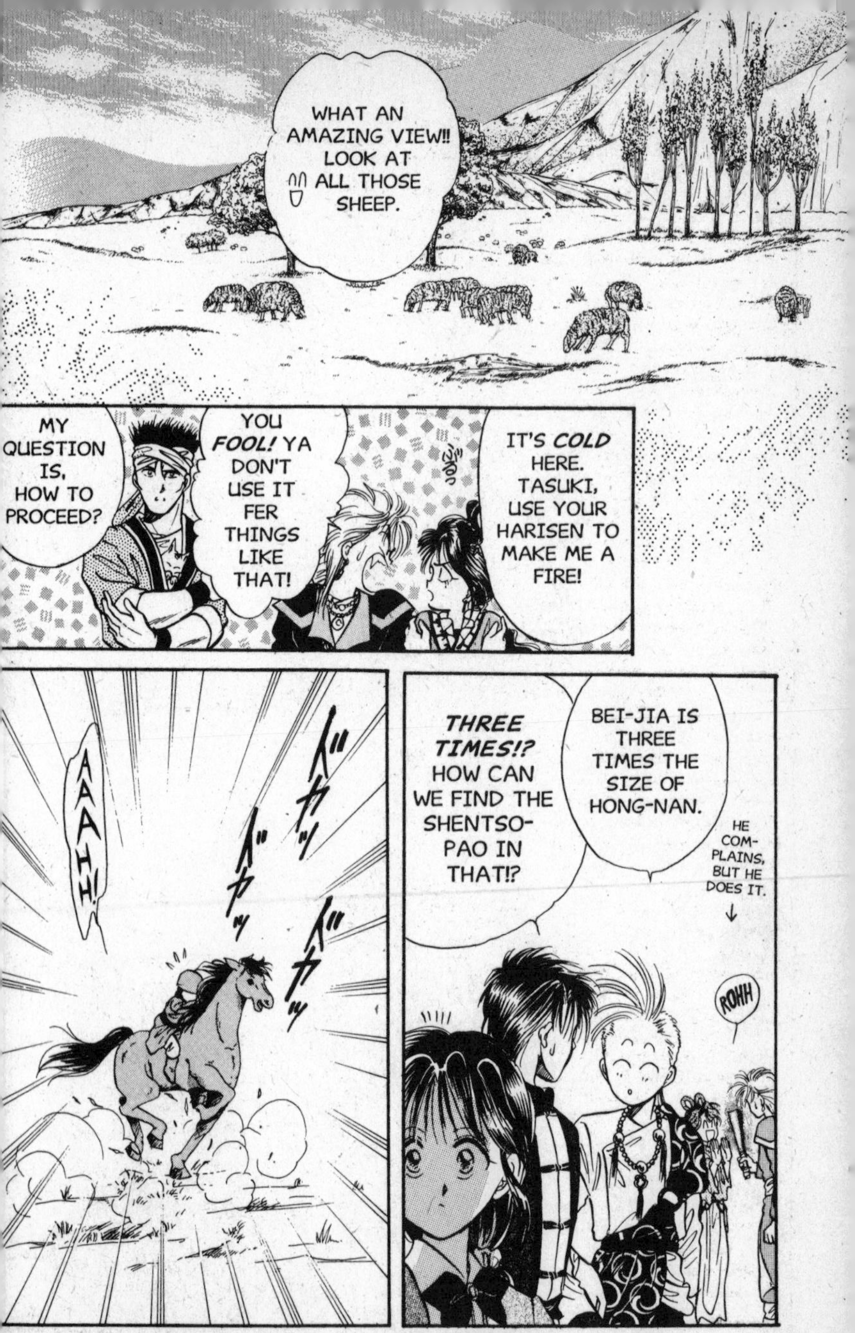
WHAT AN AMAZING VIEW!! LOOK AT ALL THOSE SHEEP.
IT'S *COLD* HERE. TASUKI, USE YOUR HARISEN TO MAKE ME A FIRE!
YOU *FOOL!* YA DON'T USE IT FER THINGS LIKE THAT!
MY QUESTION IS, HOW TO PROCEED?
BEI-JIA IS THREE TIMES THE SIZE OF HONG-NAN.
THREE TIMES!? HOW CAN WE FIND THE SHENTSO-PAO IN THAT!?
HE COM-PLAINS, BUT HE DOES IT.
ROHH
AAAHH!!

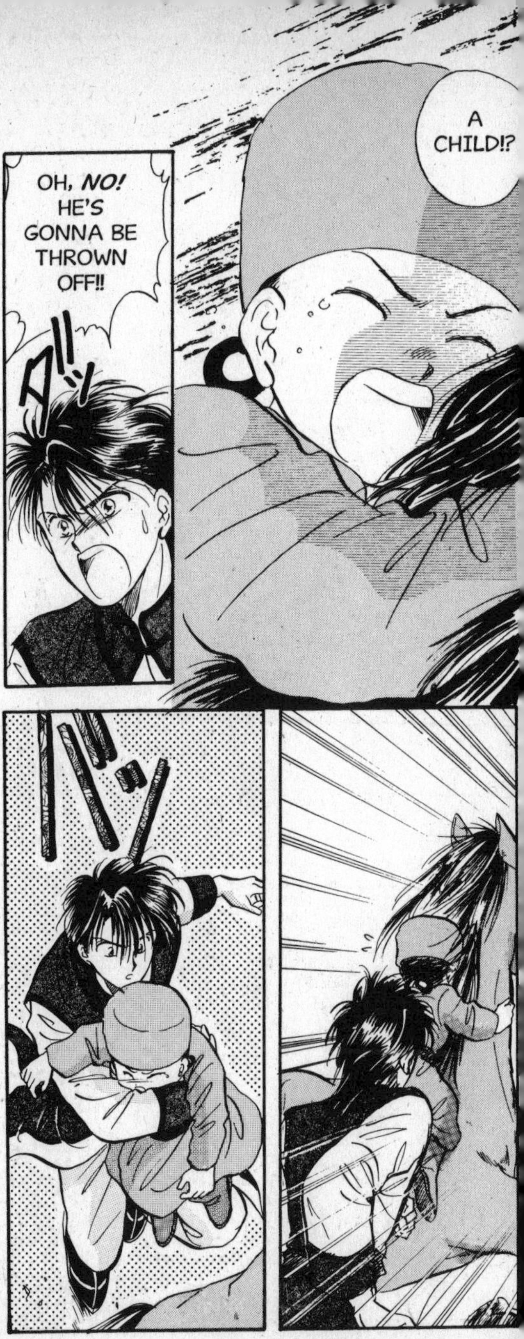
A CHILD!?
OH, *NO!* HE'S GONNA BE THROWN OFF!!

Friend

When I saw a hall I thought, "Nuriko could be here!" Looking at the Emperor's throne I'd think, "Hotohori would be sitting in that chair..." I'd see the roof and think, "Chichiri could be lying there, staring at the sky." My editor told me I was acting like an overzealous fangirl. But I think it was because I'd seen these sights so often (from research) that I almost felt at home. Though I was far from it!
I bought the coffee-table photo book of course! Hong-Nan in FY is based on the Sung dynasty, so I should have gone to see the castle in Kaifeng, but it wasn't included in the tour. The Forbidden City was built in the Ming and Ch'eng dynasties, and that's a long time after the Sung.
We passed by the HUGE walls where Pu Yi practiced riding his bike in "The Last Emperor." I bought a Chinese man's outfit at a small shop. If Tamahome really existed, I'd want him to wear this awesome-looking black outfit embroidered with a golden dragon and red ornamentation.
That night, wearing the outfit, the weird Ms. Yuu burst into a smile. The next place was the unforgettable Great Wall. At one point, we rode in a gondola car. It went up so high I was terrified. Every time it shook, little Ms. Yuu turned into which editor K ruthlessly captured on film. Our trusting relationship was called into question but we finally arrived. So it ended without the expected disaster. What disaster did I expect?
There was no one there, so the two of us walked around by ourselves for a while, and that was it. The gondola ride was much more memorable. We also visited Tientan, which served as the basis for Suzaku's temple. The altar is where the emperor prays to the heavens for a good harvest. People gathered around and prayed where the emperor used to stand.

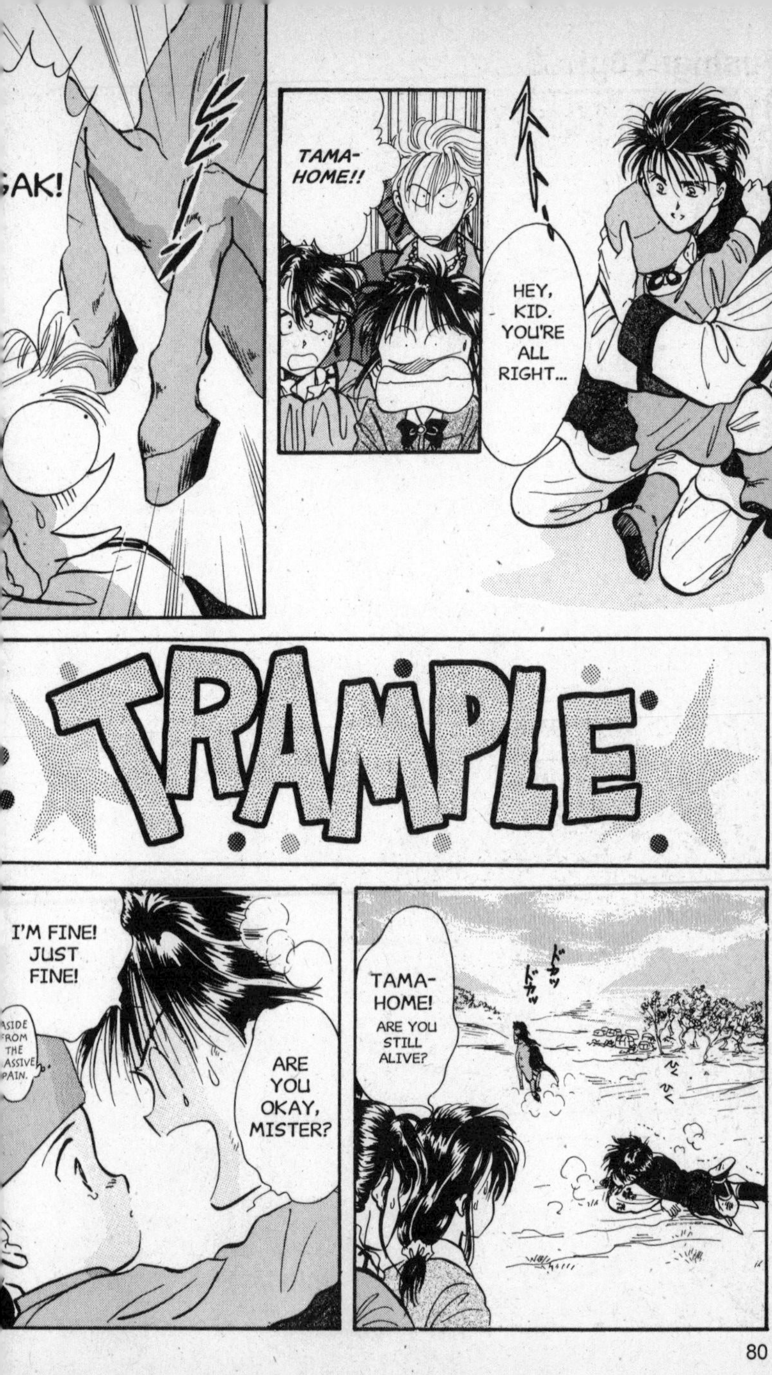
HEY, KID. YOU'RE ALL RIGHT...
TAMA-HOME!!
GAK!
TRAMPLE
TAMA-HOME! ARE YOU STILL ALIVE?
ドカッ ドカッ
ARE YOU OKAY, MISTER?
I'M FINE! JUST FINE!
ASIDE FROM THE ASSIVE PAIN.

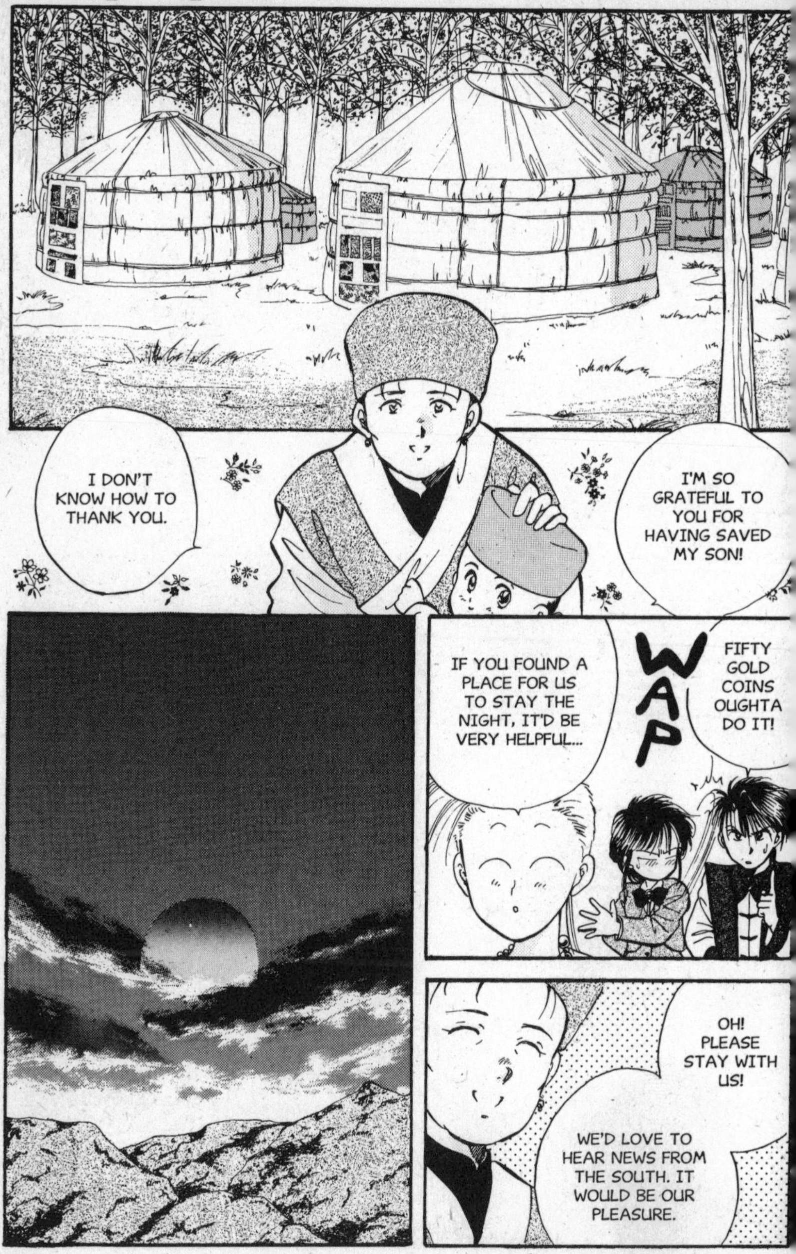
I'M SO GRATEFUL TO YOU FOR HAVING SAVED MY SON!
I DON'T KNOW HOW TO THANK YOU.
FIFTY GOLD COINS OUGHTA DO IT!
WAP
IF YOU FOUND A PLACE FOR US TO STAY THE NIGHT, IT'D BE VERY HELPFUL...
OH! PLEASE STAY WITH US!
WE'D LOVE TO HEAR NEWS FROM THE SOUTH. IT WOULD BE OUR PLEASURE.

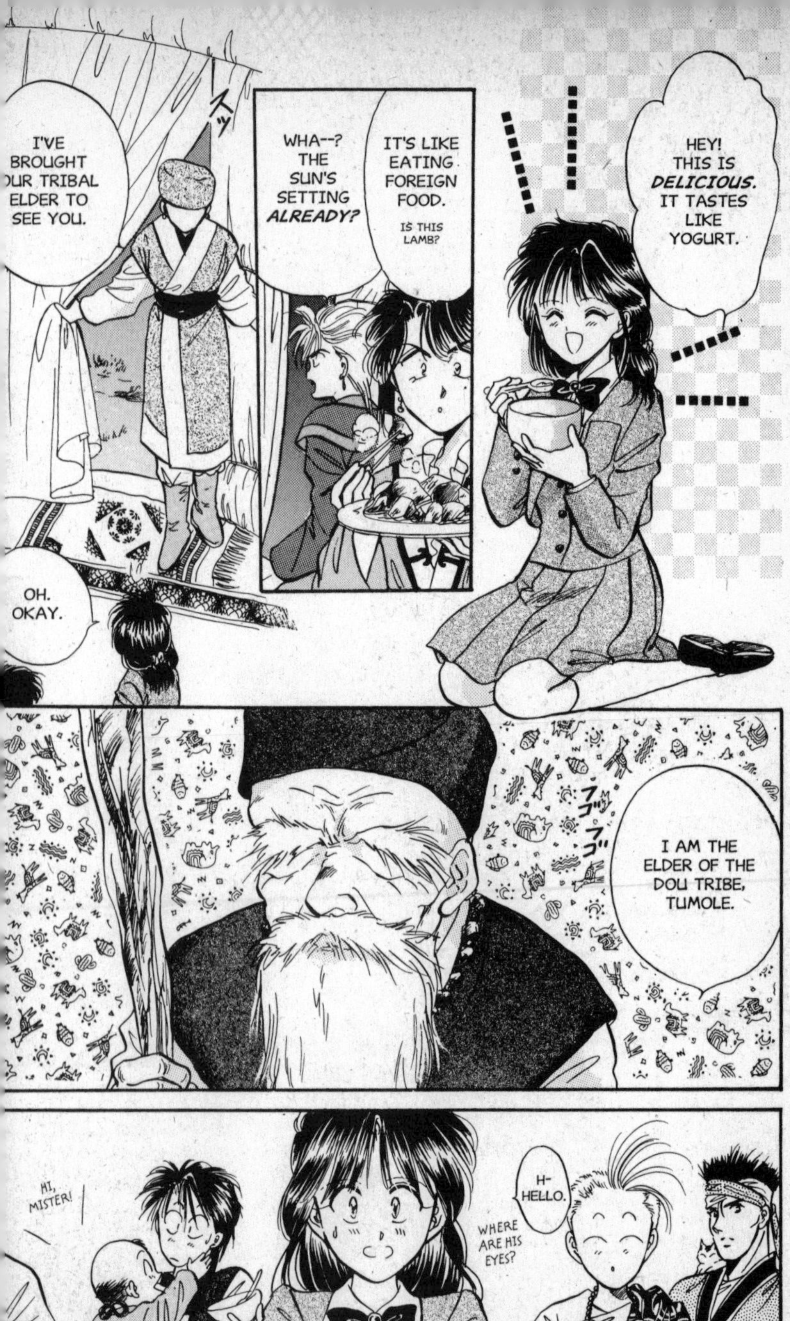
HEY! THIS IS **DELICIOUS.** IT TASTES LIKE YOGURT.
IT'S LIKE EATING FOREIGN FOOD.
IS THIS LAMB?
WHA--? THE SUN'S SETTING **ALREADY?**
スッ
I'VE BROUGHT OUR TRIBAL ELDER TO SEE YOU.
OH. OKAY.
I AM THE ELDER OF THE DOU TRIBE, TUMOLE.
フゴ フゴ
H-HELLO.
WHERE ARE HIS EYES?
HI, MISTER!

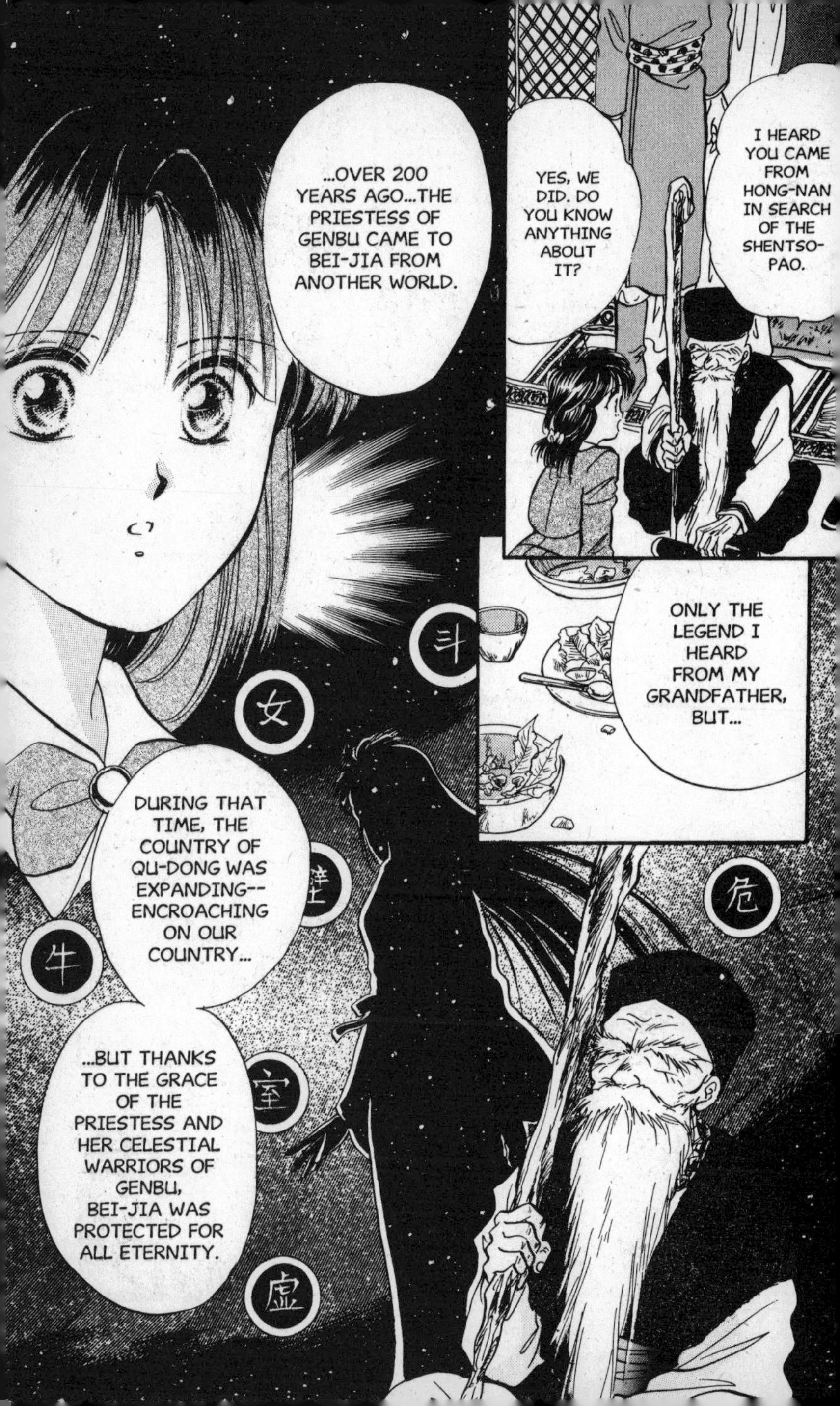
I HEARD YOU CAME FROM HONG-NAN IN SEARCH OF THE SHENTSO-PAO.
YES, WE DID. DO YOU KNOW ANYTHING ABOUT IT?
ONLY THE LEGEND I HEARD FROM MY GRANDFATHER, BUT...
...OVER 200 YEARS AGO...THE PRIESTESS OF GENBU CAME TO BEI-JIA FROM ANOTHER WORLD.
斗
女
危
DURING THAT TIME, THE COUNTRY OF QU-DONG WAS EXPANDING--ENCROACHING ON OUR COUNTRY...
牛
室
...BUT THANKS TO THE GRACE OF THE PRIESTESS AND HER CELESTIAL WARRIORS OF GENBU, BEI-JIA WAS PROTECTED FOR ALL ETERNITY.
虚

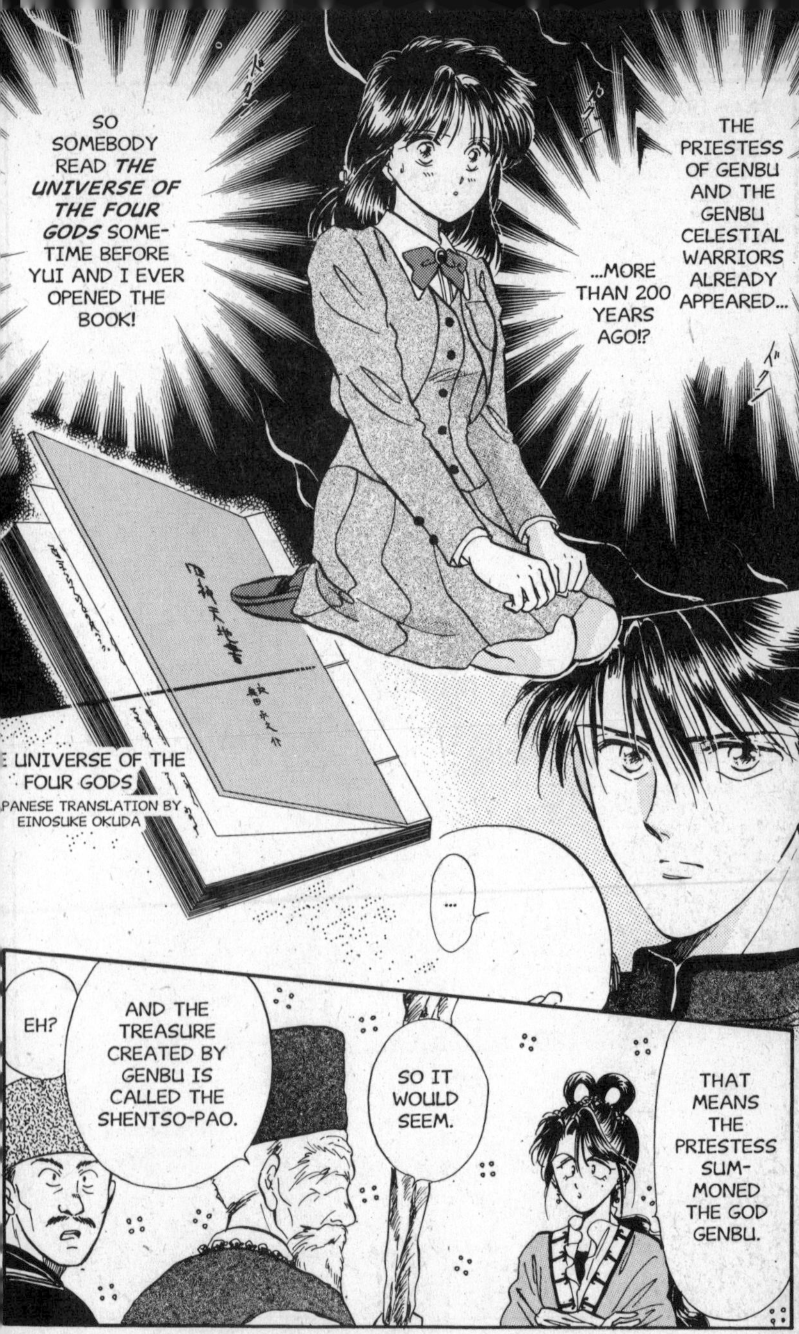
THE PRIESTESS OF GENBU AND THE GENBU CELESTIAL WARRIORS ALREADY APPEARED...
...MORE THAN 200 YEARS AGO!?
SO SOMEBODY READ *THE UNIVERSE OF THE FOUR GODS* SOMETIME BEFORE YUI AND I EVER OPENED THE BOOK!
E UNIVERSE OF THE FOUR GODS
PANESE TRANSLATION BY EINOSUKE OKUDA
...
THAT MEANS THE PRIESTESS SUMMONED THE GOD GENBU.
SO IT WOULD SEEM.
AND THE TREASURE CREATED BY GENBU IS CALLED THE SHENTSO-PAO.
EH?

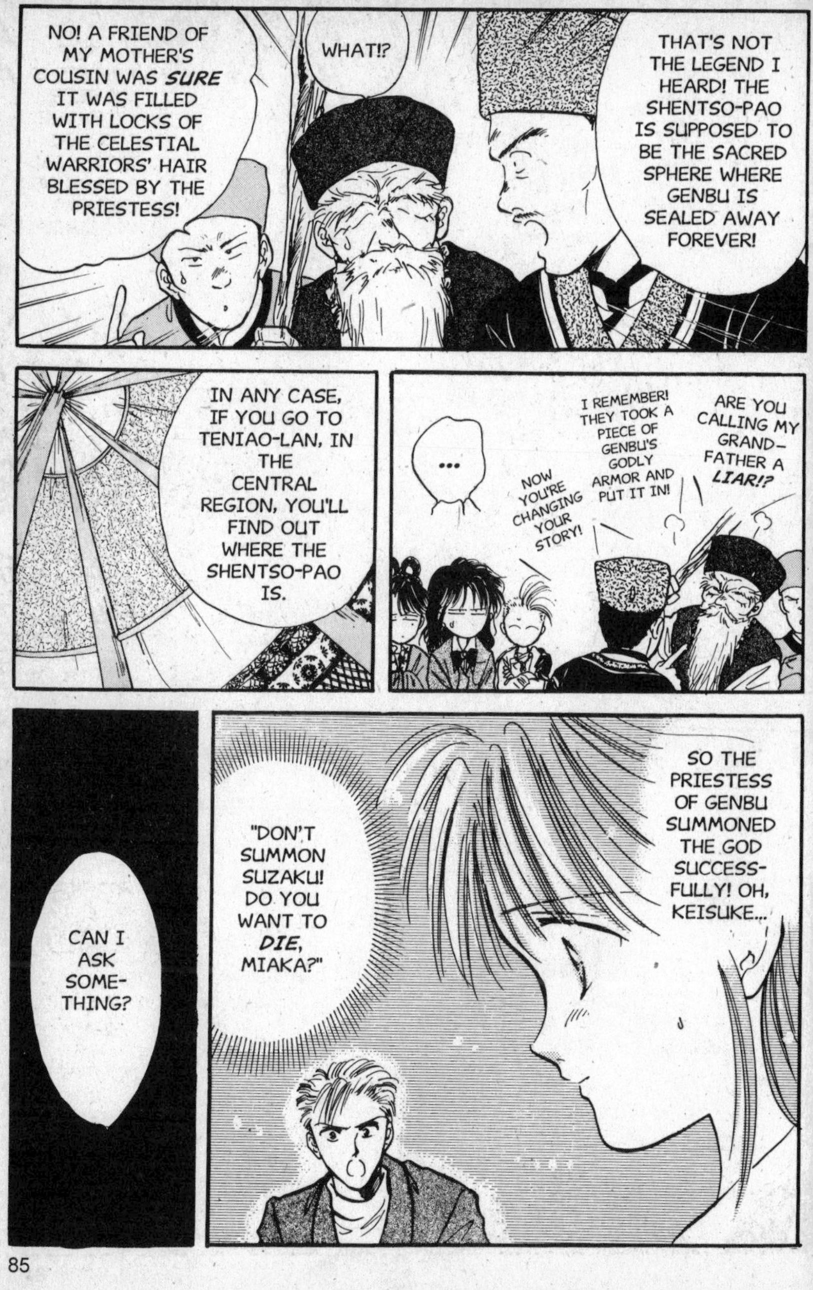
THAT'S NOT THE LEGEND I HEARD! THE SHENTSO-PAO IS SUPPOSED TO BE THE SACRED SPHERE WHERE GENBU IS SEALED AWAY FOREVER!
WHAT!?
NO! A FRIEND OF MY MOTHER'S COUSIN WAS *SURE* IT WAS FILLED WITH LOCKS OF THE CELESTIAL WARRIORS' HAIR BLESSED BY THE PRIESTESS!
ARE YOU CALLING MY GRAND-FATHER A *LIAR!?*
I REMEMBER! THEY TOOK A PIECE OF GENBU'S GODLY ARMOR AND PUT IT IN!
NOW YOU'RE CHANGING YOUR STORY!
...
IN ANY CASE, IF YOU GO TO TENIAO-LAN, IN THE CENTRAL REGION, YOU'LL FIND OUT WHERE THE SHENTSO-PAO IS.
SO THE PRIESTESS OF GENBU SUMMONED THE GOD SUCCESS-FULLY! OH, KEISUKE...
"DON'T SUMMON SUZAKU! DO YOU WANT TO *DIE*, MIAKA?"
CAN I ASK SOME-THING?

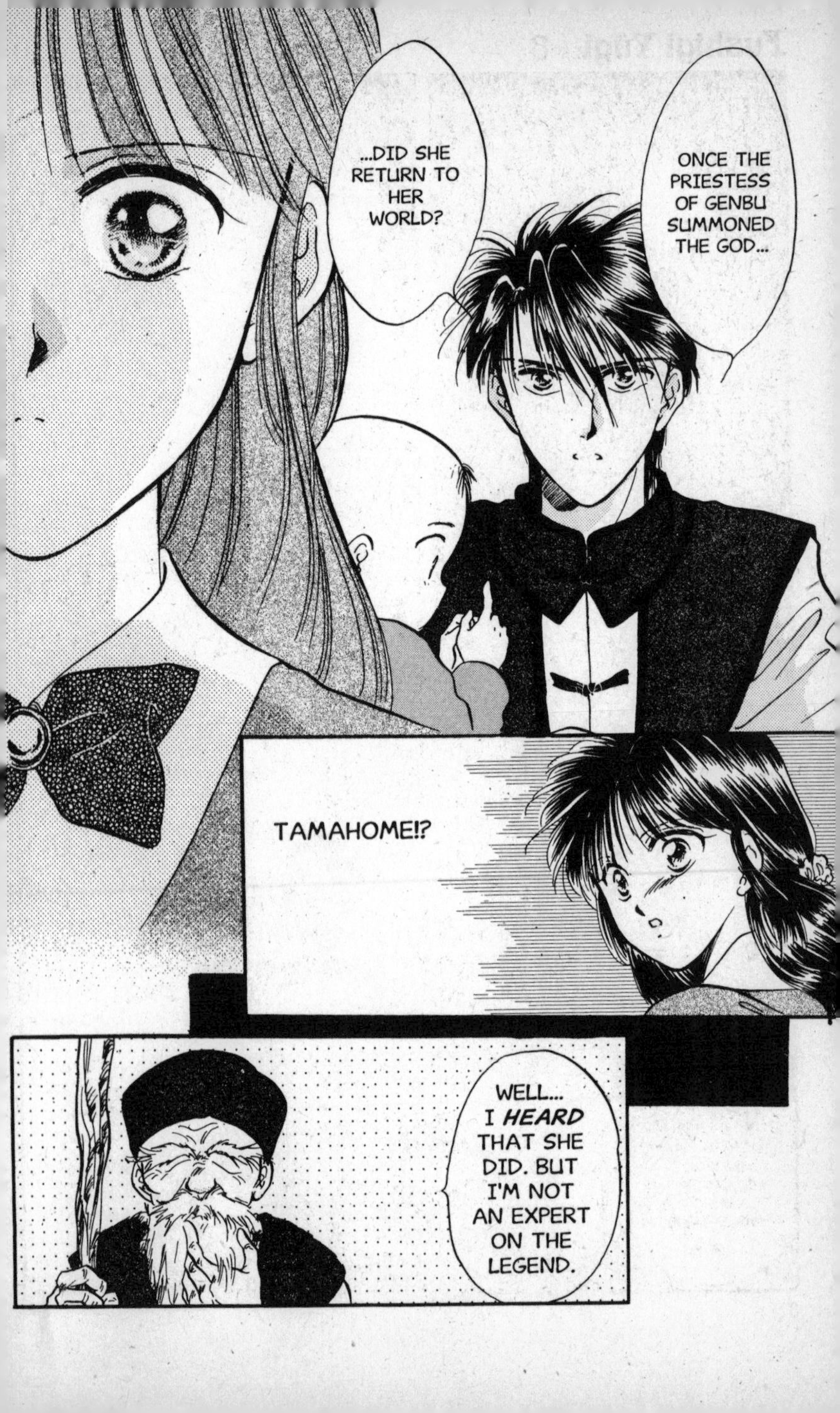
ONCE THE PRIESTESS OF GENBU SUMMONED THE GOD...
...DID SHE RETURN TO HER WORLD?
TAMAHOME!?
WELL... I *HEARD* THAT SHE DID. BUT I'M NOT AN EXPERT ON THE LEGEND.

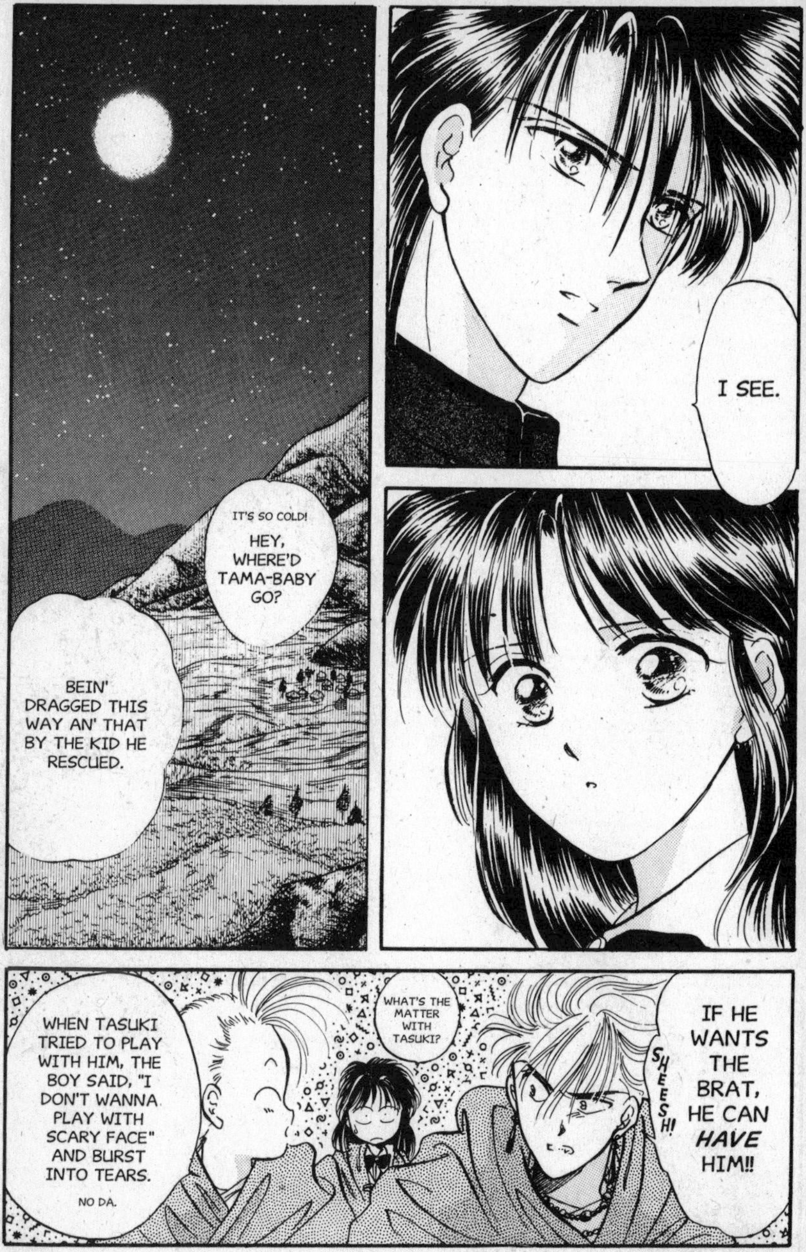
I SEE.
IT'S SO COLD!
HEY, WHERE'D TAMA-BABY GO?
BEIN' DRAGGED THIS WAY AN' THAT BY THE KID HE RESCUED.
IF HE WANTS THE BRAT, HE CAN *HAVE* HIM!!
SHEESH!
WHAT'S THE MATTER WITH TASUKI?
WHEN TASUKI TRIED TO PLAY WITH HIM, THE BOY SAID, "I DON'T WANNA PLAY WITH SCARY FACE" AND BURST INTO TEARS.
NO DA.

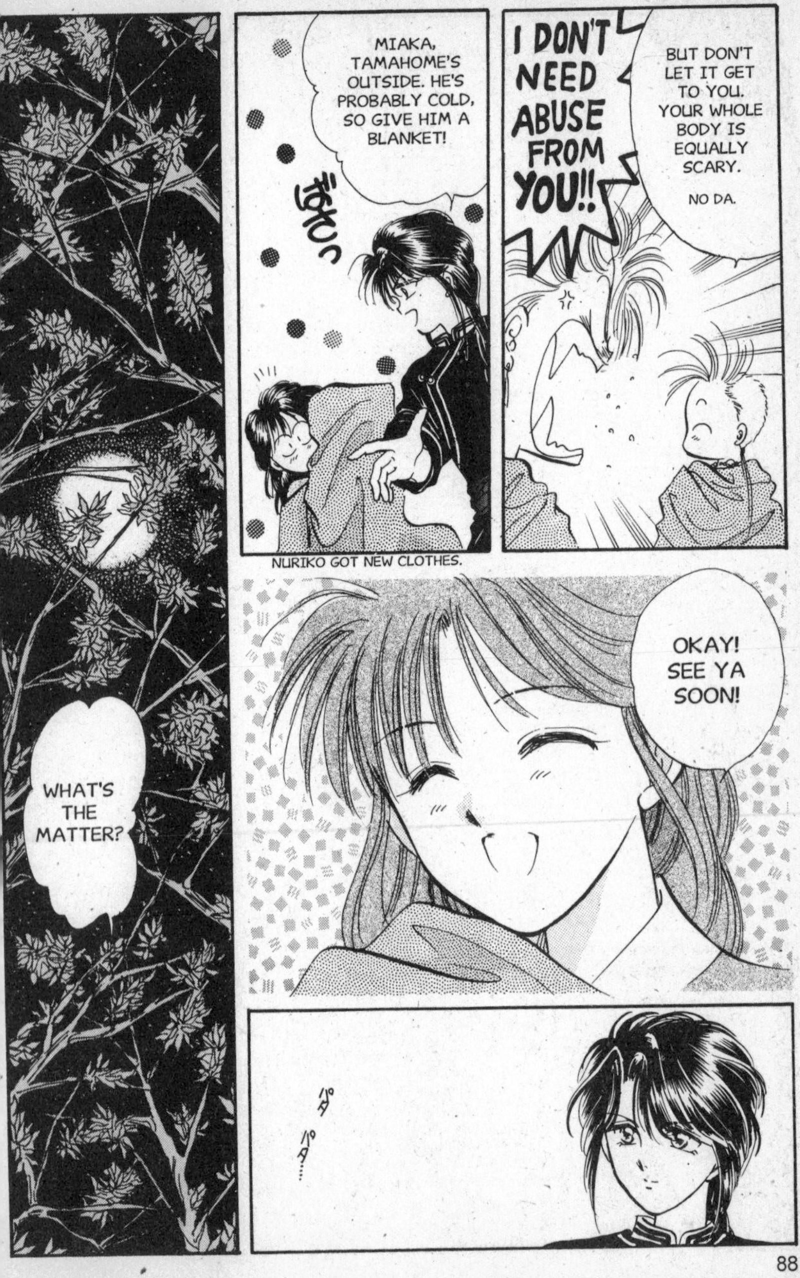
BUT DON'T LET IT GET TO YOU. YOUR WHOLE BODY IS EQUALLY SCARY.
NO DA.
I DON'T NEED ABUSE FROM YOU!!
MIAKA, TAMAHOME'S OUTSIDE. HE'S PROBABLY COLD, SO GIVE HIM A BLANKET!
ぼきっ
NURIKO GOT NEW CLOTHES.
OKAY! SEE YA SOON!
パタ
パタ……
WHAT'S THE MATTER?

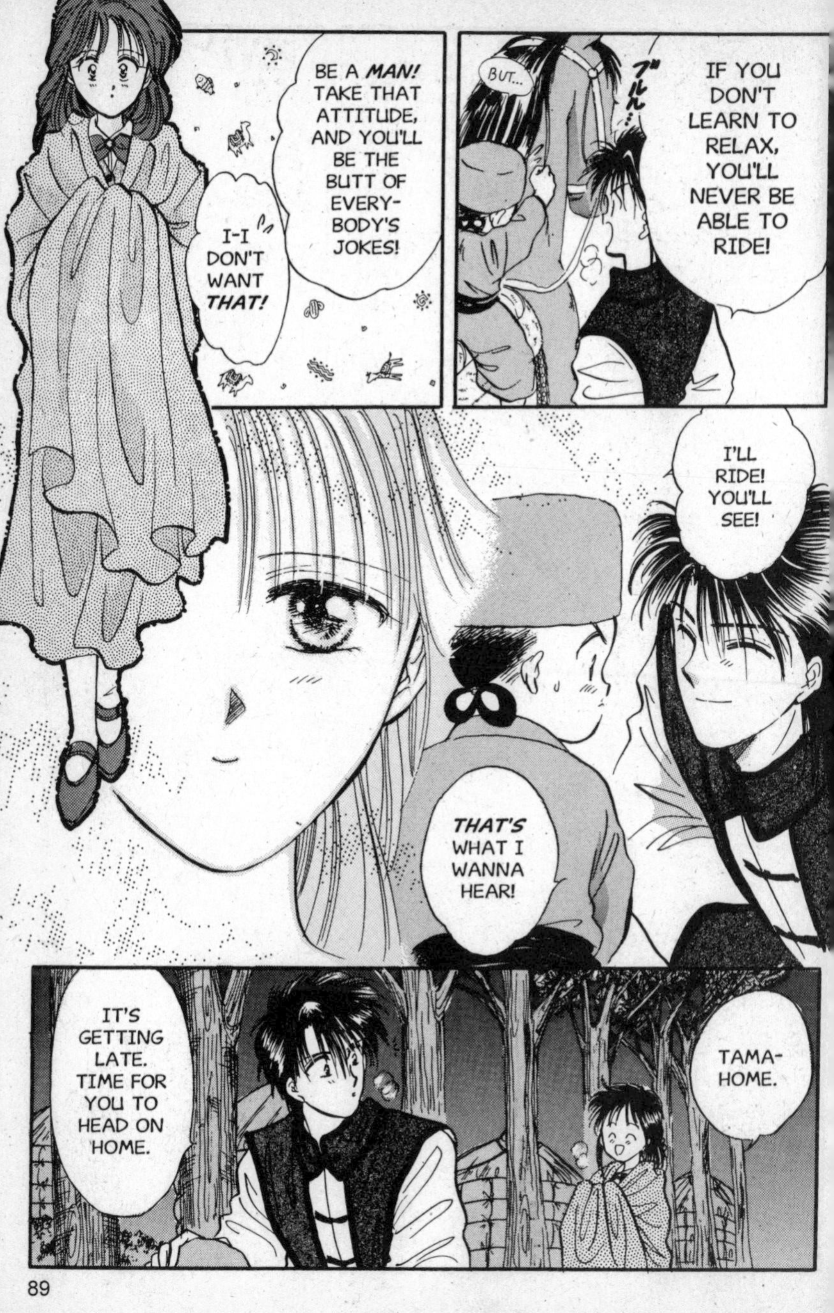
IF YOU DON'T LEARN TO RELAX, YOU'LL NEVER BE ABLE TO RIDE!
BUT...
ブルん…
BE A MAN! TAKE THAT ATTITUDE, AND YOU'LL BE THE BUTT OF EVERY-BODY'S JOKES!
I-I DON'T WANT THAT!
I'LL RIDE! YOU'LL SEE!
THAT'S WHAT I WANNA HEAR!
TAMA-HOME.
IT'S GETTING LATE. TIME FOR YOU TO HEAD ON HOME.

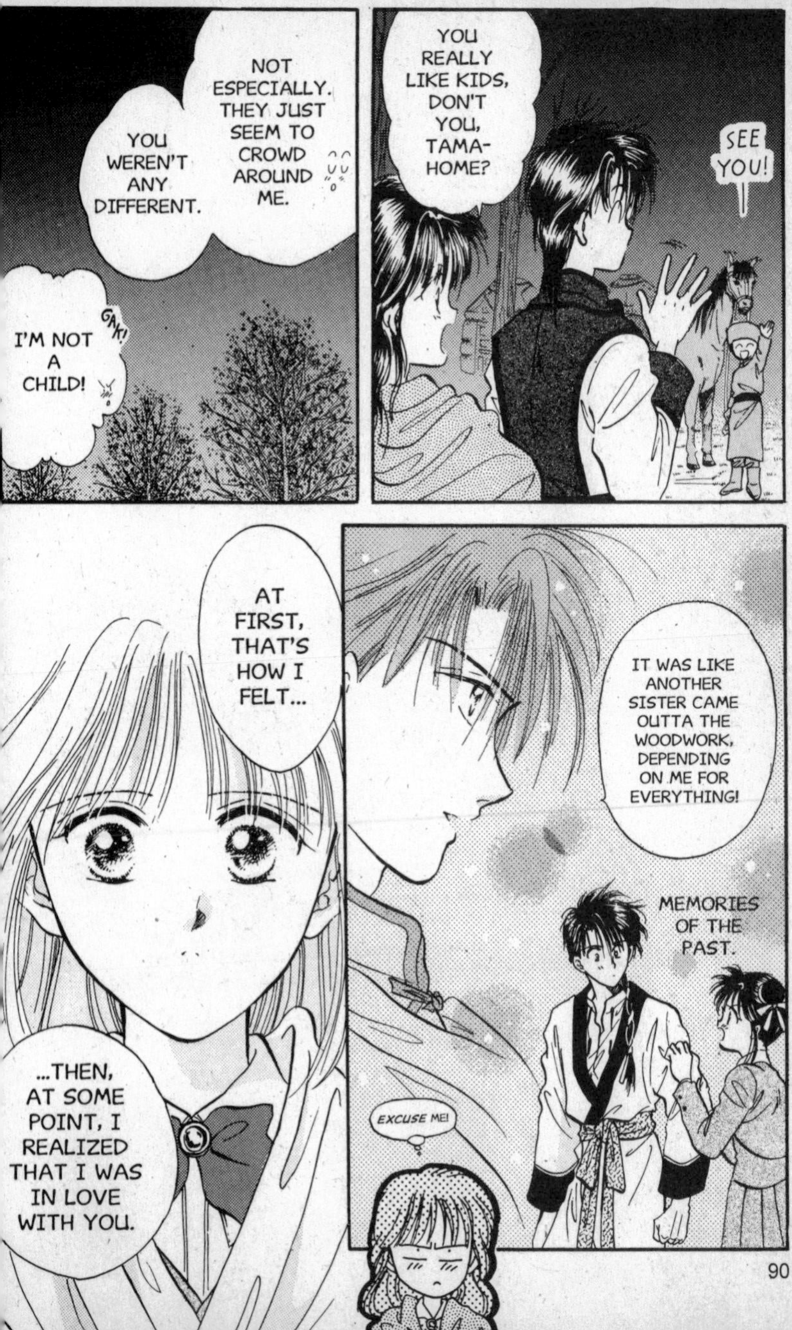
YOU REALLY LIKE KIDS, DON'T YOU, TAMA-HOME?
SEE YOU!
NOT ESPECIALLY. THEY JUST SEEM TO CROWD AROUND ME.
YOU WEREN'T ANY DIFFERENT.
GAK!
I'M NOT A CHILD!
IT WAS LIKE ANOTHER SISTER CAME OUTTA THE WOODWORK, DEPENDING ON ME FOR EVERYTHING!
MEMORIES OF THE PAST.
EXCUSE ME!
AT FIRST, THAT'S HOW I FELT...
...THEN, AT SOME POINT, I REALIZED THAT I WAS IN LOVE WITH YOU.

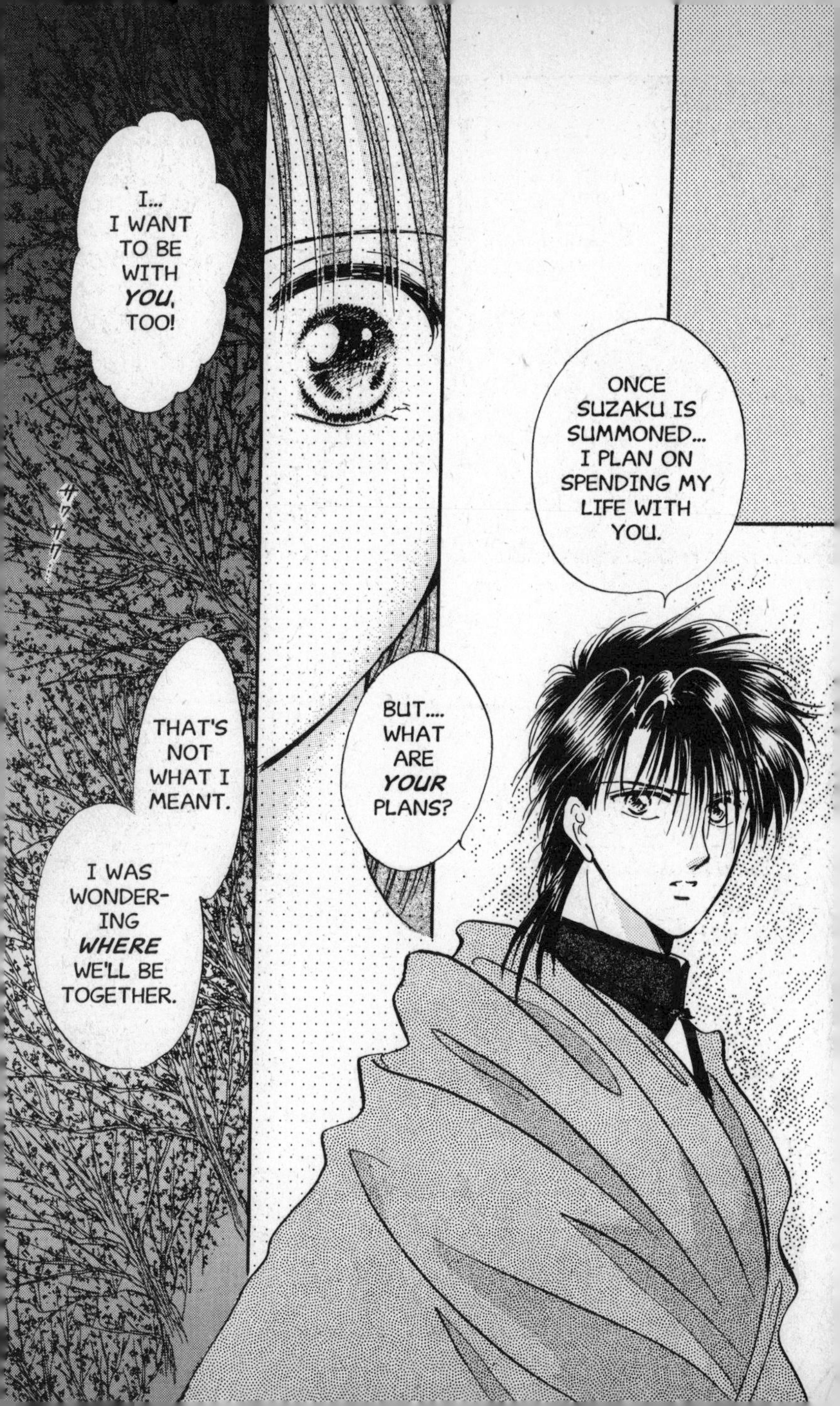

ONCE SUZAKU IS SUMMONED... I PLAN ON SPENDING MY LIFE WITH YOU.
BUT.... WHAT ARE *YOUR* PLANS?
I... I WANT TO BE WITH *YOU*, TOO!
THAT'S NOT WHAT I MEANT.
I WAS WONDERING *WHERE* WE'LL BE TOGETHER.

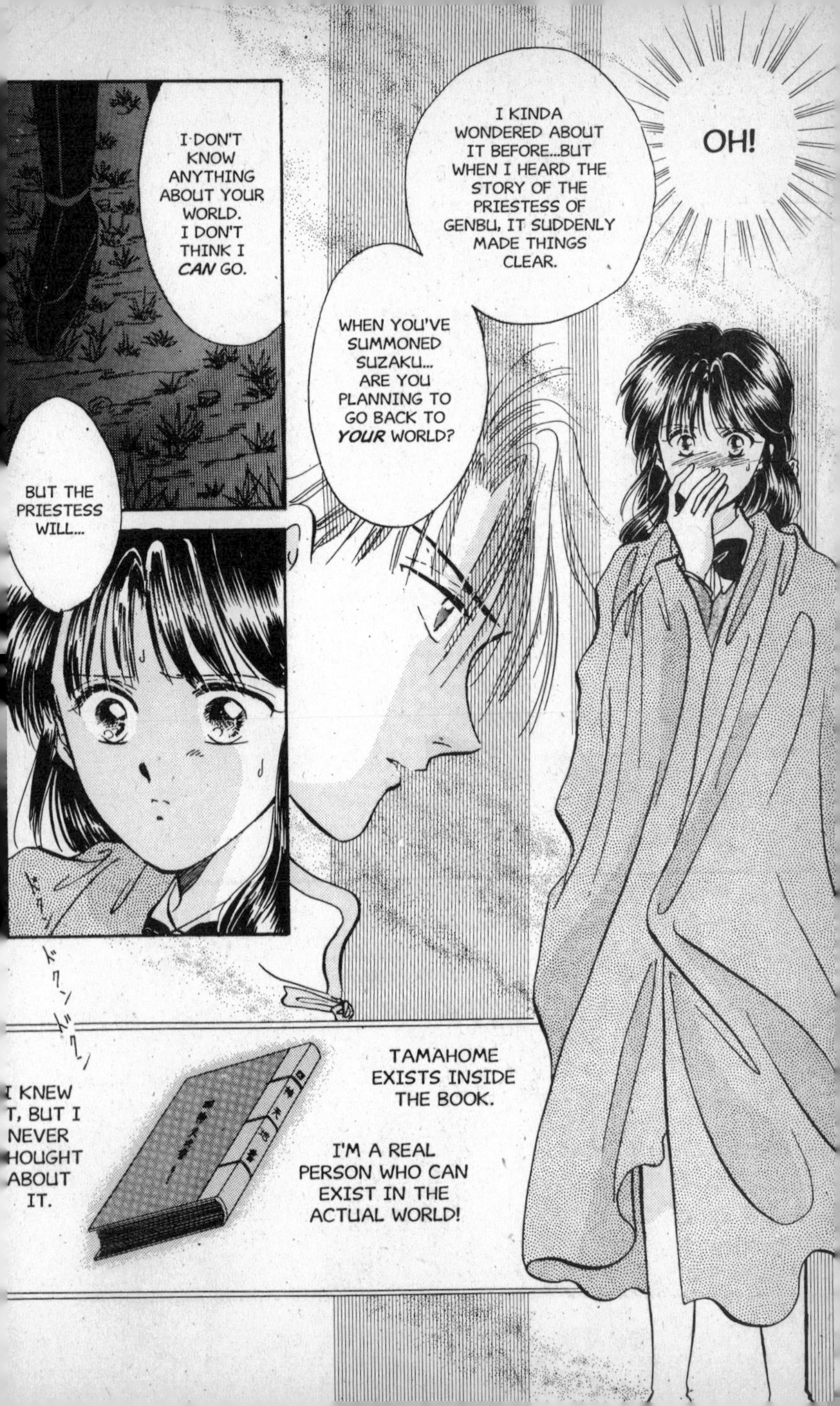
OH!
I KINDA WONDERED ABOUT IT BEFORE...BUT WHEN I HEARD THE STORY OF THE PRIESTESS OF GENBU, IT SUDDENLY MADE THINGS CLEAR.
WHEN YOU'VE SUMMONED SUZAKU... ARE YOU PLANNING TO GO BACK TO *YOUR* WORLD?
I DON'T KNOW ANYTHING ABOUT YOUR WORLD. I DON'T THINK I *CAN* GO.
BUT THE PRIESTESS WILL...
ドクン ドクン
TAMAHOME EXISTS INSIDE THE BOOK.
I'M A REAL PERSON WHO CAN EXIST IN THE ACTUAL WORLD!
I KNEW T, BUT I NEVER HOUGHT ABOUT IT.

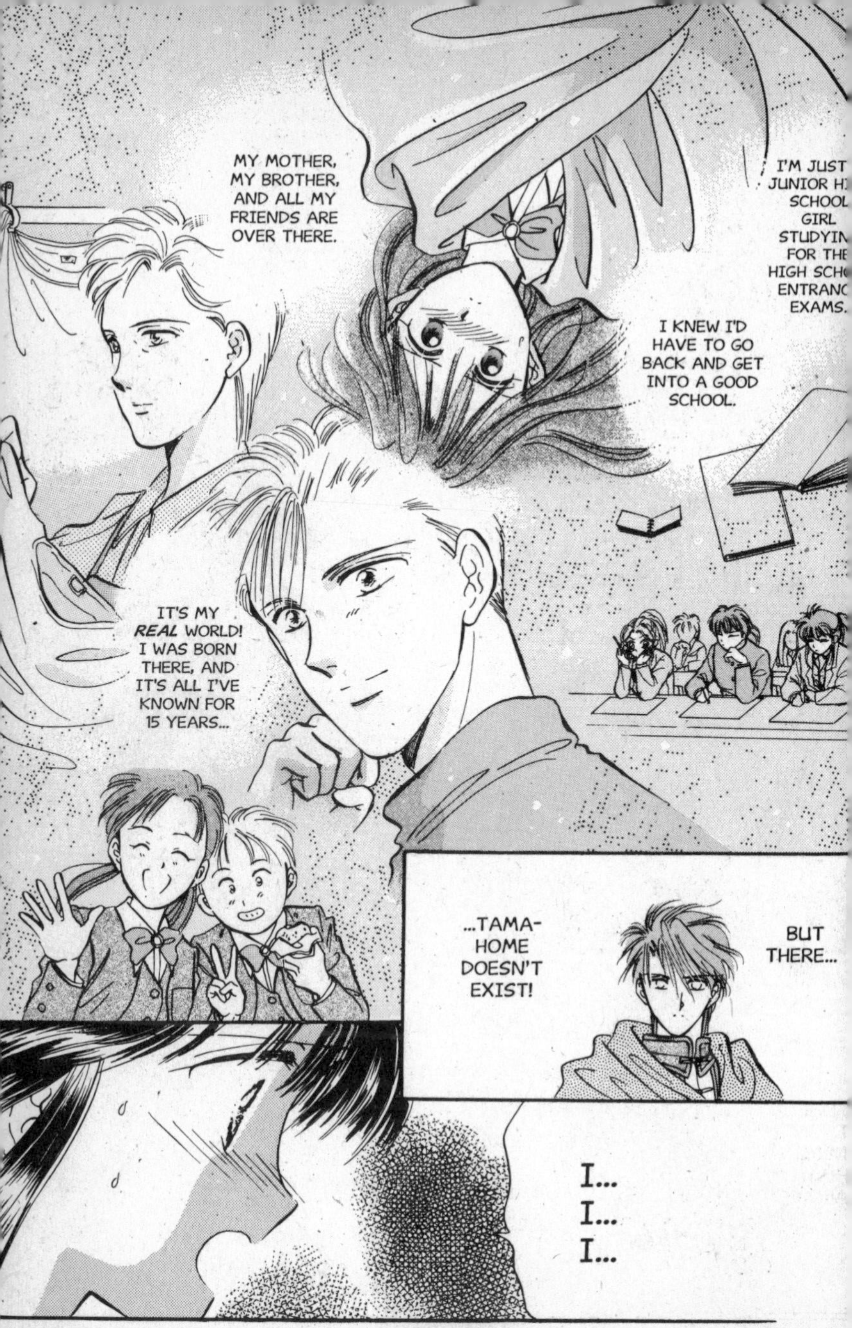

I'M JUST JUNIOR HI SCHOOL GIRL STUDYIN FOR THE HIGH SCH ENTRANC EXAMS.
I KNEW I'D HAVE TO GO BACK AND GET INTO A GOOD SCHOOL.
MY MOTHER, MY BROTHER, AND ALL MY FRIENDS ARE OVER THERE.
IT'S MY *REAL* WORLD! I WAS BORN THERE, AND IT'S ALL I'VE KNOWN FOR 15 YEARS...
BUT THERE...
...TAMA-HOME DOESN'T EXIST!
I...
I...
I...

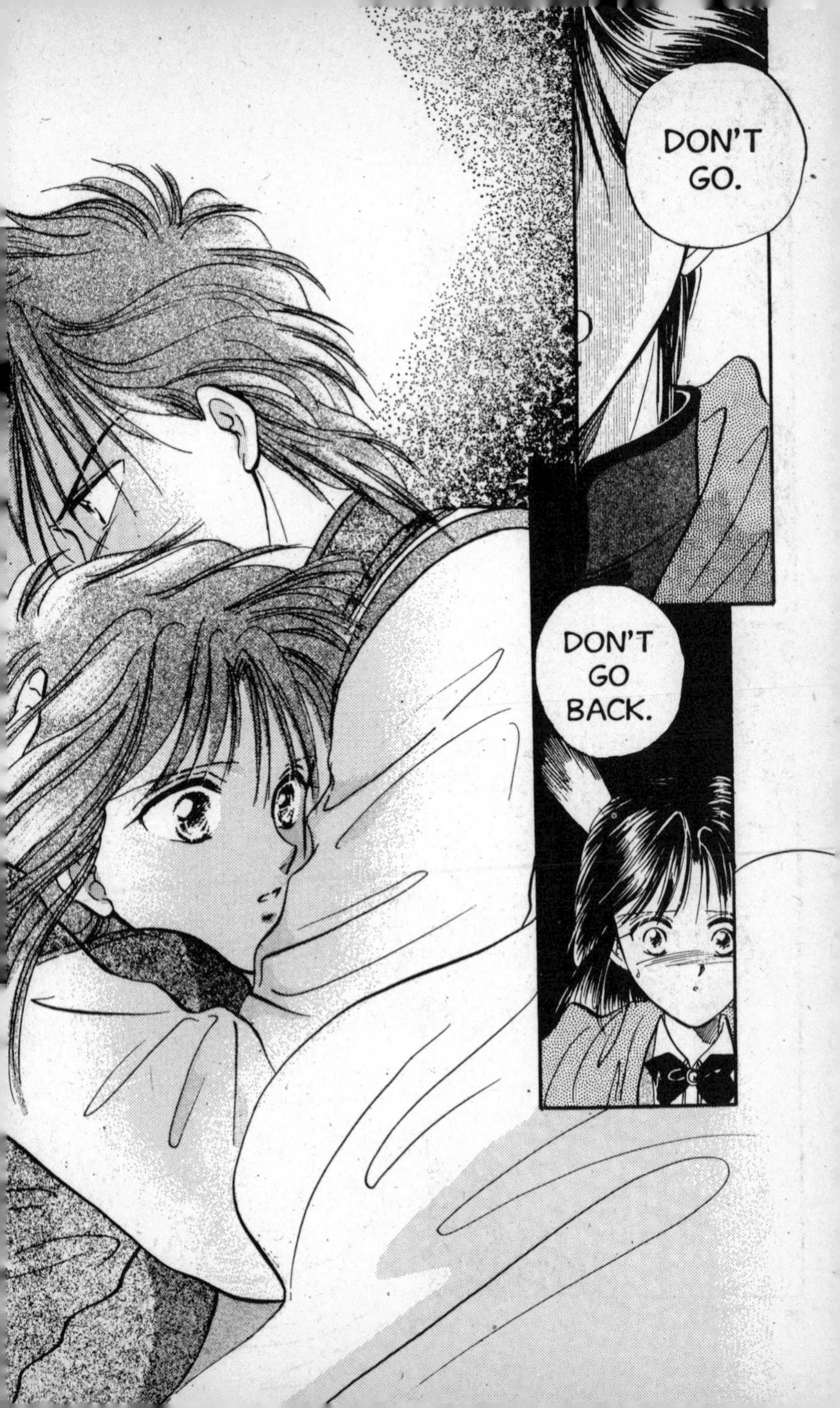
DON'T GO.
DON'T GO BACK.

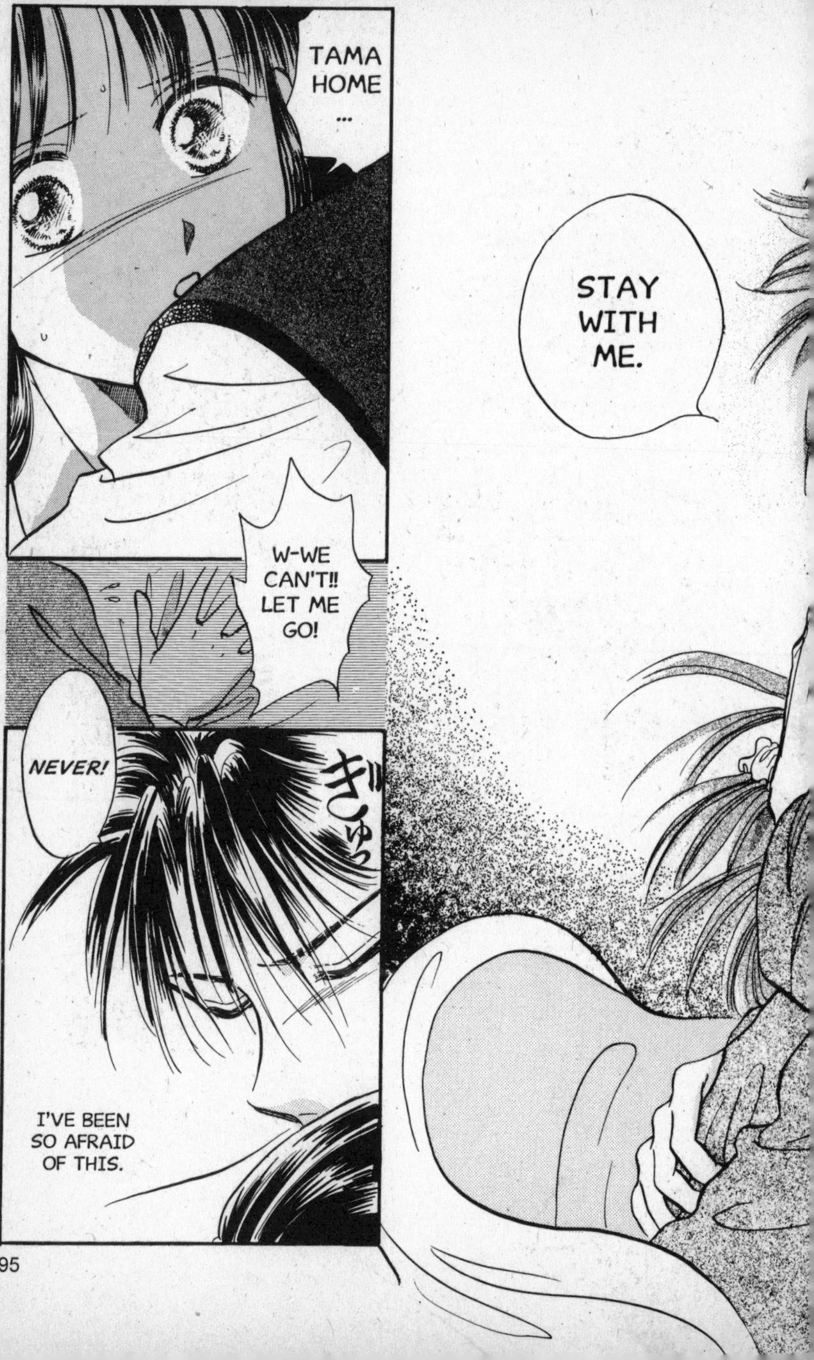
STAY WITH ME.
TAMA HOME ...
W-WE CAN'T!! LET ME GO!
NEVER!
きゅっ
I'VE BEEN SO AFRAID OF THIS.

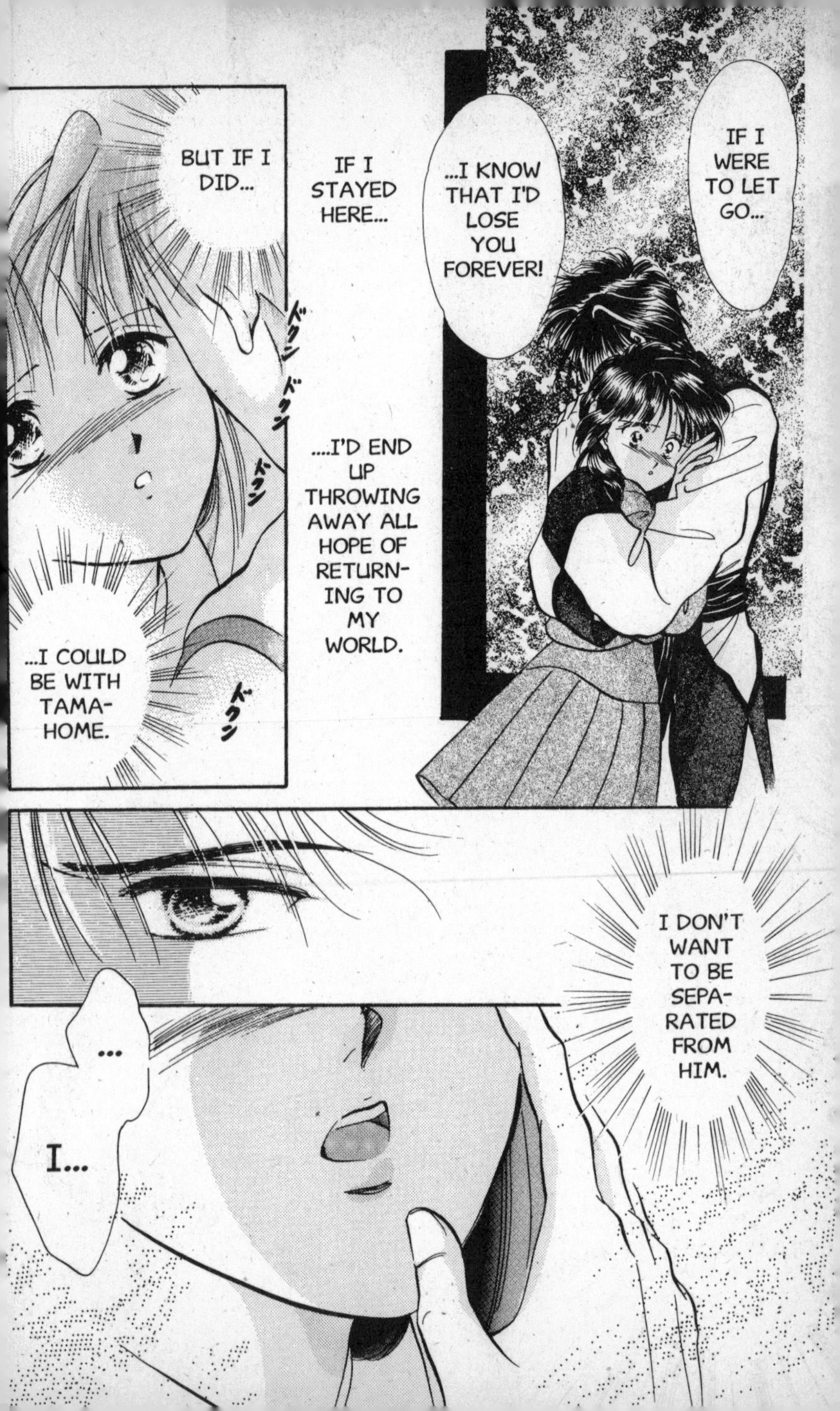
IF I WERE TO LET GO...
...I KNOW THAT I'D LOSE YOU FOREVER!
IF I STAYED HERE...
....I'D END UP THROWING AWAY ALL HOPE OF RETURN-ING TO MY WORLD.
BUT IF I DID...
ドクン
ドクン
ドクン
...I COULD BE WITH TAMA-HOME.
ドクン
I DON'T WANT TO BE SEPA-RATED FROM HIM.
...
I...

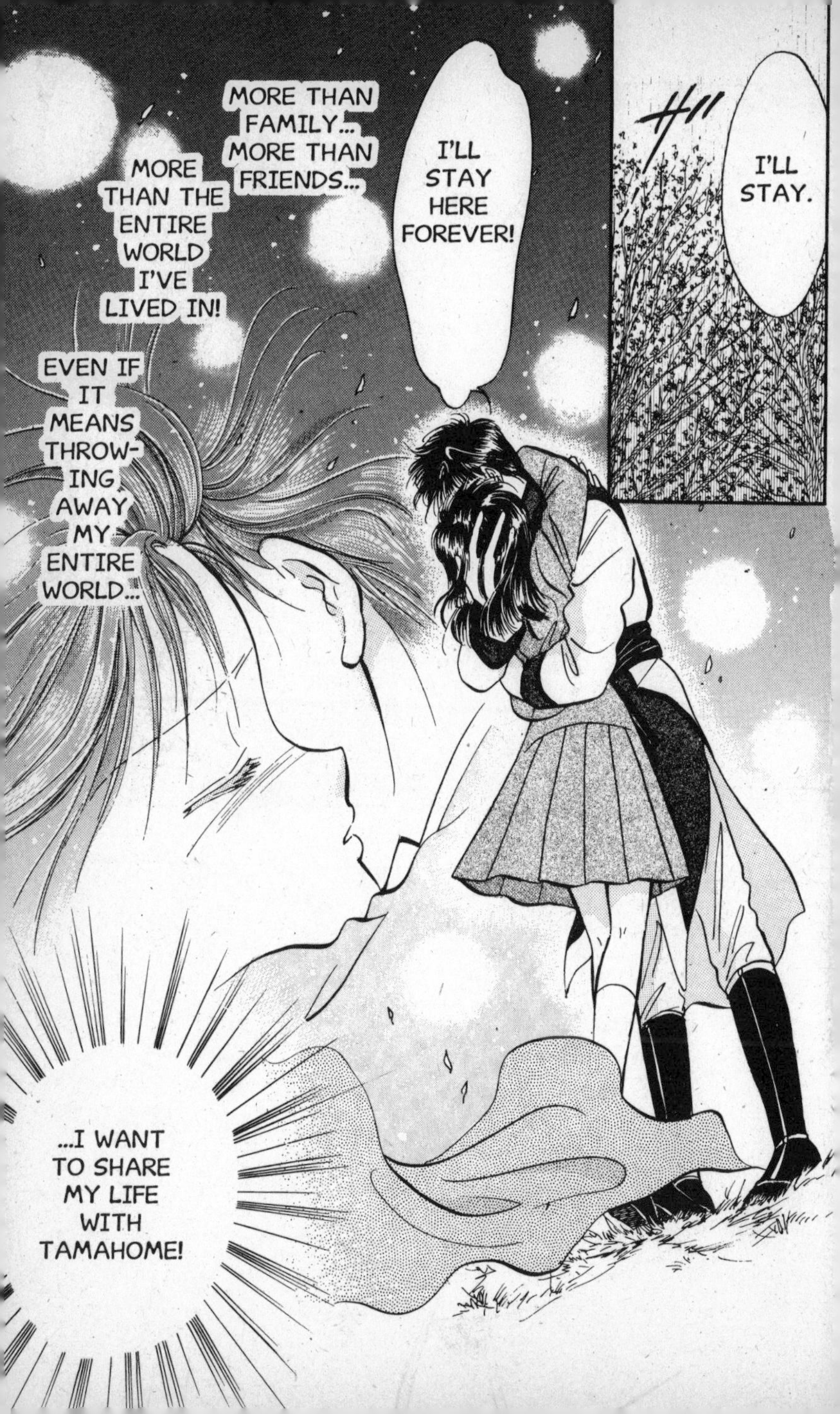
I'LL STAY.
I'LL STAY HERE FOREVER!
MORE THAN FAMILY... MORE THAN FRIENDS...
MORE THAN THE ENTIRE WORLD I'VE LIVED IN!
EVEN IF IT MEANS THROWING AWAY MY ENTIRE WORLD...
...I WANT TO SHARE MY LIFE WITH TAMAHOME!

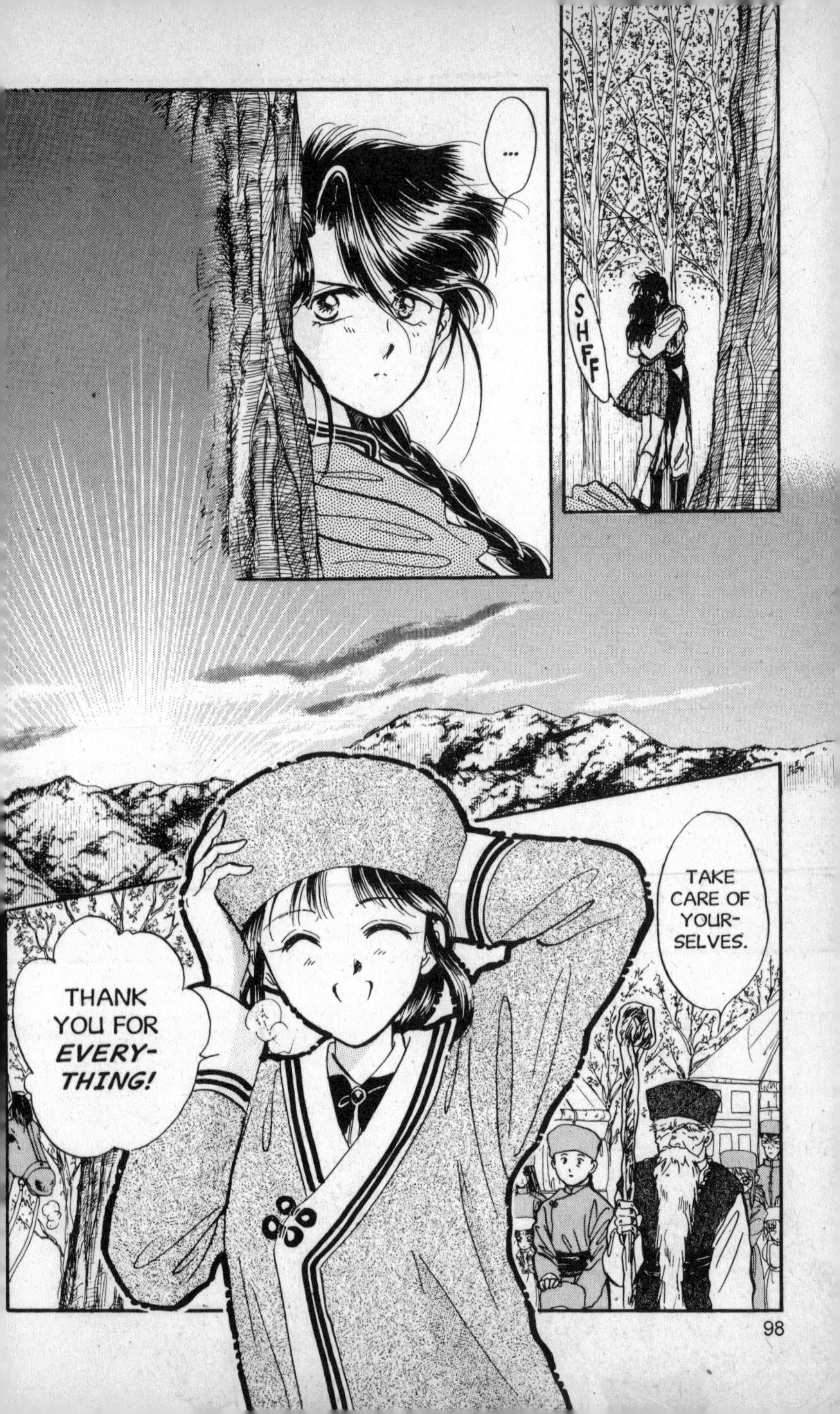
...
SHFF
TAKE CARE OF YOURSELVES.
THANK YOU FOR EVERYTHING!

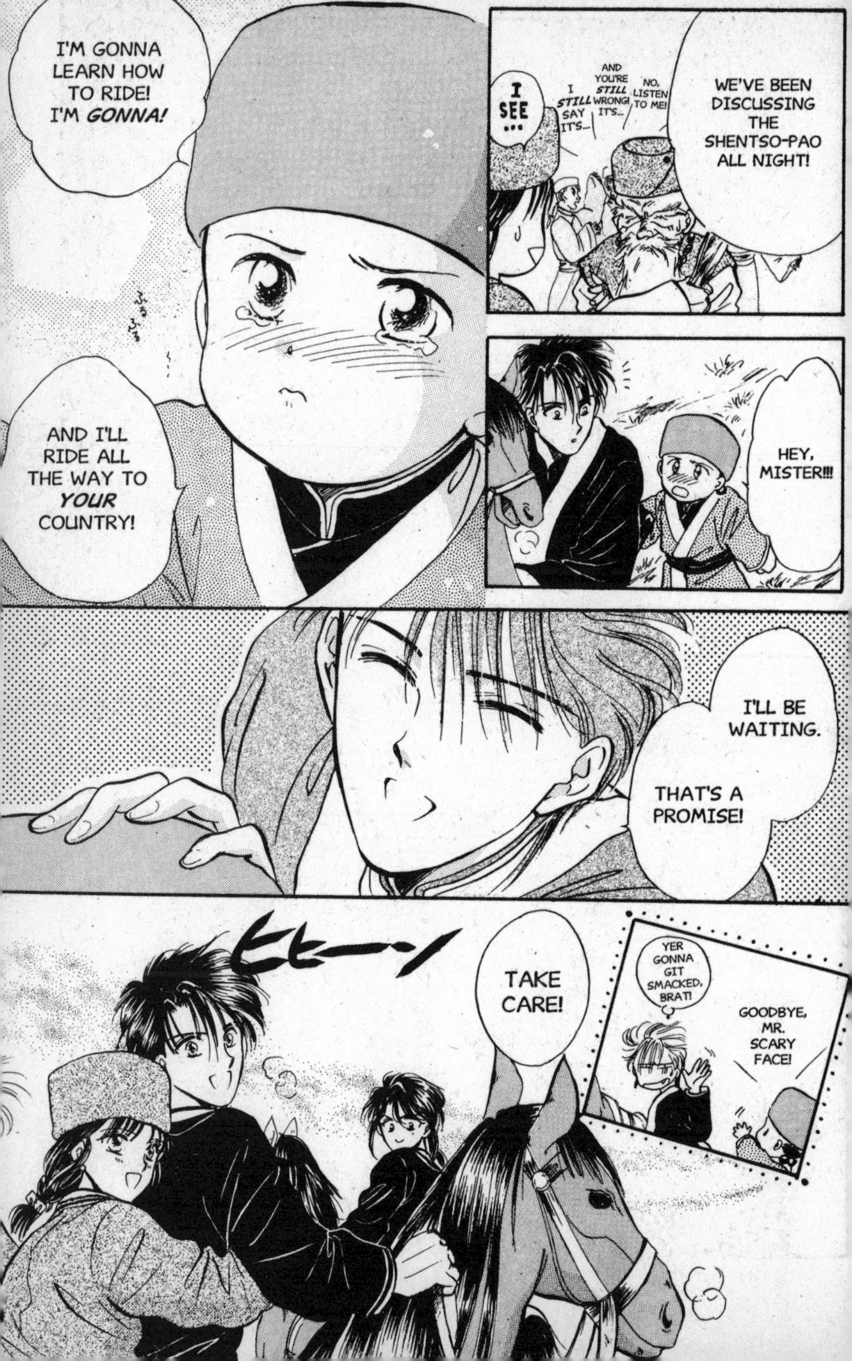

WE'VE BEEN DISCUSSING THE SHENTSO-PAO ALL NIGHT!
NO, LISTEN TO ME!
AND YOU'RE STILL WRONG! IT'S...
I STILL SAY IT'S...
I SEE...
HEY, MISTER!!!
I'M GONNA LEARN HOW TO RIDE! I'M GONNA!
AND I'LL RIDE ALL THE WAY TO YOUR COUNTRY!
I'LL BE WAITING.
THAT'S A PROMISE!
YER GONNA GIT SMACKED, BRAT!
GOODBYE, MR. SCARY FACE!
TAKE CARE!

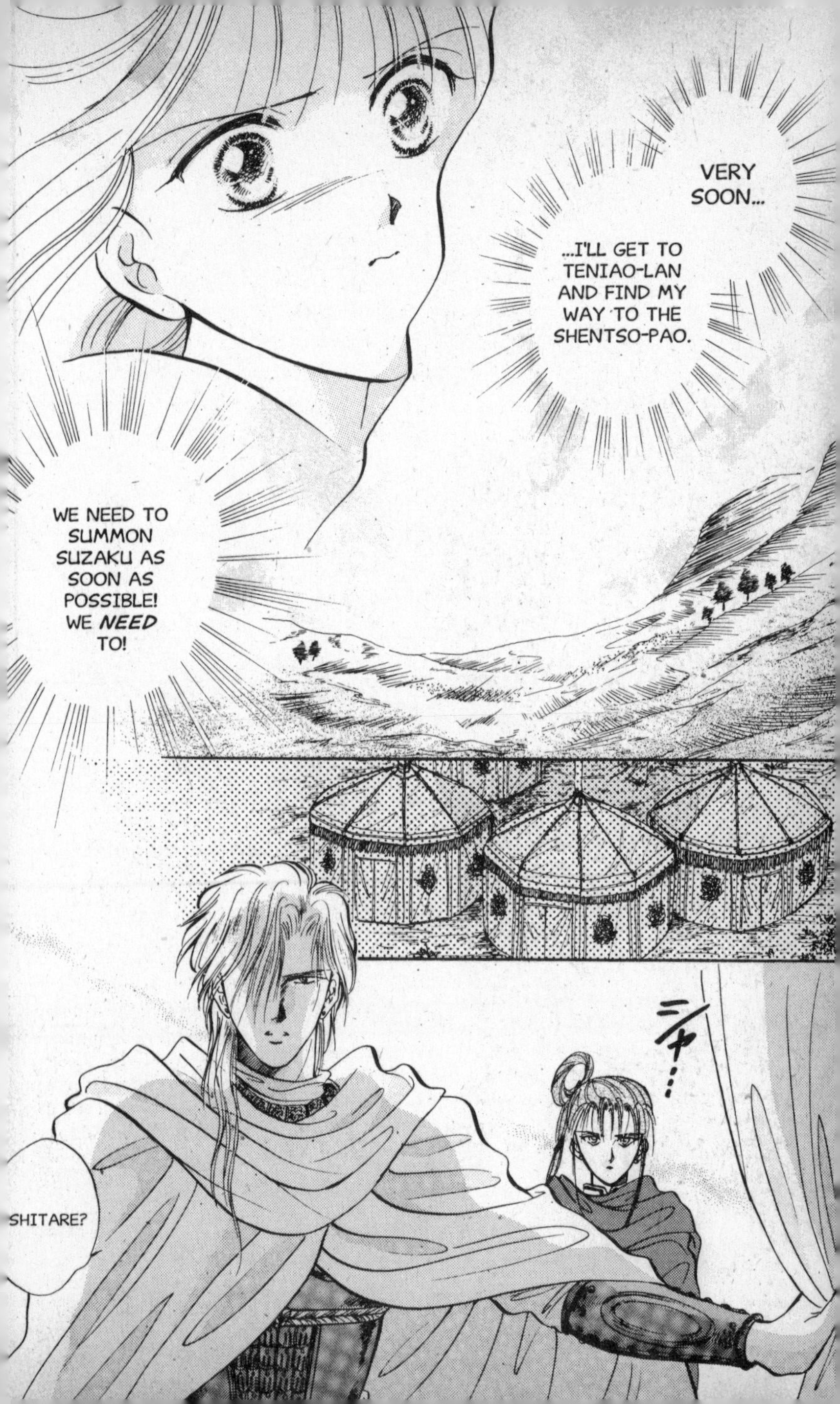
VERY SOON...
...I'LL GET TO TENIAO-LAN AND FIND MY WAY TO THE SHENTSO-PAO.
WE NEED TO SUMMON SUZAKU AS SOON AS POSSIBLE! WE *NEED* TO!
シャ...
SHITARE?

WONG 王 TAO 道 HUI 煇

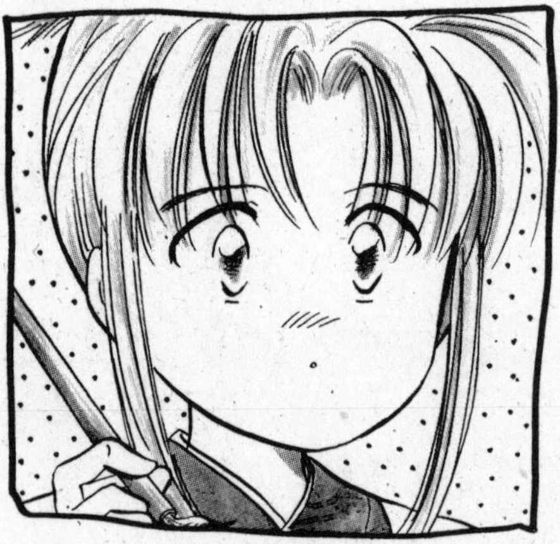

HYDRA

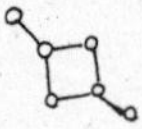

CHIRIKO

- Birthplace: Zhuang-Yuan in western Hong Nan
- Family: An elderly mother and older brother
- Height: 4' 10"
- Bloodtype: A
- Age: 13
- Power: Heightened intelligence
- Hobbies: Reading and research
- Because he's a little small for his age, he looks almost like a toddler. His incredibly high IQ gave him an interest in research from a very early age, and his experience of the world has mainly been through books and study.
  On the other hand, his intelligence is tied to the appearance of the Chinese character on his foot, and when it disappears, he is even less mentally adept than a normal child his age. He also becomes something of a crybaby. He's very sensitive about his height and his peculiar intelligence, and this has made him strive to grow up to be a "man of strength."
  He's a nice, quiet, good-student type.

Oh, in volume 7 on page 66, I said that one of the terms with digital effects was "kiseki no hito" ("miraculous one"), but when I listened closer, it turned out to be "yume" ("dream").

CHAPTER FORTY-SIX

MAELSTROM OF FEAR

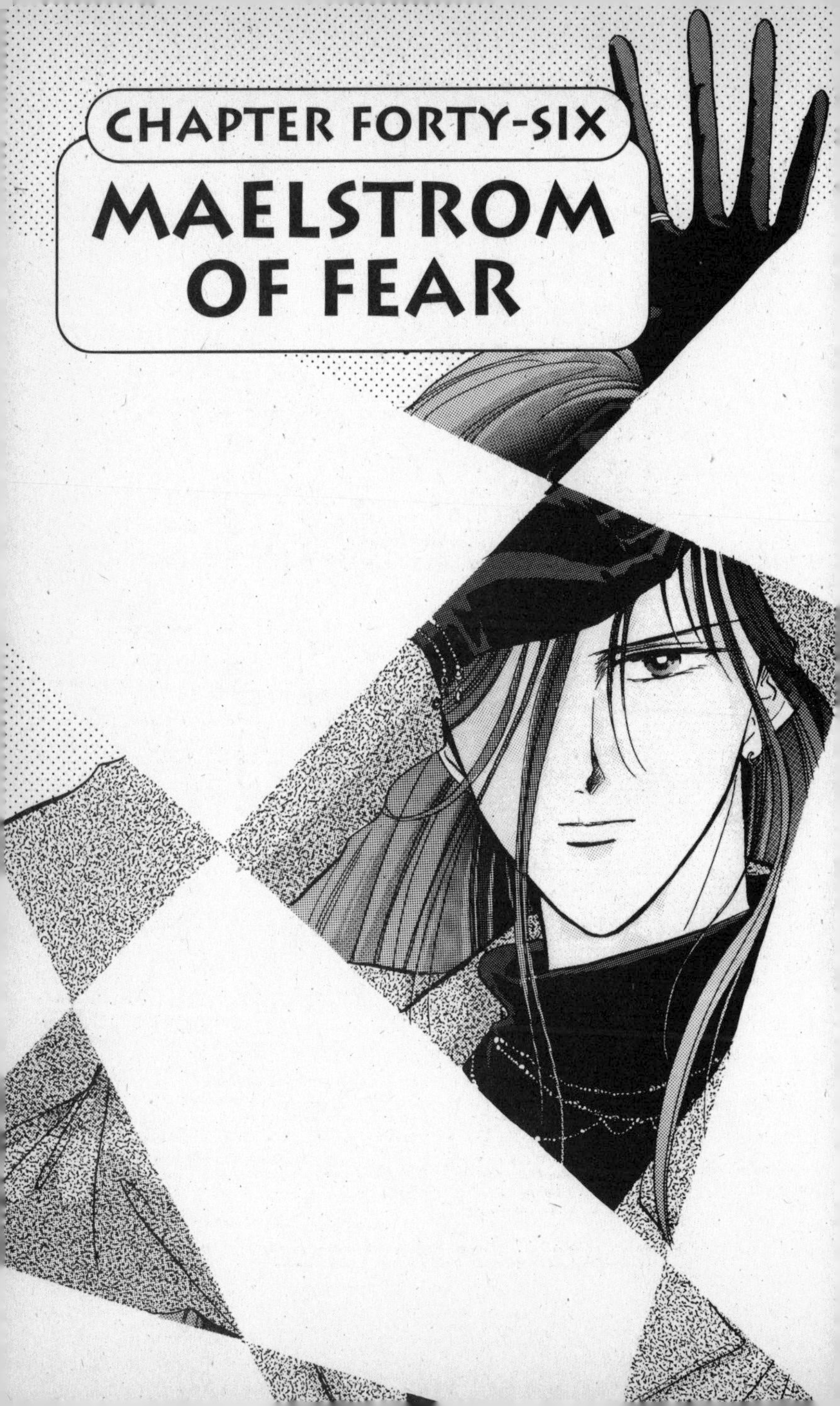

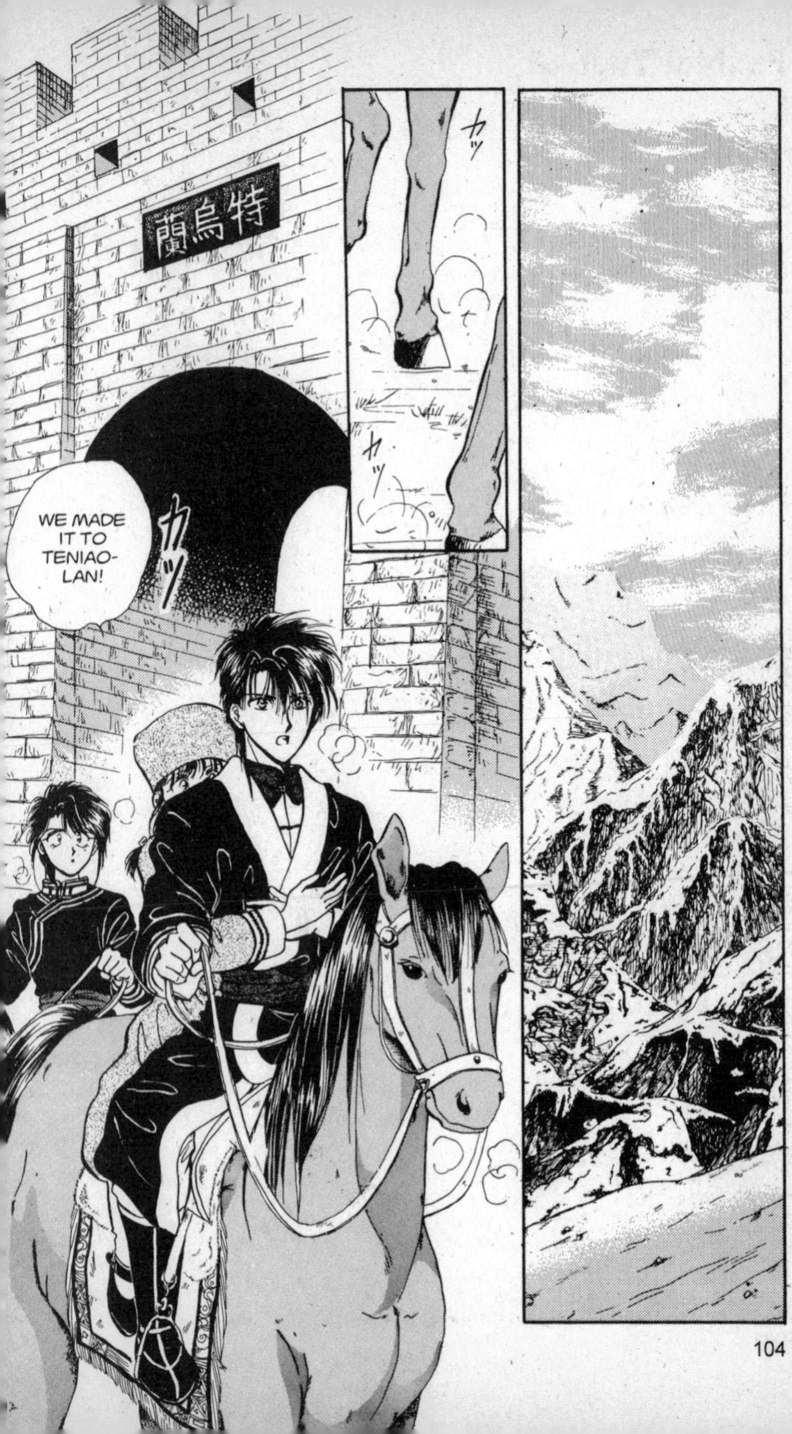

カッ
カッ
特烏蘭
カッ
WE MADE IT TO TENIAO-LAN!

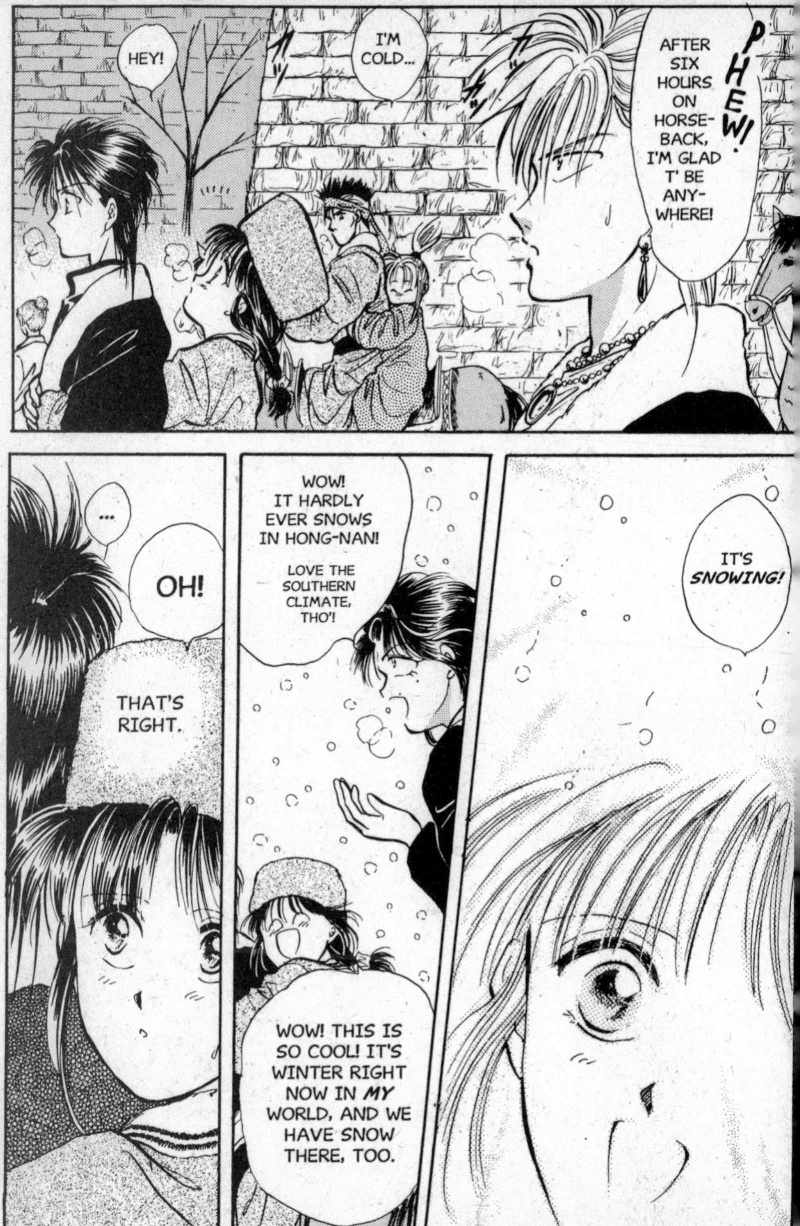
PHEW!
AFTER SIX HOURS ON HORSE-BACK, I'M GLAD T' BE ANY-WHERE!
I'M COLD...
HEY!
IT'S *SNOWING!*
WOW! IT HARDLY EVER SNOWS IN HONG-NAN!
LOVE THE SOUTHERN CLIMATE, THO'!
WOW! THIS IS SO COOL! IT'S WINTER RIGHT NOW IN *MY* WORLD, AND WE HAVE SNOW THERE, TOO.
...
OH!
THAT'S RIGHT.

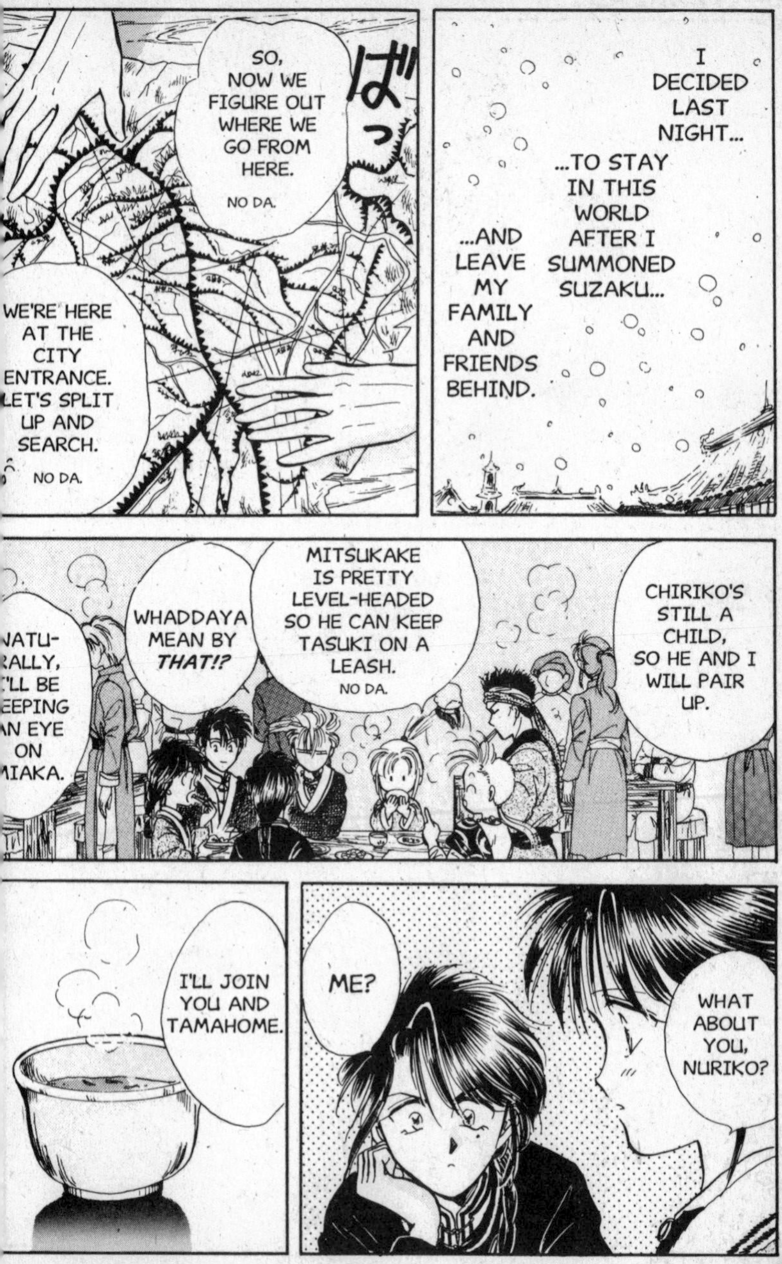
I DECIDED LAST NIGHT...
...TO STAY IN THIS WORLD AFTER I SUMMONED SUZAKU...
...AND LEAVE MY FAMILY AND FRIENDS BEHIND.
ばっ
SO, NOW WE FIGURE OUT WHERE WE GO FROM HERE. NO DA.
WE'RE HERE AT THE CITY ENTRANCE. LET'S SPLIT UP AND SEARCH. NO DA.
CHIRIKO'S STILL A CHILD, SO HE AND I WILL PAIR UP.
MITSUKAKE IS PRETTY LEVEL-HEADED SO HE CAN KEEP TASUKI ON A LEASH. NO DA.
WHADDAYA MEAN BY *THAT!?*
NATU-RALLY, I'LL BE KEEPING AN EYE ON MIAKA.
WHAT ABOUT YOU, NURIKO?
ME?
I'LL JOIN YOU AND TAMAHOME.

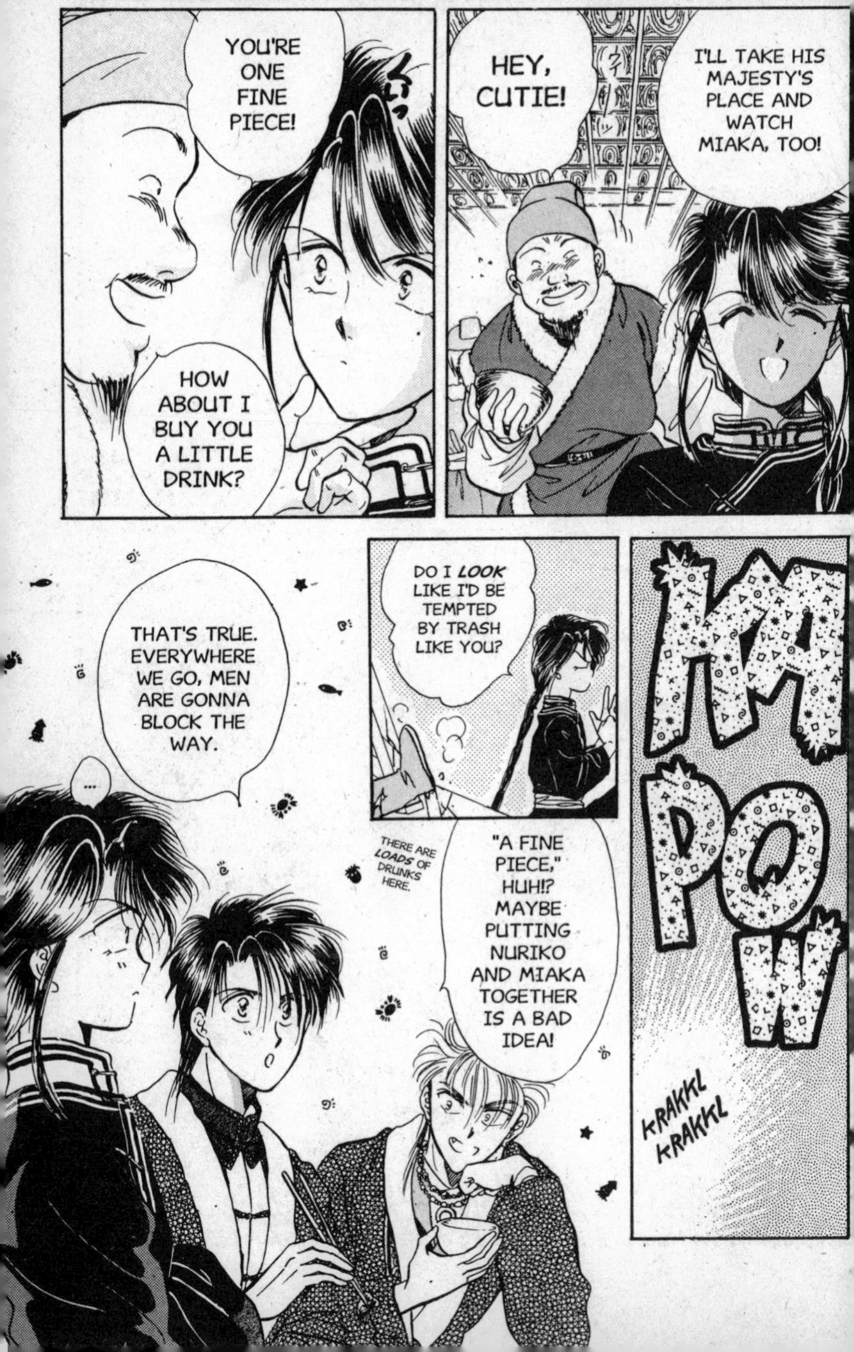
I'LL TAKE HIS MAJESTY'S PLACE AND WATCH MIAKA, TOO!
HEY, CUTIE!
YOU'RE ONE FINE PIECE!
HOW ABOUT I BUY YOU A LITTLE DRINK?
KAPOW
KRAKKL KRAKKL
DO I *LOOK* LIKE I'D BE TEMPTED BY TRASH LIKE YOU?
"A FINE PIECE," HUH!? MAYBE PUTTING NURIKO AND MIAKA TOGETHER IS A BAD IDEA!
THERE ARE *LOADS* OF DRUNKS HERE.
THAT'S TRUE. EVERYWHERE WE GO, MEN ARE GONNA BLOCK THE WAY.
...

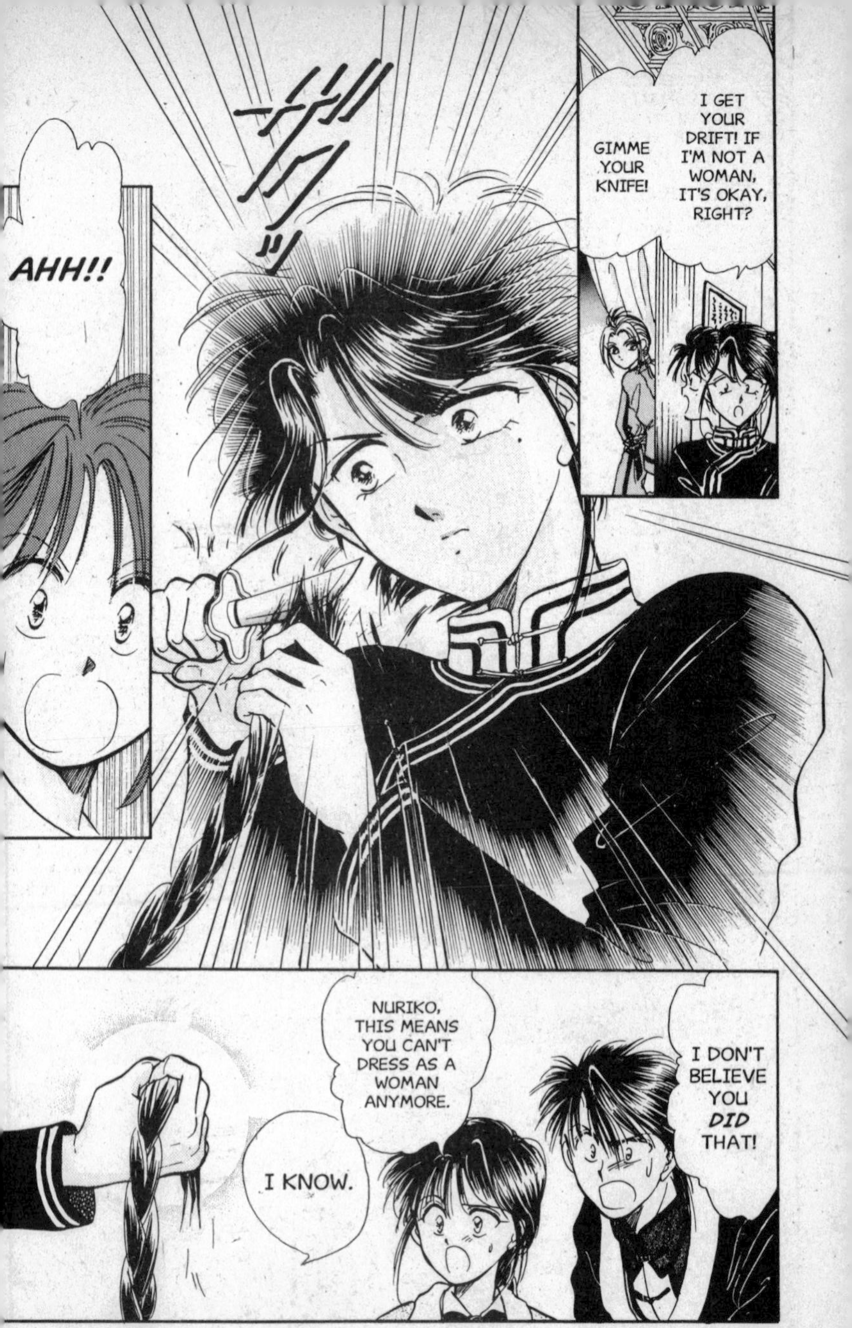
I GET YOUR DRIFT! IF I'M NOT A WOMAN, IT'S OKAY, RIGHT?
GIMME YOUR KNIFE!
AHH!!
I DON'T BELIEVE YOU *DID* THAT!
NURIKO, THIS MEANS YOU CAN'T DRESS AS A WOMAN ANYMORE.
I KNOW.

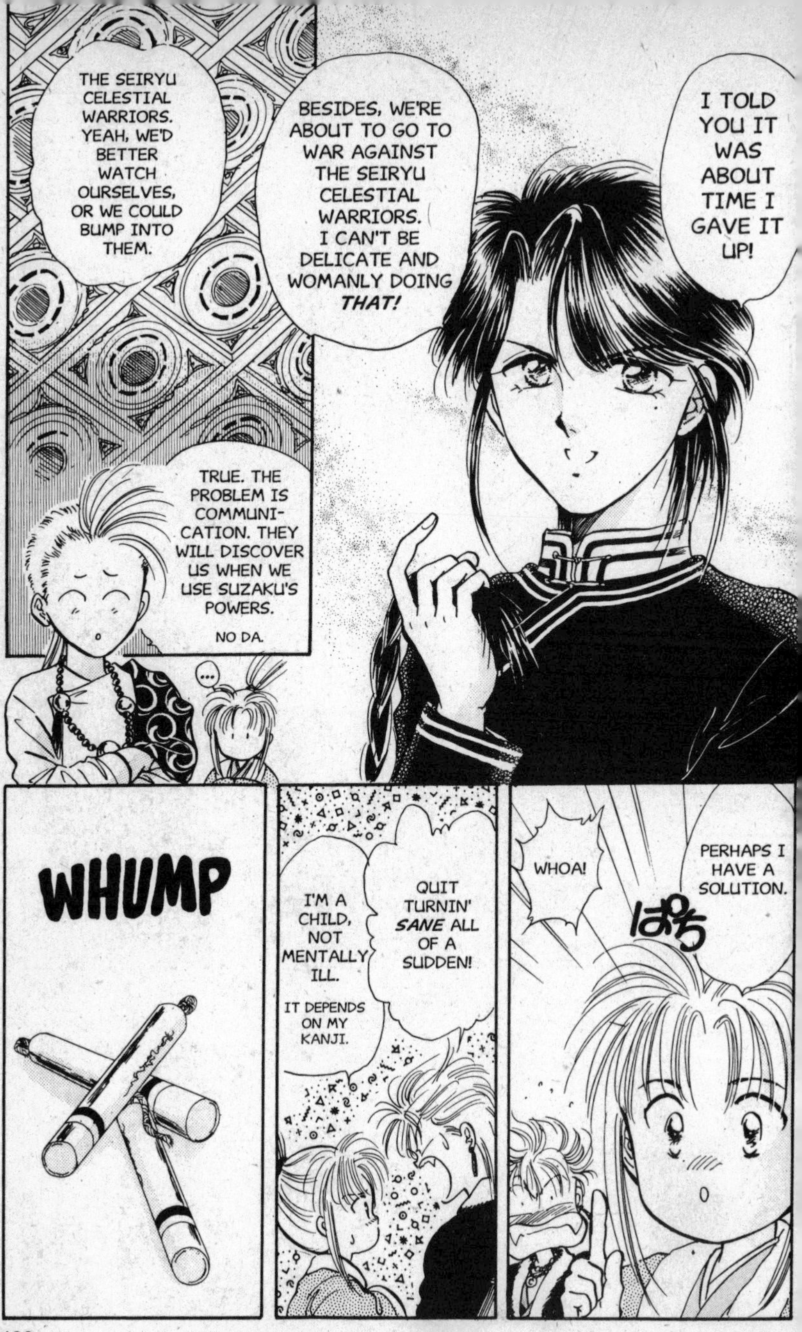

I TOLD YOU IT WAS ABOUT TIME I GAVE IT UP!
BESIDES, WE'RE ABOUT TO GO TO WAR AGAINST THE SEIRYU CELESTIAL WARRIORS. I CAN'T BE DELICATE AND WOMANLY DOING THAT!
THE SEIRYU CELESTIAL WARRIORS. YEAH, WE'D BETTER WATCH OURSELVES, OR WE COULD BUMP INTO THEM.
TRUE. THE PROBLEM IS COMMUNI-CATION. THEY WILL DISCOVER US WHEN WE USE SUZAKU'S POWERS.
NO DA.
...
PERHAPS I HAVE A SOLUTION.
WHOA!
ぱち
QUIT TURNIN' SANE ALL OF A SUDDEN!
I'M A CHILD, NOT MENTALLY ILL.
IT DEPENDS ON MY KANJI.
WHUMP

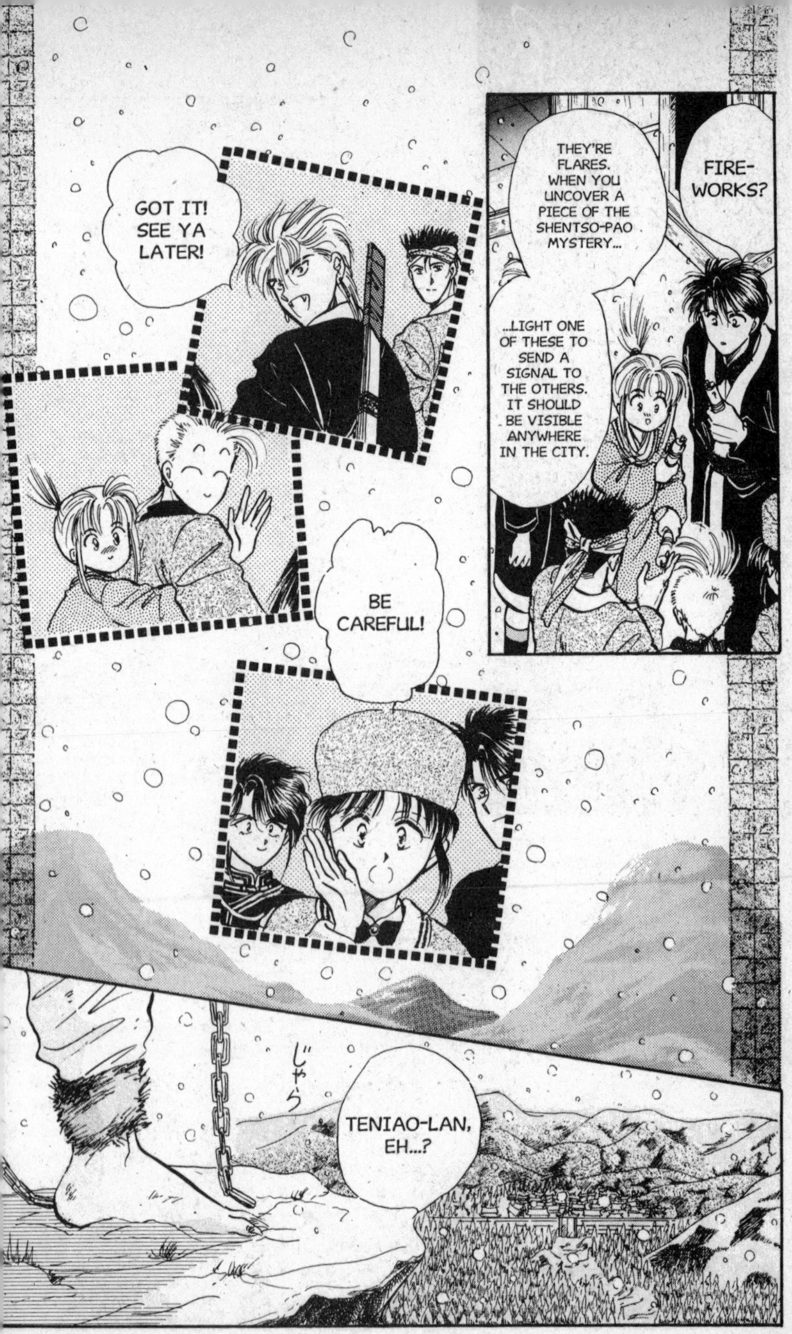
FIRE-WORKS?
THEY'RE FLARES. WHEN YOU UNCOVER A PIECE OF THE SHENTSO-PAO MYSTERY...
...LIGHT ONE OF THESE TO SEND A SIGNAL TO THE OTHERS. IT SHOULD BE VISIBLE ANYWHERE IN THE CITY.
GOT IT! SEE YA LATER!
BE CAREFUL!
じゃら
TENIAO-LAN, EH...?

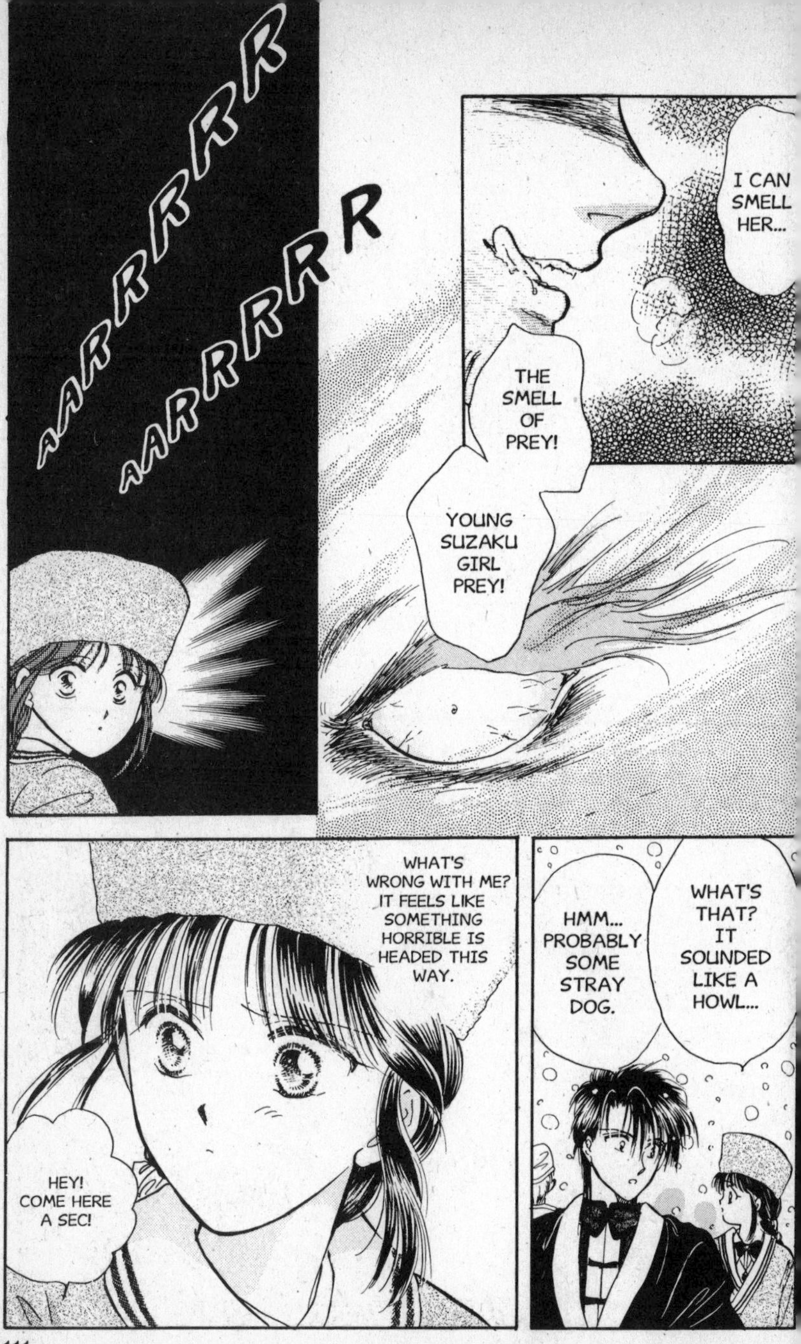

I CAN SMELL HER...
THE SMELL OF PREY!
YOUNG SUZAKU GIRL PREY!
AARRRRRR
AARRRRRR
WHAT'S THAT? IT SOUNDED LIKE A HOWL...
HMM... PROBABLY SOME STRAY DOG.
WHAT'S WRONG WITH ME? IT FEELS LIKE SOMETHING HORRIBLE IS HEADED THIS WAY.
HEY! COME HERE A SEC!

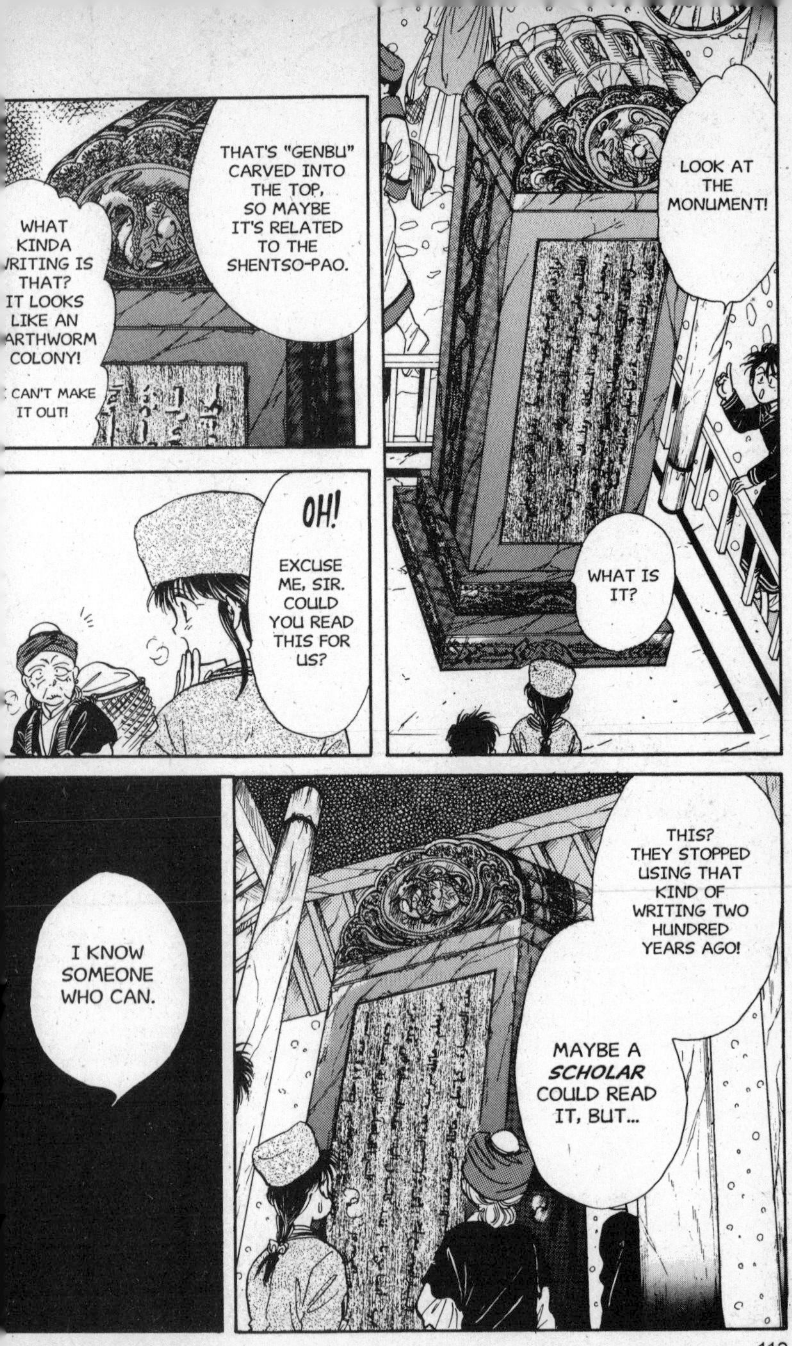
LOOK AT THE MONUMENT!
WHAT IS IT?
THAT'S "GENBU" CARVED INTO THE TOP, SO MAYBE IT'S RELATED TO THE SHENTSO-PAO.
WHAT KINDA RITING IS THAT? IT LOOKS LIKE AN ARTHWORM COLONY!
CAN'T MAKE IT OUT!
OH!
EXCUSE ME, SIR. COULD YOU READ THIS FOR US?
THIS? THEY STOPPED USING THAT KIND OF WRITING TWO HUNDRED YEARS AGO!
MAYBE A *SCHOLAR* COULD READ IT, BUT...
I KNOW SOMEONE WHO CAN.

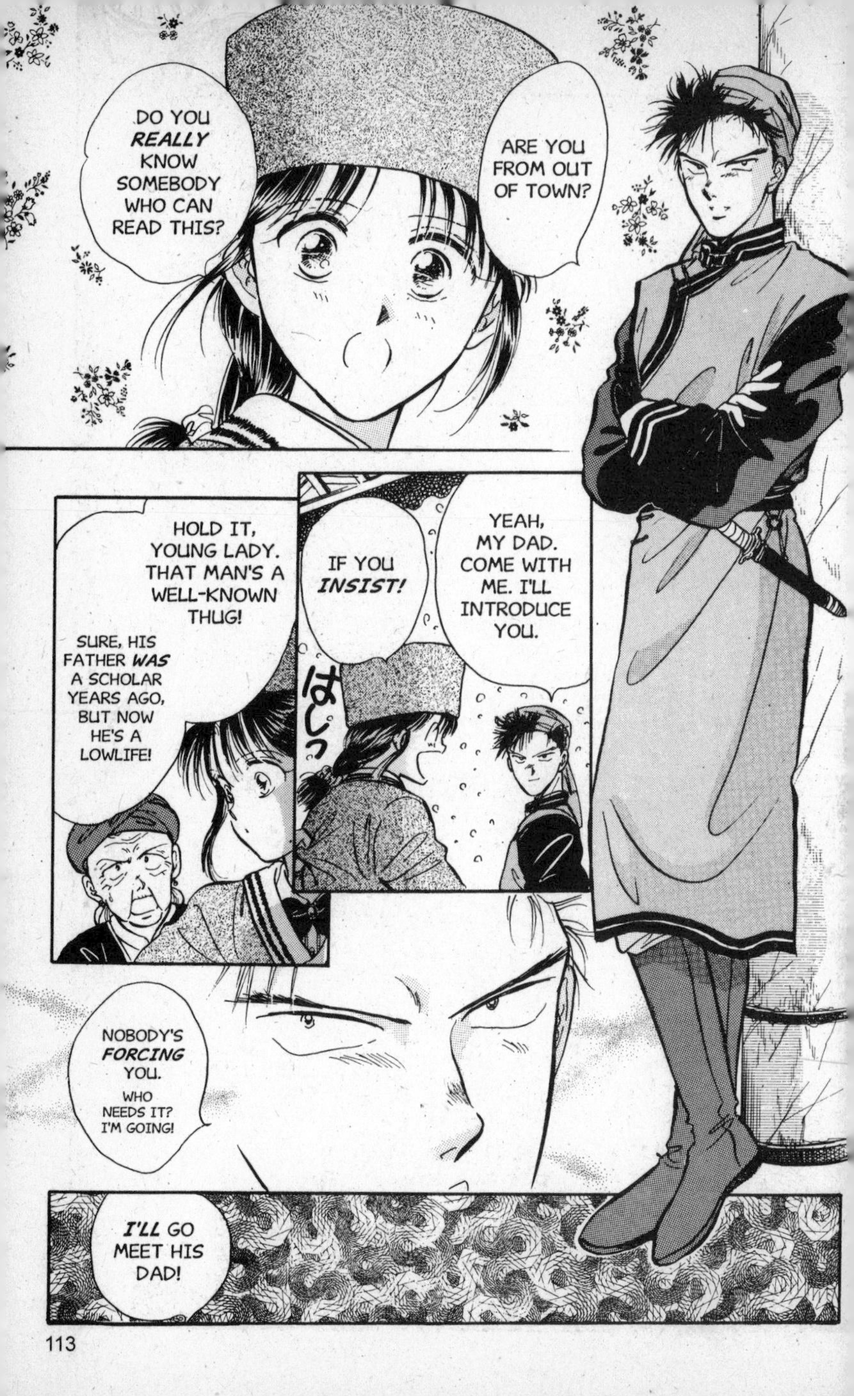
ARE YOU FROM OUT OF TOWN?
DO YOU ***REALLY*** KNOW SOMEBODY WHO CAN READ THIS?
YEAH, MY DAD. COME WITH ME. I'LL INTRODUCE YOU.
IF YOU ***INSIST!***
はしっ
HOLD IT, YOUNG LADY. THAT MAN'S A WELL-KNOWN THUG!
SURE, HIS FATHER ***WAS*** A SCHOLAR YEARS AGO, BUT NOW HE'S A LOWLIFE!
NOBODY'S ***FORCING*** YOU.
WHO NEEDS IT? I'M GOING!
I'LL GO MEET HIS DAD!

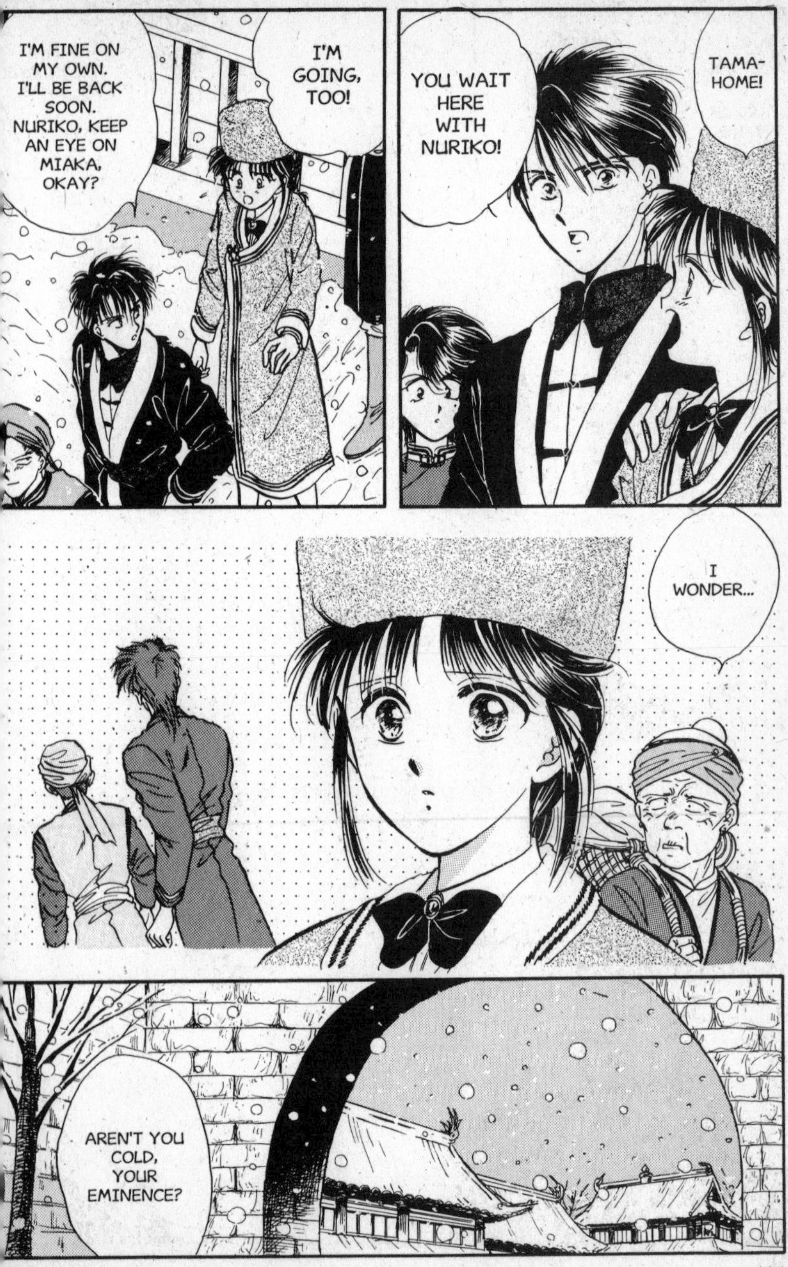
TAMA-HOME!
YOU WAIT HERE WITH NURIKO!
I'M GOING, TOO!
I'M FINE ON MY OWN. I'LL BE BACK SOON. NURIKO, KEEP AN EYE ON MIAKA, OKAY?
I WONDER...
AREN'T YOU COLD, YOUR EMINENCE?

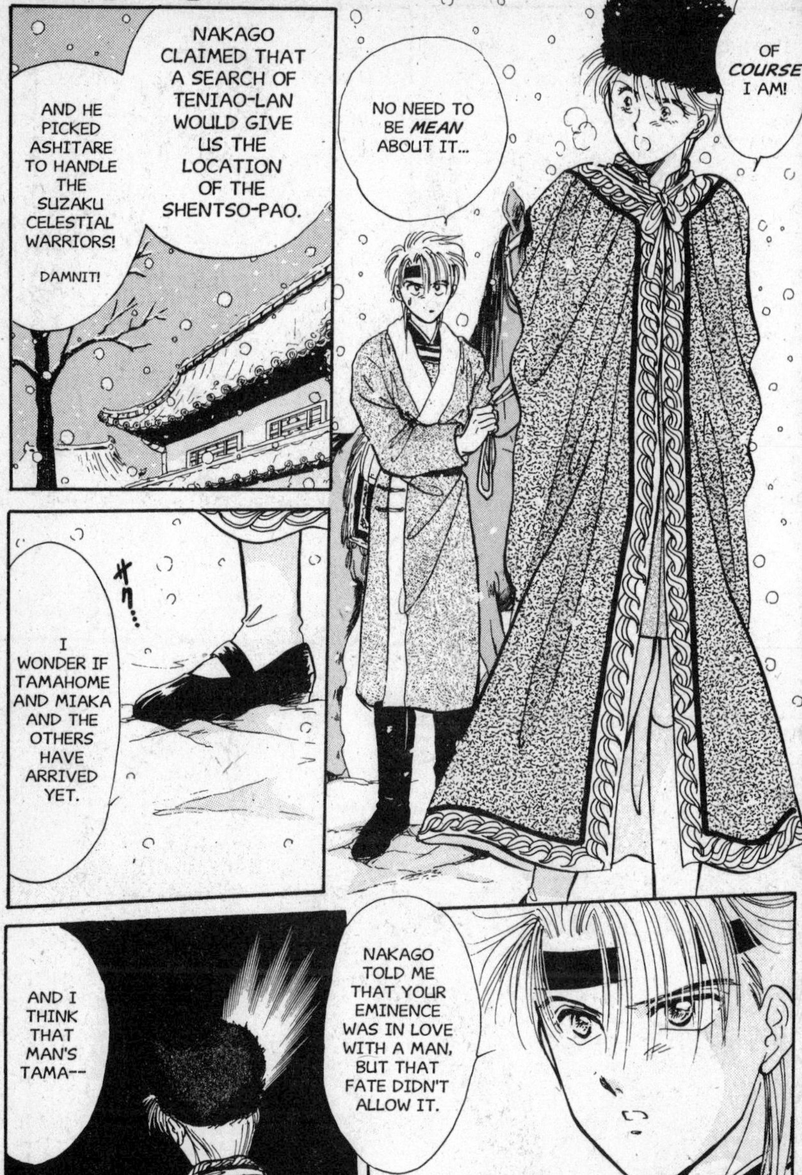
OF COURSE I AM!
NO NEED TO BE MEAN ABOUT IT...
NAKAGO CLAIMED THAT A SEARCH OF TENIAO-LAN WOULD GIVE US THE LOCATION OF THE SHENTSO-PAO.
AND HE PICKED ASHITARE TO HANDLE THE SUZAKU CELESTIAL WARRIORS!
DAMNIT!
I WONDER IF TAMAHOME AND MIAKA AND THE OTHERS HAVE ARRIVED YET.
NAKAGO TOLD ME THAT YOUR EMINENCE WAS IN LOVE WITH A MAN, BUT THAT FATE DIDN'T ALLOW IT.
AND I THINK THAT MAN'S TAMA--

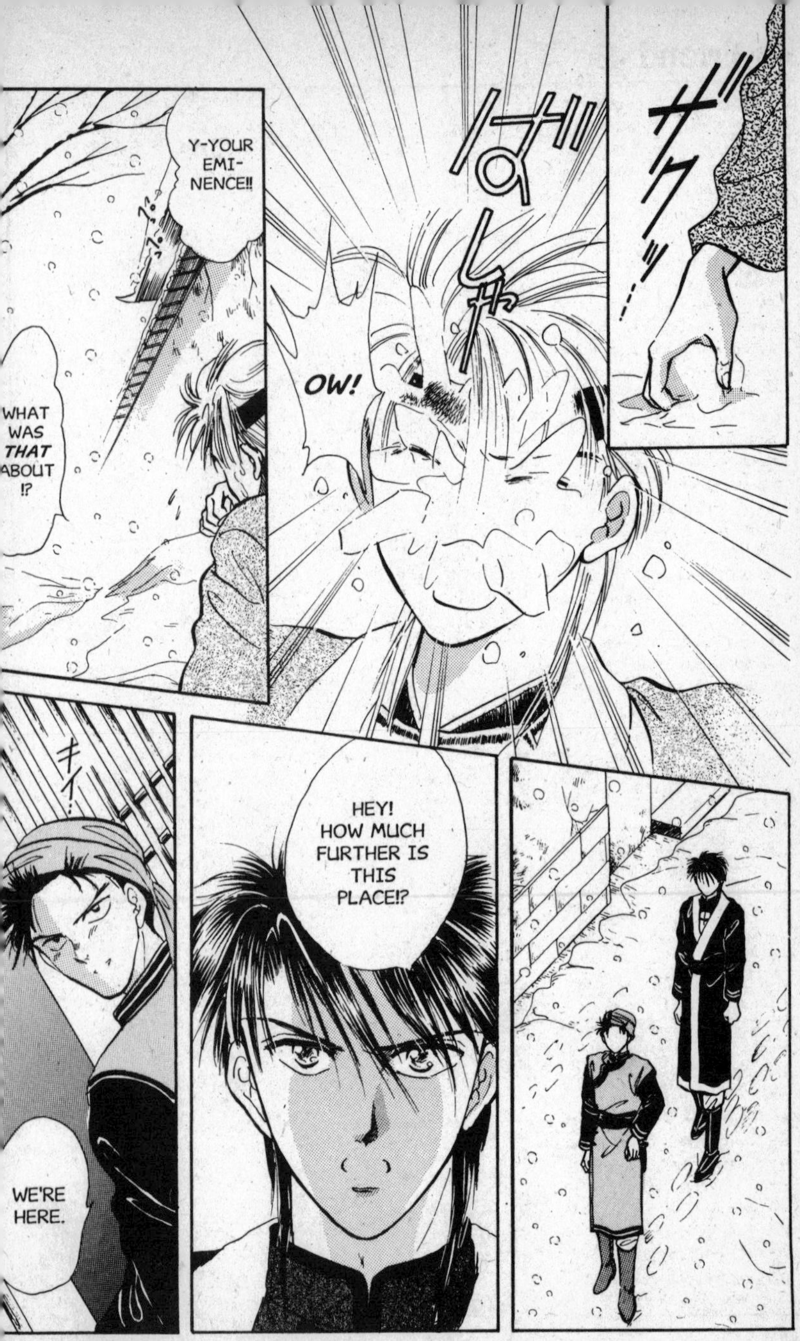
ザクッ
ばしゃ
OW!
Y-YOUR EMI-NENCE!!
WHAT WAS THAT ABOUT!?
HEY! HOW MUCH FURTHER IS THIS PLACE!?
ギイ…
WE'RE HERE.

Friend

Next, we went to Xian. By the way, Qu-Dong is based on Xian, a.k.a., the ancient capital of China, Chang'an. A super gigantic city. Kaifeng doesn't even come close! (It gave me an idea of the difference in scale between Hong-Nan and Qu-Dong.) Xian is a city of a million people with foreigners all over the place. The central "Suzaku Main Road" is supposed to have been 492 feet wide!! Narrow streets were 82 feet. You're kidding! Heijokyo (the capital of Nara-era Japan) was based on Chang'an, but it was about four times smaller. We're talking about a totally different scale here!

I wanted to see the old Imperial Palace, but it isn't there anymore. Instead, we went to the "West Gate," where Sanzo Genjo went off to Tenjiku (India). How romantic! The confrontation between Soi and Miaka was based on a photo of this area. It's not exactly the same, though.

Let's see... then there's Emperor Xuanzang and Lady Yang-gui-fei. We went to the Huaqing Hot Springs where they bathed. It was there that Lady Yang's beauty won over Xuanzang! And we have another "How romantic!" moment, which makes me think that Hotohori has rotten taste in women (I'm just kidding). It wasn't Miaka's beauty that attracted Hotohori. He fell for her innocence. Another amazing sight was the famous Terra-Cotta Warriors and Horses Pits. It's an excavation site with life-size figures of soldiers, just over a mile east of Emperor Shi-huang's mausoleum. The surprising thing is that because the statues are all based on real people, each one has a different face. They all have different bodies as well. The sight of row after row of these statues was really awesome.

They looked so real, too!

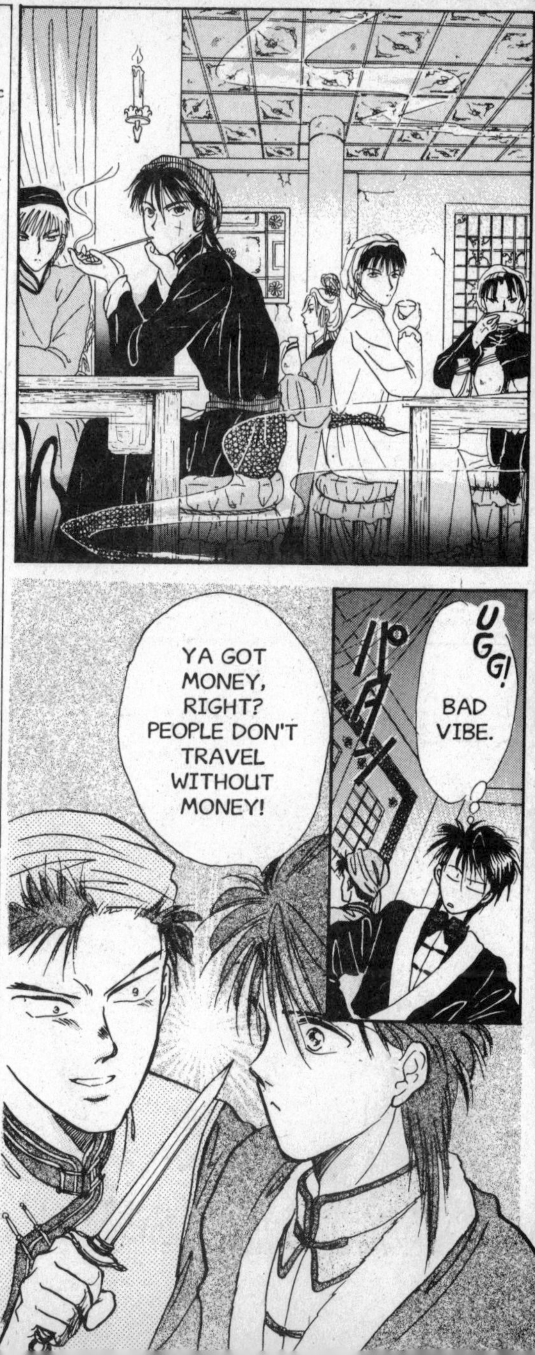
UGG!
BAD VIBE.
YA GOT MONEY, RIGHT? PEOPLE DON'T TRAVEL WITHOUT MONEY!

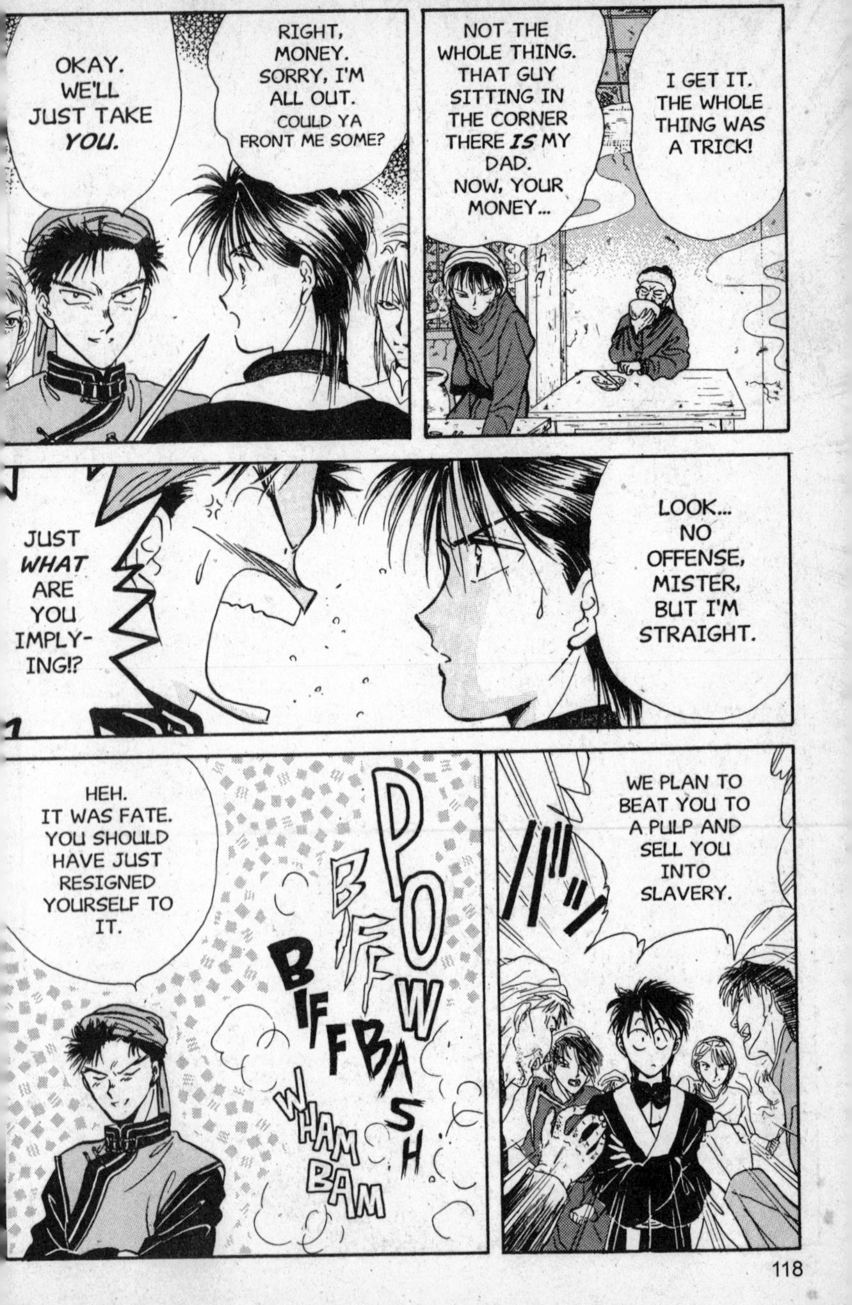
I GET IT. THE WHOLE THING WAS A TRICK!
NOT THE WHOLE THING. THAT GUY SITTING IN THE CORNER THERE *IS* MY DAD. NOW, YOUR MONEY...
RIGHT, MONEY. SORRY, I'M ALL OUT. COULD YA FRONT ME SOME?
OKAY. WE'LL JUST TAKE *YOU.*
LOOK... NO OFFENSE, MISTER, BUT I'M STRAIGHT.
JUST *WHAT* ARE YOU IMPLYING!?
WE PLAN TO BEAT YOU TO A PULP AND SELL YOU INTO SLAVERY.
HEH. IT WAS FATE. YOU SHOULD HAVE JUST RESIGNED YOURSELF TO IT.
POW
BIFF
BIFF
BASH
WHAM
BAM

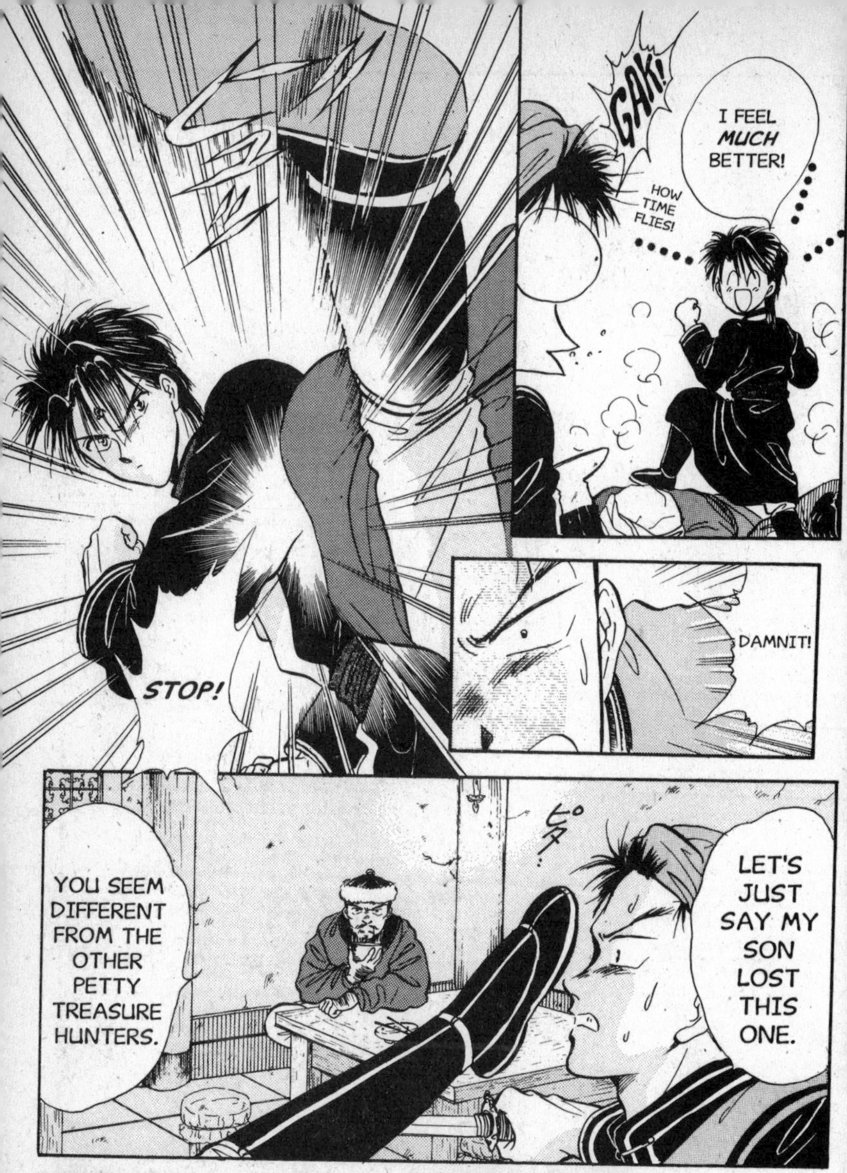
GAK!
I FEEL MUCH BETTER!
HOW TIME FLIES!
DAMNIT!
STOP!
LET'S JUST SAY MY SON LOST THIS ONE.
ピタ
YOU SEEM DIFFERENT FROM THE OTHER PETTY TREASURE HUNTERS.
YOUR POP'S TALKIN' HERE.
PAT
PAT

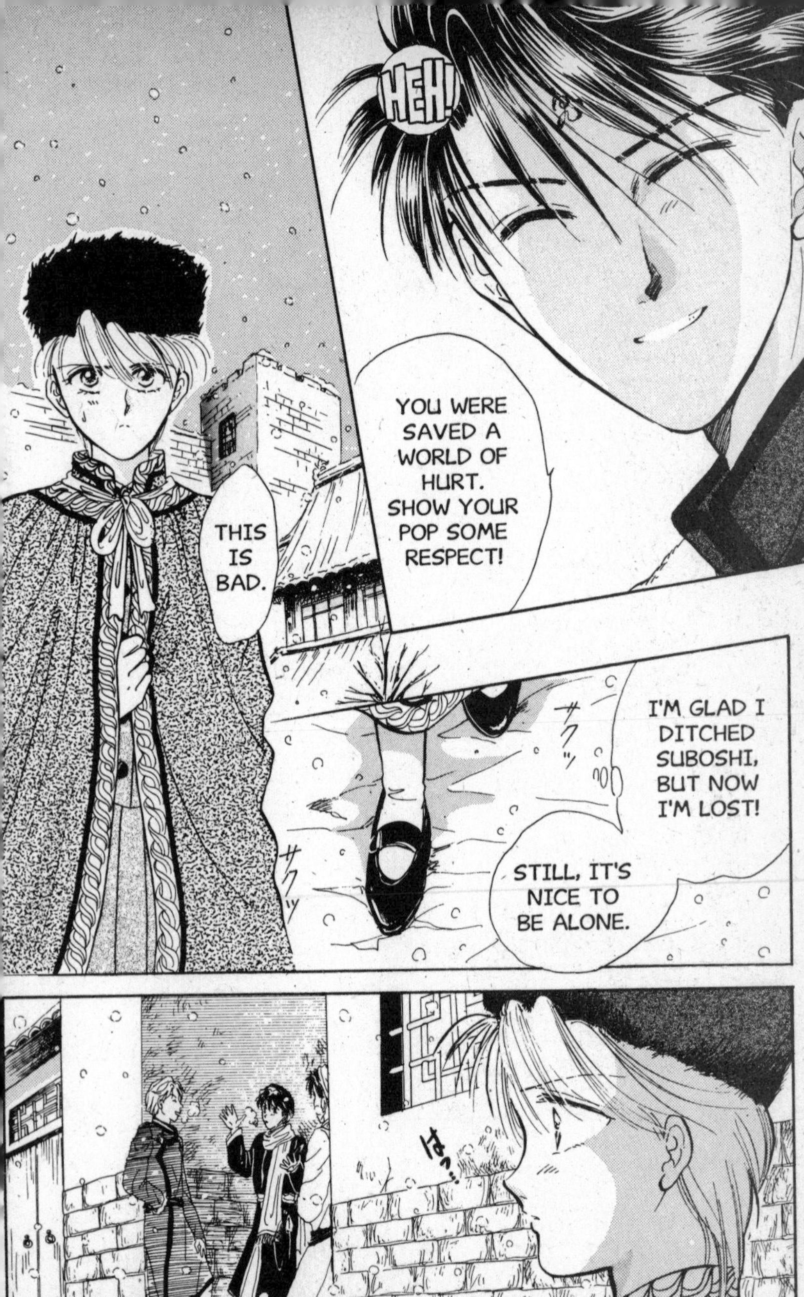
HEH!
YOU WERE SAVED A WORLD OF HURT. SHOW YOUR POP SOME RESPECT!
サクッ
サクッ
I'M GLAD I DITCHED SUBOSHI, BUT NOW I'M LOST!
STILL, IT'S NICE TO BE ALONE.
THIS IS BAD.
はっ…

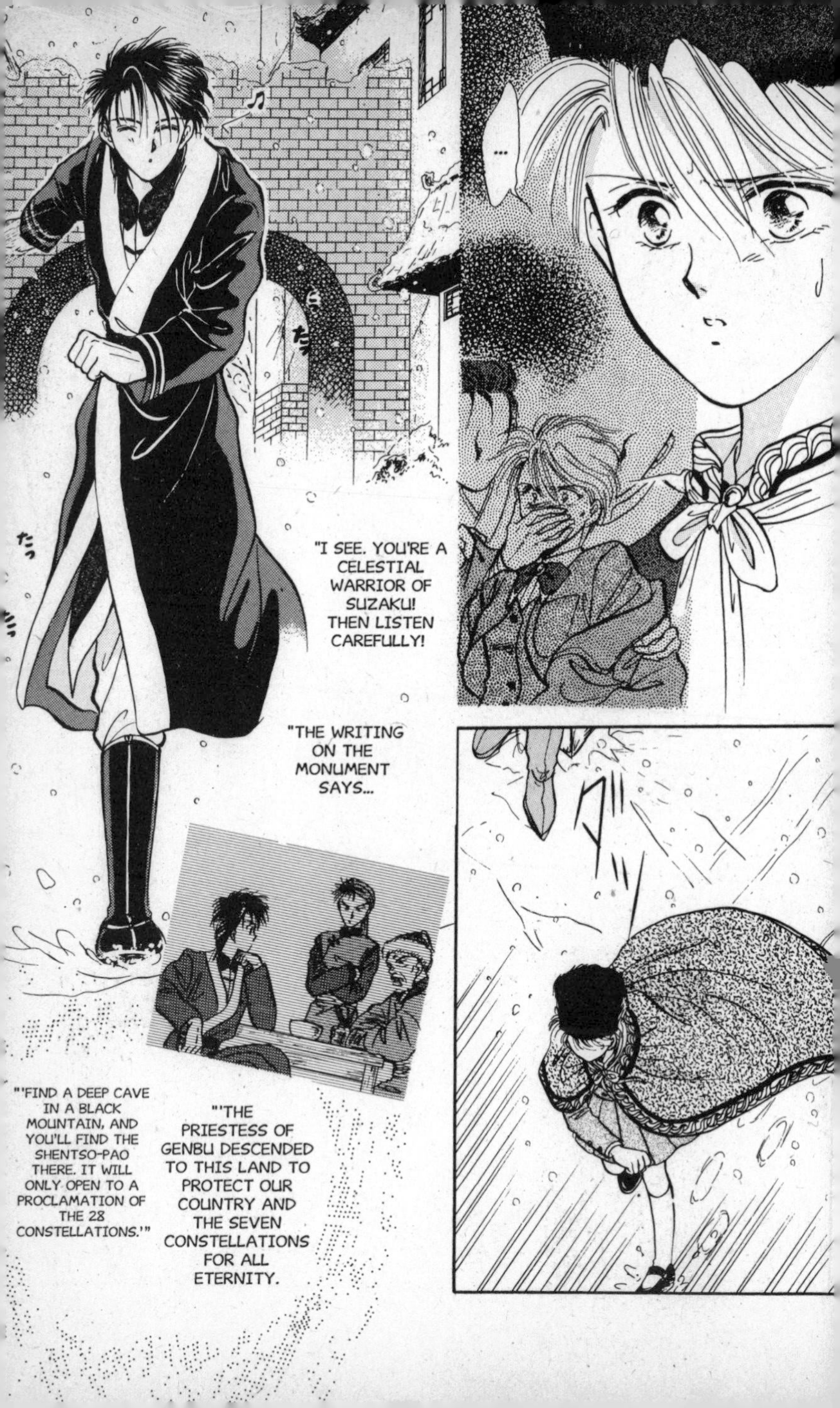
...
"I SEE. YOU'RE A CELESTIAL WARRIOR OF SUZAKU! THEN LISTEN CAREFULLY!
"THE WRITING ON THE MONUMENT SAYS...
"'THE PRIESTESS OF GENBU DESCENDED TO THIS LAND TO PROTECT OUR COUNTRY AND THE SEVEN CONSTELLATIONS FOR ALL ETERNITY.
"'FIND A DEEP CAVE IN A BLACK MOUNTAIN, AND YOU'LL FIND THE SHENTSO-PAO THERE. IT WILL ONLY OPEN TO A PROCLAMATION OF THE 28 CONSTELLATIONS.'"

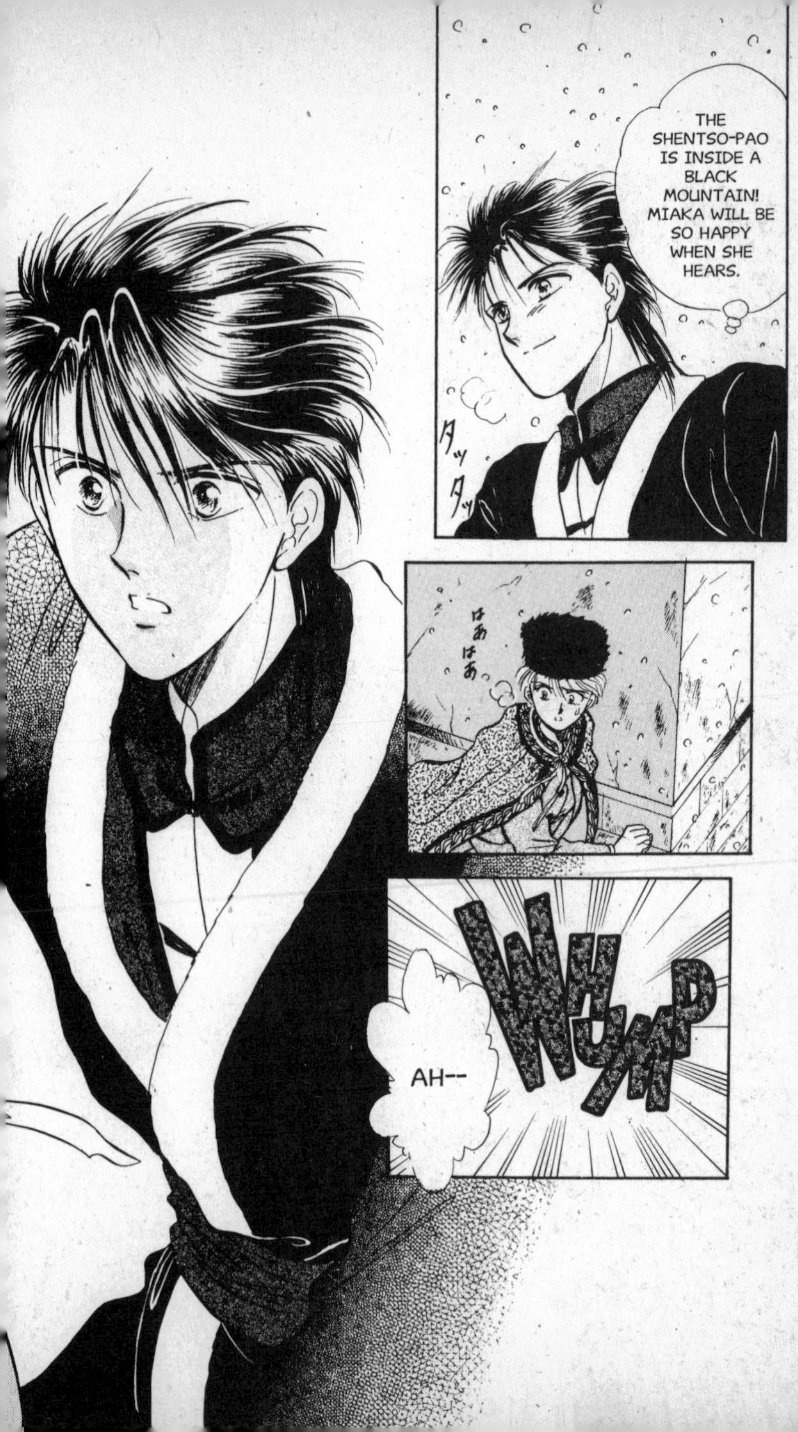
THE SHENTSO-PAO IS INSIDE A BLACK MOUNTAIN! MIAKA WILL BE SO HAPPY WHEN SHE HEARS.
タッタッ
はあはあ
WHUMP
AH--

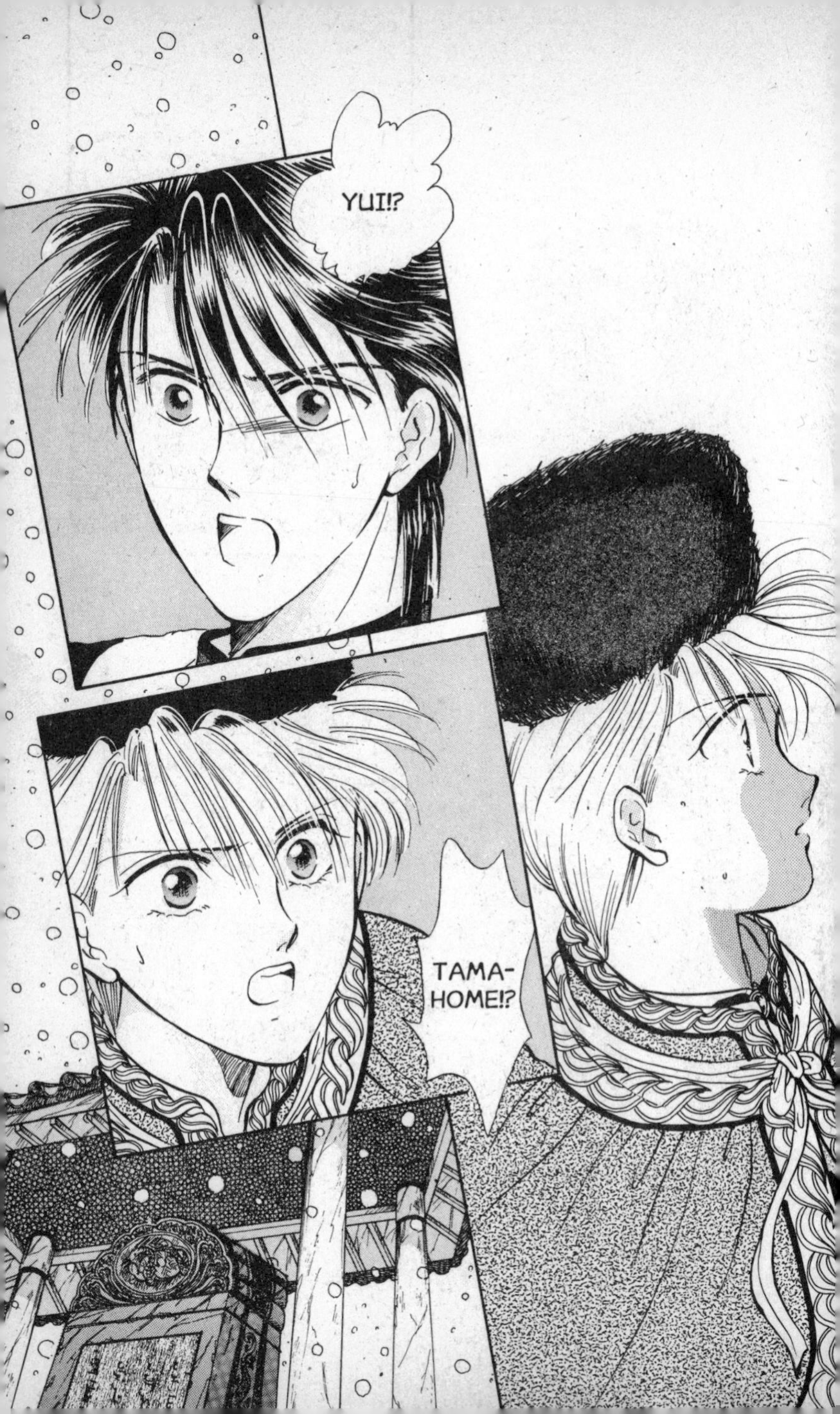
YUI!?
TAMA-
HOME!?

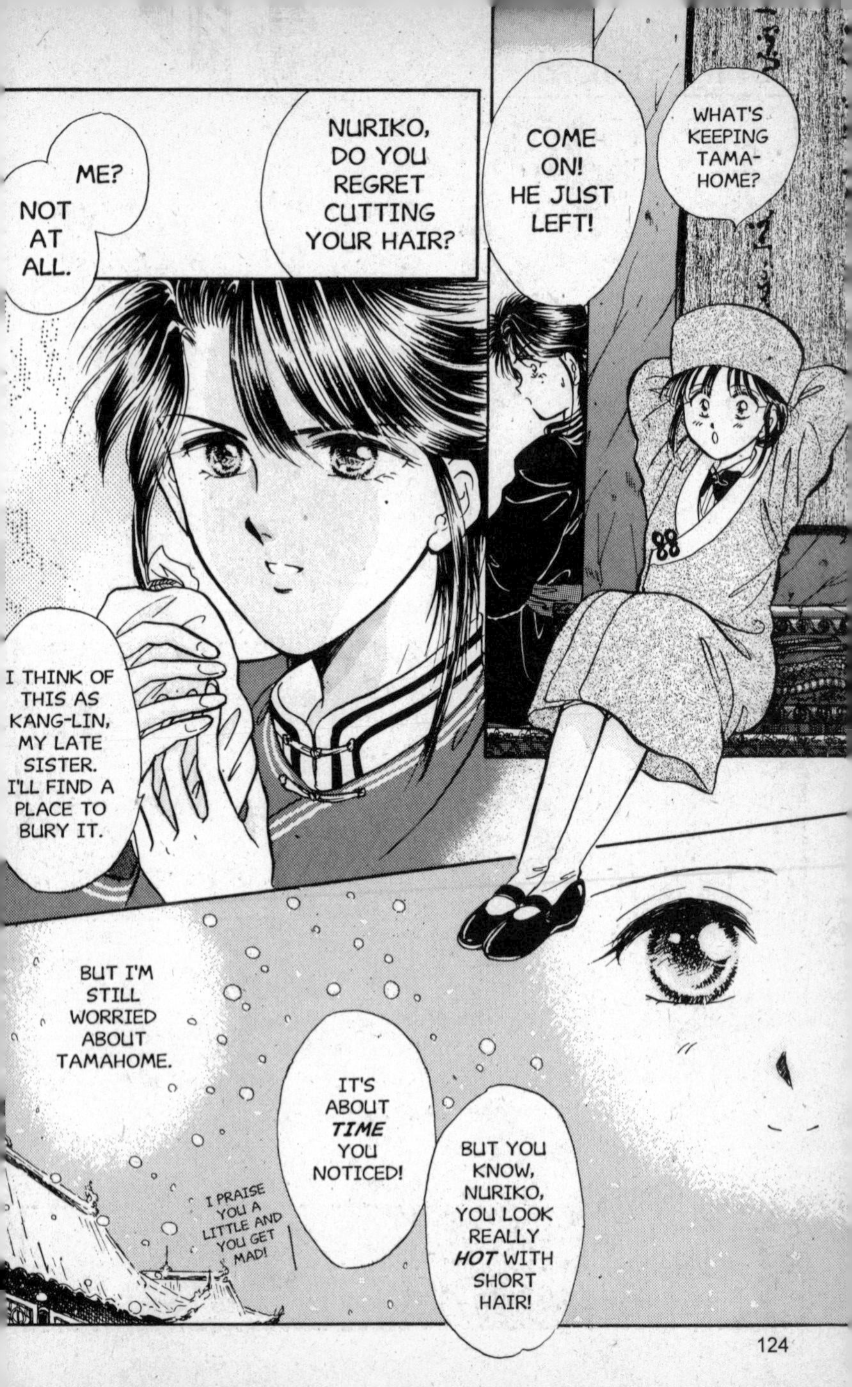
WHAT'S KEEPING TAMA-HOME?
COME ON! HE JUST LEFT!
NURIKO, DO YOU REGRET CUTTING YOUR HAIR?
ME? NOT AT ALL.
I THINK OF THIS AS KANG-LIN, MY LATE SISTER. I'LL FIND A PLACE TO BURY IT.
BUT YOU KNOW, NURIKO, YOU LOOK REALLY ***HOT*** WITH SHORT HAIR!
IT'S ABOUT ***TIME*** YOU NOTICED!
I PRAISE YOU A LITTLE AND YOU GET MAD!
BUT I'M STILL WORRIED ABOUT TAMAHOME.

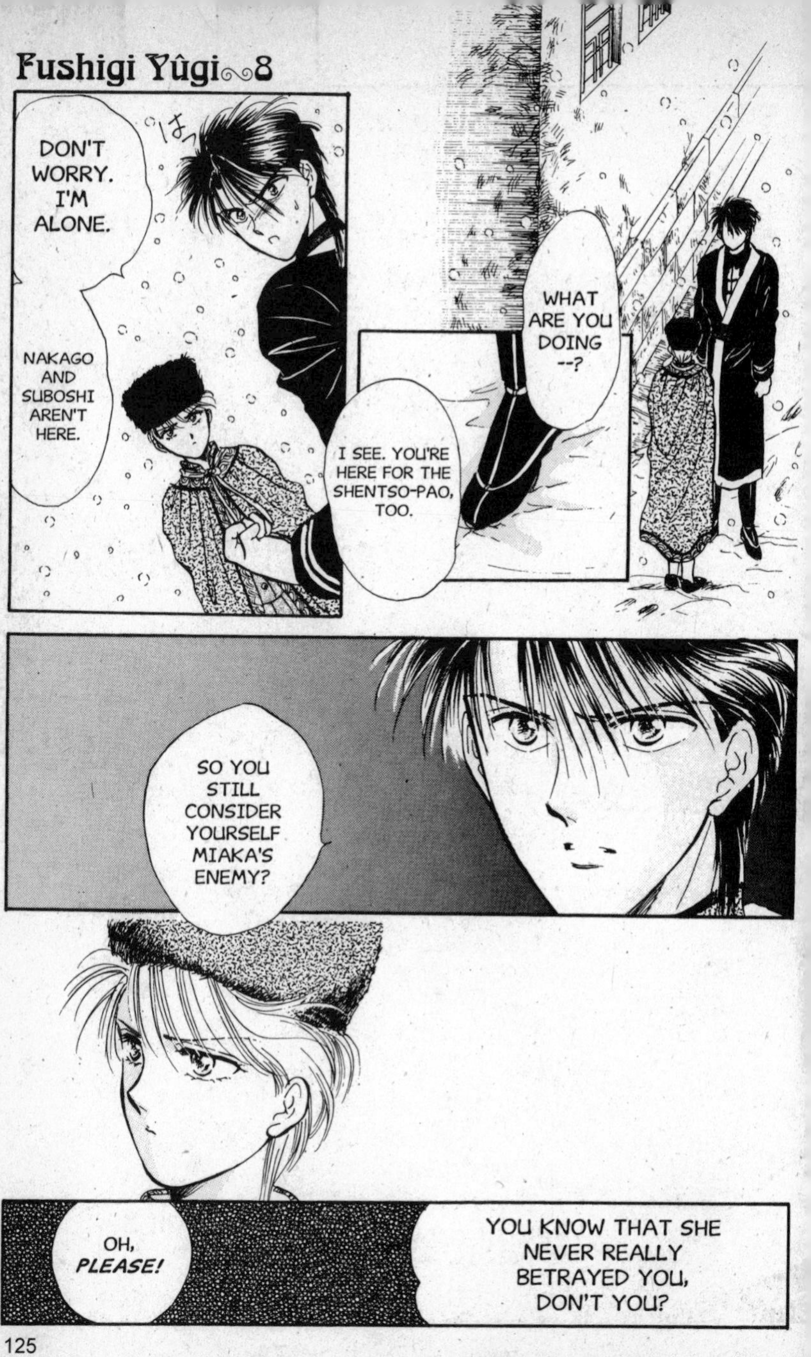
WHAT ARE YOU DOING --?
I SEE. YOU'RE HERE FOR THE SHENTSO-PAO, TOO.
はっ
DON'T WORRY. I'M ALONE.
NAKAGO AND SUBOSHI AREN'T HERE.
SO YOU STILL CONSIDER YOURSELF MIAKA'S ENEMY?
YOU KNOW THAT SHE NEVER REALLY BETRAYED YOU, DON'T YOU?
OH, *PLEASE!*

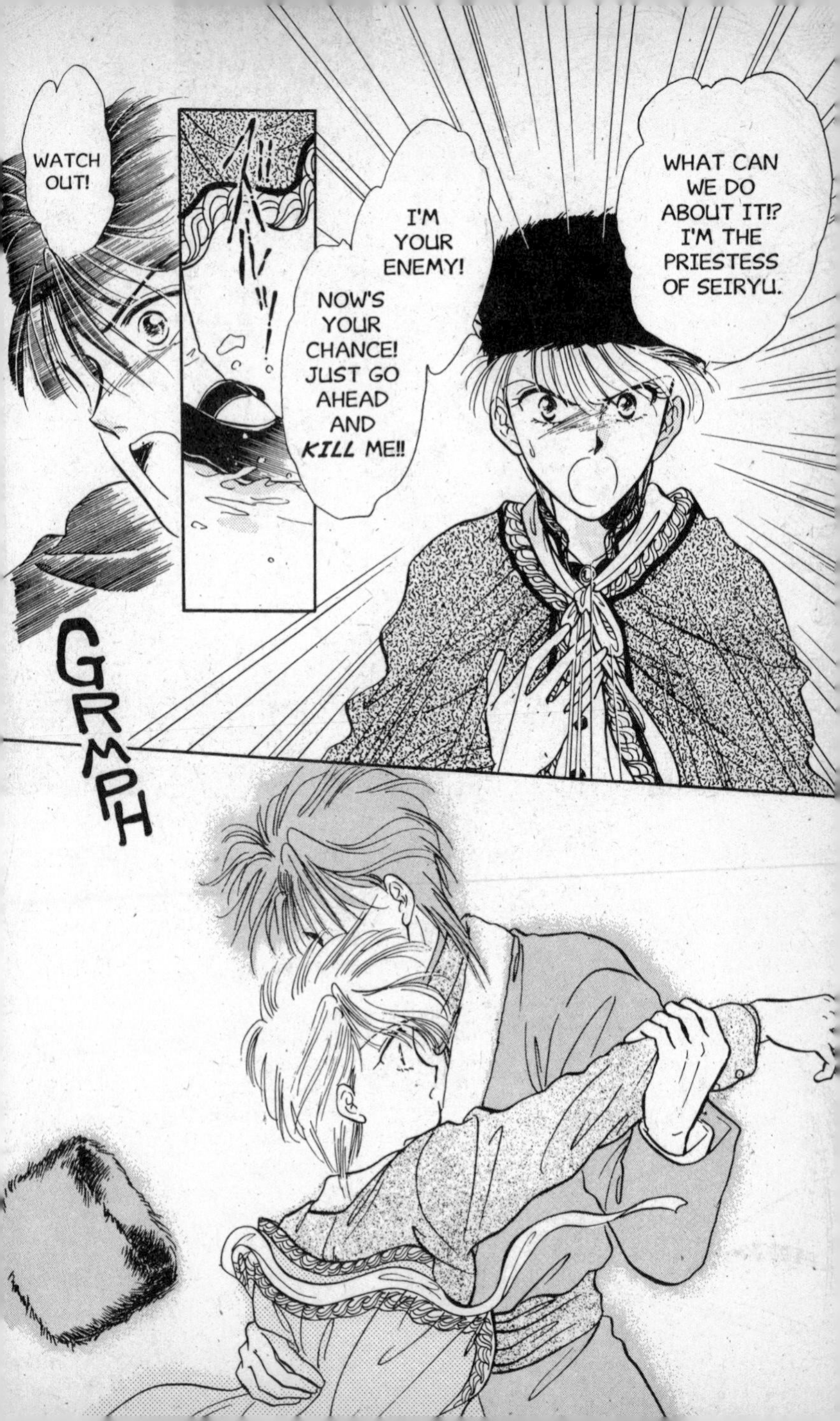
WHAT CAN WE DO ABOUT IT!? I'M THE PRIESTESS OF SEIRYU.
I'M YOUR ENEMY!
NOW'S YOUR CHANCE! JUST GO AHEAD AND *KILL* ME!!
WATCH OUT!
GRMPH

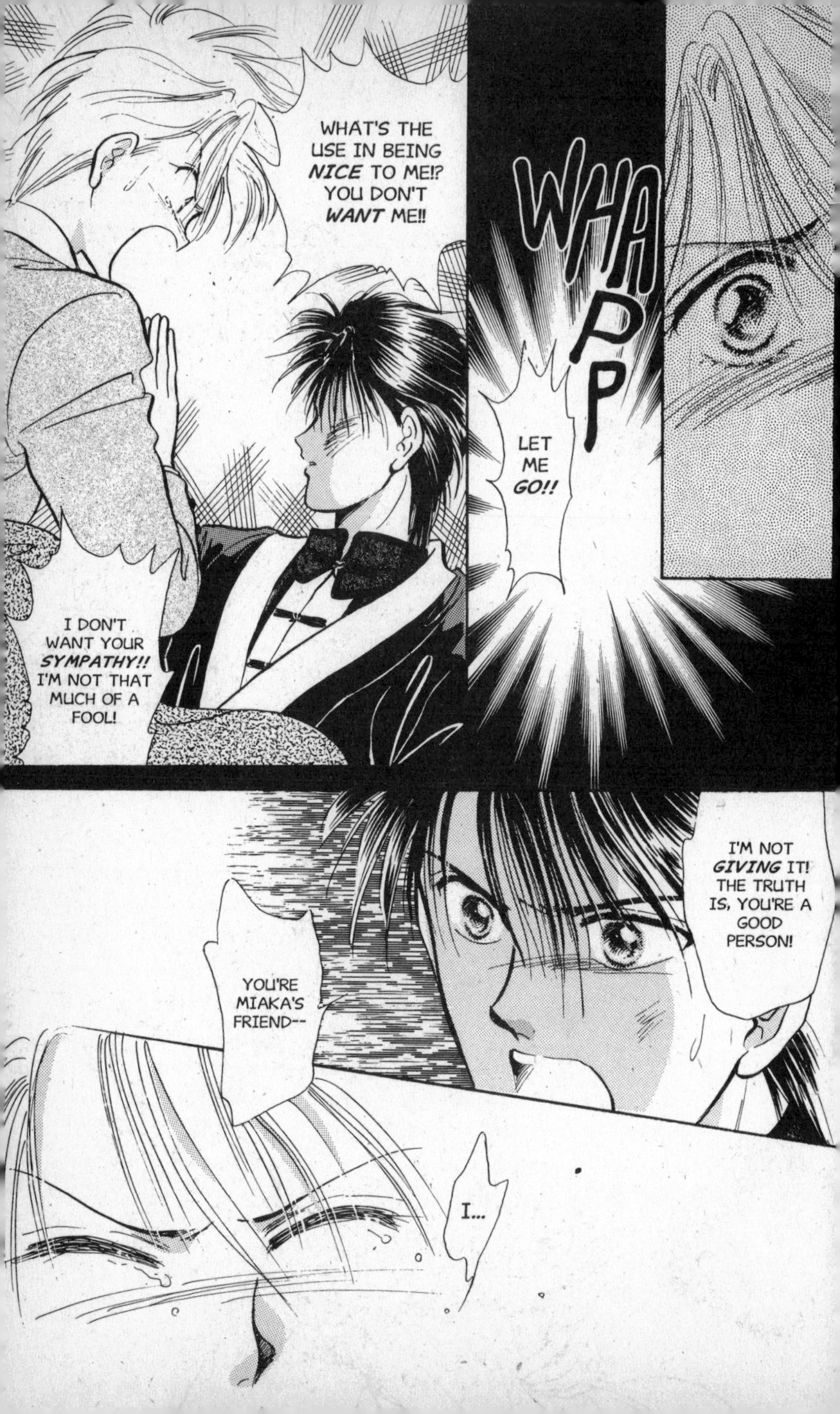
WHAPP
LET ME GO!!
WHAT'S THE USE IN BEING NICE TO ME!? YOU DON'T WANT ME!!
I DON'T WANT YOUR SYMPATHY!! I'M NOT THAT MUCH OF A FOOL!
I'M NOT GIVING IT! THE TRUTH IS, YOU'RE A GOOD PERSON!
YOU'RE MIAKA'S FRIEND--
I...

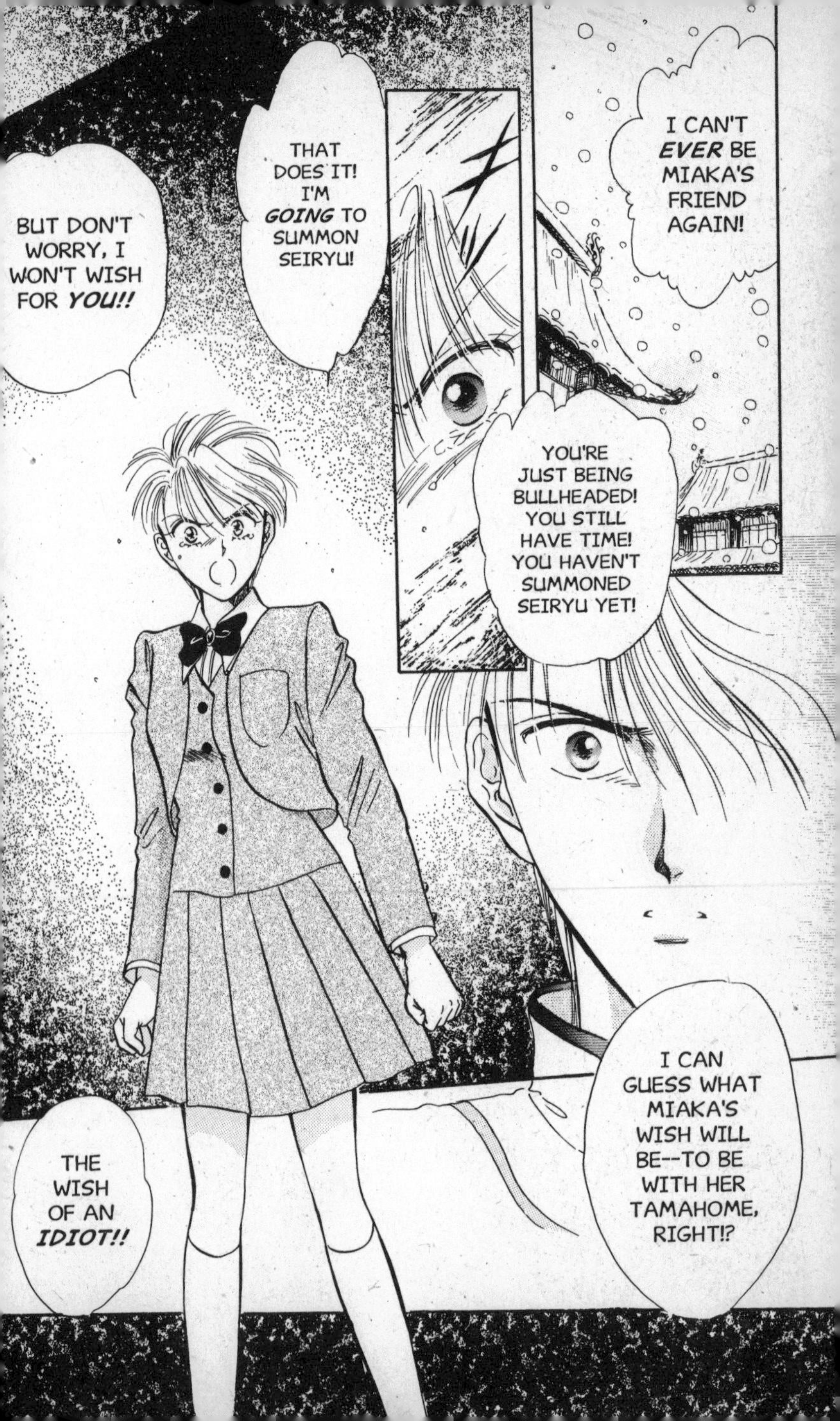
I CAN'T *EVER* BE MIAKA'S FRIEND AGAIN!
YOU'RE JUST BEING BULLHEADED! YOU STILL HAVE TIME! YOU HAVEN'T SUMMONED SEIRYU YET!
THAT DOES IT! I'M *GOING* TO SUMMON SEIRYU!
BUT DON'T WORRY, I WON'T WISH FOR *YOU!!*
I CAN GUESS WHAT MIAKA'S WISH WILL BE--TO BE WITH HER TAMAHOME, RIGHT!?
THE WISH OF AN *IDIOT!!*

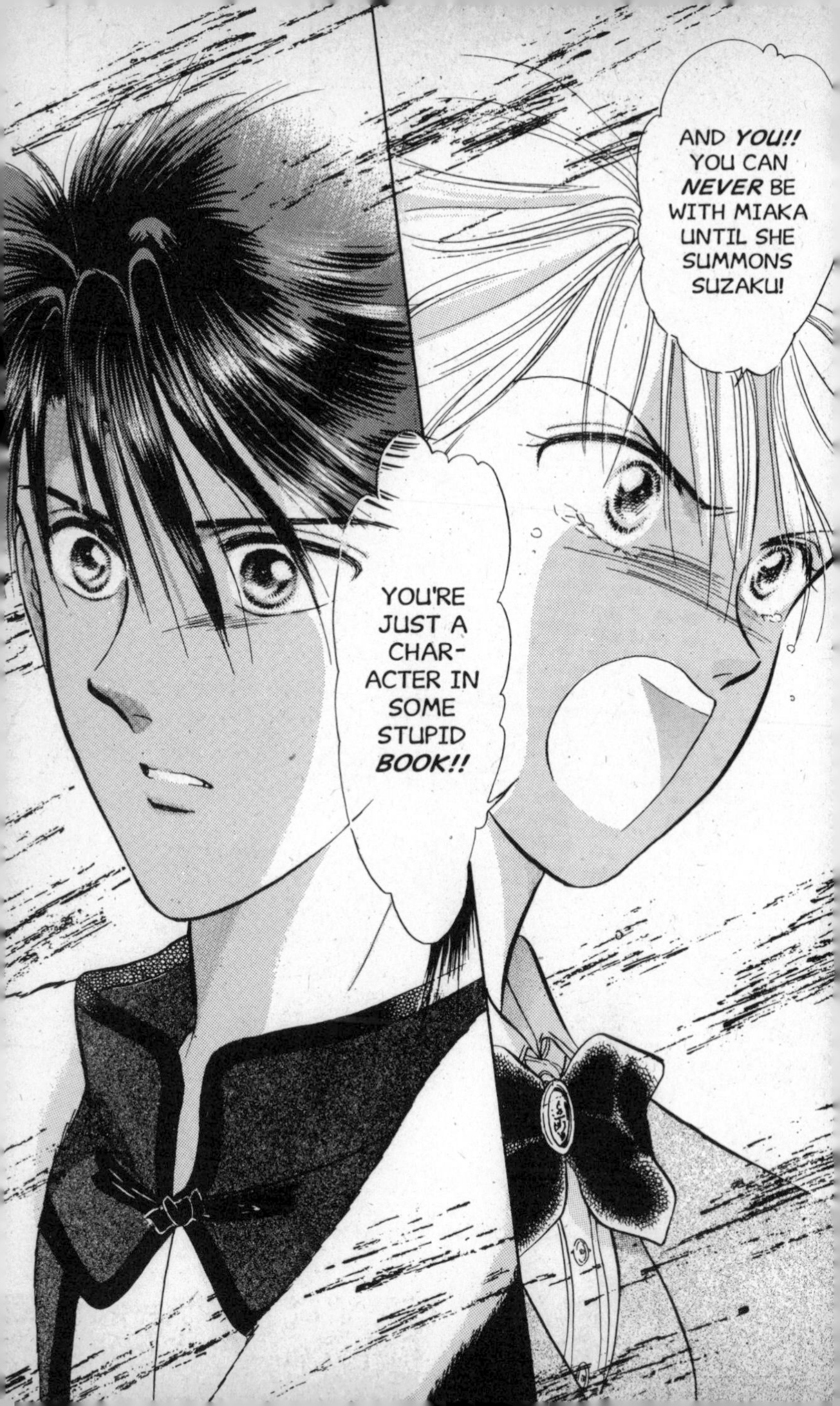
AND ***YOU!!*** YOU CAN ***NEVER*** BE WITH MIAKA UNTIL SHE SUMMONS SUZAKU!
YOU'RE JUST A CHAR-ACTER IN SOME STUPID ***BOOK!!***

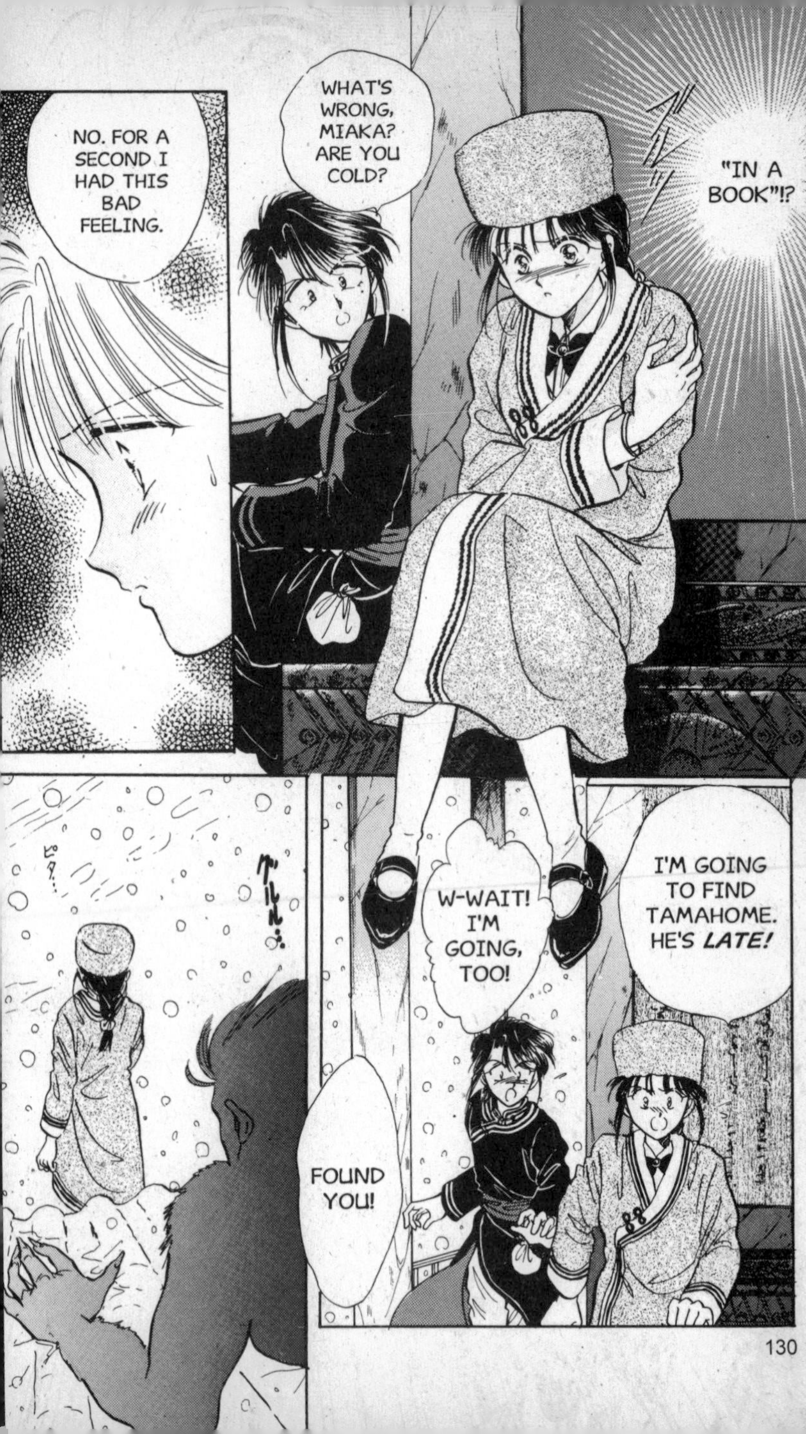

"IN A BOOK"!?
WHAT'S WRONG, MIAKA? ARE YOU COLD?
NO. FOR A SECOND I HAD THIS BAD FEELING.
I'M GOING TO FIND TAMAHOME. HE'S *LATE!*
W-WAIT! I'M GOING, TOO!
ピタ…
FOUND YOU!

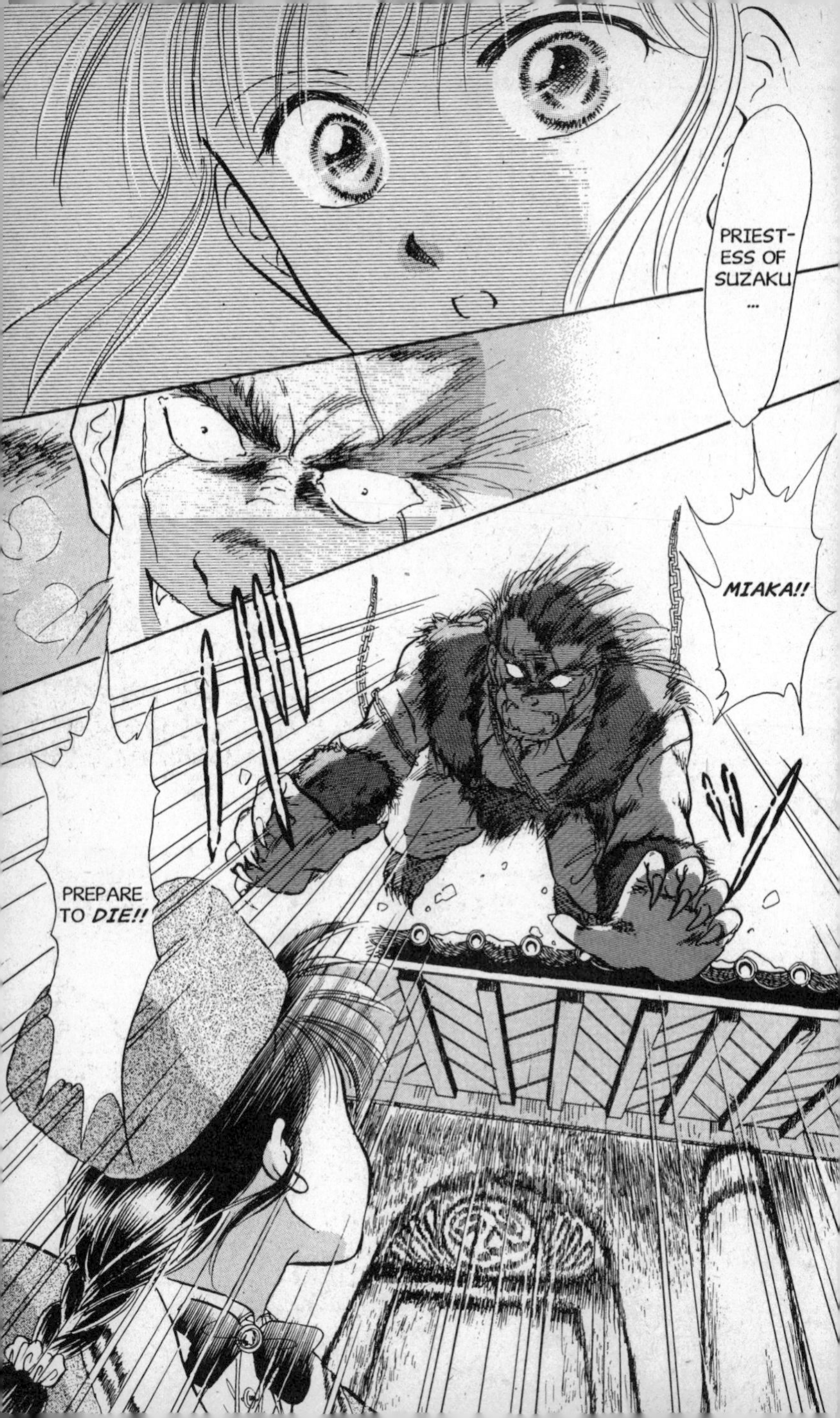

PRIEST-ESS OF SUZAKU ...
MIAKA!!
PREPARE TO *DIE!!*

SECRETS OF FUSHIGI YŪGI ①

This is a new corner that will explain the secrets and strange parts of "Fushigi Yūgi" to the fans! When you say, "This sucks! Watase, this makes no sense, damnit!" I will clear it up!

ITEM 1 What is the time difference between the world of "The Universe of the Four Gods" and the real world?

Actually, several readers tried to calculate this. Characters have spent time in the various worlds for, specifically, three days; a year and two months; and 33 years. But the true answer is this: there's no set rate. In chapter 11, Miaka spent about two hours in the real world, during which three months passed in the world of the book... And I think that most people took that as the standard rate, but here's the thing: if you read a book and a sentence reads, "And a month passed," it might take you only a second or two to read it. But in the world of the book, that's a month!

This may seem like a kind of time warp, and in the worst case, time could warp up to ten years or more, but since it takes the same few seconds to read "And three days passed" in "The Universe of the Four Gods" as it does for other time periods, there's no set rate of time passage.

ITEM 2 When Amiboshi acted as the fake Chiriko, why was he able to enter the Shrine of Suzaku with no problem?

There were no anti-Seiryu wards! Do you remember in chapter 16 when Chichiri said, "They've put up wards so none of Suzaku's chosen can get in! No do!" What *really* happened at the Seiryu Shrine was that Miaka went into the shrine, and Nakago quickly put up the wards. (That's why it took Miaka a few seconds to feel pain.)

I'm sure that Qu-Dong has laws forbidding the chosen ones of the other gods from entering the Seiryu Shrine during worship but remember there are also Genbu and Byakko shrines as well, and I'm sure the practice isn't universal.

Beyond that, even if wards had been placed in the shrine, the breaking of wards is one of the powers and chi techniques that Seiryu Celestial Warriors practice. That's one way in which Seiryu Warriors and Suzaku Warriors differ.

ITEM 3 Why did Miaka have to go out and find her Celestial Warriors when Yui had them all come to her?

This answer may seem similar to the one above, but this is one area where the Seiryu chosen and the Suzaku chosen are very different. "The Universe of the Four Gods" (the scroll version) says that the Priestess has to find her warriors, but in Yui's case, she used her chi to call her warriors to her. It could be thought of as Yui's power, but remember also that the Seiryu Celestial Warriors are very powerful! Their ability to sense the presence of another's chi goes far beyond that of the Suzaku Celestial Warriors. It's even possible that Nakago could outdo all of the Suzaku chosen by himself! The Seiryu chosen are quite a bit different from normal people (and that's how Nakago was able to locate Yui). Compared to them, in their powers and their way of life, the Suzaku chosen aren't all that different from normal people. They go around thinking, "Seven warriors? That's got nothing to do with me!" (They even forget about it!) And they just live their lives. (That difference in attitude is also reflected in Qu-Dong, which is rife with internal struggles, and Hong-Nan which is almost too peaceful.) That's one of the reasons why the Suzaku Warriors aren't very good at picking up Miaka's Priestess chi.

On the other hand, yes, Chichiri is the only warrior who can pick Miaka's chi and go to her (chapter 13), but you may have noticed something. If you think about it, the warriors were all pulled in by Miaka's chi anyway. Tamahome chose to leave his home for work just when Miaka arrived, and it was then that he got caught up in her adventures. (Until that day, he had never stepped foot outside his village.) Hotohori chose that time for his parade. Miaka's chi was behind Nuriko's decision to enter the palace as a woman and suddenly appear before her. Tasuki had left the bandits, but it was the day Miaka arrived that he decided to come back to the bandit group...and so on. It all amounts to about the same thing. There are reasons behind why Chiriko took so long to appear.

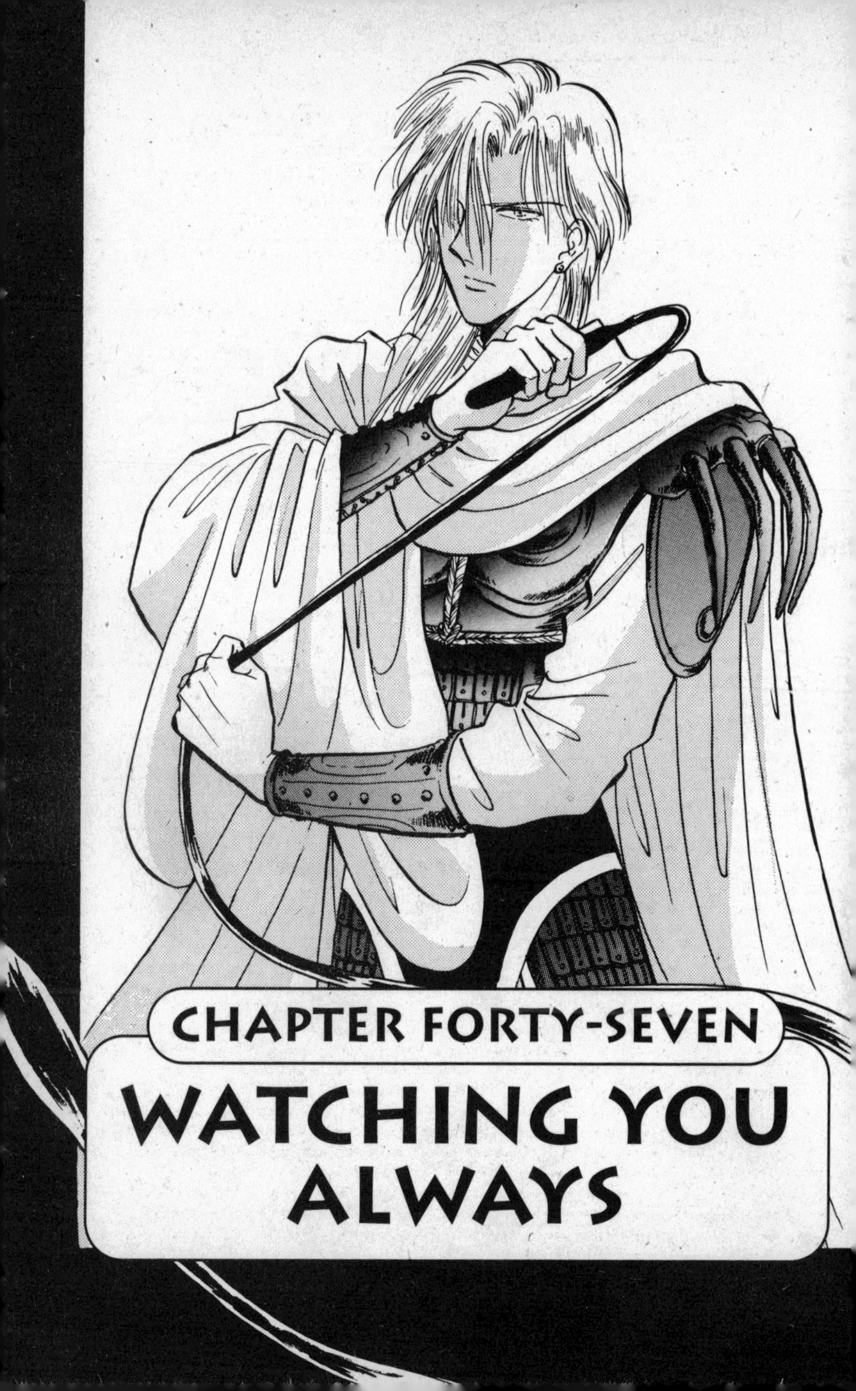

CHAPTER FORTY-SEVEN

WATCHING YOU ALWAYS

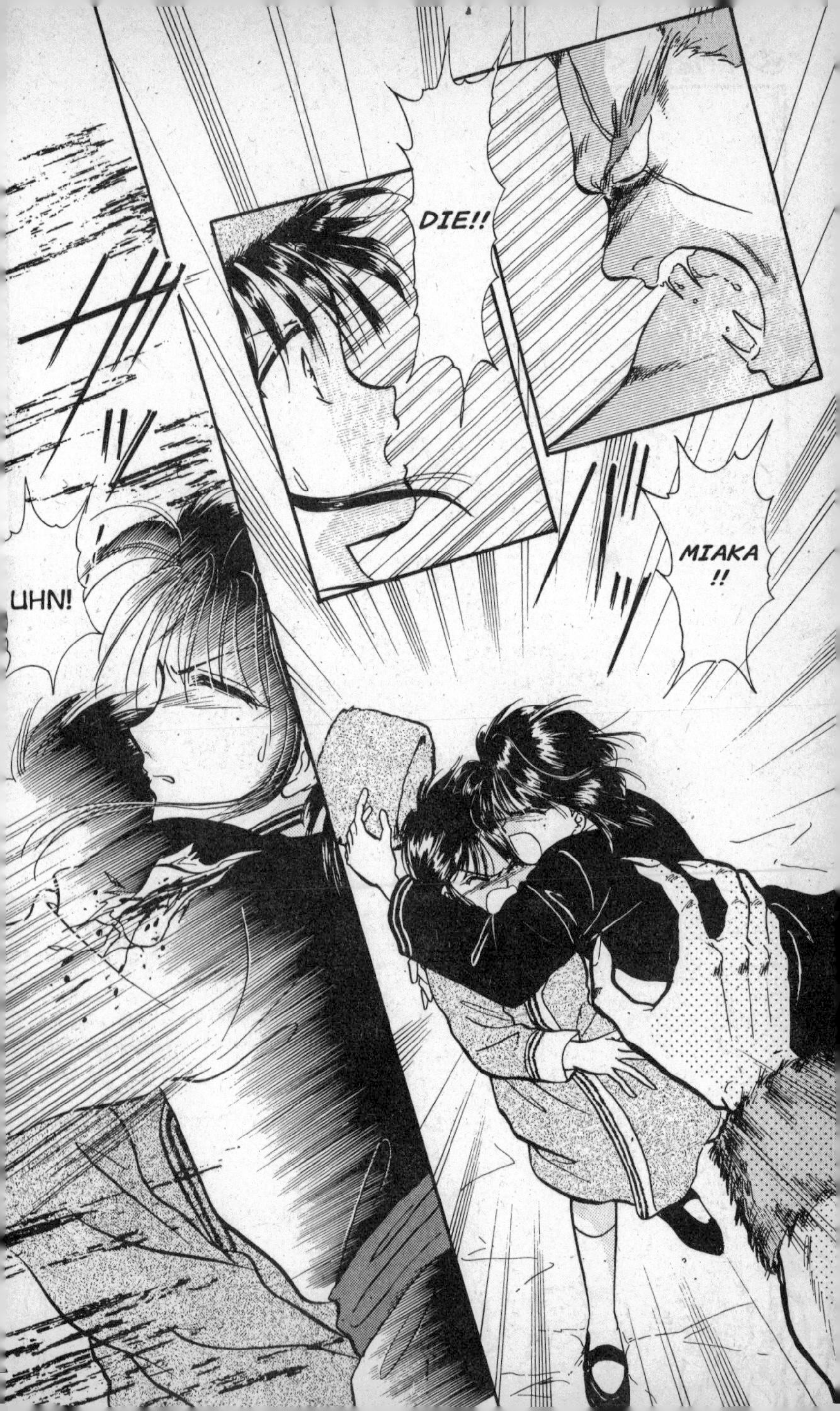
DIE!!
MIAKA !!
UHN!

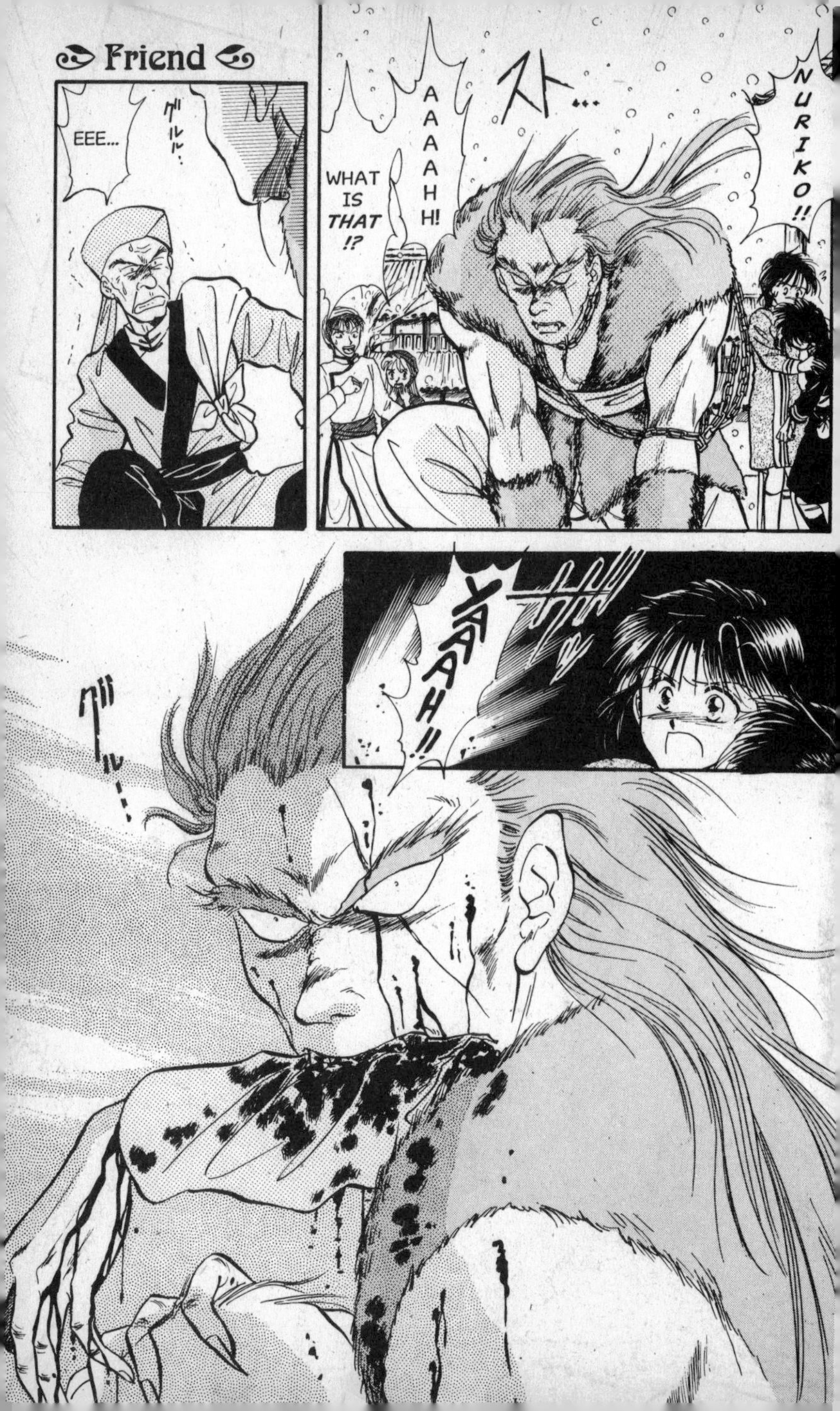
NURIKO!!
AAAAAH!
WHAT IS THAT!?
EEE...
グルル…
AAAAH!!

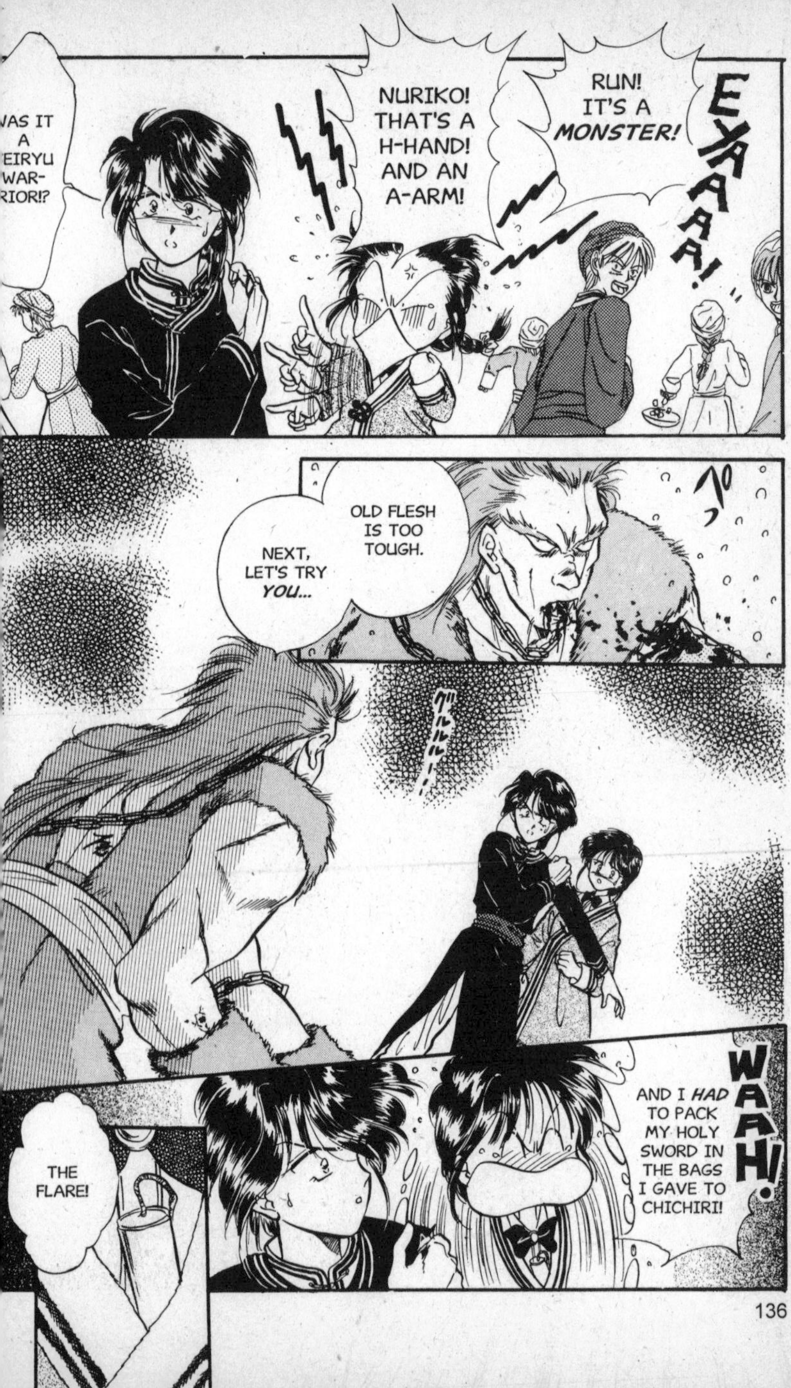
EYAAAAA!
RUN! IT'S A *MONSTER!*
NURIKO! THAT'S A H-HAND! AND AN A-ARM!
WAS IT A EIRYU WAR-RIOR!?
OLD FLESH IS TOO TOUGH.
NEXT, LET'S TRY *YOU*...
WAAH!
AND I *HAD* TO PACK MY HOLY SWORD IN THE BAGS I GAVE TO CHICHIRI!
THE FLARE!

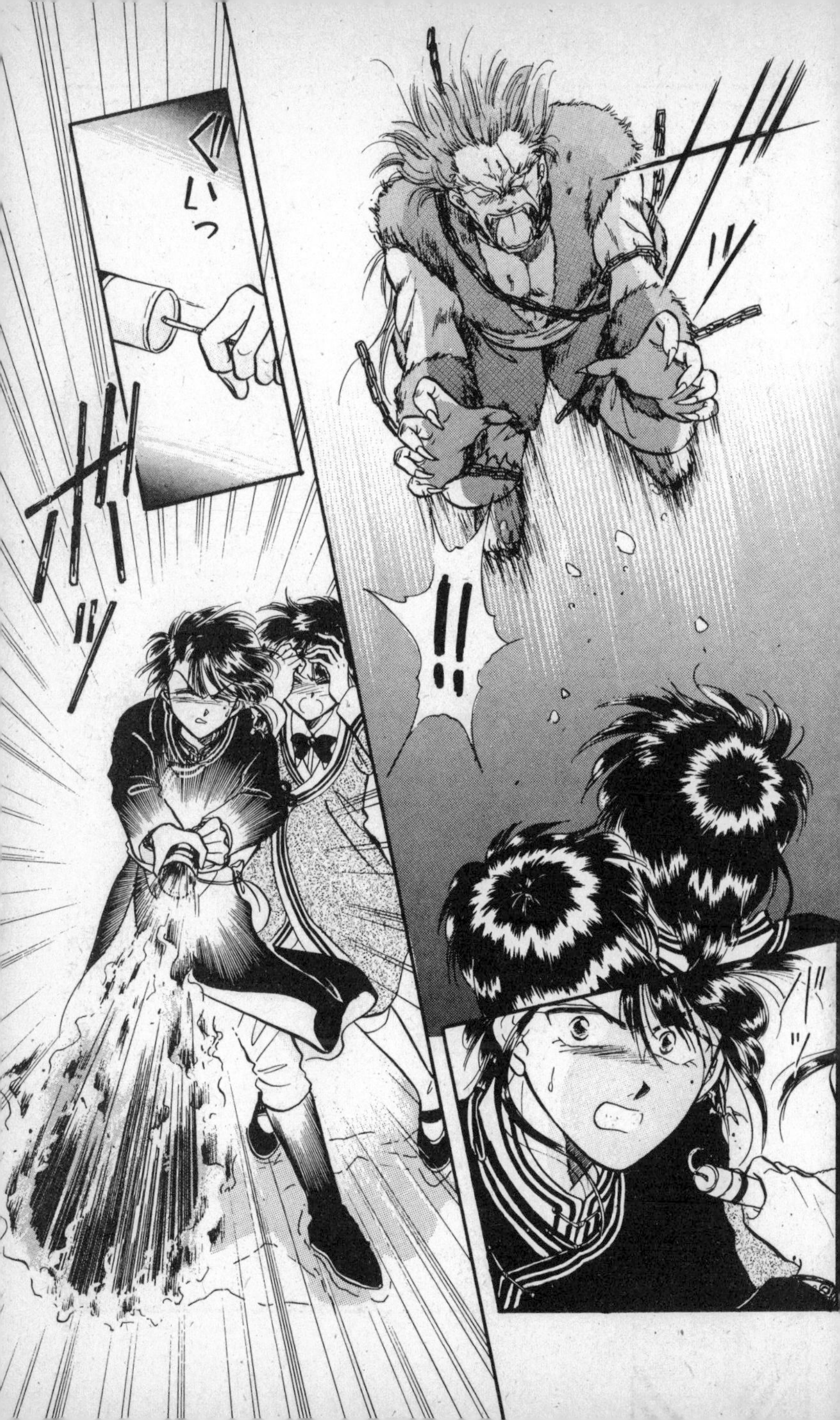
ザッ
ぐいっ
!!

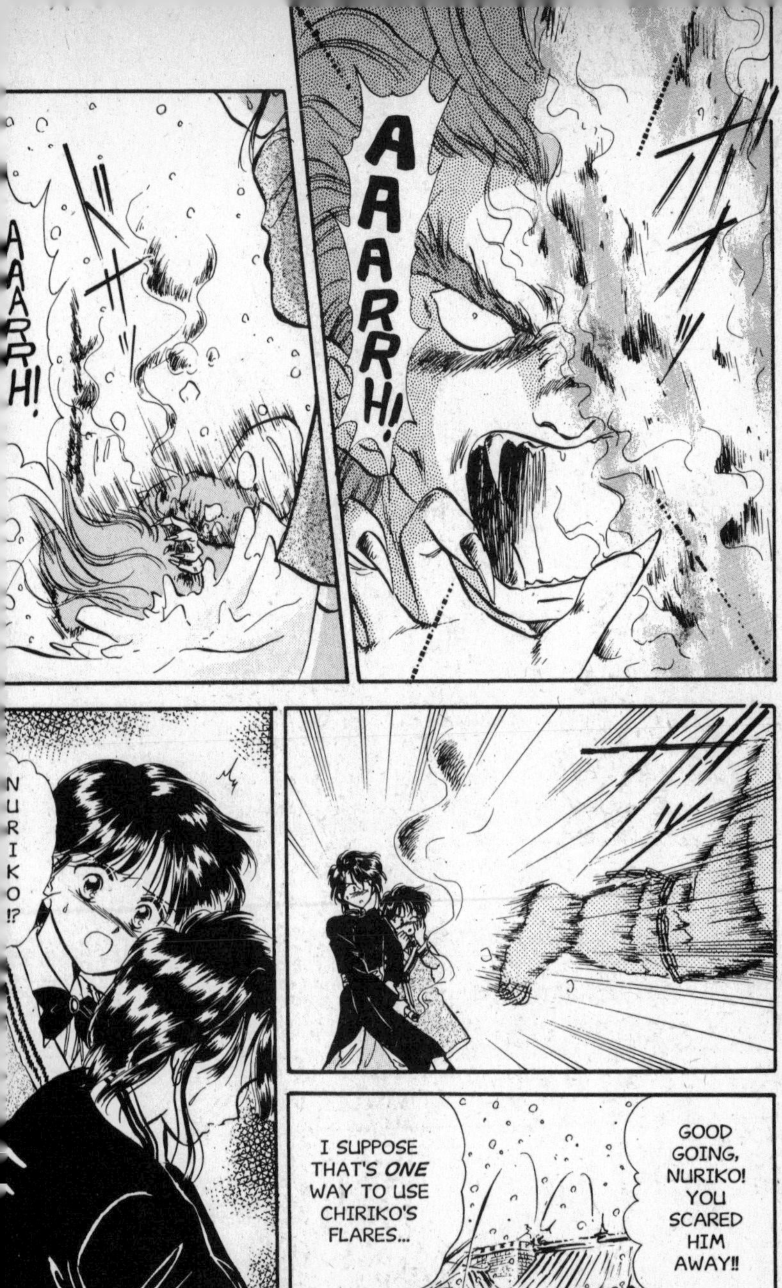
AAARRH!
AAAARRH!
NURIKO!?
GOOD GOING, NURIKO! YOU SCARED HIM AWAY!!
I SUPPOSE THAT'S *ONE* WAY TO USE CHIRIKO'S FLARES...

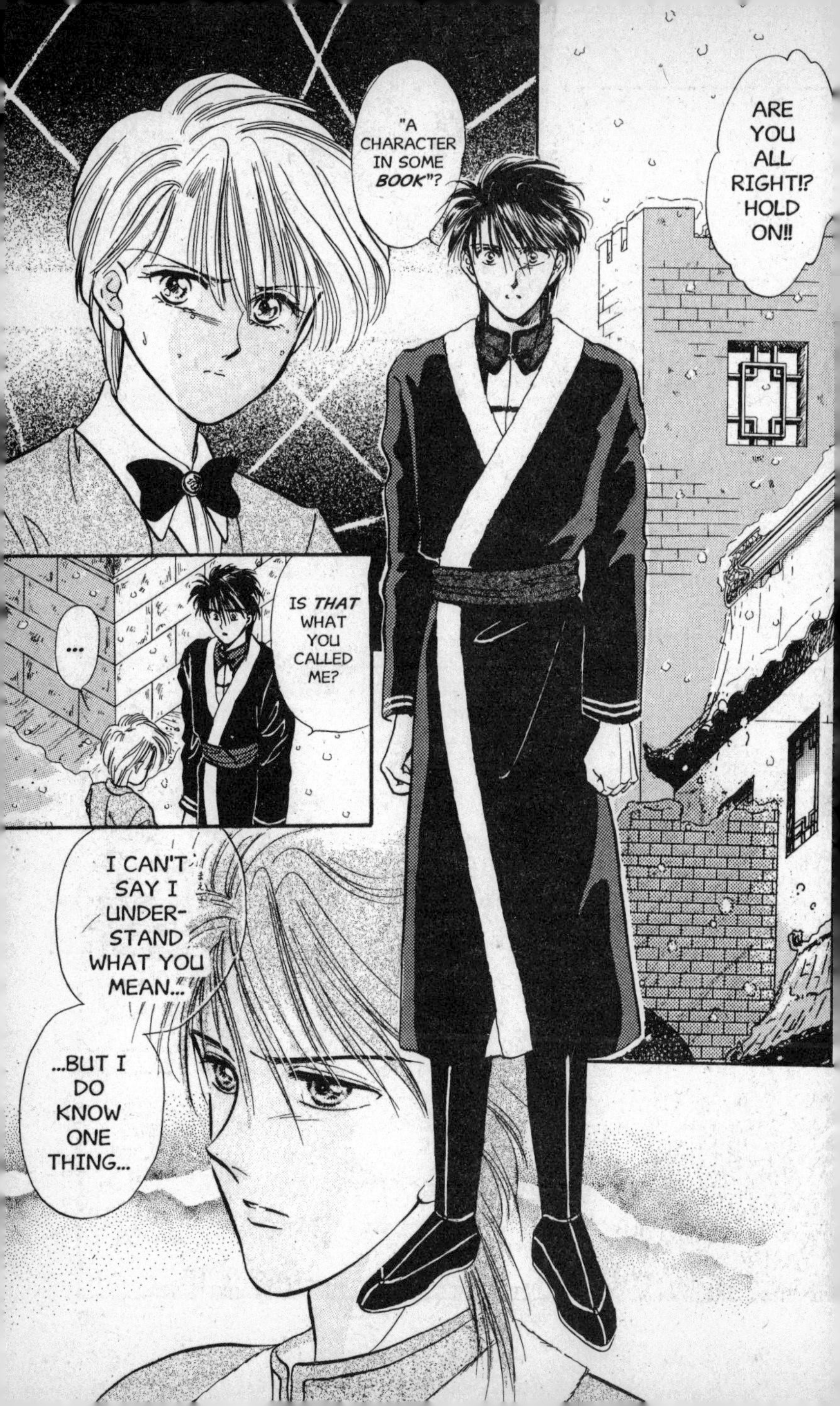
ARE YOU ALL RIGHT!? HOLD ON!!
"A CHARACTER IN SOME BOOK"?
IS THAT WHAT YOU CALLED ME?
...
I CAN'T SAY I UNDER-STAND WHAT YOU MEAN...
...BUT I DO KNOW ONE THING...

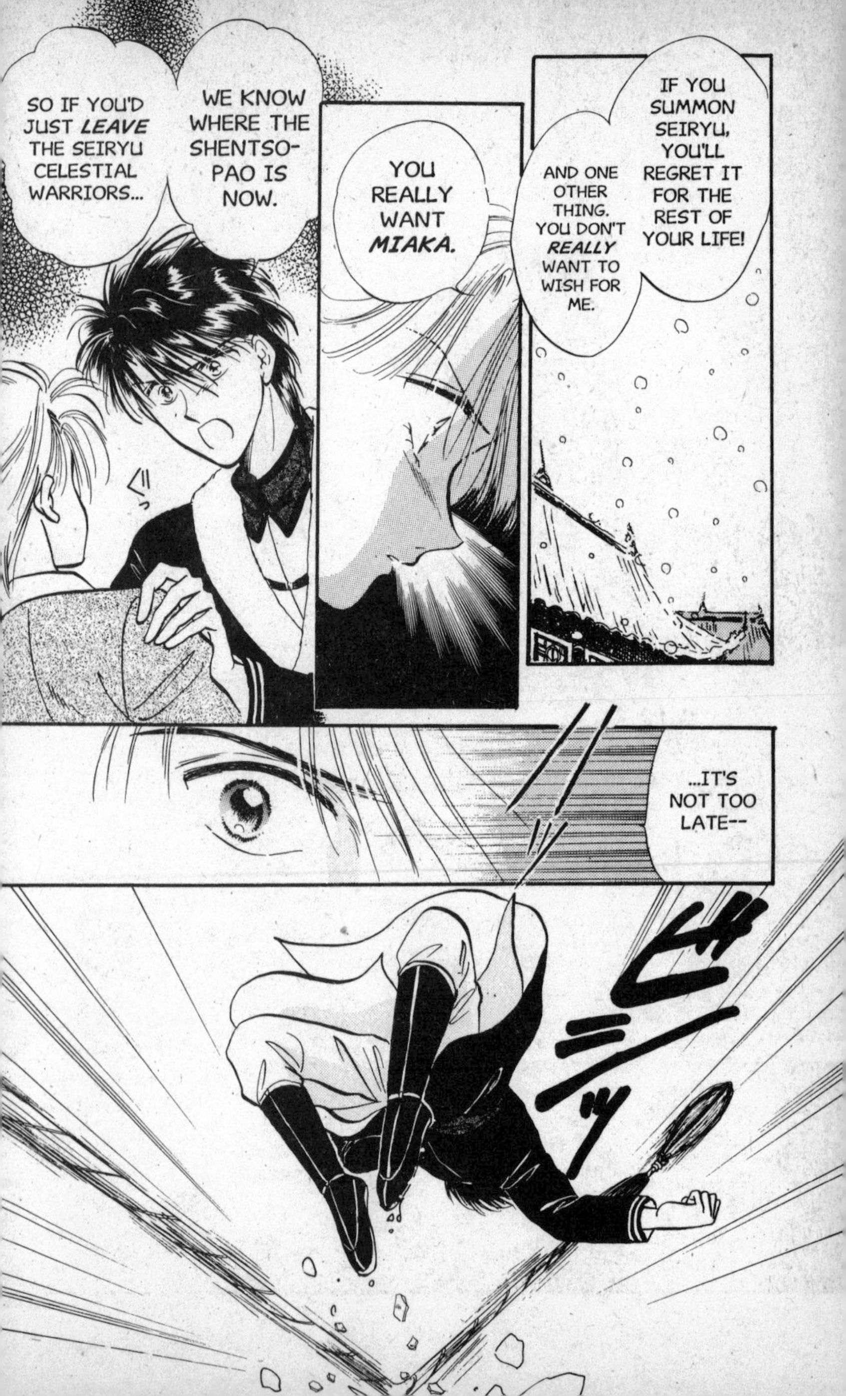
IF YOU SUMMON SEIRYU, YOU'LL REGRET IT FOR THE REST OF YOUR LIFE!
AND ONE OTHER THING. YOU DON'T *REALLY* WANT TO WISH FOR ME.
YOU REALLY WANT *MIAKA.*
WE KNOW WHERE THE SHENTSO-PAO IS NOW.
SO IF YOU'D JUST *LEAVE* THE SEIRYU CELESTIAL WARRIORS...
...IT'S NOT TOO LATE--

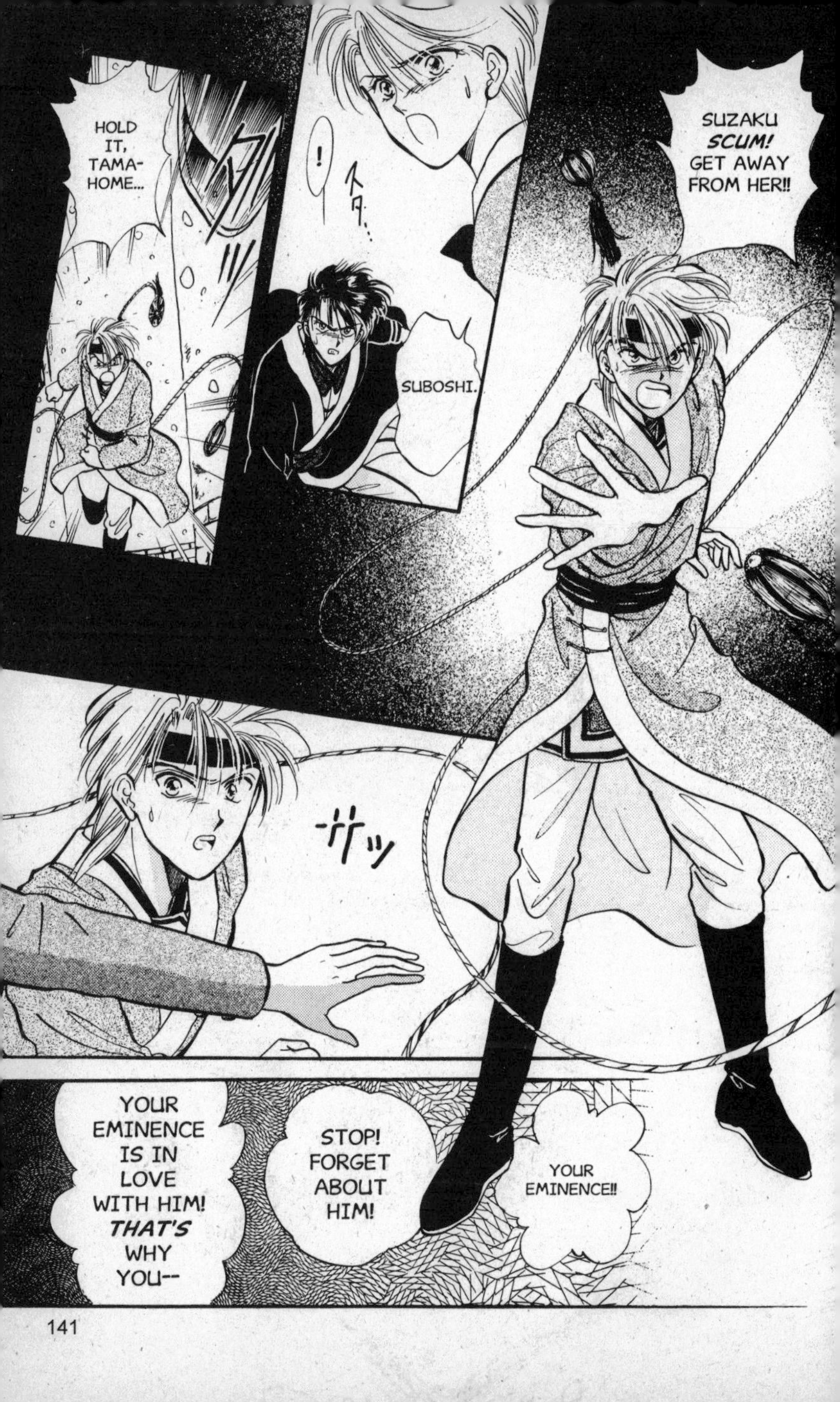

SUZAKU SCUM! GET AWAY FROM HER!!
!
スタ…
SUBOSHI.
HOLD IT, TAMA-HOME...
サッ
YOUR EMINENCE!!
STOP! FORGET ABOUT HIM!
YOUR EMINENCE IS IN LOVE WITH HIM! THAT'S WHY YOU--

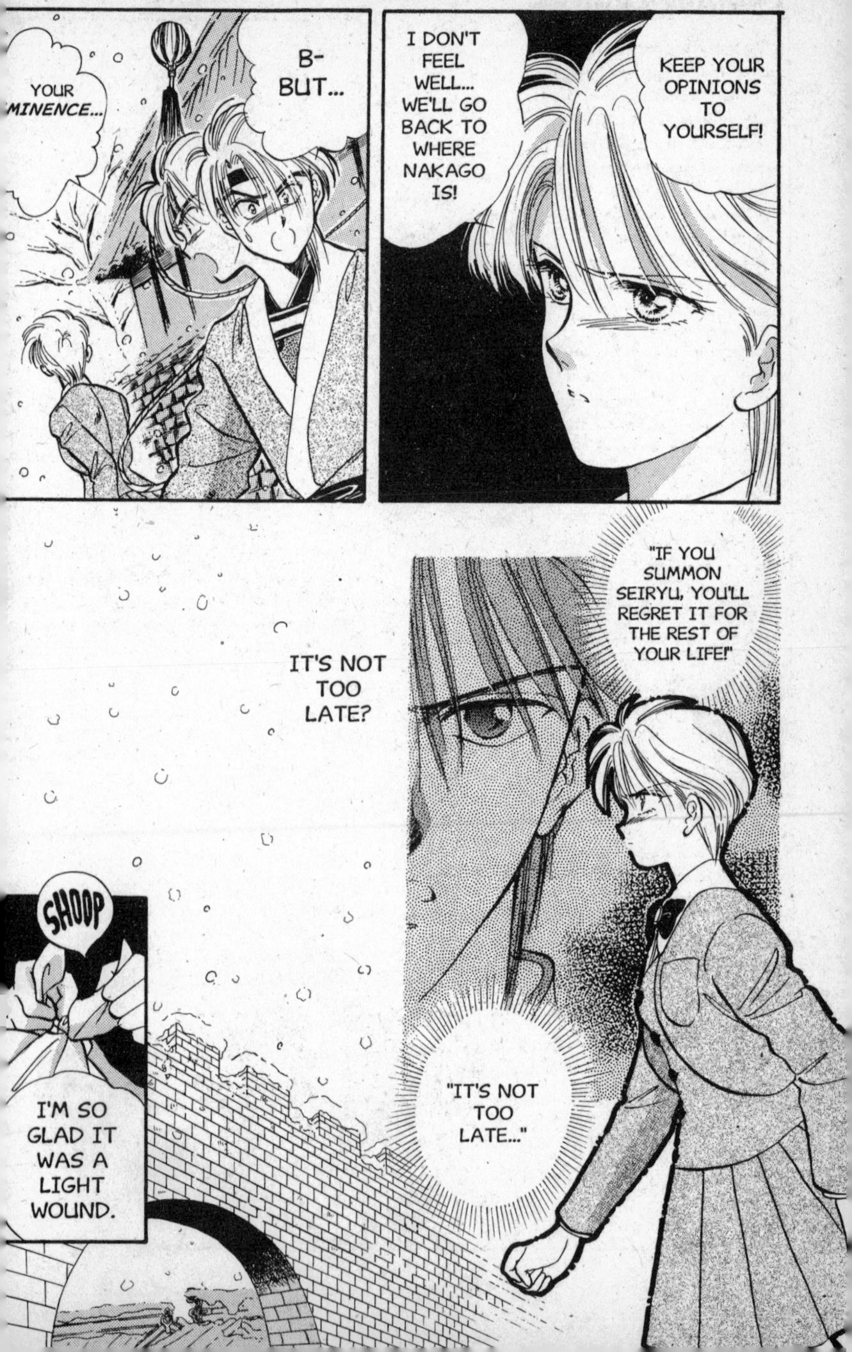

KEEP YOUR OPINIONS TO YOURSELF!
I DON'T FEEL WELL... WE'LL GO BACK TO WHERE NAKAGO IS!
B-BUT...
YOUR MINENCE...
"IF YOU SUMMON SEIRYU, YOU'LL REGRET IT FOR THE REST OF YOUR LIFE!"
IT'S NOT TOO LATE?
"IT'S NOT TOO LATE..."
SHOOP
I'M SO GLAD IT WAS A LIGHT WOUND.

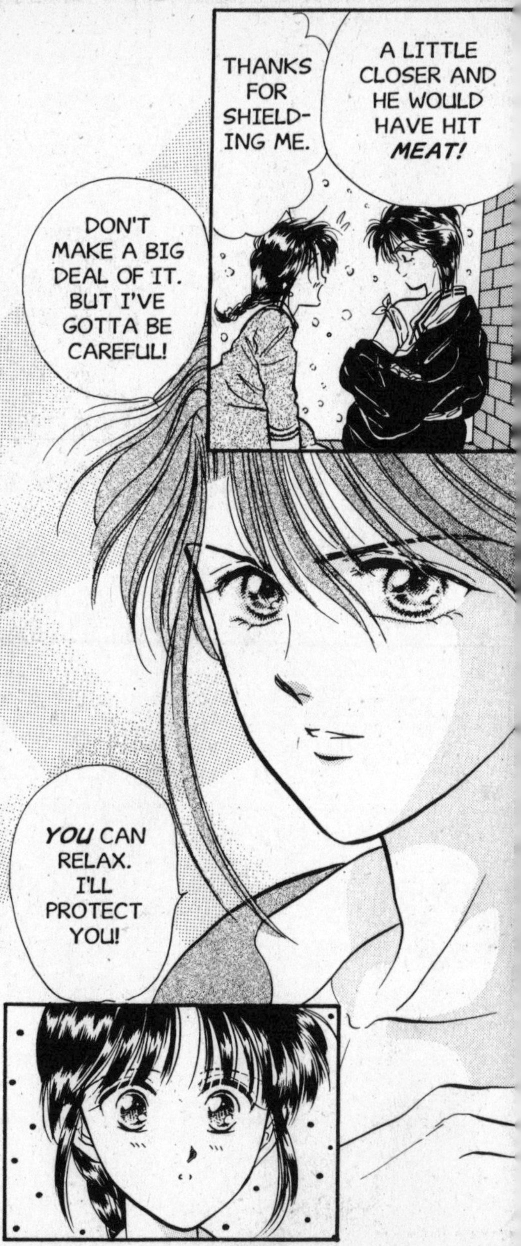
A LITTLE CLOSER AND HE WOULD HAVE HIT *MEAT!*
THANKS FOR SHIELD-ING ME.
DON'T MAKE A BIG DEAL OF IT. BUT I'VE GOTTA BE CAREFUL!
YOU CAN RELAX. I'LL PROTECT YOU!

These statues are around 70 inches tall. I guess people were taller back then. I heard something about how the more civilization advances and the smarter we are, the shorter we get. Really? Which would mean there were men as tall as Tasuki and Tamahome. That's thousands of years ago! And guys like them were walking the Earth! Ba-dump! Ba-dump! But before these statues were made, living soldiers were buried alive in the emperor's tomb. I bet it was awful! Or did their loyalty numb the pain? The Chinese are said to be very loyal. Once they've committed, they go all the way, even risking their lives. On the other hand, they have a reputation of being merciless and wily. I'll bet most readers (me included) have a notion of China that's based on the clothes worn in Hong Kong kung fu movies. A pseudo-Chinese look. (Can you guess what I'm trying to say?) But the real China seems more earthy and alive! It's a land where you get the feeling that a lot of people have given their blood and tears in endless wars. This isn't something to be taken lightly. It's a man's country where tough women have survived in their shadows. "Fushigi Yûgi" has gradually evolved from having a pseudo-Chinese feel to a more realistic one. I'd like to draw a story that's both sweet and serious. Oops, I got side-tracked. I'll continue with my travels next time.

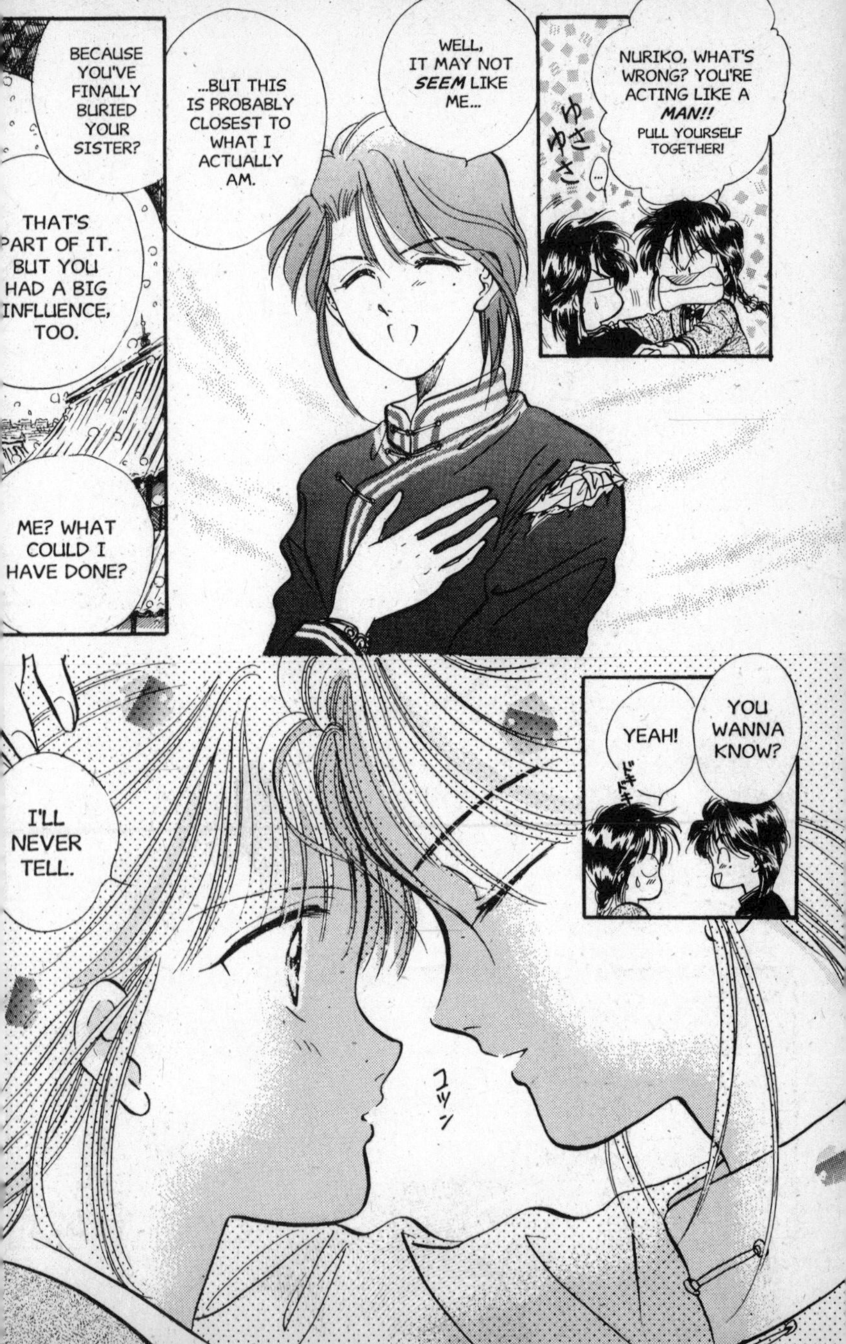
NURIKO, WHAT'S WRONG? YOU'RE ACTING LIKE A *MAN!!* PULL YOURSELF TOGETHER!
ゆさゆさ
...
WELL, IT MAY NOT *SEEM* LIKE ME...
...BUT THIS IS PROBABLY CLOSEST TO WHAT I ACTUALLY AM.
BECAUSE YOU'VE FINALLY BURIED YOUR SISTER?
THAT'S PART OF IT. BUT YOU HAD A BIG INFLUENCE, TOO.
ME? WHAT COULD I HAVE DONE?
YOU WANNA KNOW?
YEAH!
ドキドキ
I'LL NEVER TELL.
コツン

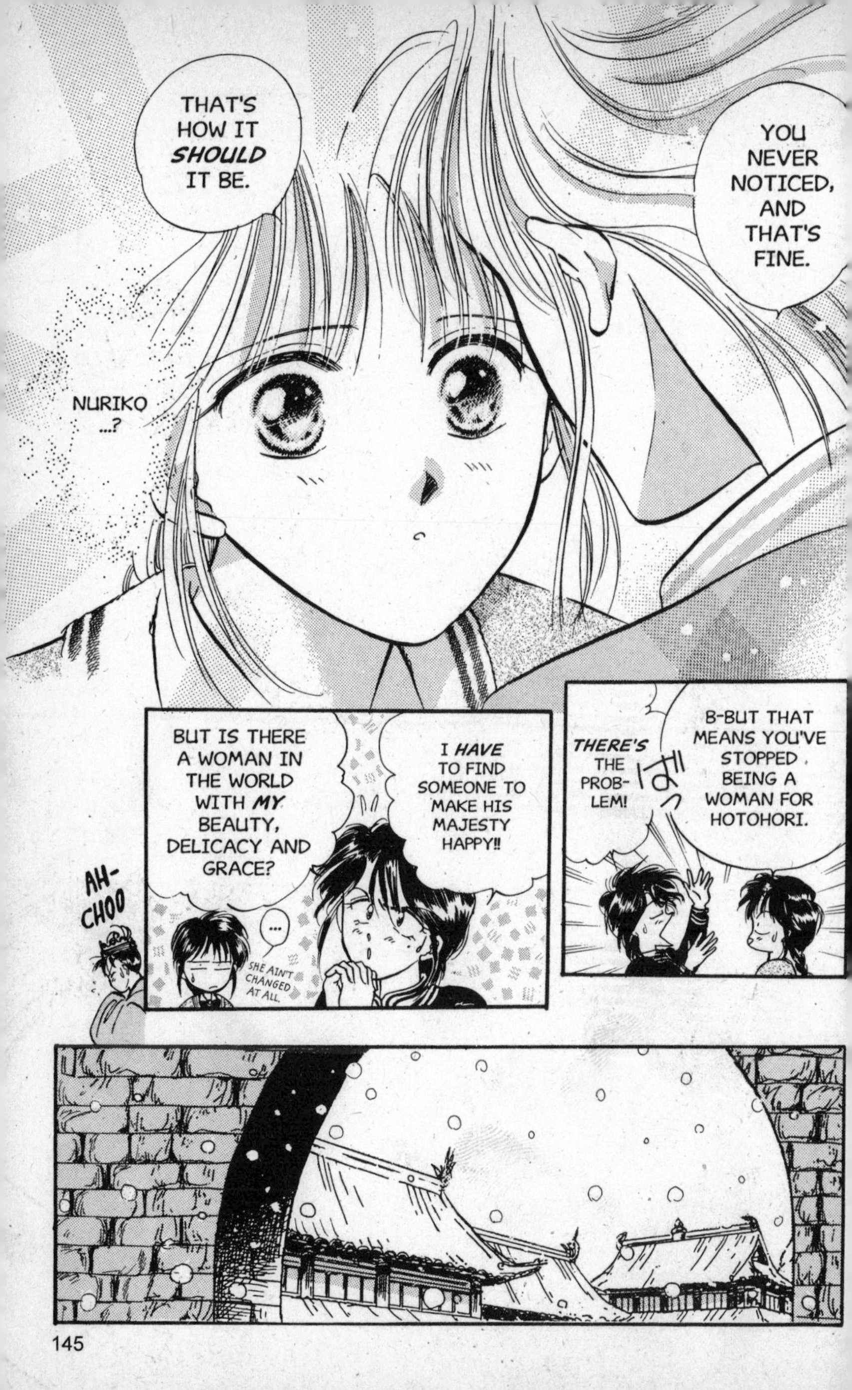

YOU NEVER NOTICED, AND THAT'S FINE.
THAT'S HOW IT *SHOULD* IT BE.
NURIKO ...?
B-BUT THAT MEANS YOU'VE STOPPED BEING A WOMAN FOR HOTOHORI.
ぱっ
THERE'S THE PROB-LEM!
I *HAVE* TO FIND SOMEONE TO MAKE HIS MAJESTY HAPPY!!
BUT IS THERE A WOMAN IN THE WORLD WITH *MY* BEAUTY, DELICACY AND GRACE?
...
SHE AIN'T CHANGED AT ALL.
AH-CHOO

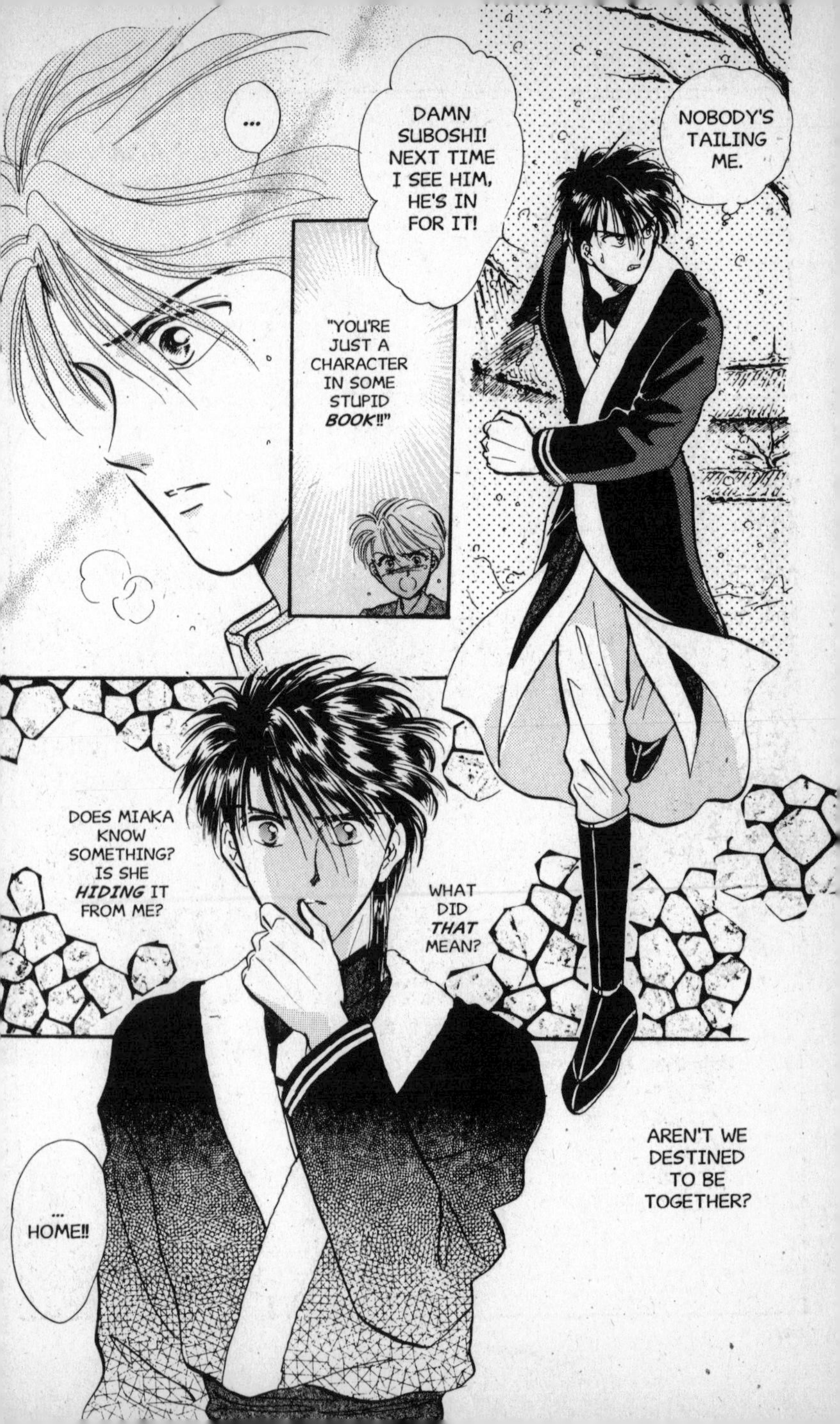
NOBODY'S TAILING ME.
DAMN SUBOSHI! NEXT TIME I SEE HIM, HE'S IN FOR IT!
...
"YOU'RE JUST A CHARACTER IN SOME STUPID *BOOK*!!"
WHAT DID *THAT* MEAN?
DOES MIAKA KNOW SOMETHING? IS SHE *HIDING* IT FROM ME?
AREN'T WE DESTINED TO BE TOGETHER?
... HOME!!

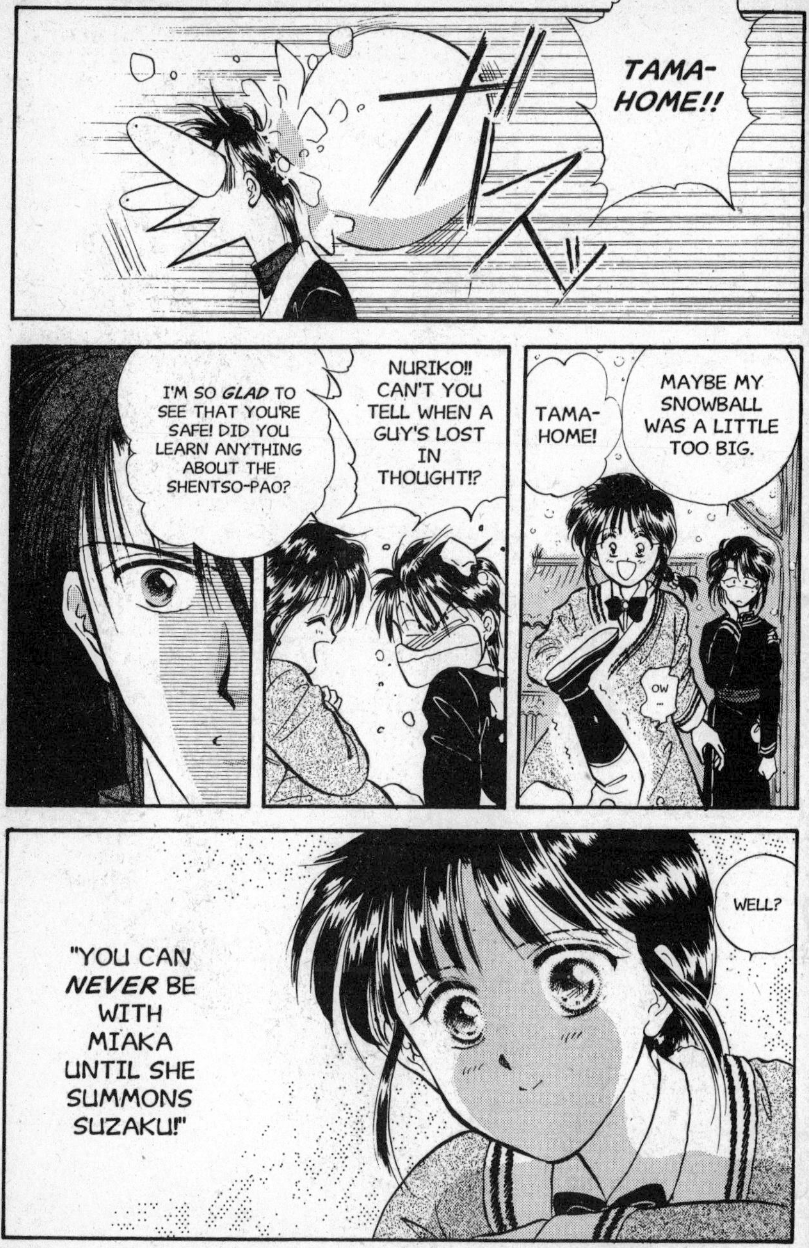

TAMA-HOME!!
MAYBE MY SNOWBALL WAS A LITTLE TOO BIG.
TAMA-HOME!
OW ...
NURIKO!! CAN'T YOU TELL WHEN A GUY'S LOST IN THOUGHT!?
I'M SO GLAD TO SEE THAT YOU'RE SAFE! DID YOU LEARN ANYTHING ABOUT THE SHENTSO-PAO?
WELL?
"YOU CAN NEVER BE WITH MIAKA UNTIL SHE SUMMONS SUZAKU!"

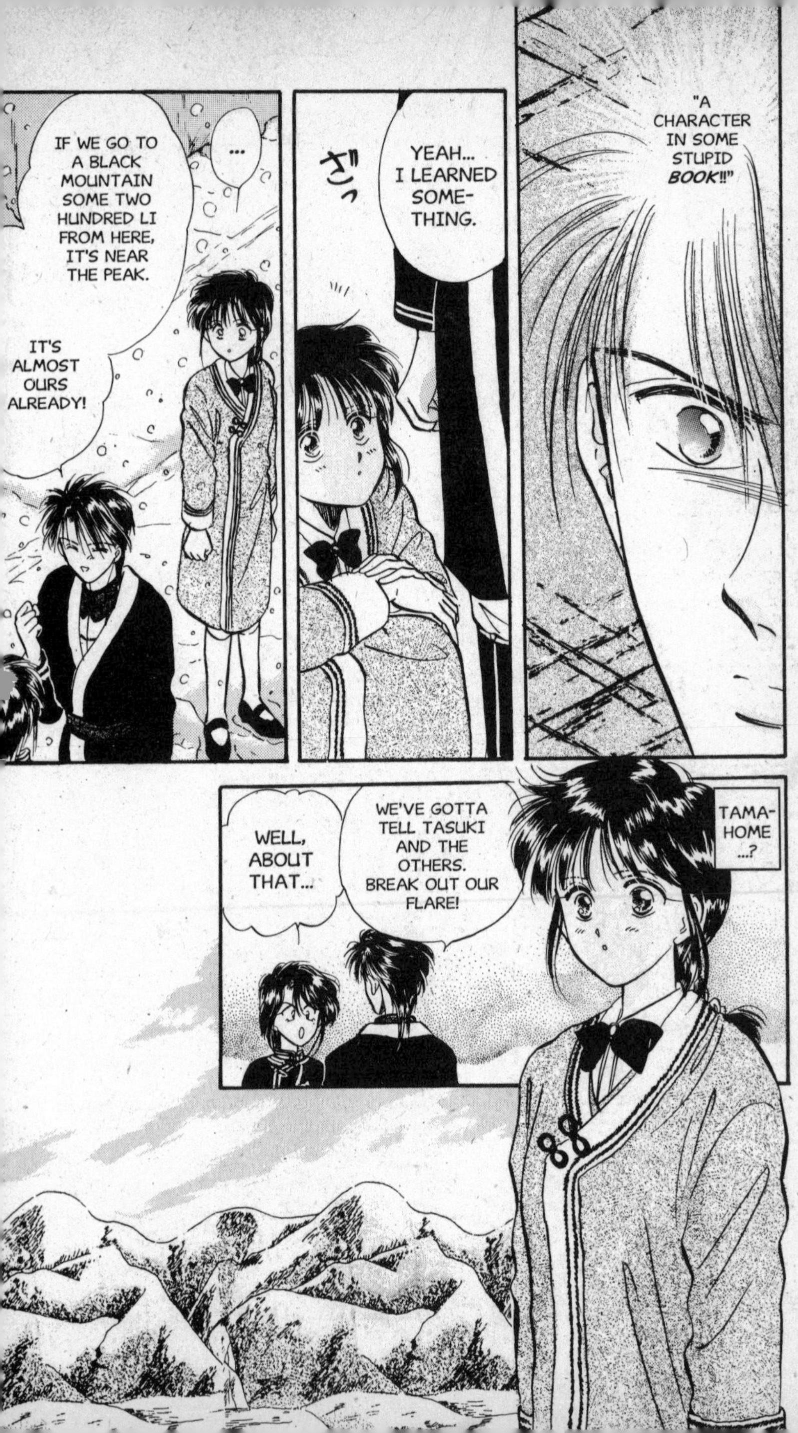
"A CHARACTER IN SOME STUPID *BOOK*!!"
YEAH... I LEARNED SOME-THING.
ざっ
...
IF WE GO TO A BLACK MOUNTAIN SOME TWO HUNDRED LI FROM HERE, IT'S NEAR THE PEAK.
IT'S ALMOST OURS ALREADY!
TAMA-HOME ...?
WE'VE GOTTA TELL TASUKI AND THE OTHERS. BREAK OUT OUR FLARE!
WELL, ABOUT THAT...

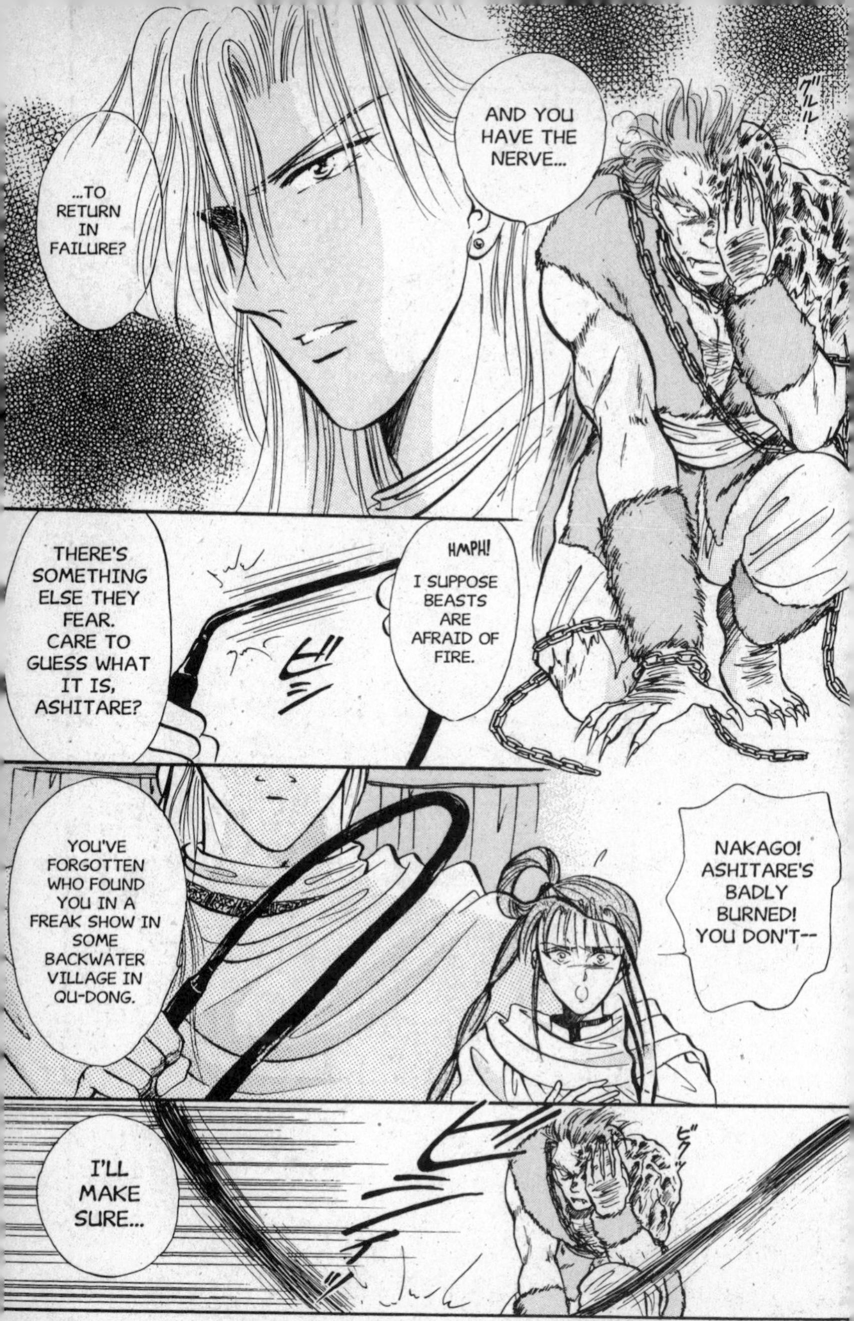
AND YOU HAVE THE NERVE...
...TO RETURN IN FAILURE?
HMPH! I SUPPOSE BEASTS ARE AFRAID OF FIRE.
THERE'S SOMETHING ELSE THEY FEAR. CARE TO GUESS WHAT IT IS, ASHITARE?
NAKAGO! ASHITARE'S BADLY BURNED! YOU DON'T--
YOU'VE FORGOTTEN WHO FOUND YOU IN A FREAK SHOW IN SOME BACKWATER VILLAGE IN QU-DONG.
I'LL MAKE SURE...

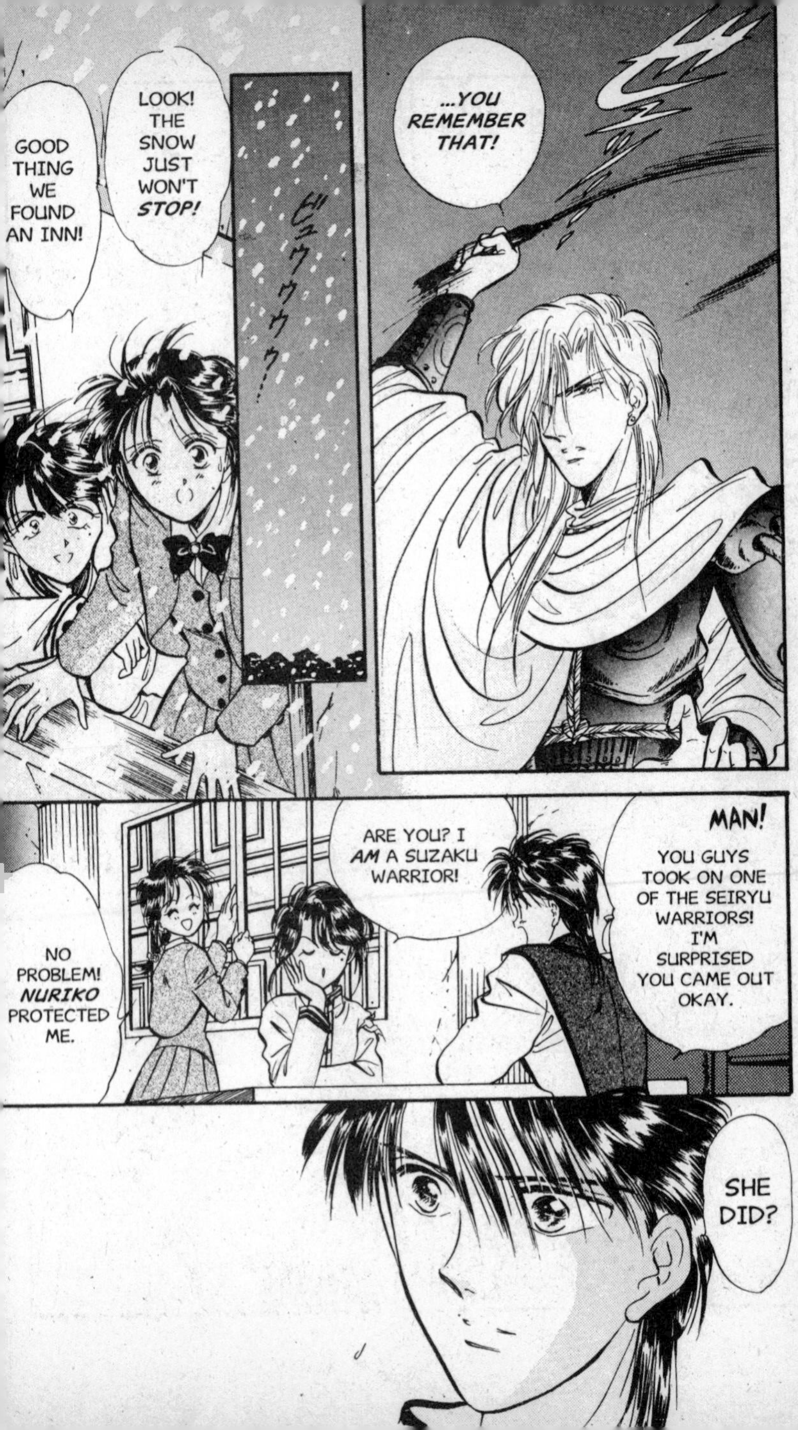

...YOU REMEMBER THAT!
LOOK! THE SNOW JUST WON'T *STOP!*
GOOD THING WE FOUND AN INN!
MAN! YOU GUYS TOOK ON ONE OF THE SEIRYU WARRIORS! I'M SURPRISED YOU CAME OUT OKAY.
ARE YOU? I *AM* A SUZAKU WARRIOR!
NO PROBLEM! *NURIKO* PROTECTED ME.
SHE DID?

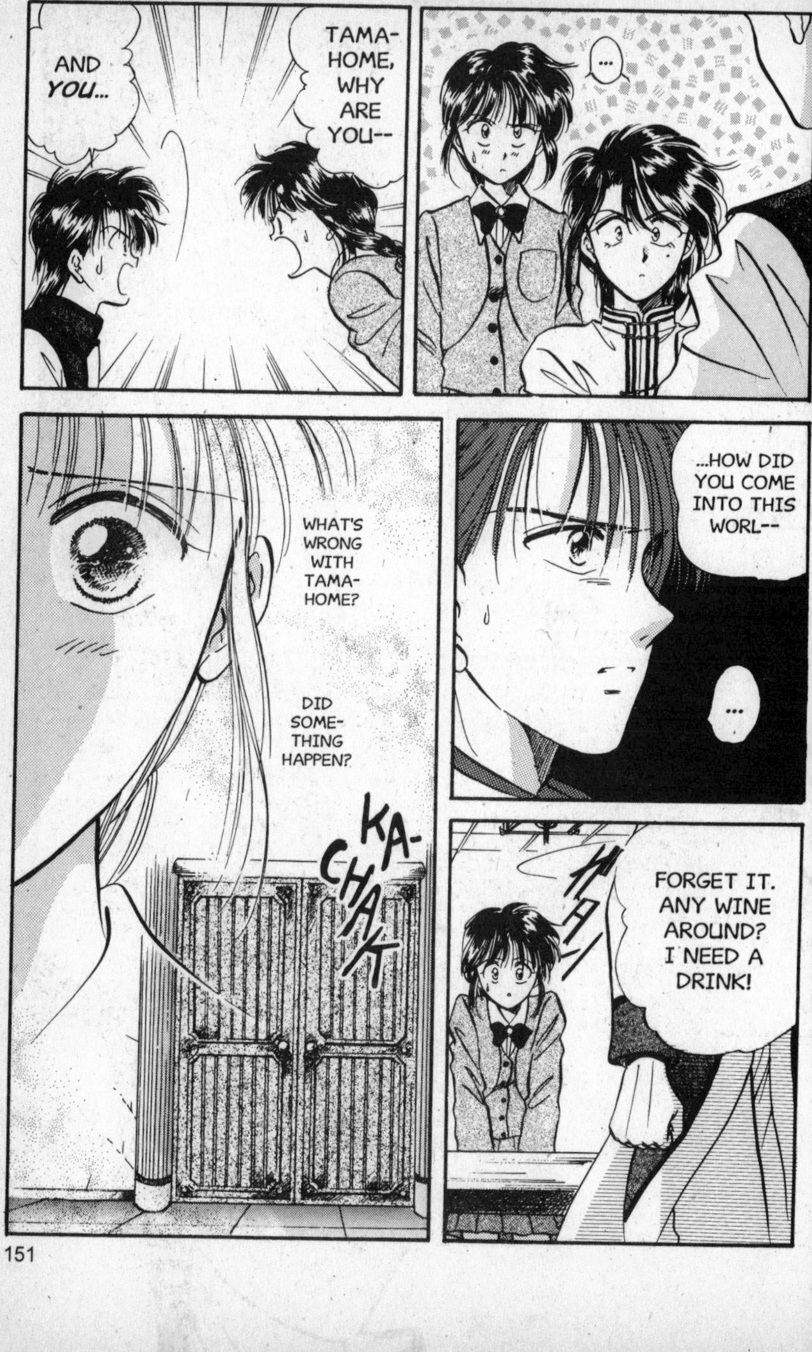
...
TAMA-HOME, WHY ARE YOU--
AND *YOU*...
...HOW DID YOU COME INTO THIS WORL--
...
FORGET IT. ANY WINE AROUND? I NEED A DRINK!
WHAT'S WRONG WITH TAMA-HOME?
DID SOMETHING HAPPEN?
KA-CHAK

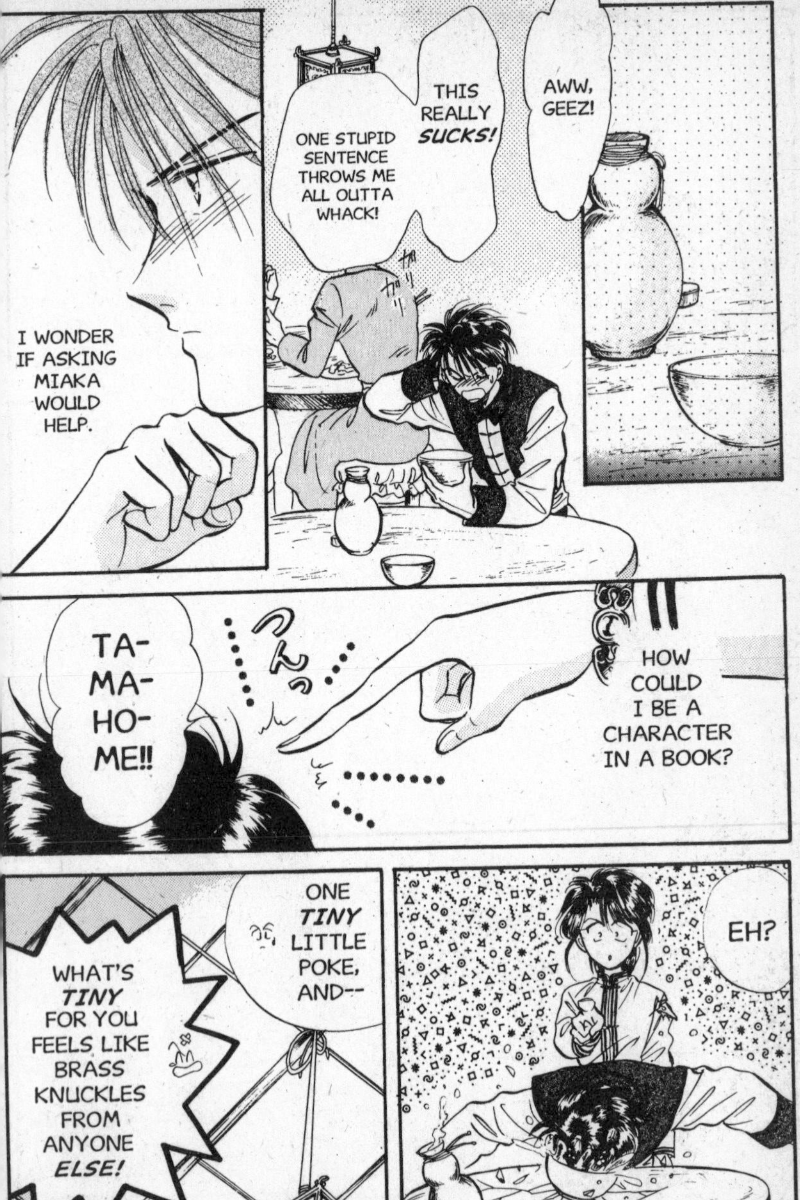
AWW, GEEZ!
THIS REALLY SUCKS!
ONE STUPID SENTENCE THROWS ME ALL OUTTA WHACK!
I WONDER IF ASKING MIAKA WOULD HELP.
HOW COULD I BE A CHARACTER IN A BOOK?
つんっ
TA-MA-HO-ME!!
EH?
ONE TINY LITTLE POKE, AND--
WHAT'S TINY FOR YOU FEELS LIKE BRASS KNUCKLES FROM ANYONE ELSE!

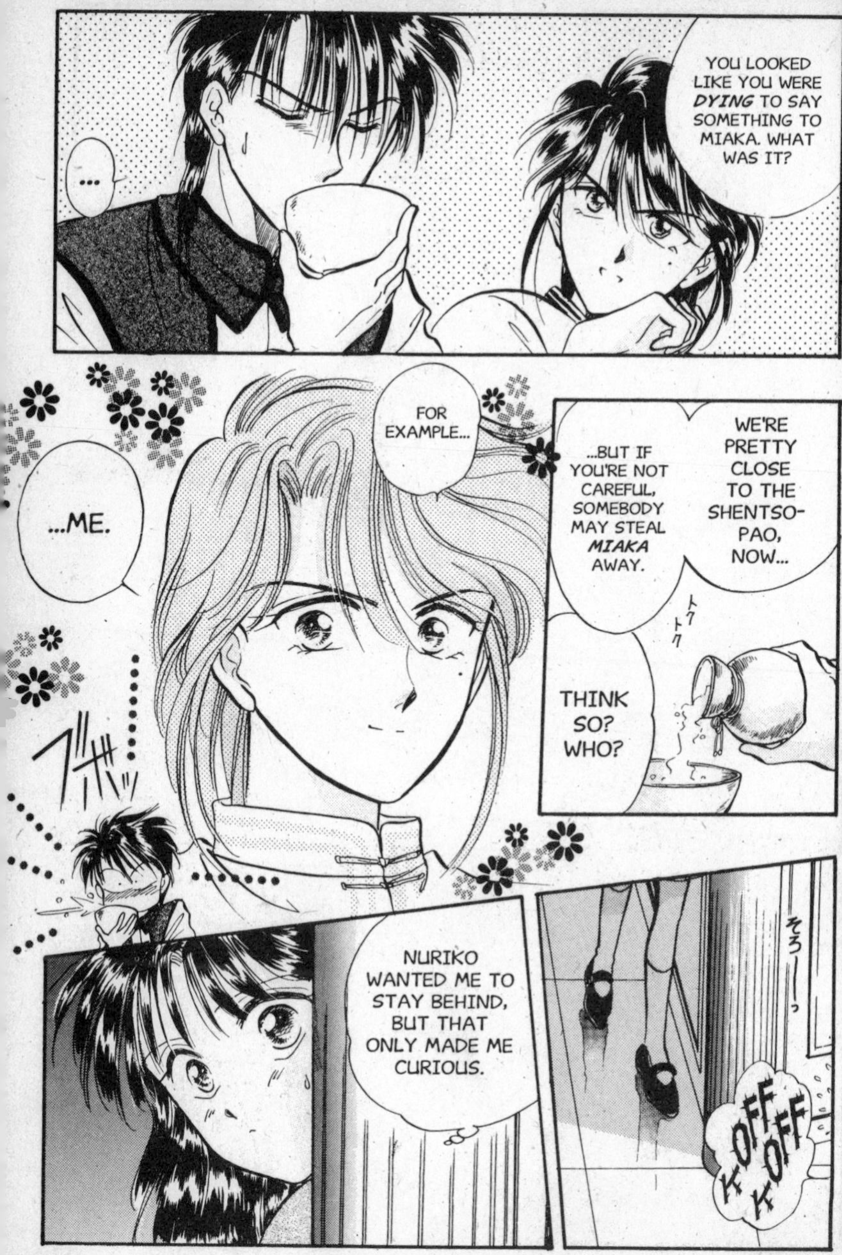
YOU LOOKED LIKE YOU WERE *DYING* TO SAY SOMETHING TO MIAKA. WHAT WAS IT?
...
WE'RE PRETTY CLOSE TO THE SHENTSO-PAO, NOW...
...BUT IF YOU'RE NOT CAREFUL, SOMEBODY MAY STEAL *MIAKA* AWAY.
THINK SO? WHO?
FOR EXAMPLE...
...ME.
KOFF KOFF
NURIKO WANTED ME TO STAY BEHIND, BUT THAT ONLY MADE ME CURIOUS.

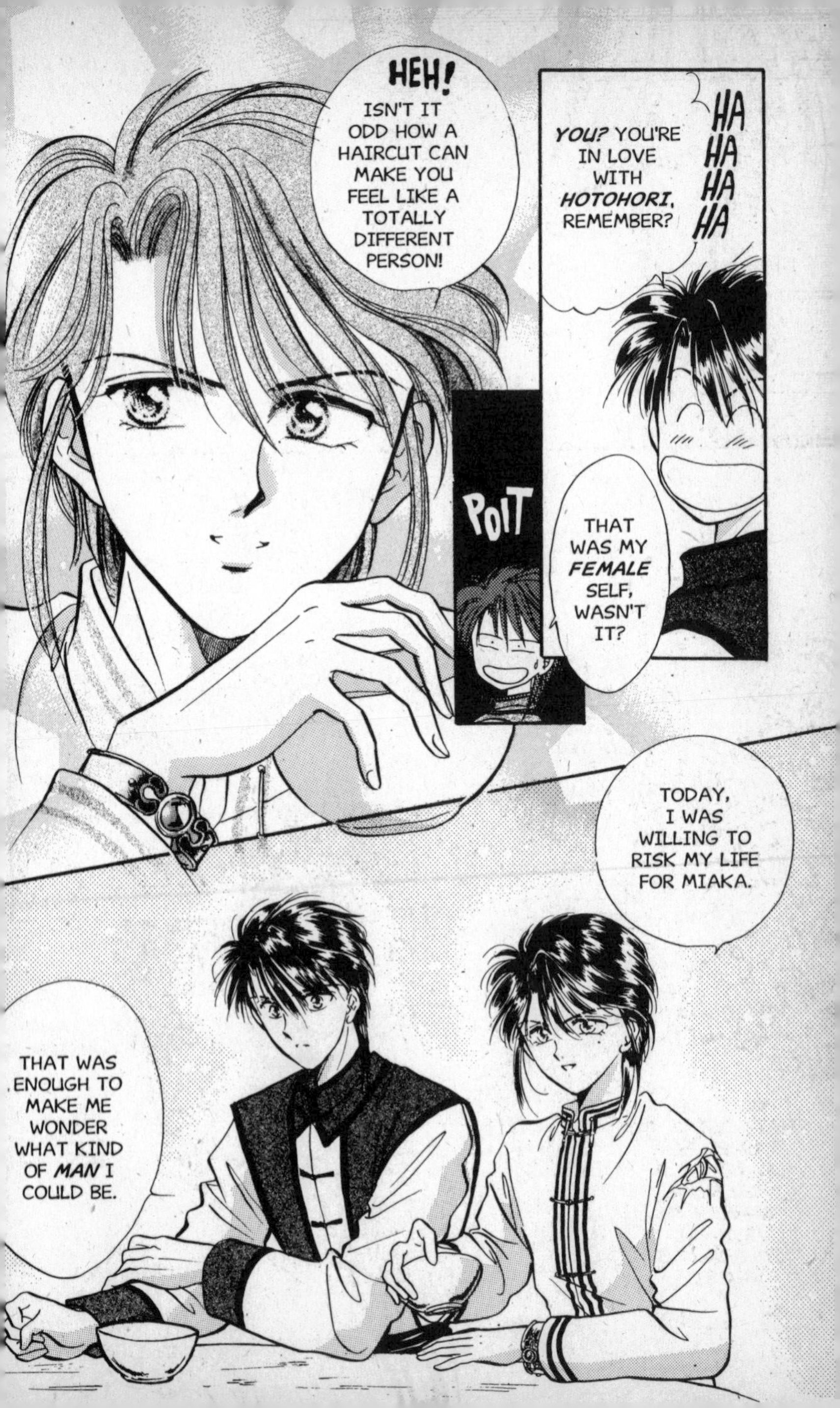
HA HA HA HA
YOU? YOU'RE IN LOVE WITH HOTOHORI, REMEMBER?
POIT
THAT WAS MY FEMALE SELF, WASN'T IT?
HEH!
ISN'T IT ODD HOW A HAIRCUT CAN MAKE YOU FEEL LIKE A TOTALLY DIFFERENT PERSON!
TODAY, I WAS WILLING TO RISK MY LIFE FOR MIAKA.
THAT WAS ENOUGH TO MAKE ME WONDER WHAT KIND OF MAN I COULD BE.

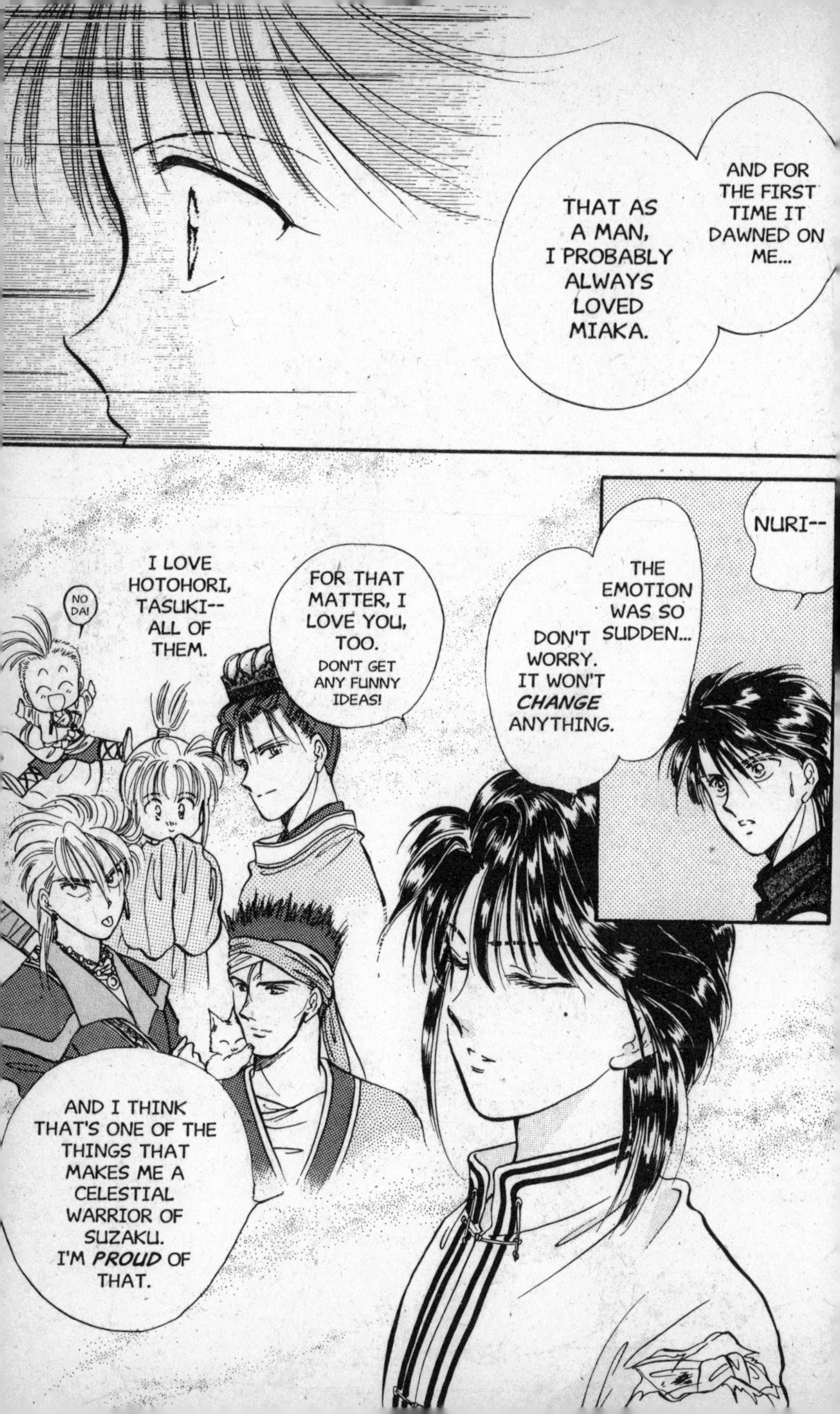

AND FOR THE FIRST TIME IT DAWNED ON ME...
THAT AS A MAN, I PROBABLY ALWAYS LOVED MIAKA.
NURI--
THE EMOTION WAS SO SUDDEN...
DON'T WORRY. IT WON'T *CHANGE* ANYTHING.
FOR THAT MATTER, I LOVE YOU, TOO.
DON'T GET ANY FUNNY IDEAS!
I LOVE HOTOHORI, TASUKI-- ALL OF THEM.
NO DA!
AND I THINK THAT'S ONE OF THE THINGS THAT MAKES ME A CELESTIAL WARRIOR OF SUZAKU. I'M *PROUD* OF THAT.

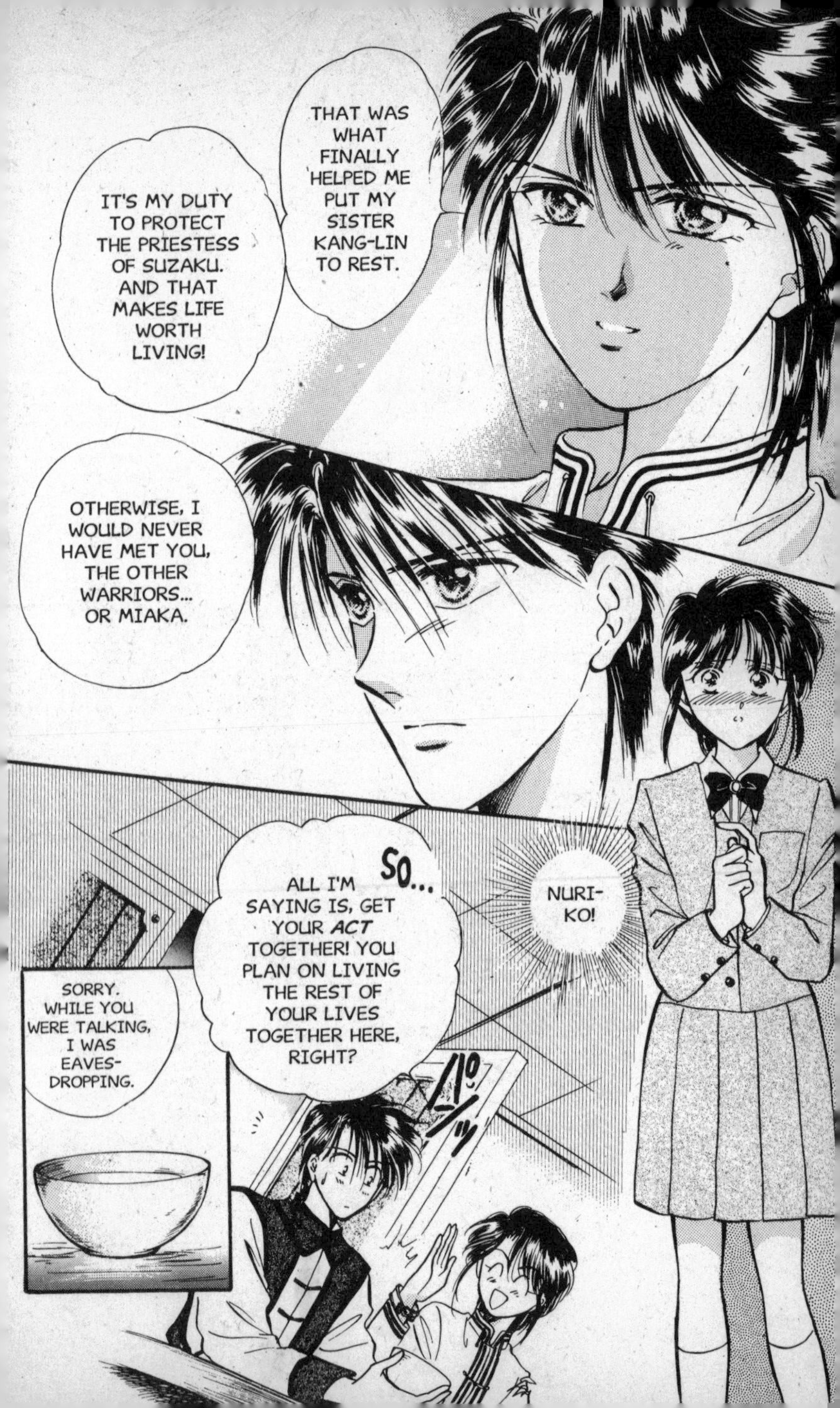

THAT WAS WHAT FINALLY HELPED ME PUT MY SISTER KANG-LIN TO REST.
IT'S MY DUTY TO PROTECT THE PRIESTESS OF SUZAKU. AND THAT MAKES LIFE WORTH LIVING!
OTHERWISE, I WOULD NEVER HAVE MET YOU, THE OTHER WARRIORS... OR MIAKA.
NURI-KO!
SO...
ALL I'M SAYING IS, GET YOUR *ACT* TOGETHER! YOU PLAN ON LIVING THE REST OF YOUR LIVES TOGETHER HERE, RIGHT?
SORRY. WHILE YOU WERE TALKING, I WAS EAVES-DROPPING.

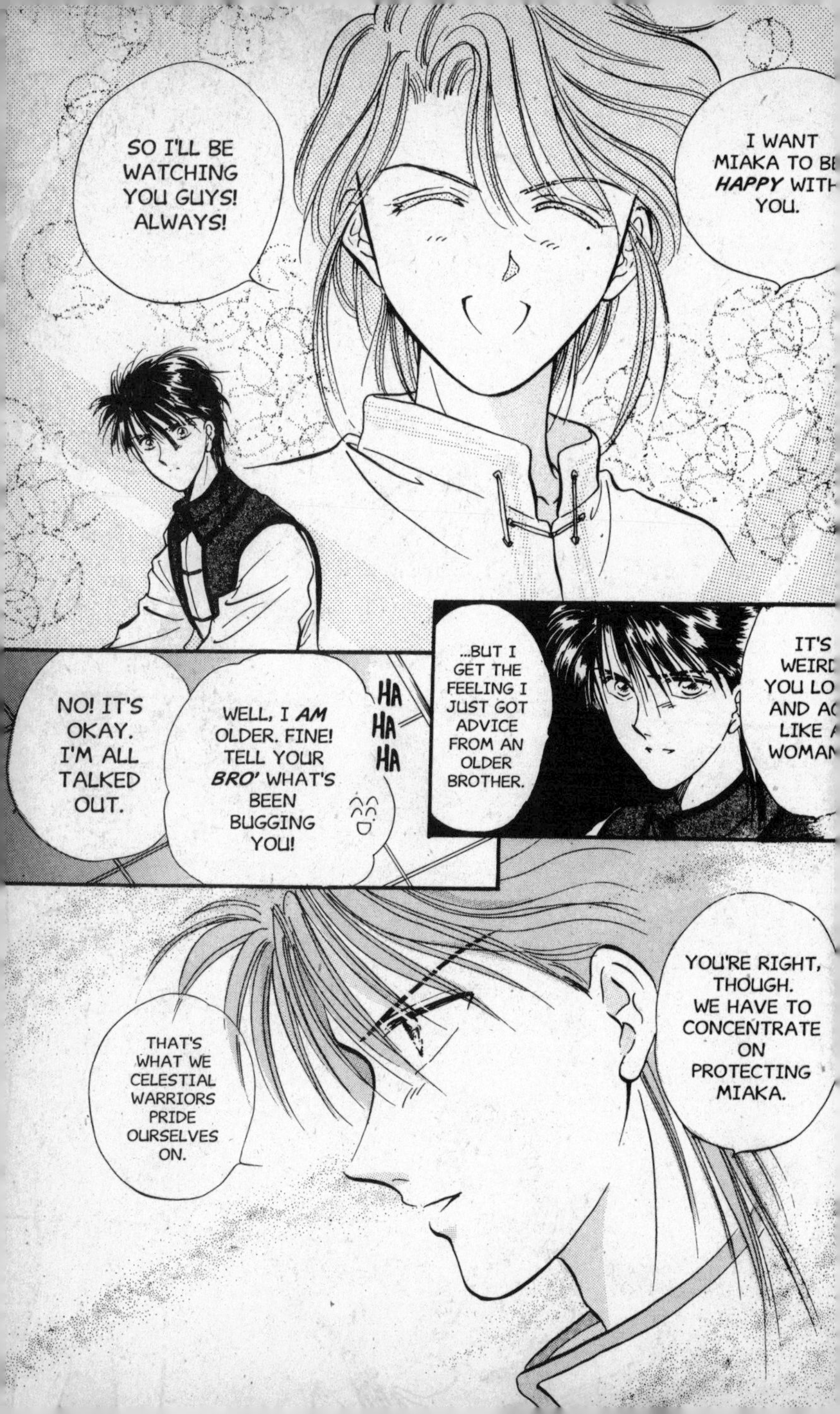
I WANT MIAKA TO BE *HAPPY* WITH YOU.
SO I'LL BE WATCHING YOU GUYS! ALWAYS!
IT'S WEIRD YOU LO AND AC LIKE A WOMAN
...BUT I GET THE FEELING I JUST GOT ADVICE FROM AN OLDER BROTHER.
HA HA HA
WELL, I *AM* OLDER. FINE! TELL YOUR *BRO'* WHAT'S BEEN BUGGING YOU!
NO! IT'S OKAY. I'M ALL TALKED OUT.
YOU'RE RIGHT, THOUGH. WE HAVE TO CONCENTRATE ON PROTECTING MIAKA.
THAT'S WHAT WE CELESTIAL WARRIORS PRIDE OURSELVES ON.

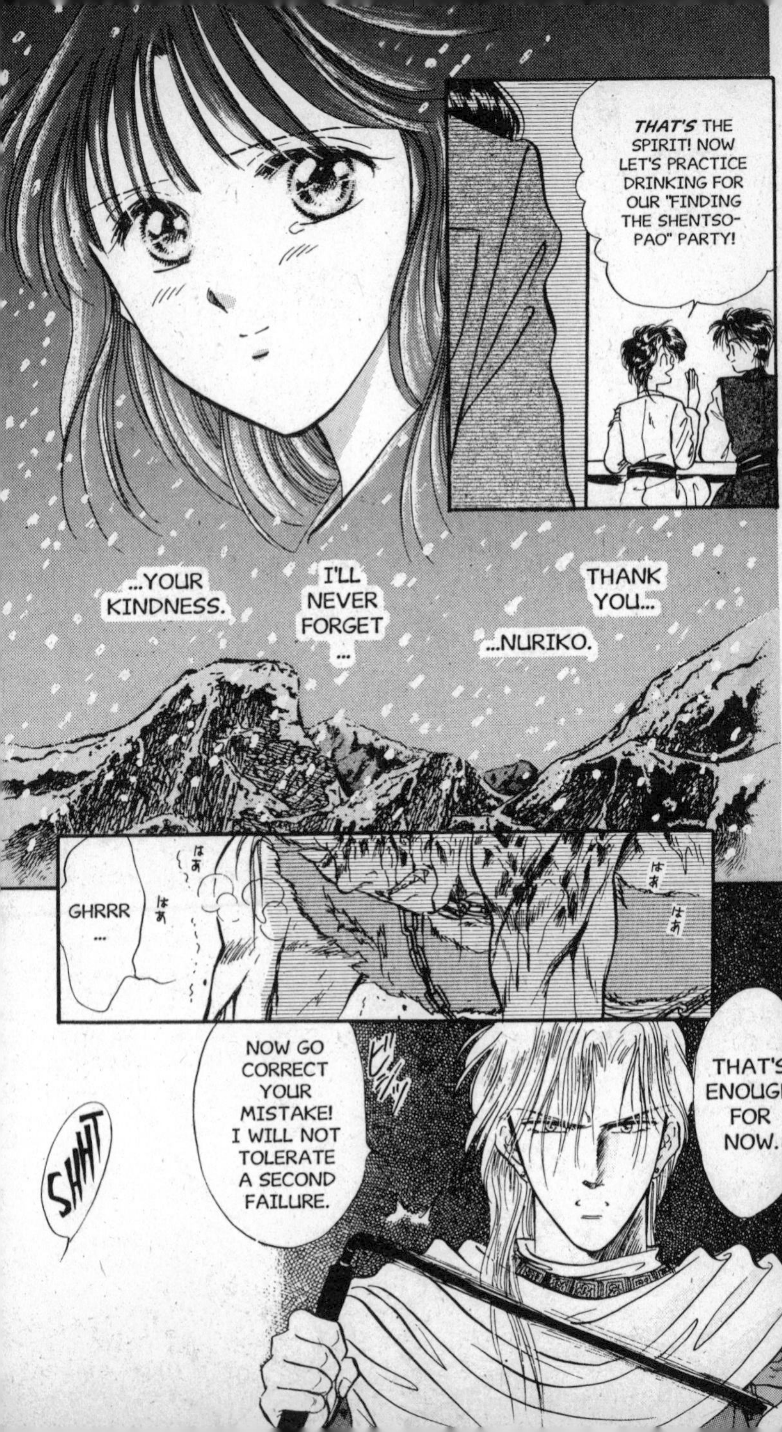

THAT'S THE SPIRIT! NOW LET'S PRACTICE DRINKING FOR OUR "FINDING THE SHENTSO-PAO" PARTY!
THANK YOU...
...NURIKO.
I'LL NEVER FORGET ...
...YOUR KINDNESS.
はあ
はあ
はあ
はあ
GHRRR ...
THAT'S ENOUGH FOR NOW.
NOW GO CORRECT YOUR MISTAKE! I WILL NOT TOLERATE A SECOND FAILURE.
SHHT

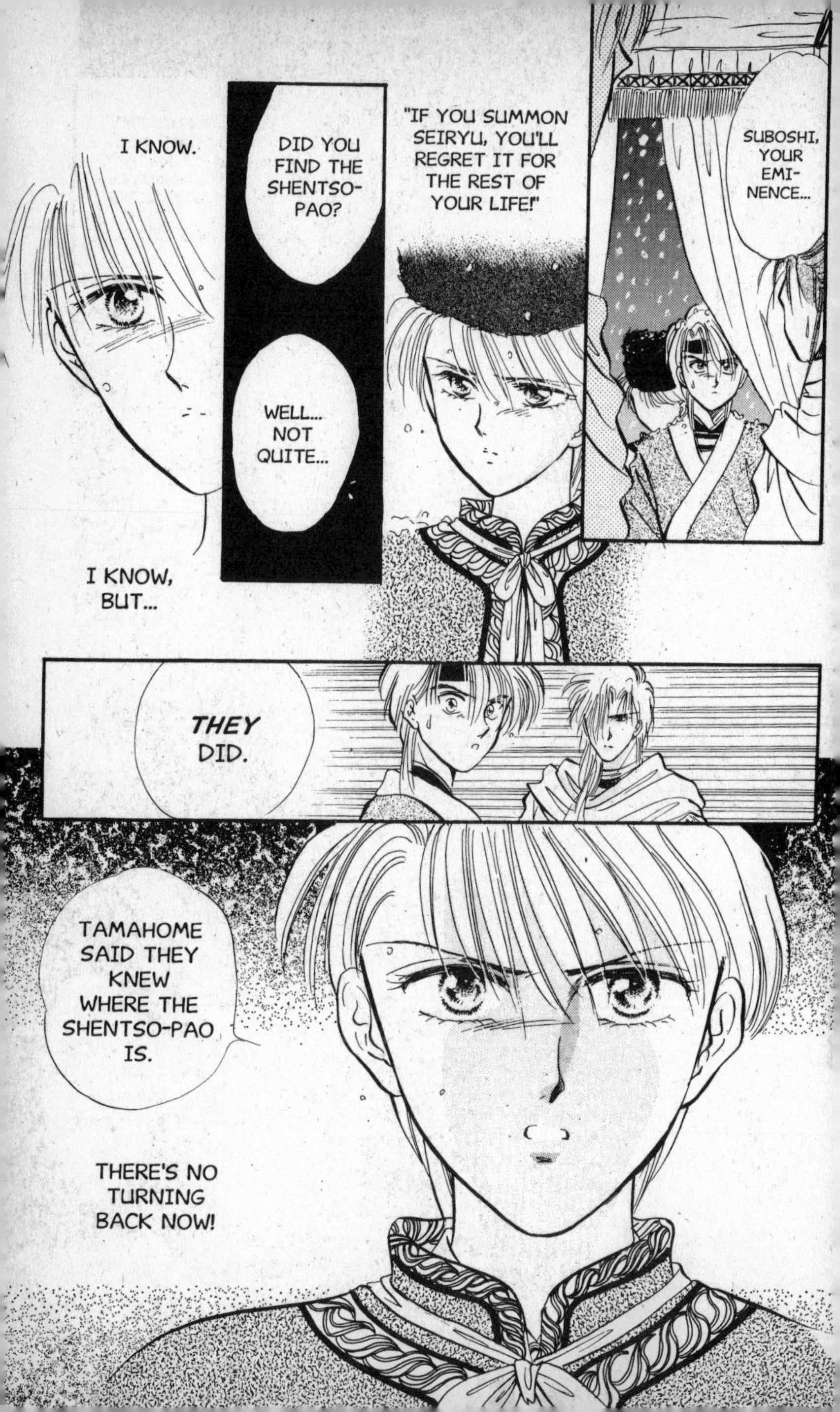
SUBOSHI, YOUR EMINENCE...
"IF YOU SUMMON SEIRYU, YOU'LL REGRET IT FOR THE REST OF YOUR LIFE!"
DID YOU FIND THE SHENTSO-PAO?
WELL... NOT QUITE...
I KNOW.
I KNOW, BUT...
THEY DID.
TAMAHOME SAID THEY KNEW WHERE THE SHENTSO-PAO IS.
THERE'S NO TURNING BACK NOW!

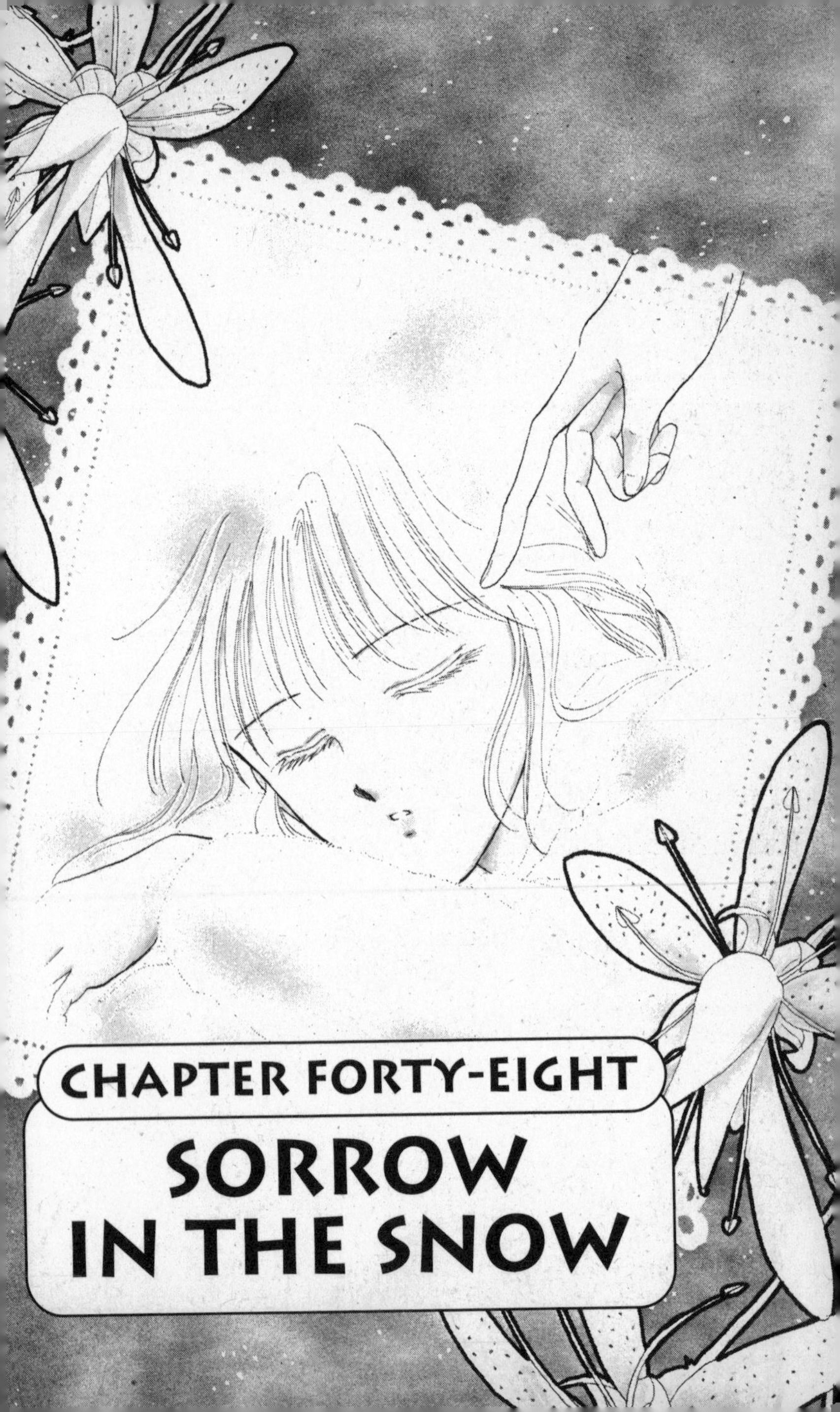
CHAPTER FORTY-EIGHT
SORROW IN THE SNOW

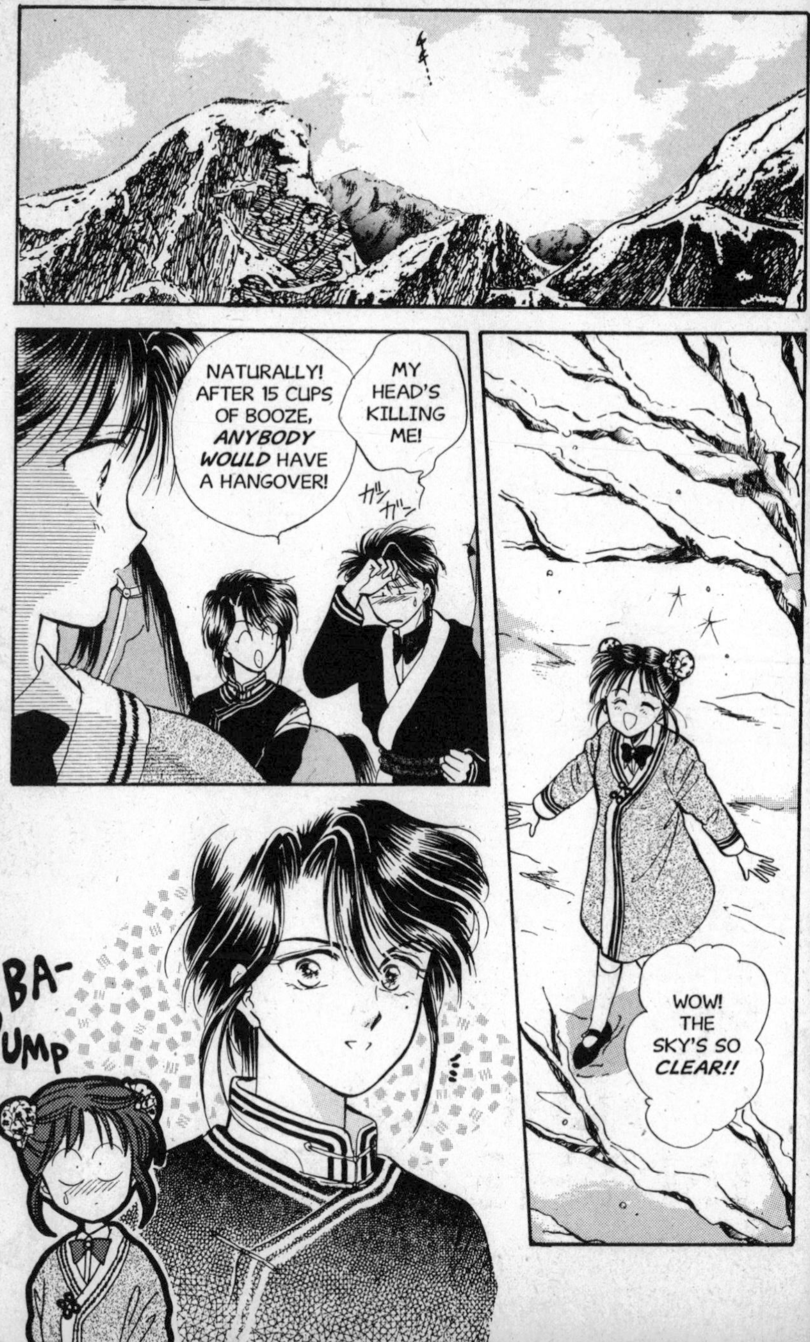
WOW! THE SKY'S SO CLEAR!!
MY HEAD'S KILLING ME!
ガンガン
NATURALLY! AFTER 15 CUPS OF BOOZE, ANYBODY WOULD HAVE A HANGOVER!
BA-DUMP

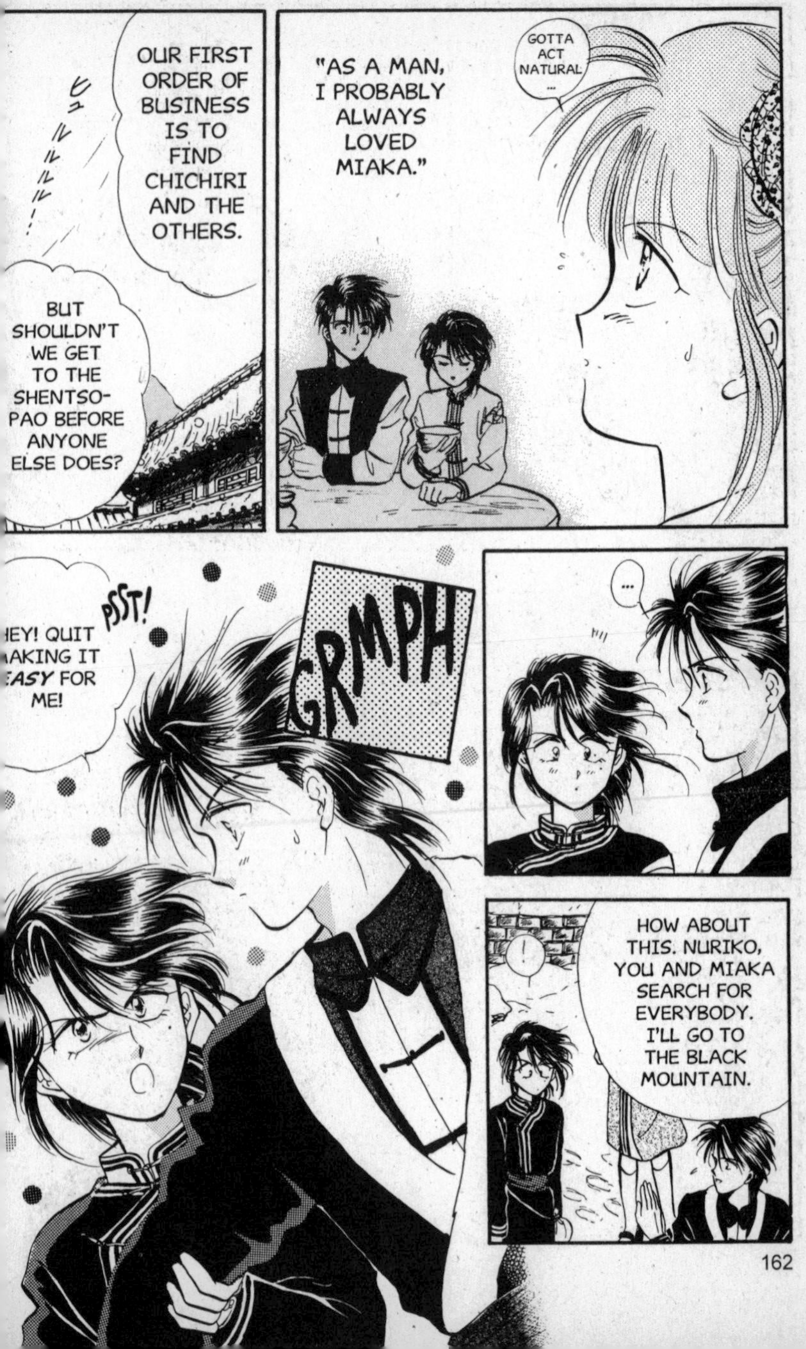
GOTTA ACT NATURAL ...
"AS A MAN, I PROBABLY ALWAYS LOVED MIAKA."
OUR FIRST ORDER OF BUSINESS IS TO FIND CHICHIRI AND THE OTHERS.
BUT SHOULDN'T WE GET TO THE SHENTSO-PAO BEFORE ANYONE ELSE DOES?
...
!
HOW ABOUT THIS. NURIKO, YOU AND MIAKA SEARCH FOR EVERYBODY. I'LL GO TO THE BLACK MOUNTAIN.
GRMPH
PSST!
EY! QUIT AKING IT ASY FOR ME!

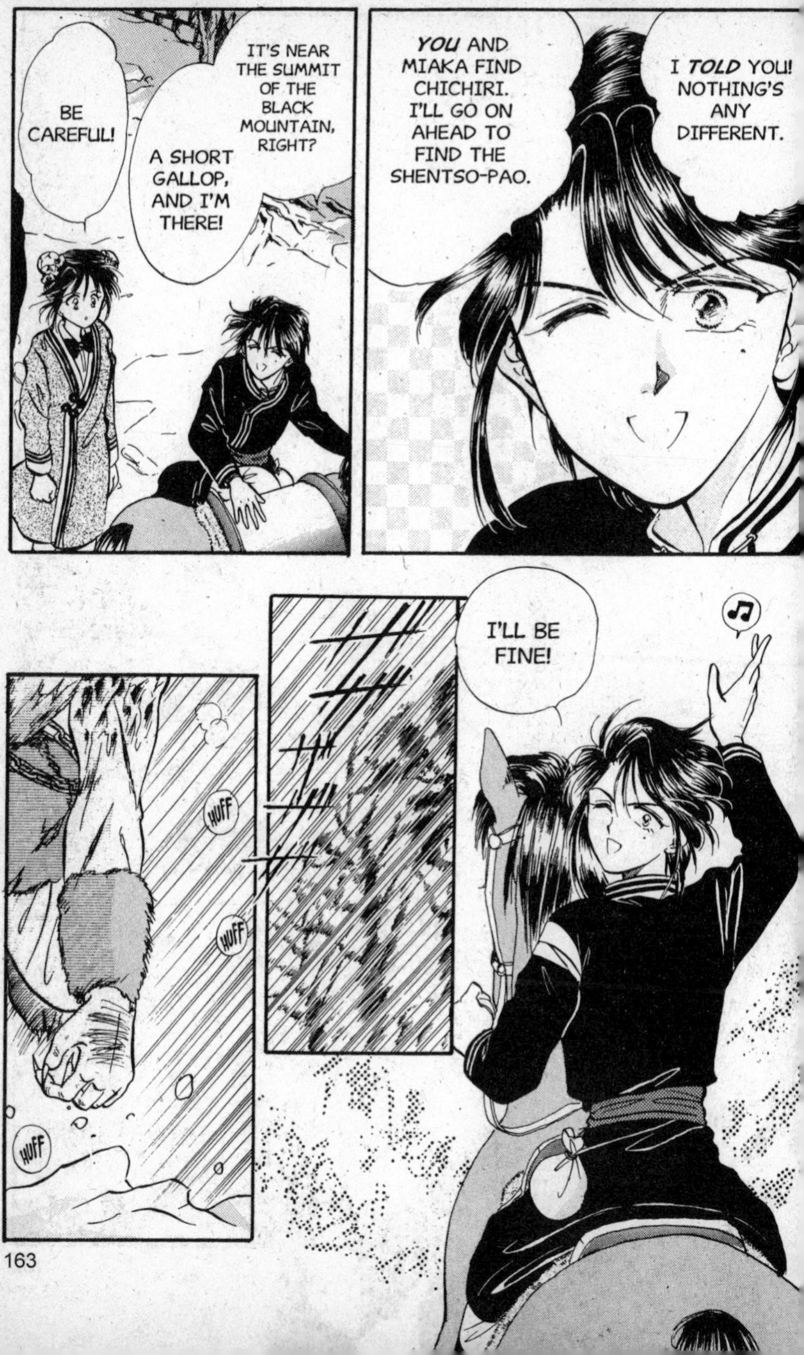
I *TOLD* YOU! NOTHING'S ANY DIFFERENT.
YOU AND MIAKA FIND CHICHIRI. I'LL GO ON AHEAD TO FIND THE SHENTSO-PAO.
IT'S NEAR THE SUMMIT OF THE BLACK MOUNTAIN, RIGHT?
A SHORT GALLOP, AND I'M THERE!
BE CAREFUL!
I'LL BE FINE!
♫
HUFF
HUFF
HUFF

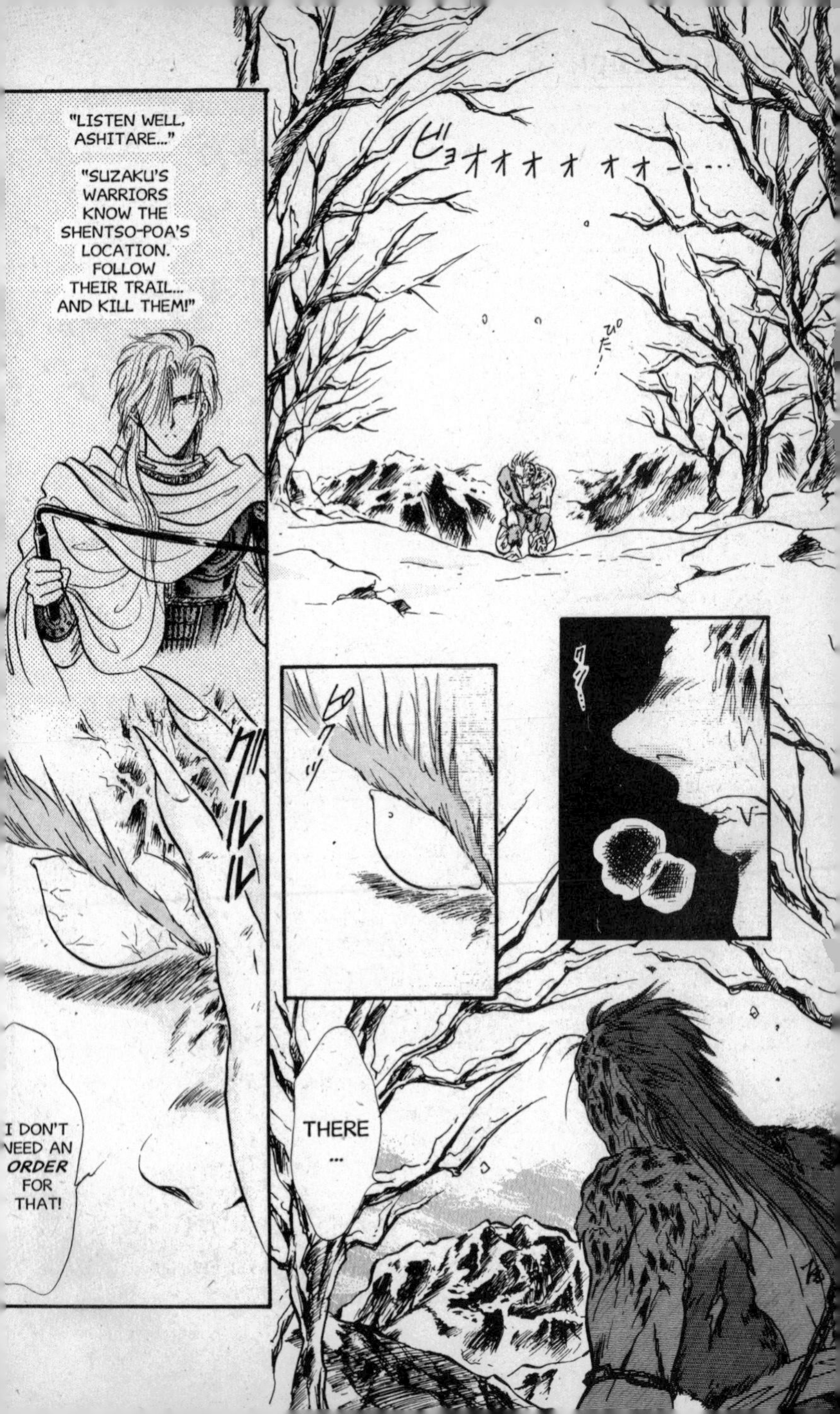
ビョオオオオ オオオー……
THERE ...
"LISTEN WELL, ASHITARE..."
"SUZAKU'S WARRIORS KNOW THE SHENTSO-POA'S LOCATION. FOLLOW THEIR TRAIL... AND KILL THEM!"
I DON'T NEED AN *ORDER* FOR THAT!

This is the last chat section of this volume. I'll share some recent letters that surprised me. One writer observed, "Doesn't Ashitare look like Blanka from 'Street Fighter II'?" I just burst out laughing! I didn't do it on purpose! But maybe in my subconscious, I wanted revenge for all the fights where Blanka beat me! However, Ashitare had nothing at all to do with that! Bei-Jia is based on Mongolia. Mongolia got me thinking of Genghis Khan, which got me thinking of his nickname "Blue Wolf," and I went from there to *wolf*!! It's a pretty simple idea. What if I based a human character on a wolf? Ha ha ha. Next time I'll play Ashitare and defeat Blanka!

The next letter was more serious. It mentioned that the cover of my graphic novel "Suna no Tiara" ("Tiara of Sand") looked just like an anime calendar!! That was a total coincidence! The cover for the graphic novel was simply taken from the cover of the "Shôjo Comic" anthology magazine that "Suna no Tiara" was printed in two years ago! I usually draw new art for each graphic novel, but back then, I was just too busy (I mean it was already early August), so my editor came up with the idea of using the magazine cover for the graphic novel. (I had them wait for the back cover illustration, which was an original.) But I'm not implying that the guys who made the animation calendar stole my idea. Given how much manga and anime there is in the world, it's only a matter of time before two people come up with the same design independently. So don't let it phase you!

Besides, I don't have the guts to plagiarize! ☺ I'm too much of a coward to lie. And I'm such a terrible writer, I'll bet I'm giving you wrong impressions even in a partial-page chat section! ☺

Thank you for all your letters and presents! To the fan from Aomori, I know it's a little late, but thank you! Your gift was delicious! Geez! I got it more than half a year ago! And I'll try to keep my stress to a minimum, but I'll still be working hard!!

See you next time!!

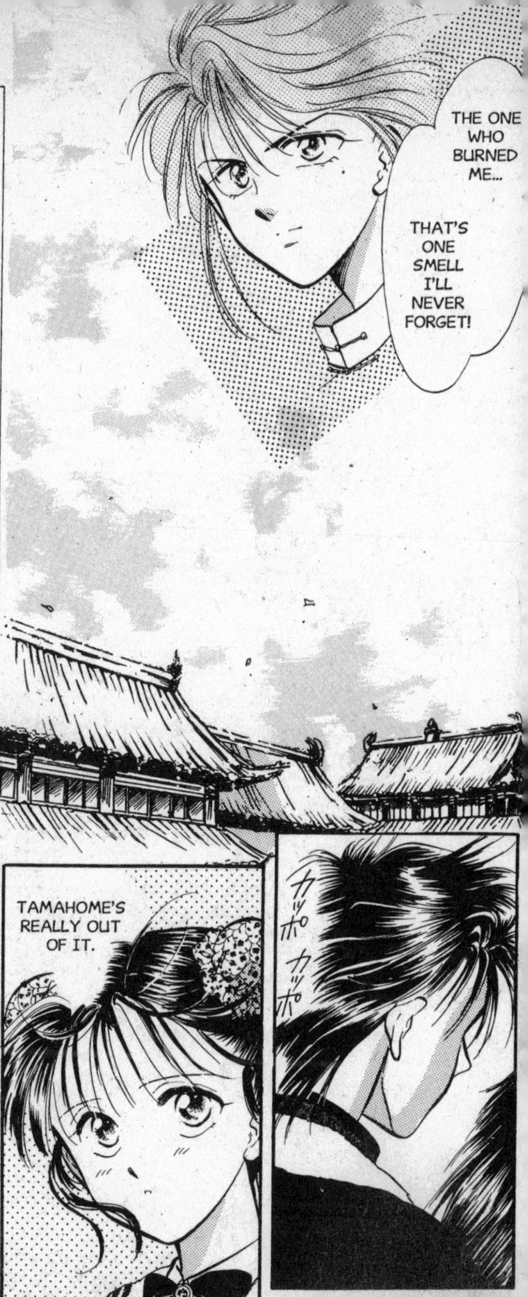
THE ONE WHO BURNED ME...
THAT'S ONE SMELL I'LL NEVER FORGET!
カッポ カッポ
TAMAHOME'S REALLY OUT OF IT.

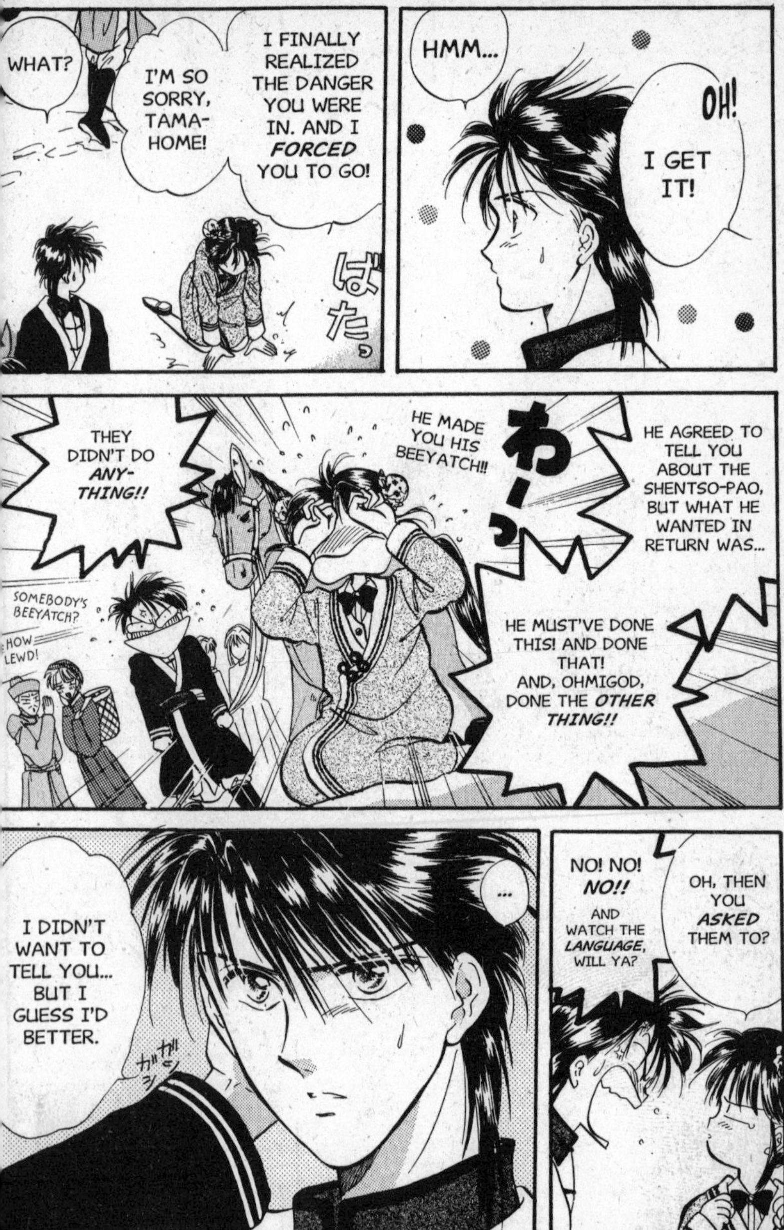
HMM...
OH!
I GET IT!
I FINALLY REALIZED THE DANGER YOU WERE IN. AND I *FORCED* YOU TO GO!
I'M SO SORRY, TAMA-HOME!
WHAT?
ばたっ
HE AGREED TO TELL YOU ABOUT THE SHENTSO-PAO, BUT WHAT HE WANTED IN RETURN WAS...
わーっ
HE MADE YOU HIS BEEYATCH!!
THEY DIDN'T DO *ANYTHING!!*
HE MUST'VE DONE THIS! AND DONE THAT! AND, OHMIGOD, DONE THE *OTHER THING!!*
SOMEBODY'S BEEYATCH?
HOW LEWD!
OH, THEN YOU *ASKED* THEM TO?
NO! NO! *NO!!* AND WATCH THE *LANGUAGE*, WILL YA?
...
I DIDN'T WANT TO TELL YOU... BUT I GUESS I'D BETTER.

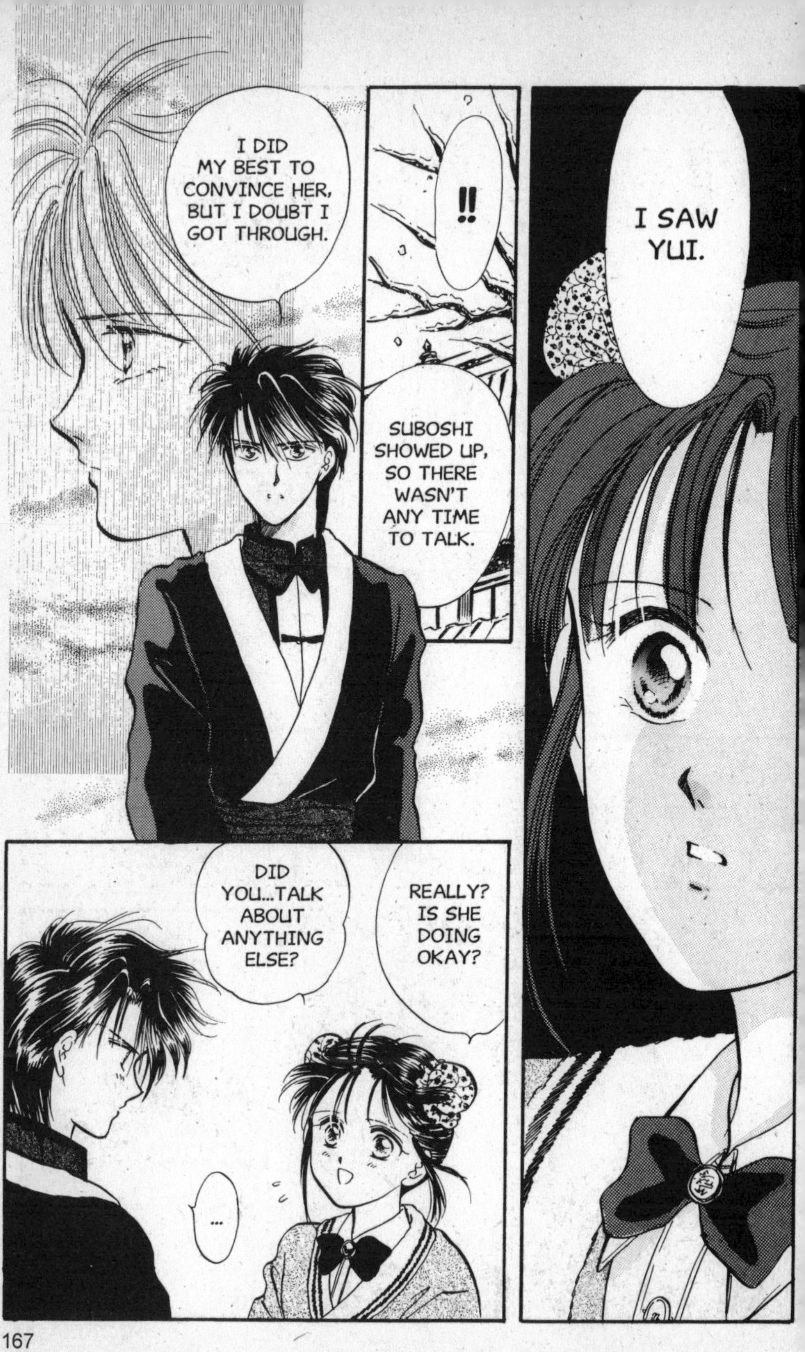
I SAW YUI.
!!
SUBOSHI SHOWED UP, SO THERE WASN'T ANY TIME TO TALK.
I DID MY BEST TO CONVINCE HER, BUT I DOUBT I GOT THROUGH.
REALLY? IS SHE DOING OKAY?
DID YOU...TALK ABOUT ANYTHING ELSE?
...

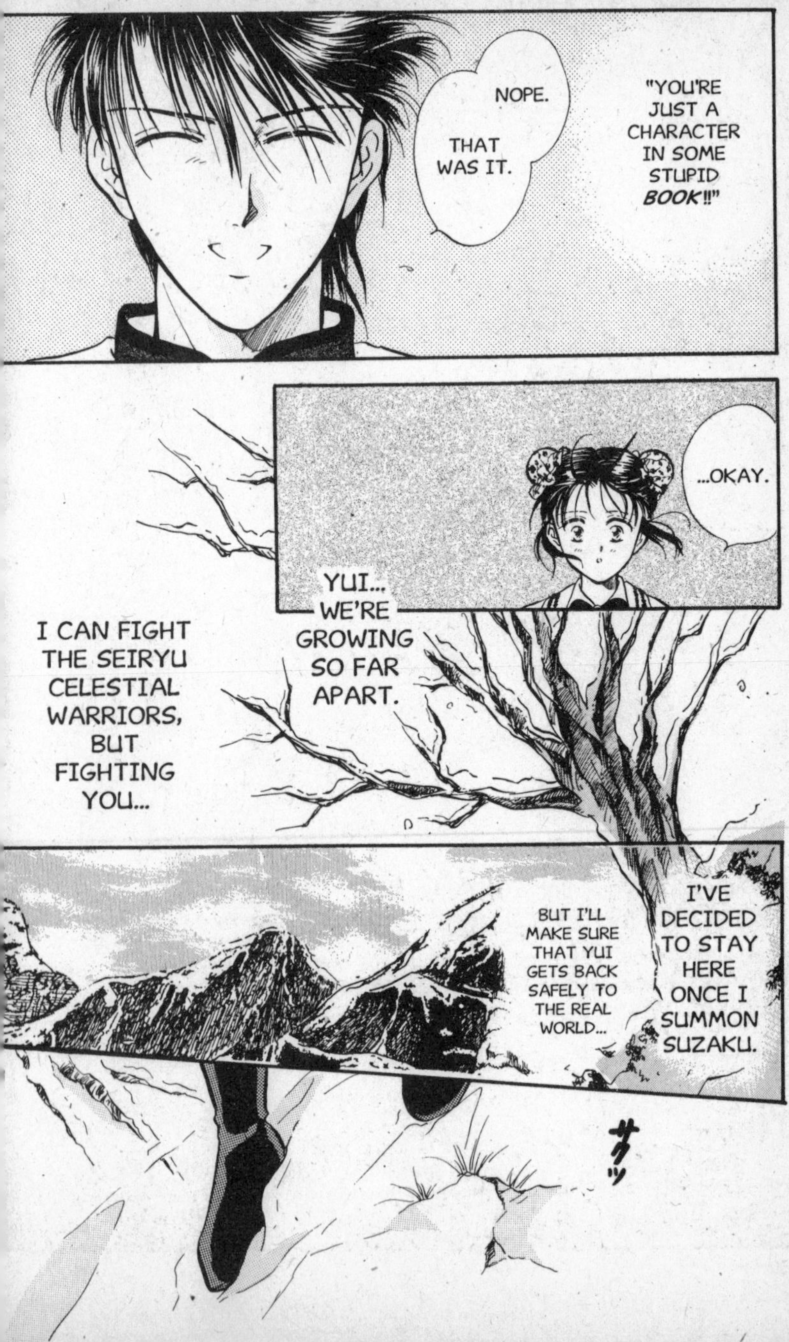
"YOU'RE JUST A CHARACTER IN SOME STUPID *BOOK*!!"
NOPE. THAT WAS IT.
...OKAY.
YUI... WE'RE GROWING SO FAR APART.
I CAN FIGHT THE SEIRYU CELESTIAL WARRIORS, BUT FIGHTING YOU...
I'VE DECIDED TO STAY HERE ONCE I SUMMON SUZAKU.
BUT I'LL MAKE SURE THAT YUI GETS BACK SAFELY TO THE REAL WORLD...
サクッ

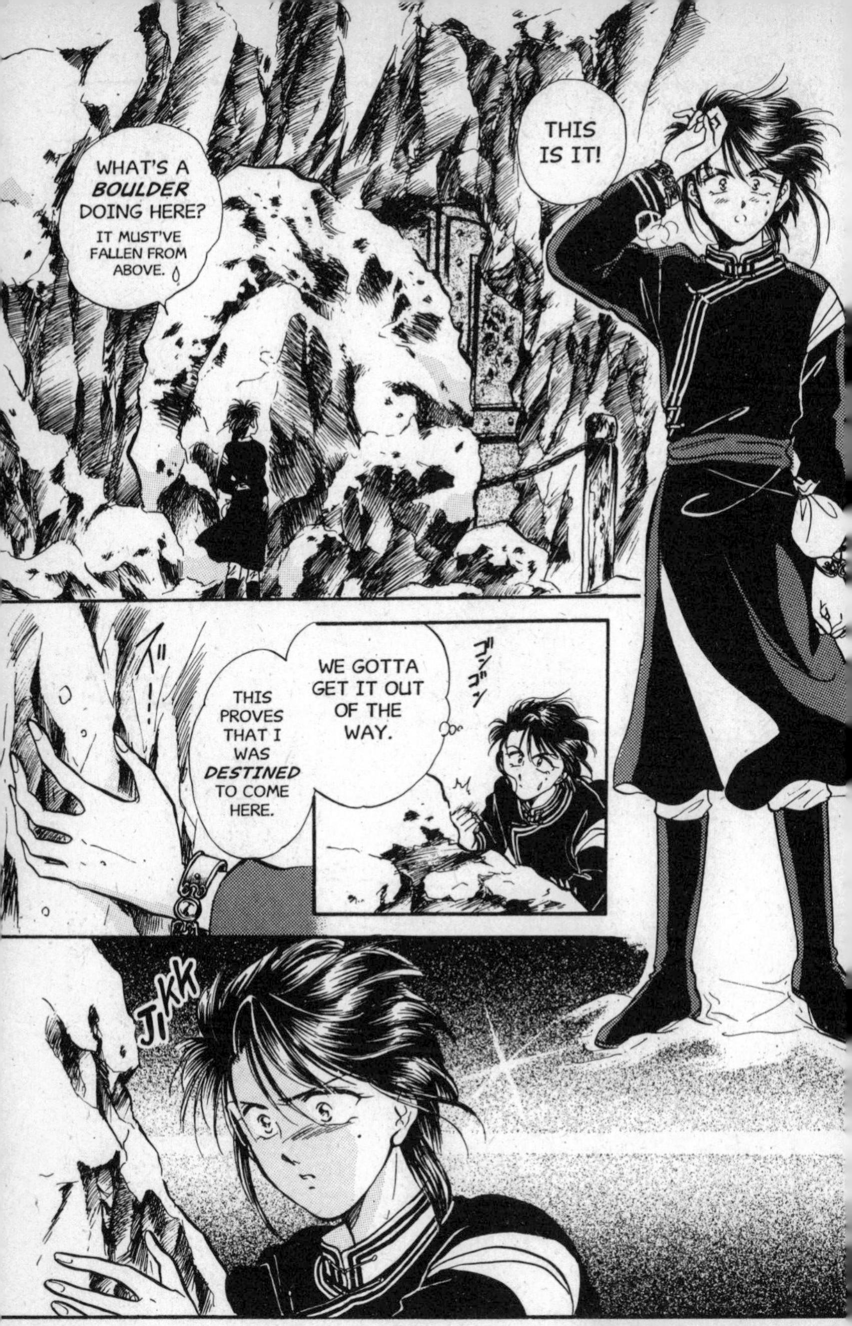

THIS IS IT!
WHAT'S A *BOULDER* DOING HERE?
IT MUST'VE FALLEN FROM ABOVE.
ゴン ゴン
WE GOTTA GET IT OUT OF THE WAY.
THIS PROVES THAT I WAS *DESTINED* TO COME HERE.
JIKK

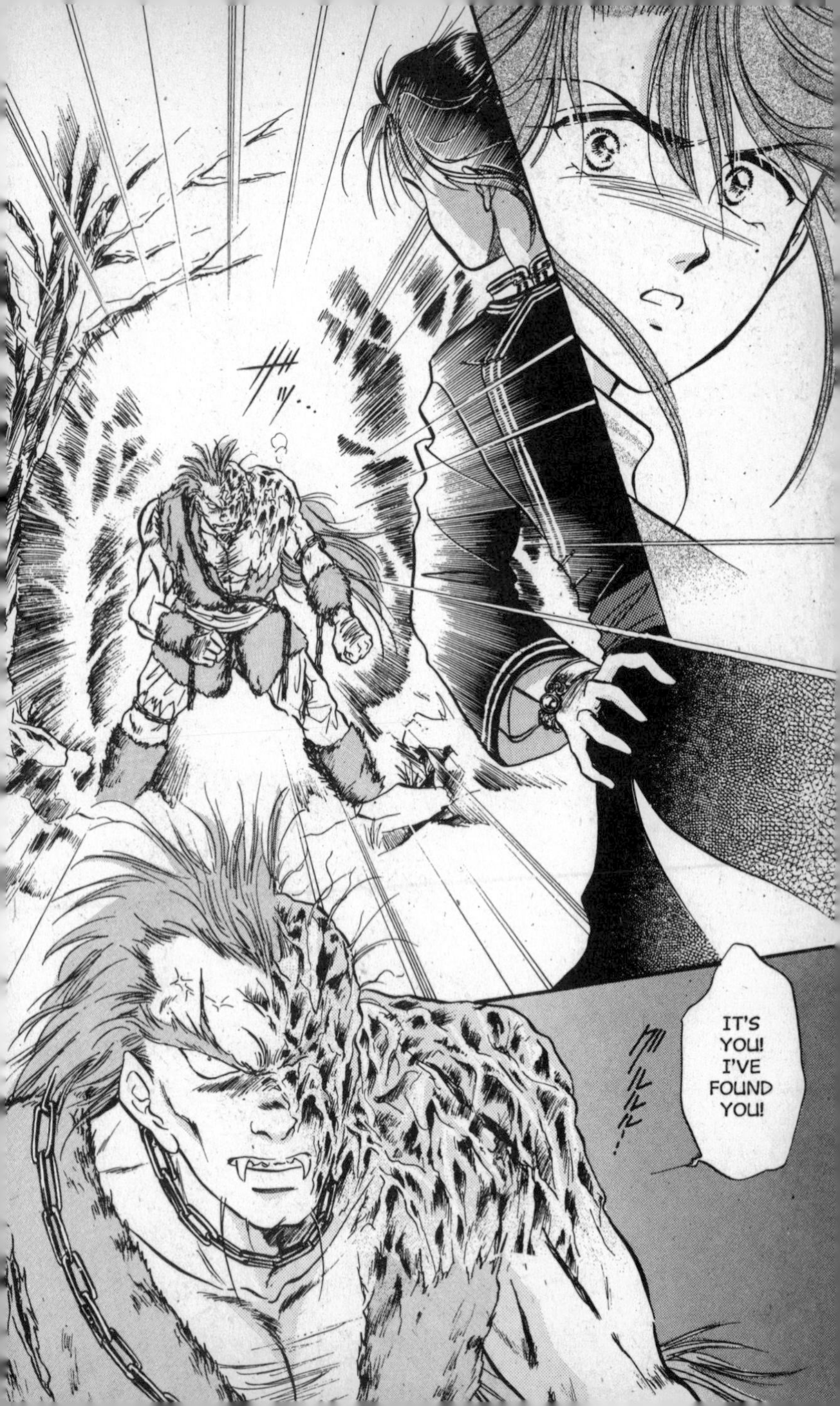
IT'S YOU! I'VE FOUND YOU!

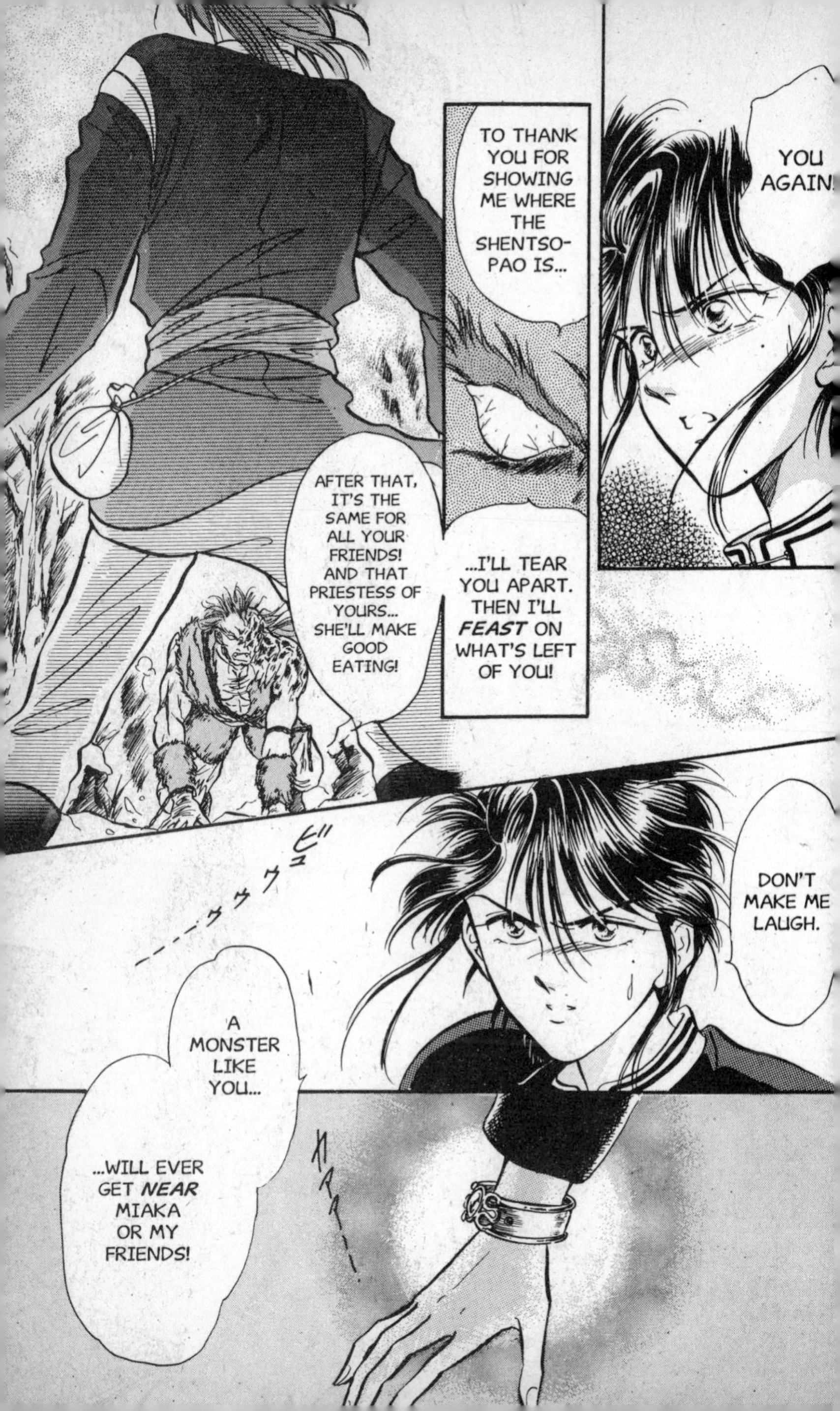
YOU AGAIN!
TO THANK YOU FOR SHOWING ME WHERE THE SHENTSO-PAO IS...
...I'LL TEAR YOU APART. THEN I'LL *FEAST* ON WHAT'S LEFT OF YOU!
AFTER THAT, IT'S THE SAME FOR ALL YOUR FRIENDS! AND THAT PRIESTESS OF YOURS... SHE'LL MAKE GOOD EATING!
DON'T MAKE ME LAUGH.
ビュウウウ
A MONSTER LIKE YOU...
...WILL EVER GET *NEAR* MIAKA OR MY FRIENDS!

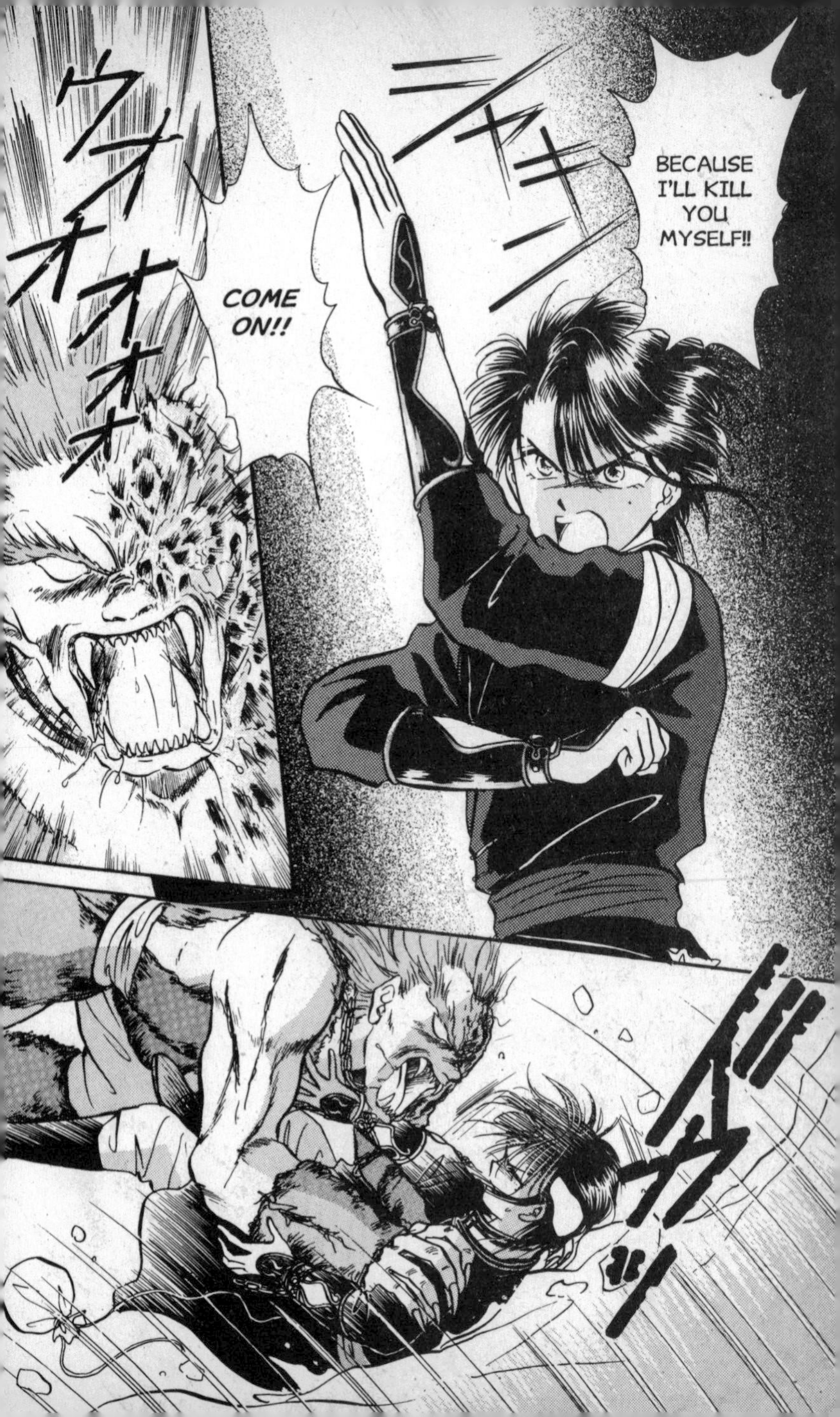
BECAUSE I'LL KILL YOU MYSELF!!
シャキーン
COME ON!!
ウオオオオ
ドスッ!

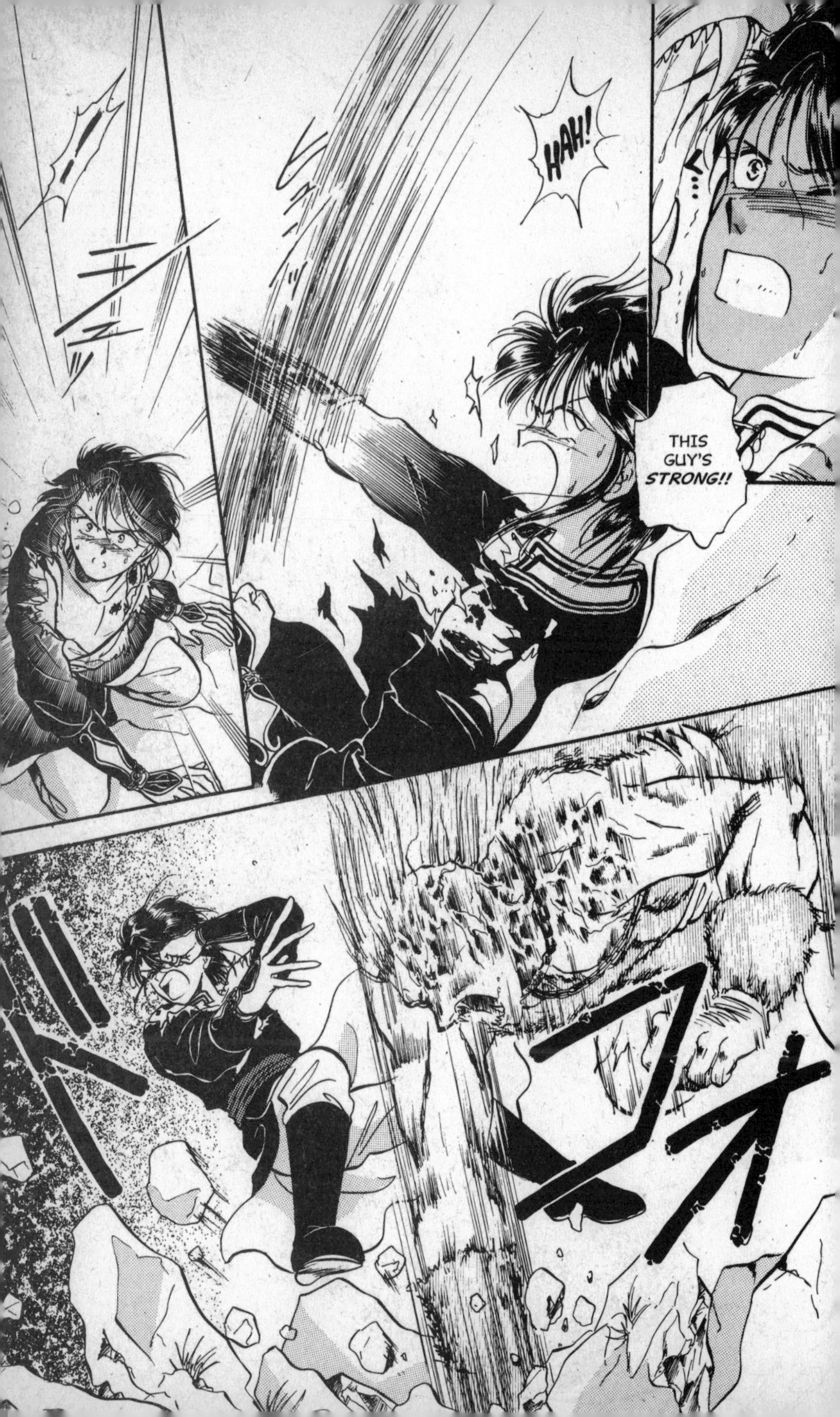
THIS GUY'S *STRONG!!*
HAH!

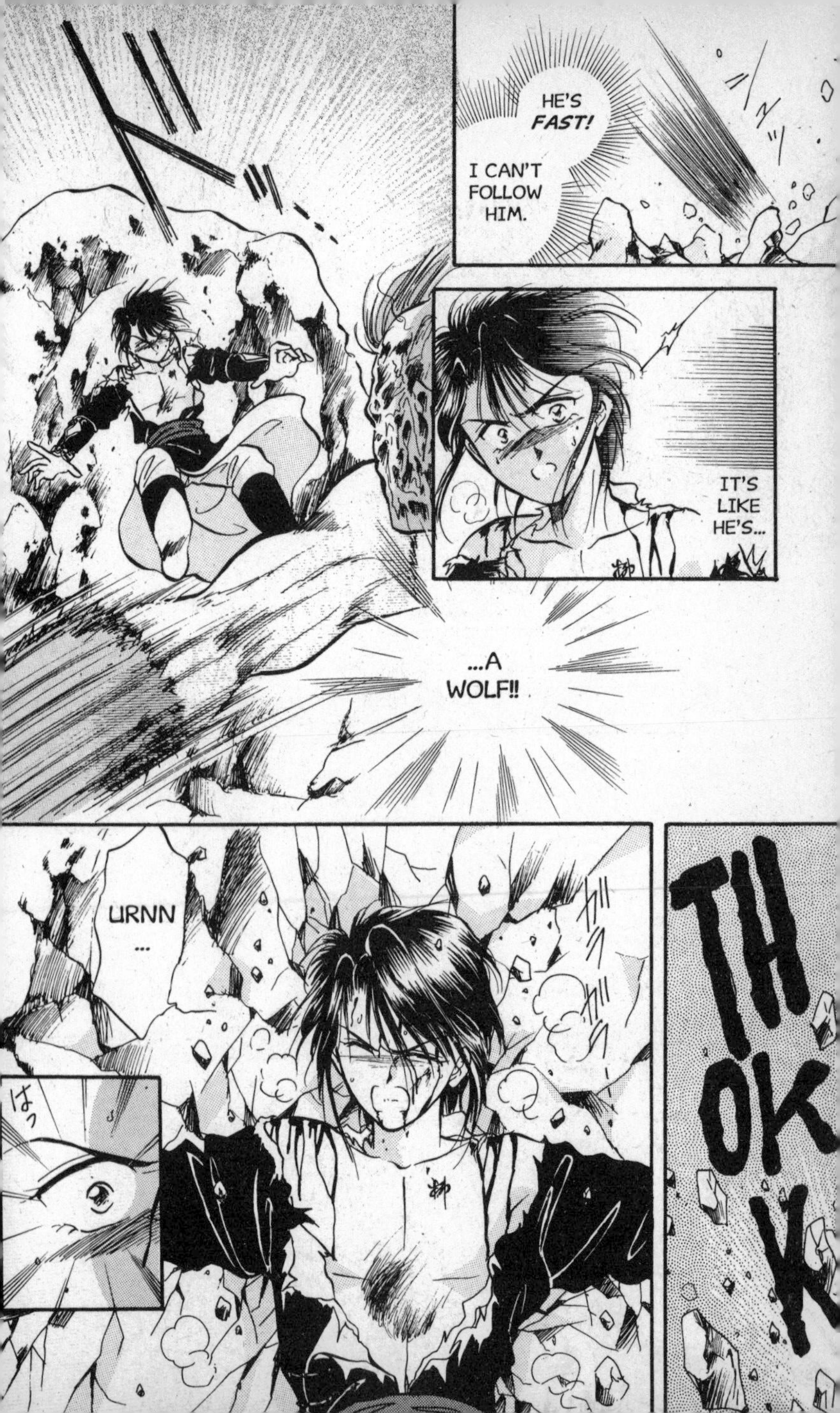

HE'S FAST!
I CAN'T FOLLOW HIM.
IT'S LIKE HE'S...
...A WOLF!!
THOKK
URNN ...
はっ

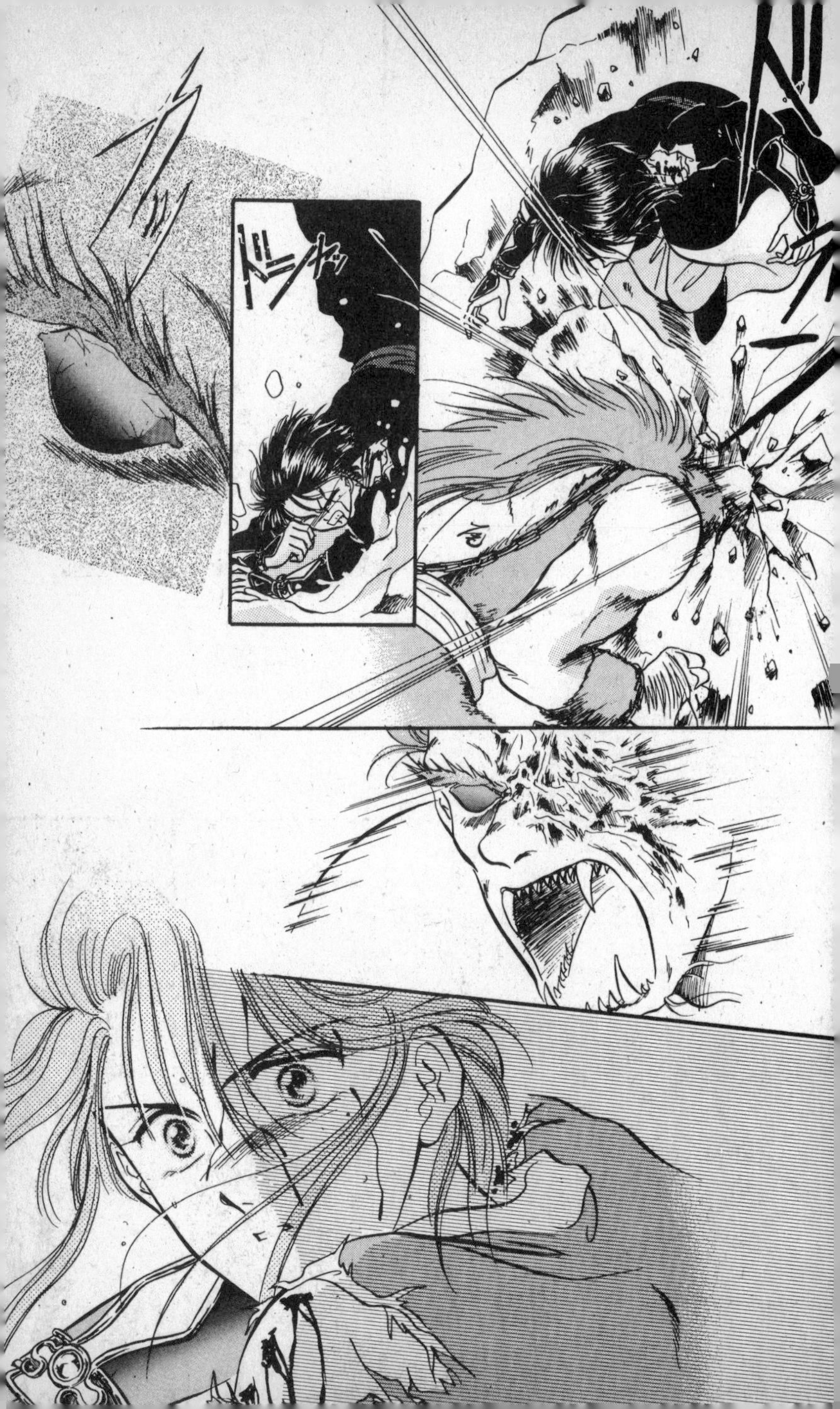

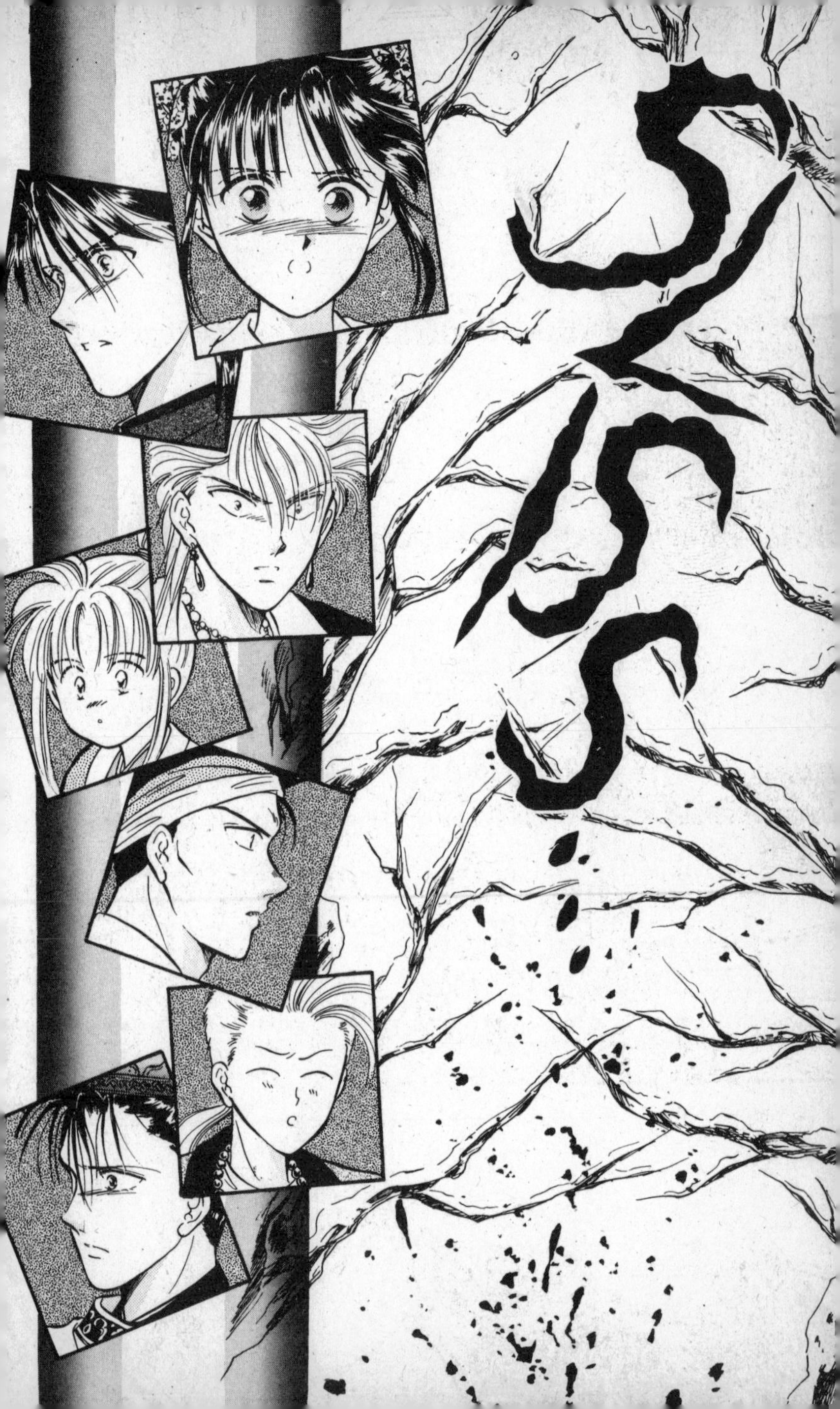

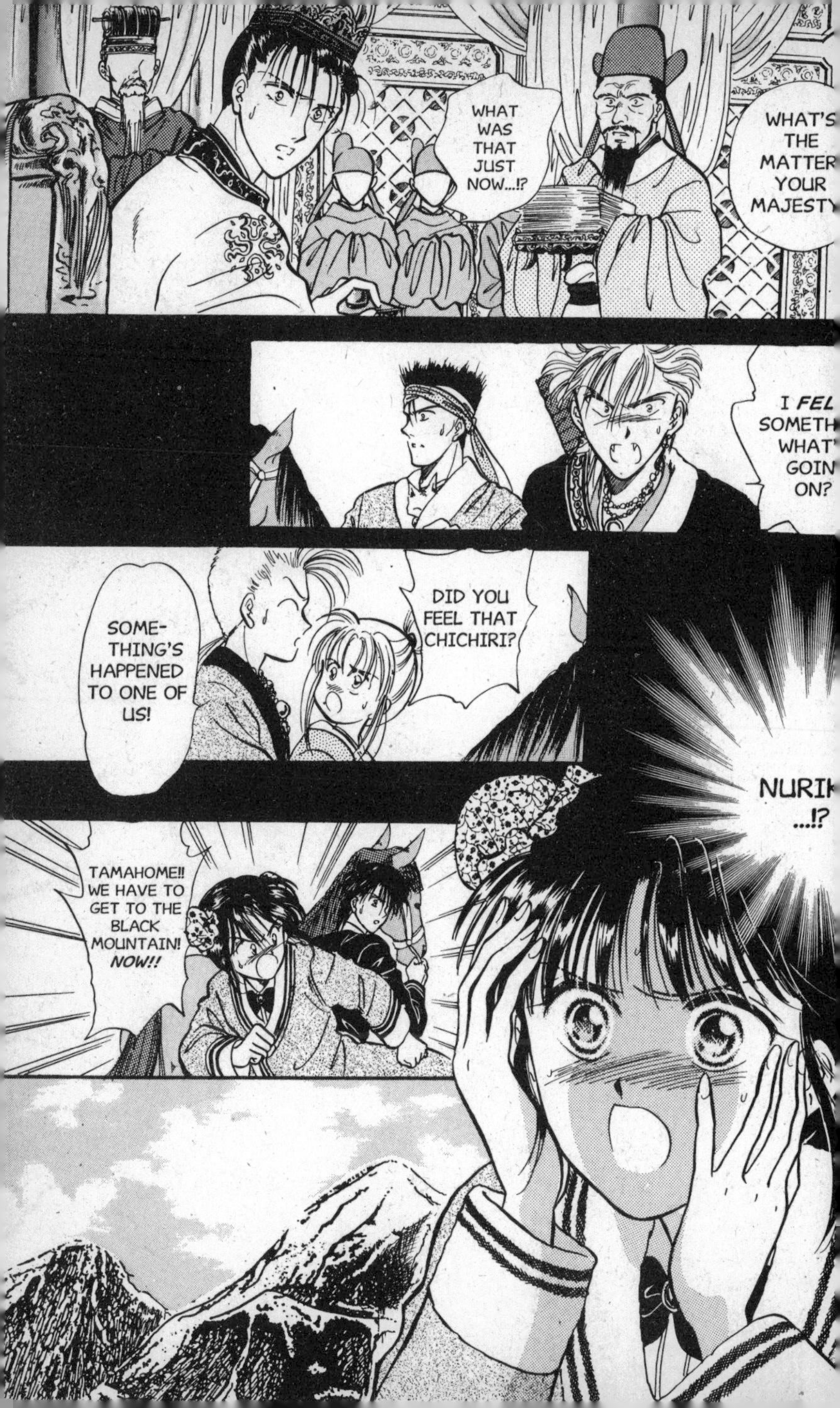
WHAT'S THE MATTER YOUR MAJESTY
WHAT WAS THAT JUST NOW...!?
I FEL SOMETH WHAT' GOIN ON?
DID YOU FEEL THAT CHICHIRI?
SOME-THING'S HAPPENED TO ONE OF US!
NURIK ...!?
TAMAHOME!! WE HAVE TO GET TO THE BLACK MOUNTAIN! NOW!!

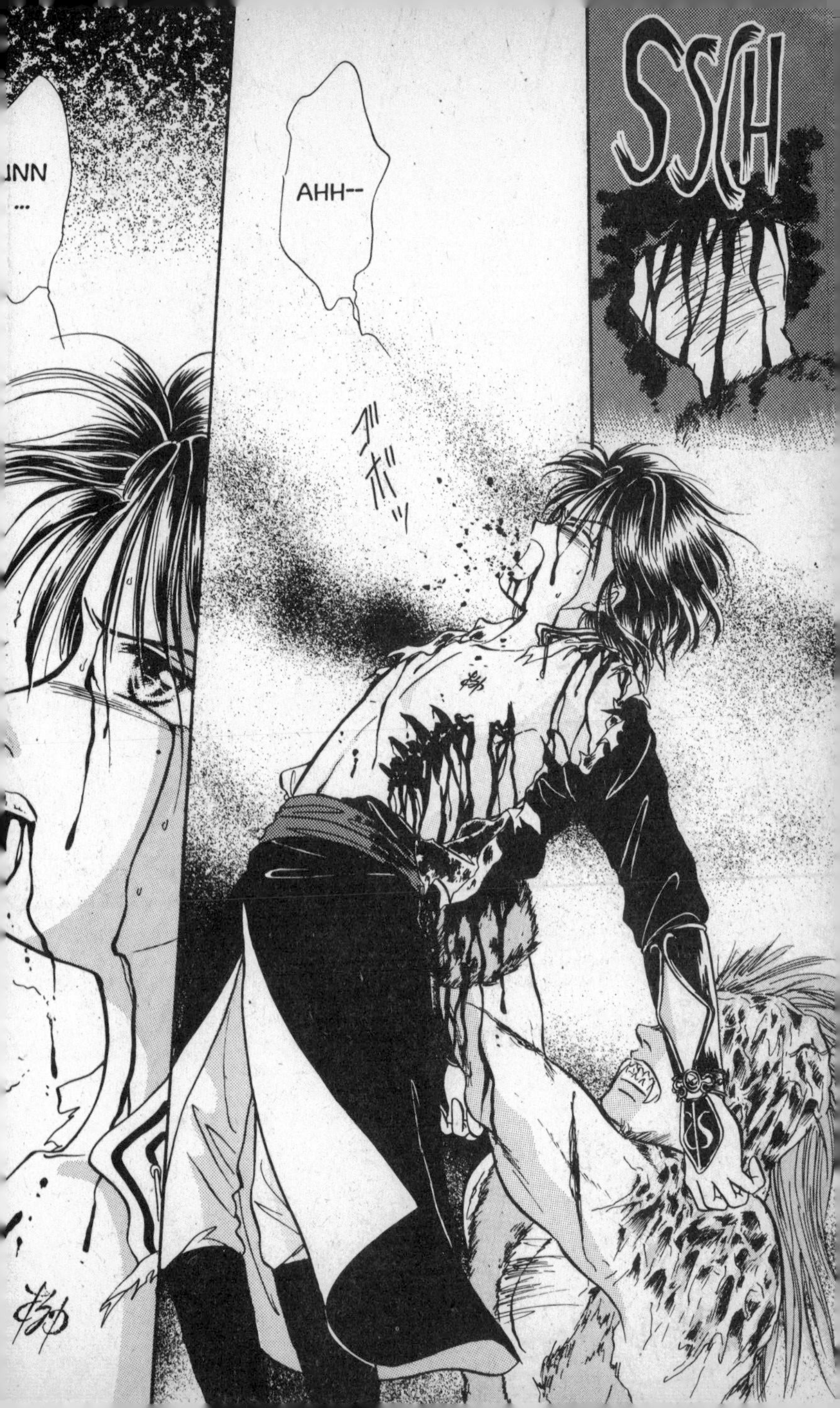
SSCH
AHH--
ゴボッ
NN
...

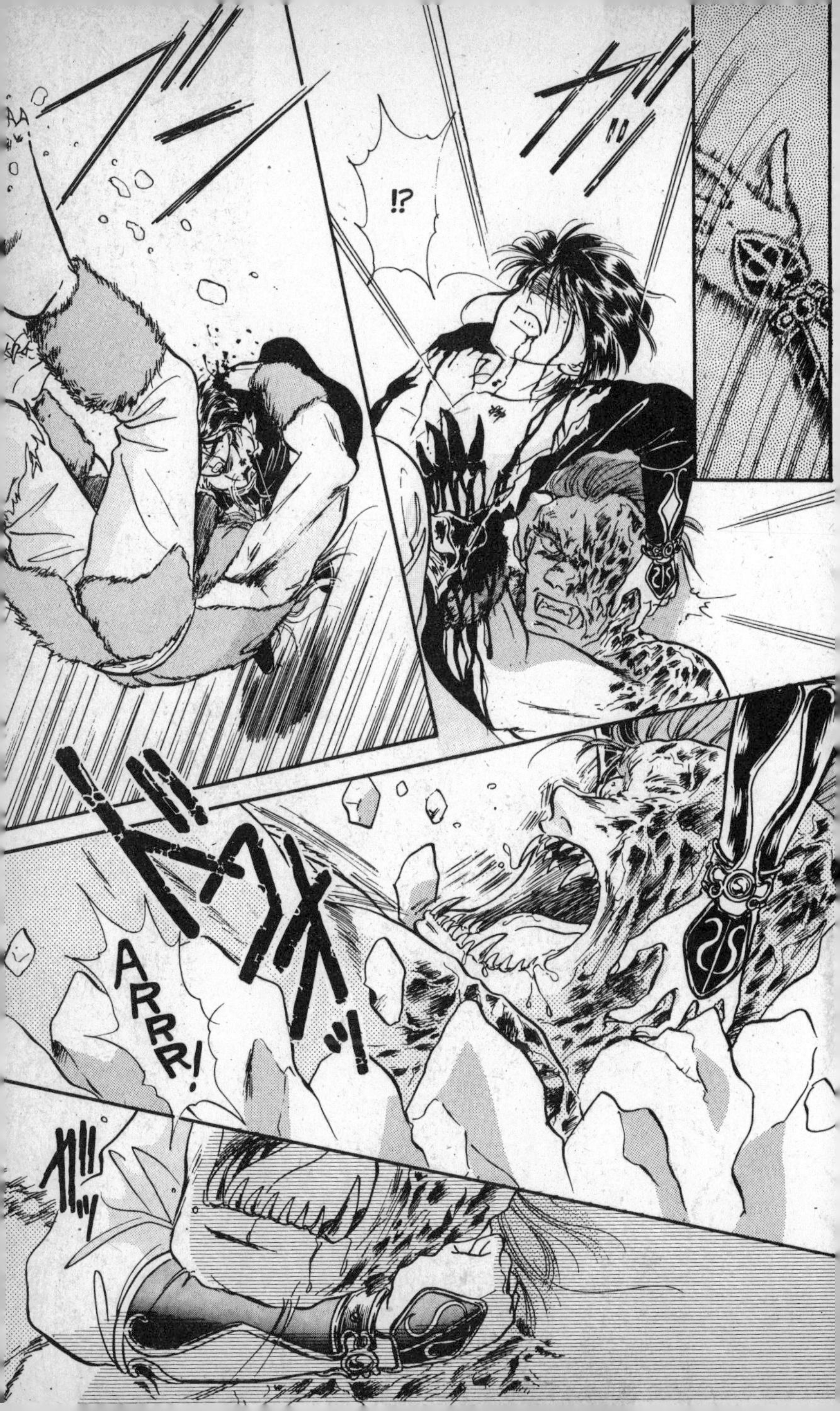

!?
ARRR!

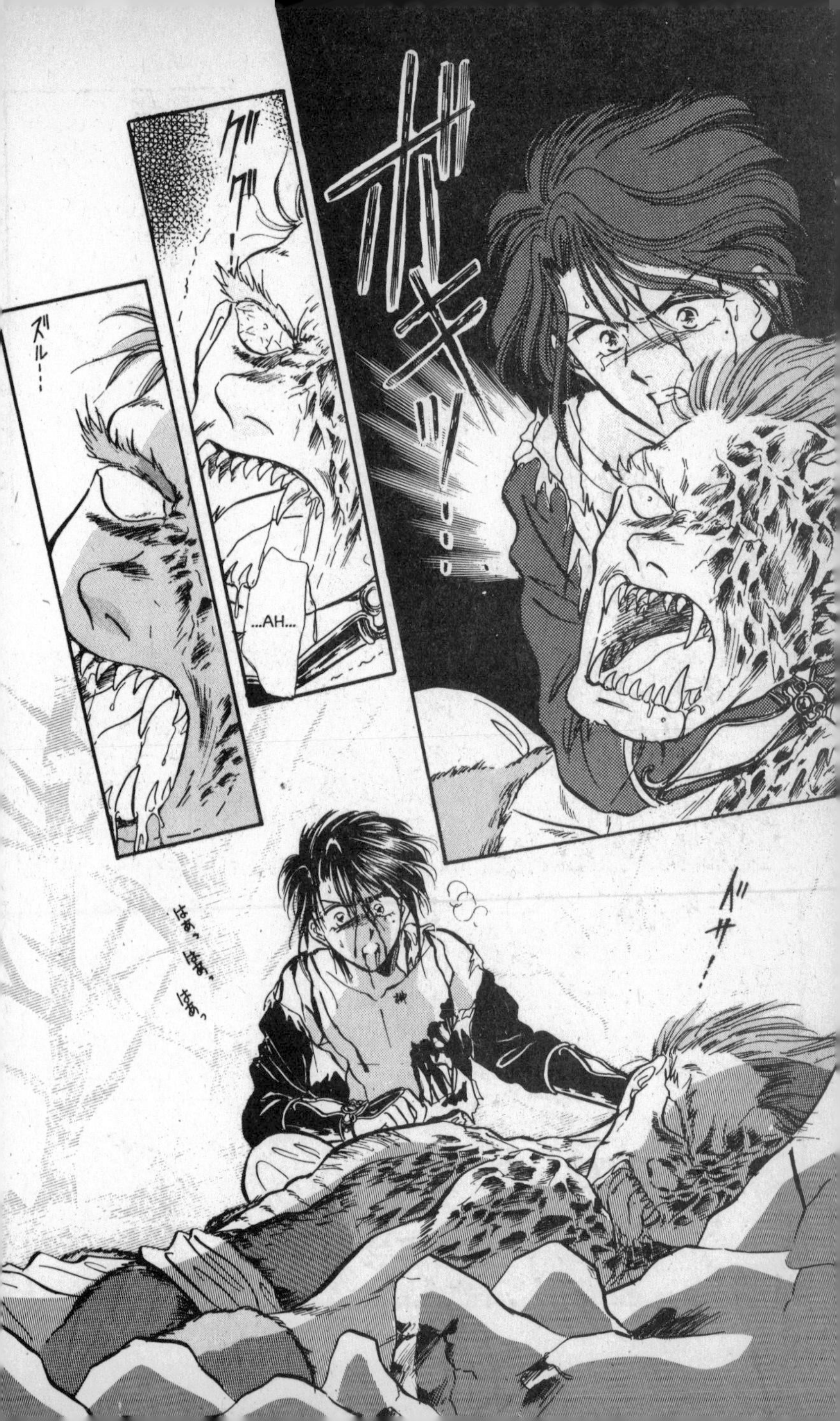
ガキッ!…
ググ…
…AH…
ズル…
ドサ…!
はぁっ はぁっ はぁっ

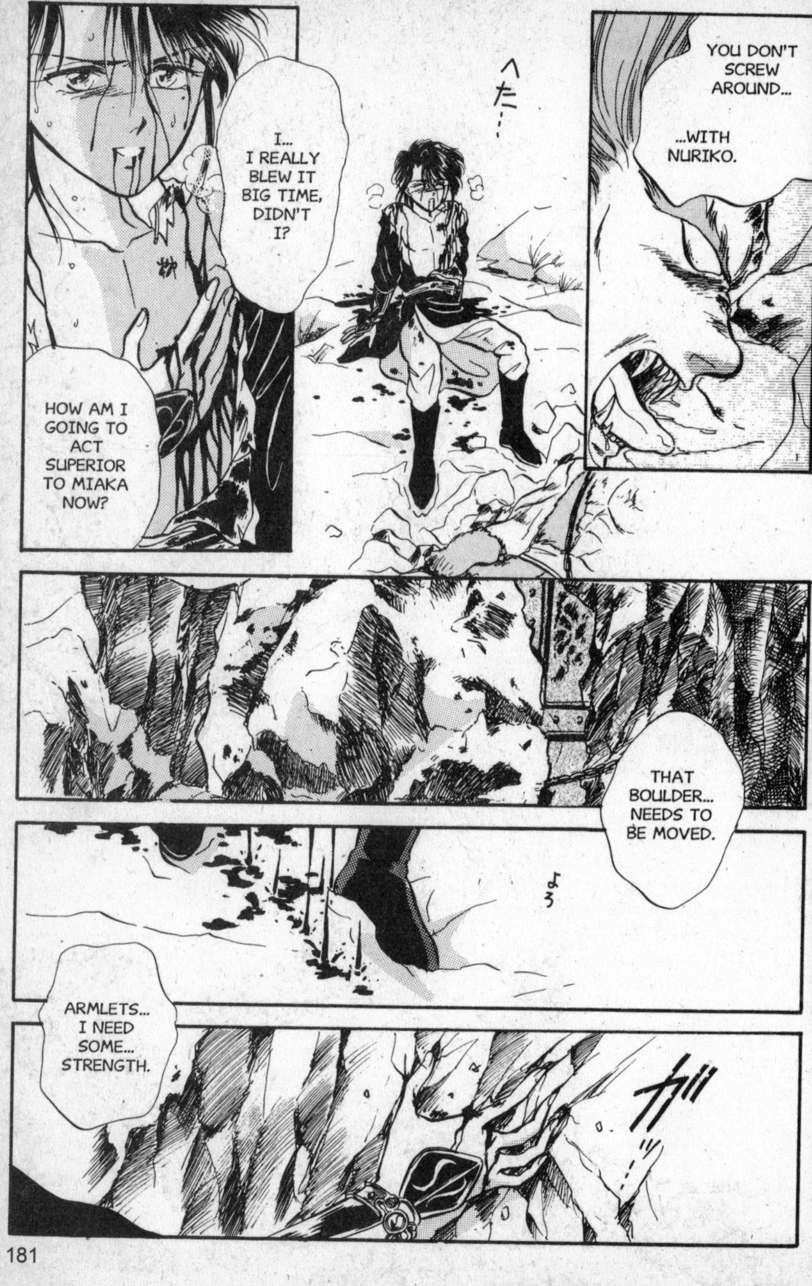
YOU DON'T SCREW AROUND...
...WITH NURIKO.
へた…
I... I REALLY BLEW IT BIG TIME, DIDN'T I?
HOW AM I GOING TO ACT SUPERIOR TO MIAKA NOW?
THAT BOULDER... NEEDS TO BE MOVED.
よろ
ARMLETS... I NEED SOME... STRENGTH.
ガッ

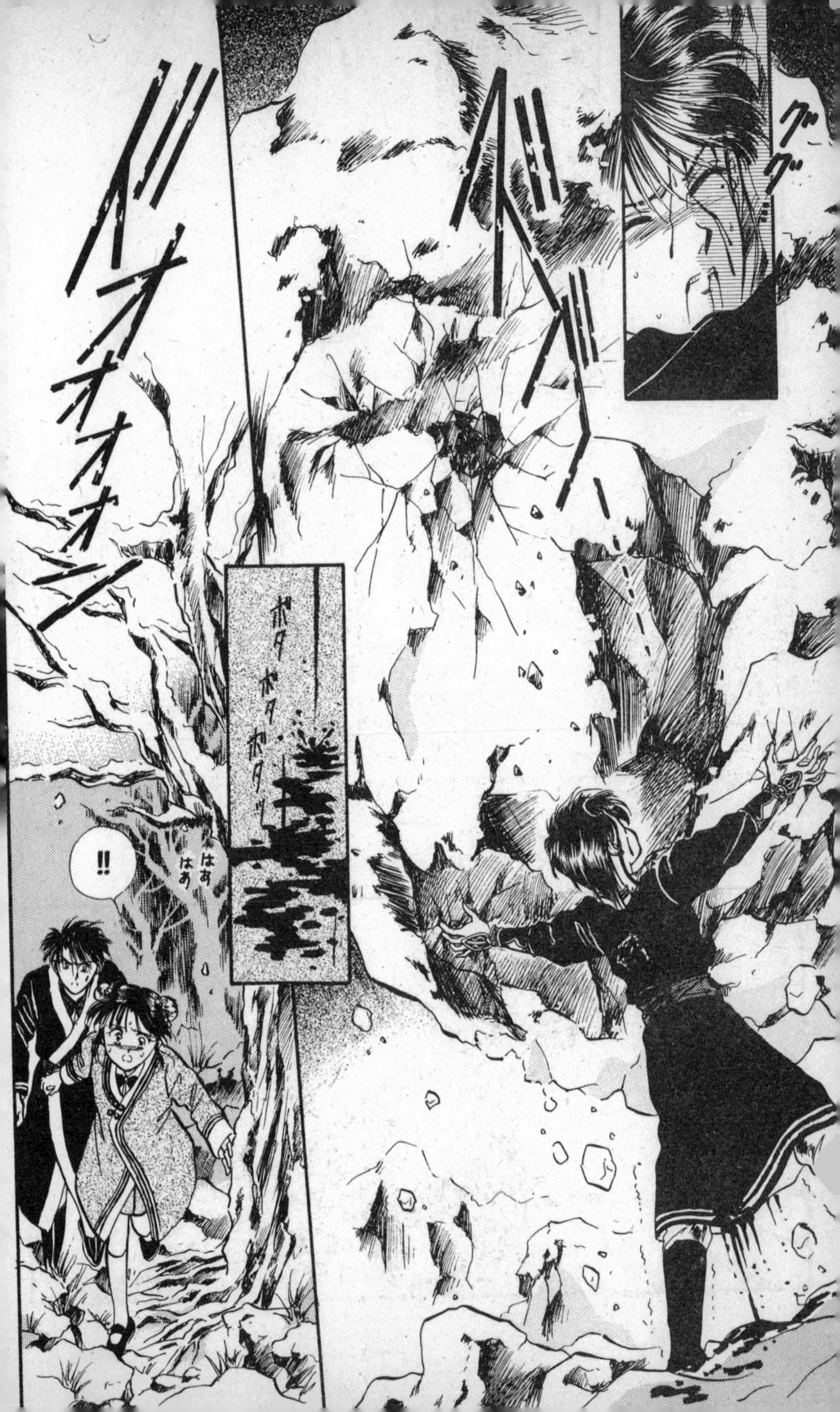
グ…グ
ポタ ポタ ポタッ
バオオオオン
はぁ はぁ
!!

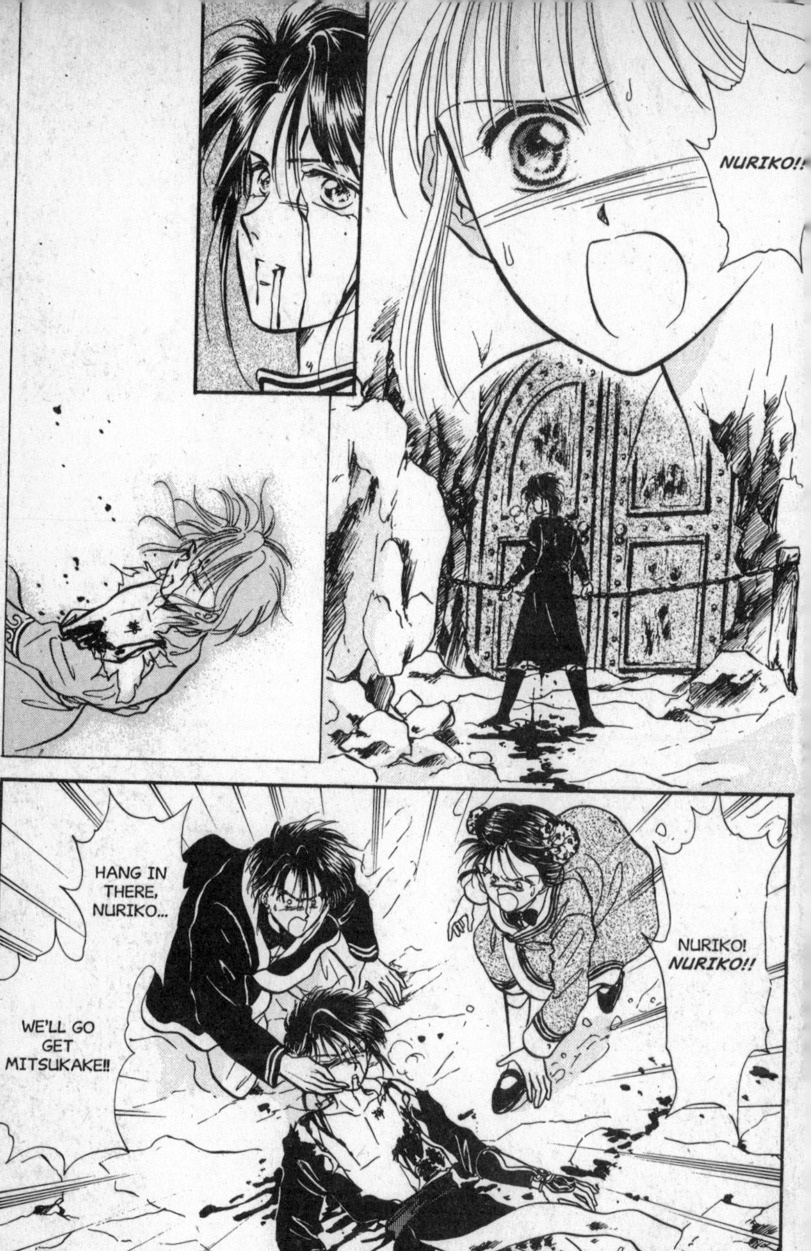
NURIKO!!
NURIKO! NURIKO!!
HANG IN THERE, NURIKO...
WE'LL GO GET MITSUKAKE!!

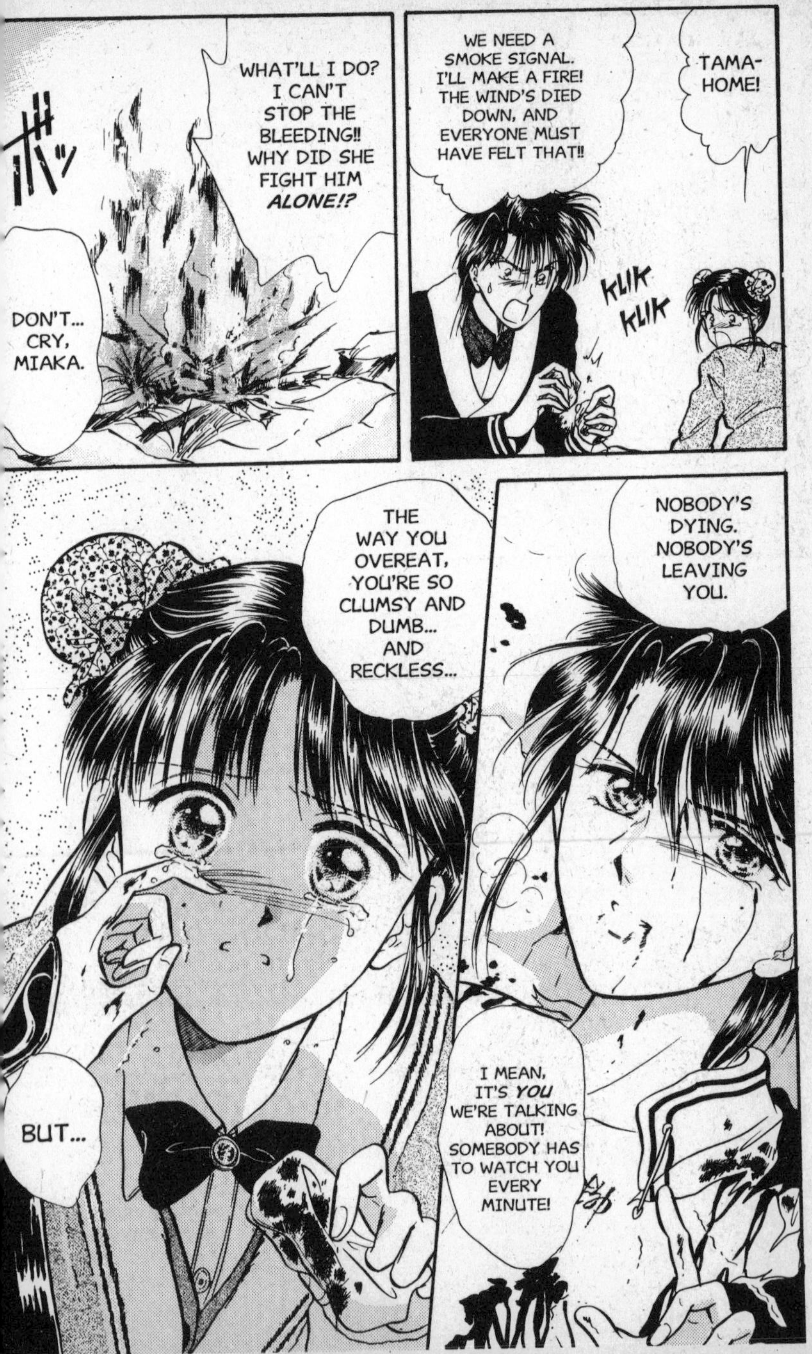
TAMA-HOME!
WE NEED A SMOKE SIGNAL. I'LL MAKE A FIRE! THE WIND'S DIED DOWN, AND EVERYONE MUST HAVE FELT THAT!!
KLIK KLIK
ボッ
WHAT'LL I DO? I CAN'T STOP THE BLEEDING!! WHY DID SHE FIGHT HIM *ALONE!?*
DON'T... CRY, MIAKA.
NOBODY'S DYING. NOBODY'S LEAVING YOU.
I MEAN, IT'S *YOU* WE'RE TALKING ABOUT! SOMEBODY HAS TO WATCH YOU EVERY MINUTE!
THE WAY YOU OVEREAT, YOU'RE SO CLUMSY AND DUMB... AND RECKLESS...
BUT...

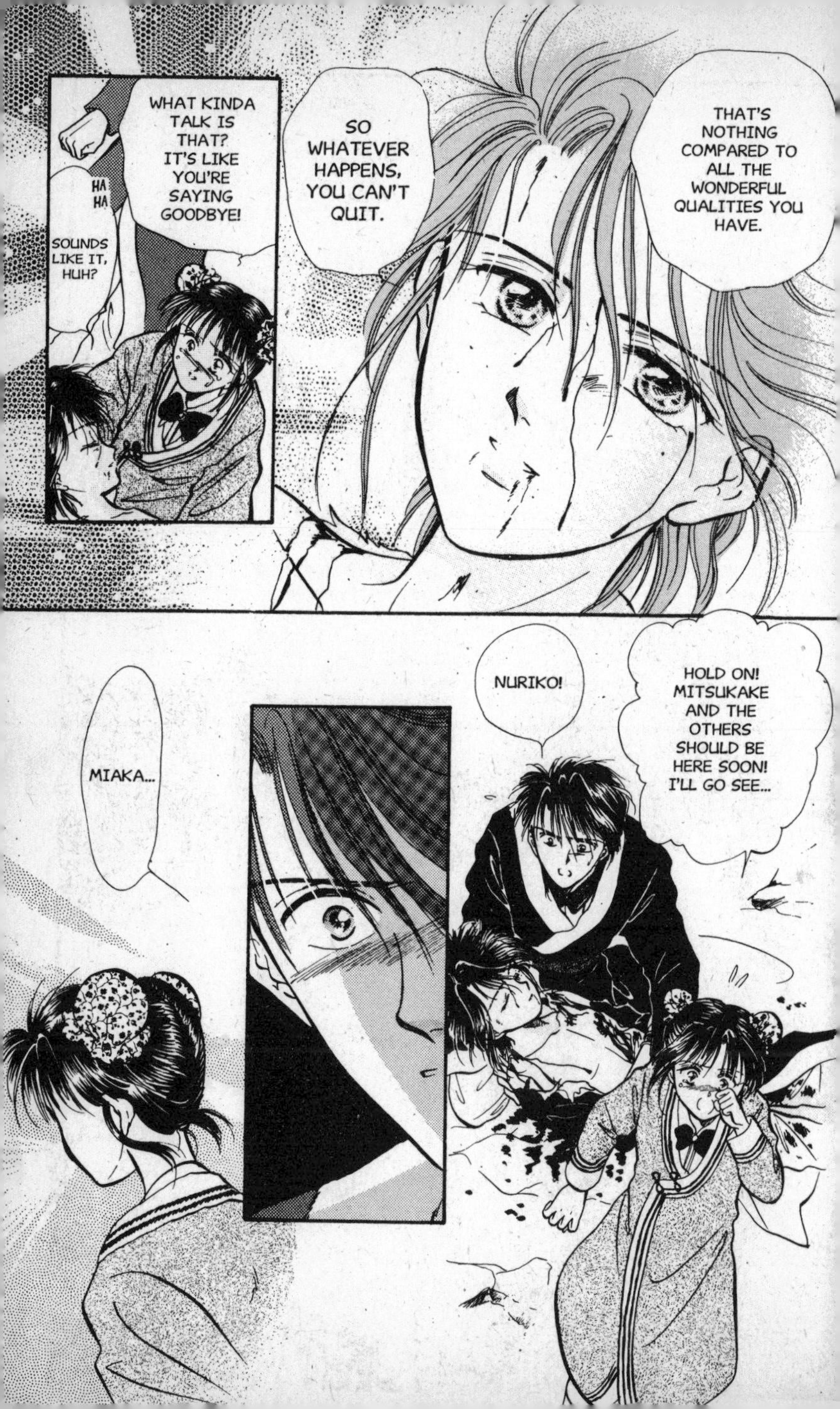
THAT'S NOTHING COMPARED TO ALL THE WONDERFUL QUALITIES YOU HAVE.
SO WHATEVER HAPPENS, YOU CAN'T QUIT.
WHAT KINDA TALK IS THAT? IT'S LIKE YOU'RE SAYING GOODBYE!
HA HA
SOUNDS LIKE IT, HUH?
HOLD ON! MITSUKAKE AND THE OTHERS SHOULD BE HERE SOON! I'LL GO SEE...
NURIKO!
MIAKA...

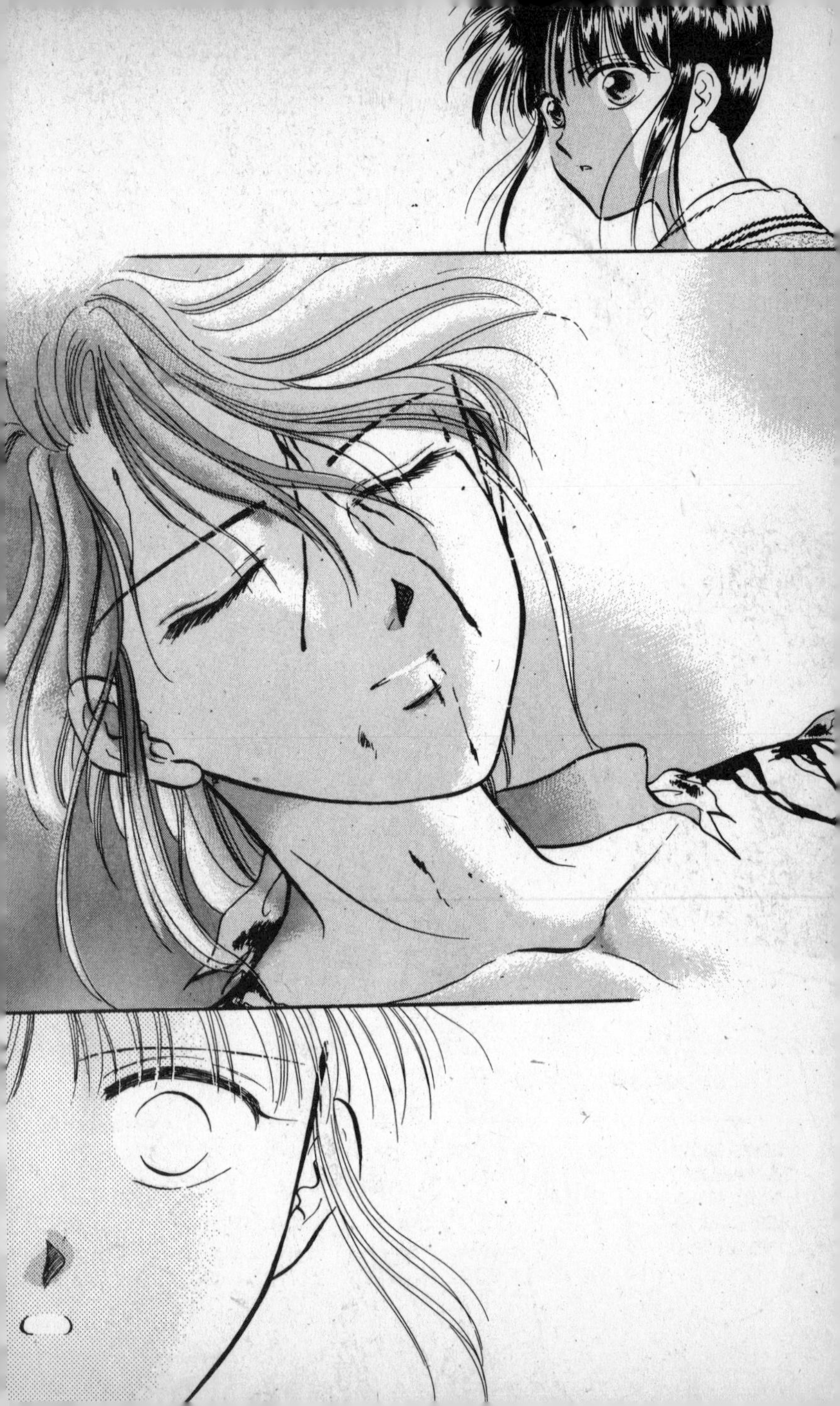

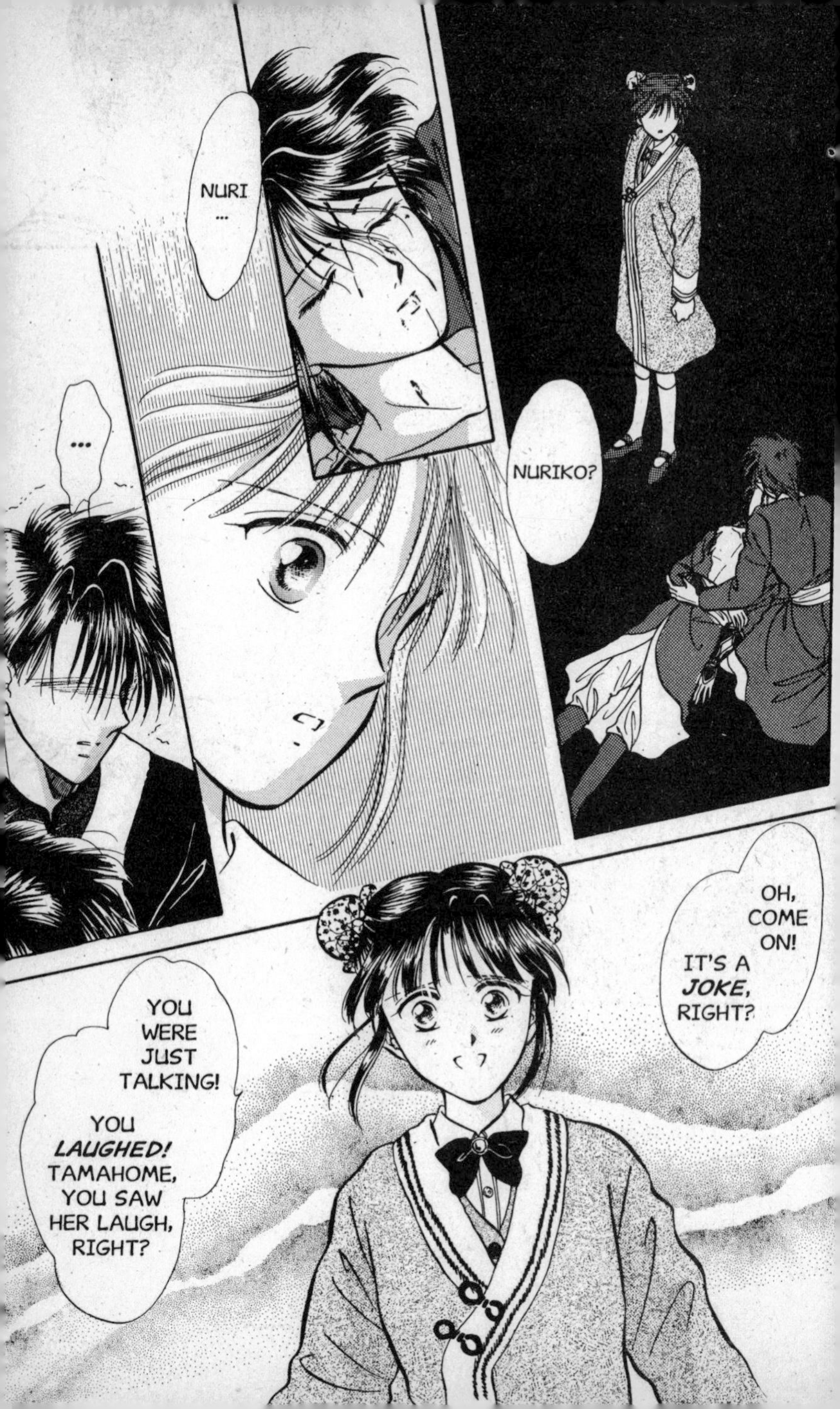
NURIKO?
NURI ...
...
OH, COME ON! IT'S A *JOKE*, RIGHT?
YOU WERE JUST TALKING!
YOU *LAUGHED!* TAMAHOME, YOU SAW HER LAUGH, RIGHT?

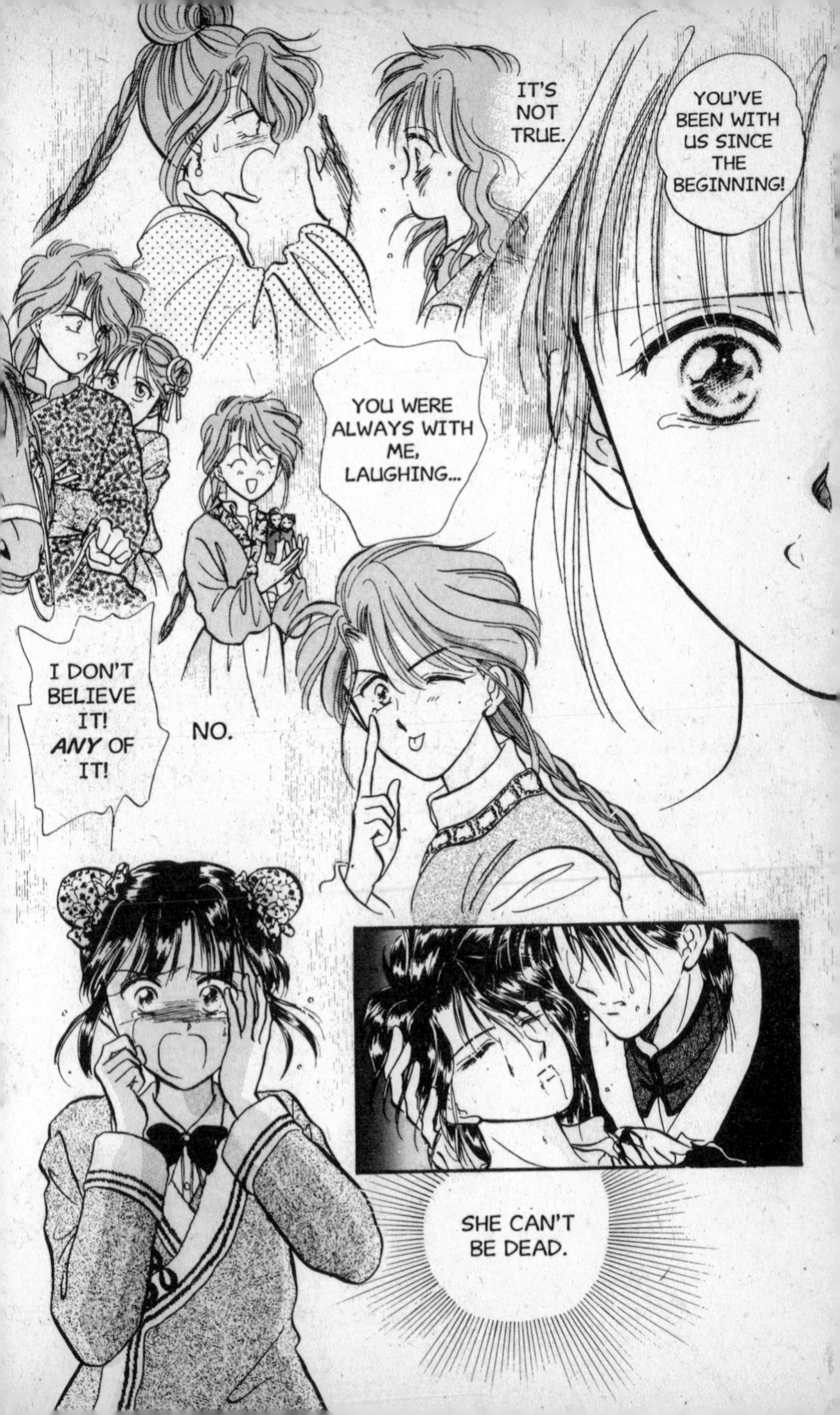
YOU'VE BEEN WITH US SINCE THE BEGINNING!
IT'S NOT TRUE.
YOU WERE ALWAYS WITH ME, LAUGHING...
NO.
I DON'T BELIEVE IT! ANY OF IT!
SHE CAN'T BE DEAD.

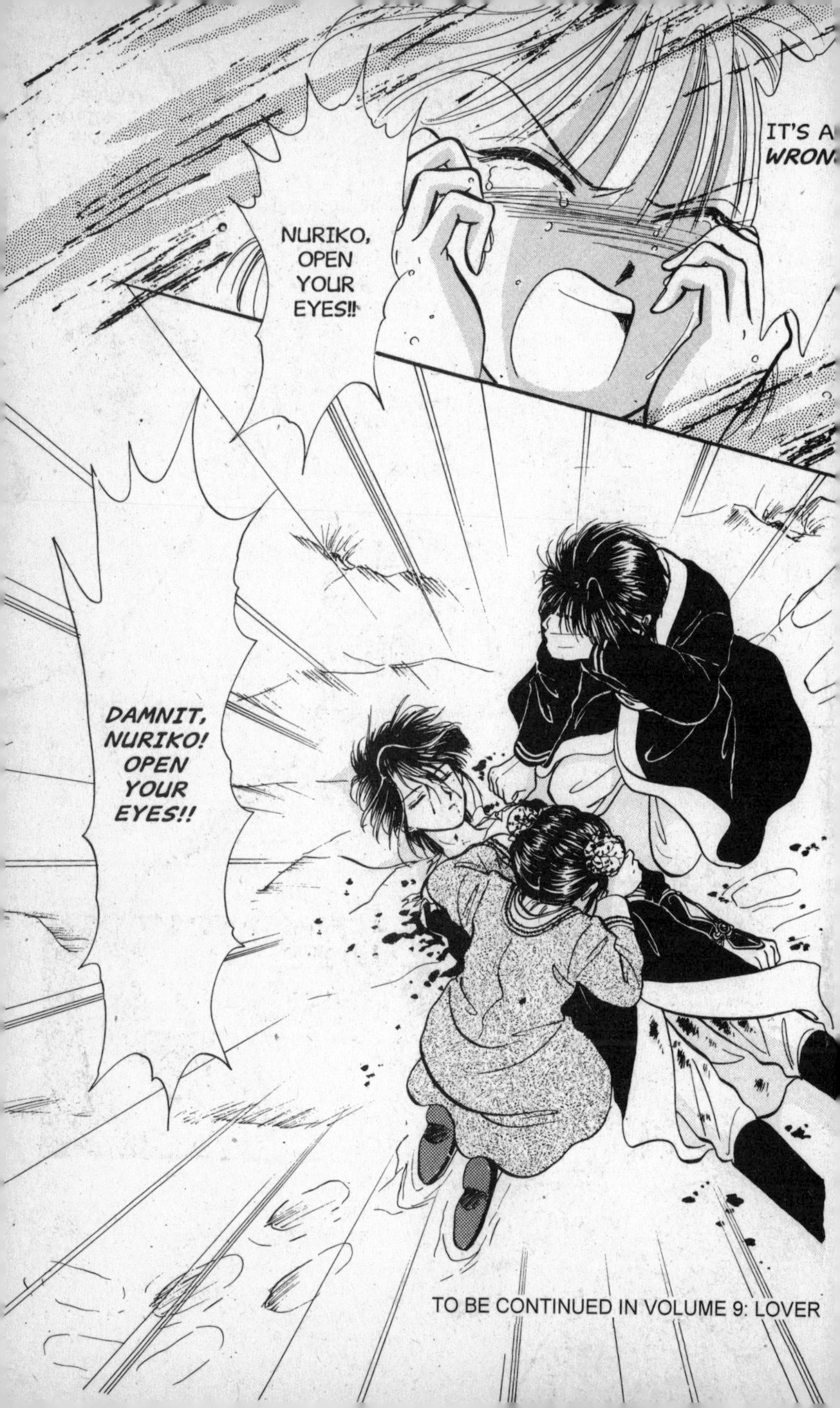
IT'S A
WRON
NURIKO, OPEN YOUR EYES!!
DAMNIT, NURIKO! OPEN YOUR EYES!!
TO BE CONTINUED IN VOLUME 9: LOVER

EDITOR'S RECOMMENDATIONS

If you enjoyed this volume of **fushigi yûgi**™ then here's some more manga you might be interested in.

Boys Over Flowers

Meet Tsukushi Makino, a poor girl at elite Eitoku Academy who becomes the target of the school bullies—four extremely rich and good-looking guys known as the F4. But when Tsukushi decides to fight back, she discovers that the bullies aren't everything they appear to be...

Doubt!!

When a cruel classmate humiliates her in public, plain Ai Maekawa retools her image and starts over at a new school. But while the new Ai is a hit with the boys, she finds there's more to reinventing herself than changing her looks.

Imadoki! Nowadays

In this popular Yuu Watase series, Tanpopo Yamazaki finds life at exclusive Meio Academy out of her league. The aristocratic student body snubs her, and the cute boy she noticed won't even acknowledge her existence. How will she survive in a school where superficiality reigns supreme?

The Fushigi Yûgi Guide to Sound Effects

Most of the sound effects in FUSHIGI YÛGI are the way Yuu Watase created them, in their original Japanese.

We created this glossary for a page-by-page, panel-by-panel explanation of the action and background noises. By using this guide, you may even learn some Japanese.

The glossary lists page and panel number. For example, page 1, panel 3, would be listed as 1.3.

23.4 FX: Ba (bwah)
24.1 FX: Golon (roll)
25.2 FX: Potsun (whisper)
26.1 FX: Gyu (squeeze)
26.1 FX: Bikun (jolt)
28.1-2 FX: Dokun dokun dokun dokun (ba-dump ba-dump ba-dump ba-dump)
29.2 FX: Ha (gasp)
29.4 FX: Shiiin (silence)
29.5 FX: Kukaaaa (zzzz)
30.1 FX: Suuu (zzz)
30.4 FX: Booo (aduuuuh)
31.1 FX: Su (fsh)
31.2 FX: Pacchiri (blink)
31.5 FX: Ta ta ta ta (pitter patter pitter patter)

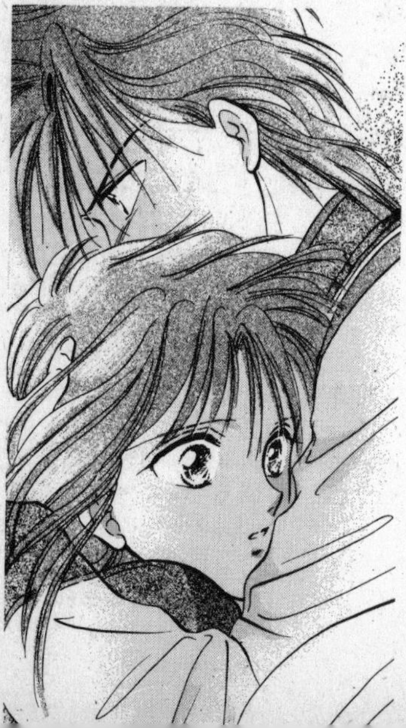

CHAPTER FORTY-THREE: THE SEALED CASTLE WALL

7.6 FX: Gushi gushi (rub rub)
8.3 FX: Gusu gusu (whimper)
8.5 FX: Gala gala (gttnk gttnk)
9.1 FX: Katsu katsu (clop clop)
9.5 FX: Zukin (zing)
11.1 FX: Ba (pwof)
11.1 FX: Pachi pachi (clap clap)
11.3 FX: Hyoko (stumble)
12.1 FX: Musuu (mrrrgh)
12.2 FX: Buuu (bwooooppt)
13.3 FX: Doki doki doki (ba-dump ba-dump ba-dump)
13.4 FX: Za (zsh)
14.3 FX: Gikuuu (shock)
17.2 FX: Za (zsh)
17.3 FX: Fu (heh)
17.4 FX: Kopopopo (glug glug)
18.1 FX: Baku baku baku baku (chomp chomp chomp chomp)
18.2 FX: Doki (ba-dump)
18.3 FX: Dogimagi (flustered)
18.3 FX: Mu (grr)
18.4 FX: Doka (boot)
19.2 FX: Ke (ha)
19.5 FX: Bu (ptooey)
20.3 FX: Hiso hiso (whisper whisper)
21.1 FX: Gui (push)
21.3 FX: Nikkori (smile)
21.4 FX: Gyu (squeeze)
21.4 FX: Mu (grr)
23.1 FX: Kulu (fwp)
23.2 FX: Gachan (gchnk)
23.3 FX: Shulu (shwf)
23.3 FX: Basa basa (bwaf bwaf)

61.3 FX: Yoro (wobble)
61.4 FX: Ta (tmp)
63.3 FX: Za (zsh)

CHAPTER FORTY-FIVE: HEARTLAND

66.1 FX: Hyulululululu (hwooooh)
67.5 FX: Shulu (shwrl)
68.1 FX: Ba (bwah)
68.2 FX: Gaaaan (gooong)
68.3 FX: Doboooon doboooon (dbooosh dboosh)
68.4 FX: Zaba (zwwoosh)
69.1 FX: Ba (pounce)
70.1 FX: Zazazaza (zshhhhhhwoooh)
70.3 FX: Zaa (zwoosh)
70.4 FX: A (whoa)
71.2 FX: Su (shww)
71.3 FX: Booo (aduuh)
74.4 FX: Sha (shwsh)
75.3 FX: Ba (turning away)
78.2 FX: Bulu (shiver)
78.4 FX: Doka doka doka (dwf dwf dwf)
79.2 FX: Da (dash)
79.4 FX: Ba (grab)
80.1 FX: Suto (stnk)
80.5 FX: Hiku hiku (twitch twitch)
80.5 FX: Doka doka (klop klop)
82.3 FX: Su (shw)
82.4 FX: Fugo fugo (hm hm)
88.2 FX: Basa (bwaf)
88.4 FX: Pata pata (pitter patter)
89.1 FX: Bululu (brrrr)
91.4 FX: Sawa sawa (fwooh)
92.4 FX: Dokun dokun dokun (ba-dump ba-dump ba-dump)

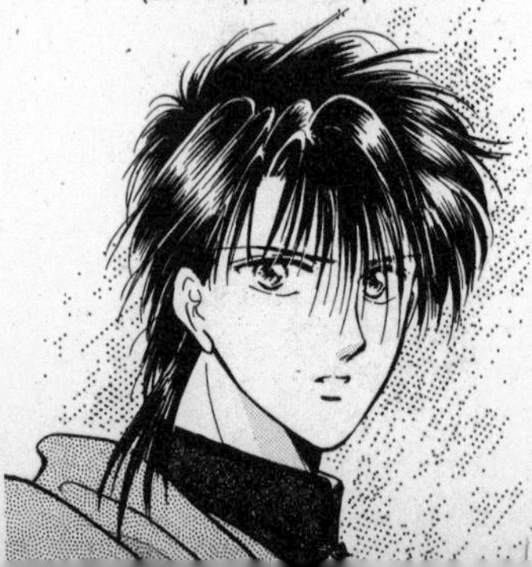

CHAPTER FORTY-FOUR: THE SPARK OF COMBAT

37.1 FX: Bun bun (shake shake)
37.2 FX: Don don don (bang bang bang)
37.3 FX: Don don (bang bang)
38.2 FX: Bashi (bzap)
38.3 FX: Ha (gasp)
38.4 FX: Ban (bam)
40.2 FX: Buuu (bwaaap)
40.3 FX: Dota dota (stomp stomp)
40.3 FX: Waaa (yaaaaagh)
40.4 FX: Kacha (kcht)
40.5 FX: Tatatata (tmptmptmptmp)
41.1 FX: Waaaaa (yraaaaagh)
42.1 FX: Hyun hyun (vwip vwip)
44.1 FX: Ha ha (huff huff)
44.3 FX: Kasa (rustle)
44.4 FX: Su (shw)
44.5 FX: Gui (yank)
45.2 FX: Muku (mwk)
46.1 FX: Bata bata (tmp tmp)
46.2 FX: Niko (smile)
48.4 FX: Ha (gasp)
50.2 FX: Ka (flash)
51.4 FX: Shuuuu (fshhh)
51.4 FX: Busu busu busu (crackle bshh bshh)
52.1 FX: Zee haa zee (wheeze huff huff)
52.2 FX: Hyuuu (hwoooh)
52.4 FX: Basa (bwsh)
54.1 FX: Ka (flash)
54.3 FX: Babababababa (bzapzapzapzap)
55.5 FX: Ha ha (huff huff)
55.5 FX: Bali bali (crackle crackle)
56.1 FX: Ha (gasp)
56.2 FX: Chaki (chkn)
57.1 FX: Niha (sneer)
57.2 FX: Ka (flash)
57.3 FX: Pishaaaa (pshiiiiing)
58.2 FX: Bali bali bali (crackle crackle crackle)
58.3 FX: Ka (flash)
59.2 FX: Bua (vwooooomsh)
60.1 FX: Bali bali bali (crackle crackle crackle)
60.2 FX: Shuuu (fshhhh)

CHAPTER FORTY-SEVEN: WATCHING YOU ALWAYS

134.3 FX: Ba (shove)
134.4 FX: Za (zoosh)
135.1 FX: Suto (stnk)
135.2 FX: Gululu (grrrrrowl)
135.3 FX: Za (zwsh)
135.4 FX: Gulu (grrrrr)
136.1 FX: Kyaaaa (aaaaaah)
136.2 FX: Pe (ptooey)
136.3 FX: Gululu (grrrrrowl)
136.4 FX: Waaan (waaaah)
137.1 FX: Za (zwosh)
137.2 FX: Ba (bwh)
137.3 FX: Gui (yank)
137.4 FX: Bo (vwooh)
138.1 FX: Boo (vwooosh)
138.2 FX: Dosa (thud)
138.3 FX: Za (zsh)
140.3 FX: Gu (grip)
140.4 FX: Ha (gasp)
140.5 FX: Bishi (vwpsh)
141.2 FX: Suta (shtk)
141.3 FX: Da (dash)
141.4 FX: Sa (halt)
144.1 FX: Yusa yusa (shake shake)
144.4 FX: Doki doki (ba-dump ba-dump)
144.5 FX: Kotsun (konk)
145.2 FX: Ba (jerk)
147.1 FX: Bosu (boff)
148.2 FX: Za (zsh)
149.1 FX: Gululu (grrrrr)
149.3 FX: Bishi (bwpsh)

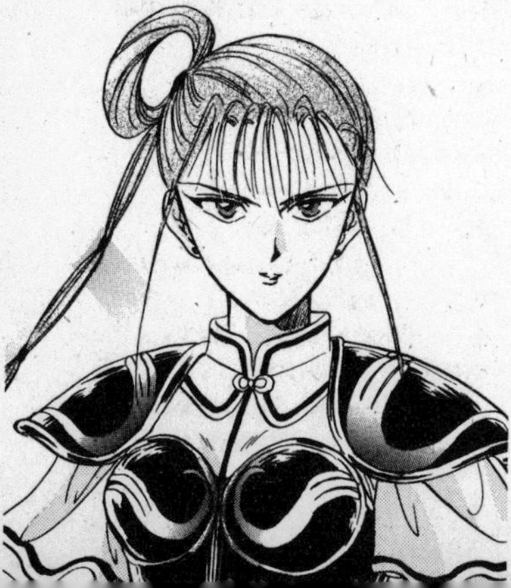

94-5.6 FX: Gyu (squeeze)
96.2 FX: Dokun dokun dokun dokun (ba-dump ba-dump ba-dump ba-dump)
97.1 FX: Za (rustle)
99.3 FX: Fulu fulu (tremble)
99.6 FX: Hihiiiin (whinny)
100.3 FX: Sha (shwsh)
101.2 FX: Jala (klink)
101.3 FX: Gulululu (grrrrr)

CHAPTER FORTY-SIX: MAELSTROM OF FEAR

104.2 FX: Ka ka (klp klp)
104.3 FX: Ka (klp)
106.2 FX: Ba (bwap)
107.2 FX: Kui (tug)
108.2 FX: Zaku (hack)
109.4 FX: Pachi (blink)
110.6 FX: Jala (klink)
113.3 FX: Hashi (rustle)
115.3 FX: Saku (shkt)
116.1 FX: Zaku (zksh)
116.2 FX: Basha (bwap)
116.3 FX: Pe pe (pwut phoo)
116.6 FX: Kii (creee)
117.2 FX: Patan (tnk)
118.1 FX: Kata (ktnk)
118.4 FX: Ba (dash)
119.3 FX: Byu (vwosh)
119.4 FX: Pita (freeze)
120.3 FX: Saku saku (shik shik)
120.4 FX: Ha (gasp)
121.2 FX: Da (dash)
121.3 FX: Ta ta (tmp tmp)
122-3.1 FX: Ta ta (tmp tmp)
122-3.2 FX: Ha ha (huff huff)
125.3 FX: Ha (gasp)
126.2 FX: Zulu (slip)
126.4 FX: Gui (pull)
128.2 FX: Ki (glare)
130.1 FX: Bulu (shiver)
130.5 FX: Gululu (grrrrrowl)
130.5 FX: Pita (freeze)
131.3 FX: Ba (bwah)

173.1 FX: Ku (straining)
173.1 FX: Gili gili (gnhhh)
173.2 FX: Hyun (hwoosh)
173.3 FX: Shu (shwah)
173.4 FX: Dokoo (pounding)
174.1 FX: Shu (shwish)
174.3 FX: Do (dboom)
174.4 FX: Doka (dwk)
174.5 FX: Gala gala (glnk glnk)
174.6 FX: Ha (gasp)
175.1 FX: Doon (doom)
175.2 FX: Dosha (thud)
175.3 FX: Ka (glint)
178.2 FX: Goho (gah)
179.2 FX: Ga (grab)
179.3 FX: Bun (hurl)
179.4 FX: Dokoo (dwak)
179.5 FX: Ga (ghik)
180.1 FX: Boki (crack)
180.2 FX: Gugu (choking)
180.3 FX: Zulu (zlish)
180.4 FX: Dosa (thud)
180.4 FX: Ha ha ha (huff huff huff)
181.2 FX: Heta (slump)
181.5 FX: Yoro (wobble)
181.6 FX: Ga (grip)
182.1 FX: Gugu (ghhhnn)
182.2 FX: Zugo (zgwooh)
182.3 FX: Pota pota pota (drip drip drip)
182.4 FX: Dooоon (da-booom)
182.4 FX: Ha ha (huff huff)
184.2 FX: Bo (bwoh)

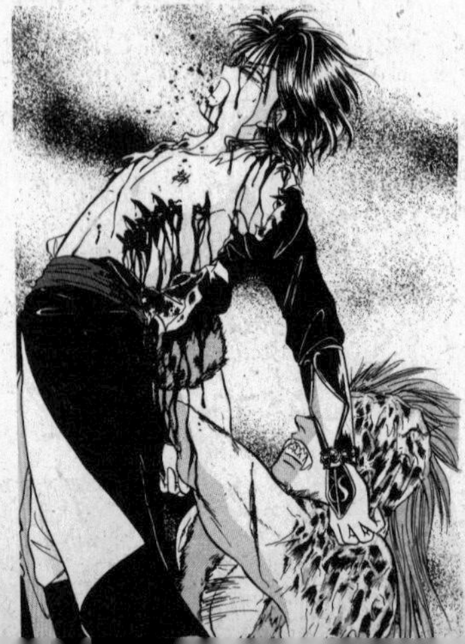

149.5 FX: Biku (jolt)
149.5 FX: Bishi (bwpsh)
150.1 FX: Byu (vwip)
150.2 FX: Byuuuu (fwooooh)
151.4 FX: Gatan (gtnk)
152.2 FX: Gali gali (scratch scratch)
152.4 FX: Tsun (tonk)
153.2 FX: Doku doku (plk plk)
153.3 FX: Buho (splurt)
153.4 FX: Solooo (tiptoe)
154.1 FX: Hahahaha (hahahaha)
154.2 FX: Pita (freeze)
156.3 FX: Pan (smack)
158.3 FX: Ha ha ha ha (huff huff huff huff)
158.4 FX: Bishi (snap)

CHAPTER FORTY-EIGHT: SORROW IN THE SNOW

161.1 FX: Chichi (chirp chirp)
161.3 FX: Gan gan (pound pound)
162.2 FX: Hyulululu (hwooooh)
162.6 FX: Koso (whisper)
163.2 FX: Zazazazaza (zshhzshzshzsh)
164.1 FX: Byooooo (vwooooooh)
164.1 FX: Pita (freeze)
164.2 FX: Kun (sniff)
164.3 FX: Piku (ping)
164.5 FX: Gululu (grrrrr)
165.2 FX: Kapo kapo (clop clop)
166.1 FX: Boso (mumble)
166.2 FX: Bata (whmp)
166.3 FX: Waaa (waaaah)
166.3 FX: Zawa zawa (chatter chatter)
166.3 FX: Hiso hiso (whisper whisper)
166.5 FX: Gashi gashi (scratch scratch)
168.5 FX: Saku (ksh)
169.2 FX: Gon gon (gonk gonk)
169.3 FX: Zu (zhmm)
169.4 FX: Biku (shudder)
170.2 FX: Za (zsh)
170.3 FX: Gulululu (grrrrr)
171.4 FX: Byuuu (vwoooooosh)
171.5 FX: Kaaa (glow)
172.1 FX: Shakin (shwching)
172.2 FX: Uoooooo (grooooaaah)
172.3 FX: Doka (slam)

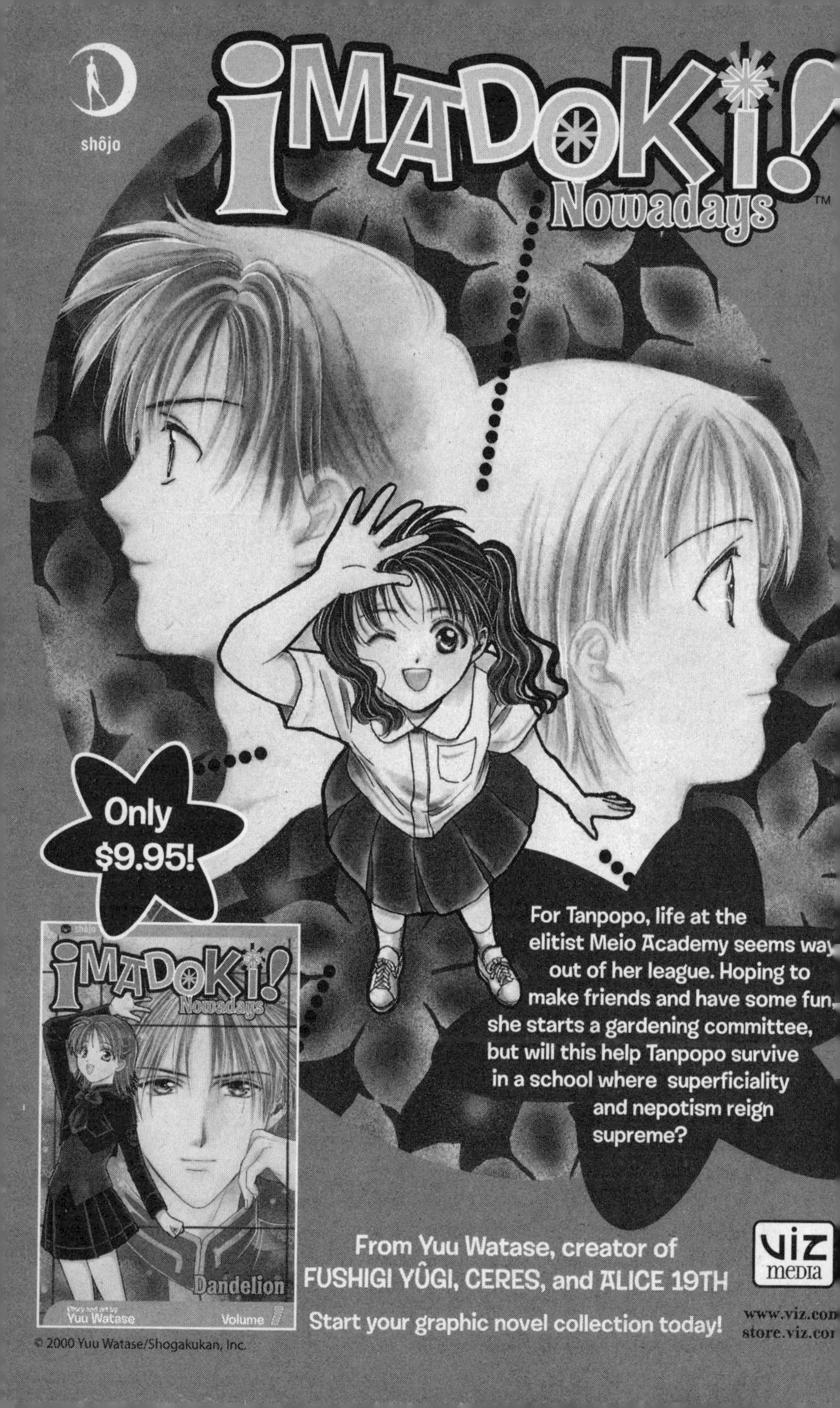

a Heavenly Maiden
From Yuu Watase, creator of ALICE 19TH, FUSHIGI YÛGI, and IMADOKI!–complete your collection today!
CERES
Celestial Legend
Manga only $9.95
VIZ MEDIA
www.viz.com
store.viz.com
© 1997 Yuu Watase/Shogakukan, Inc.

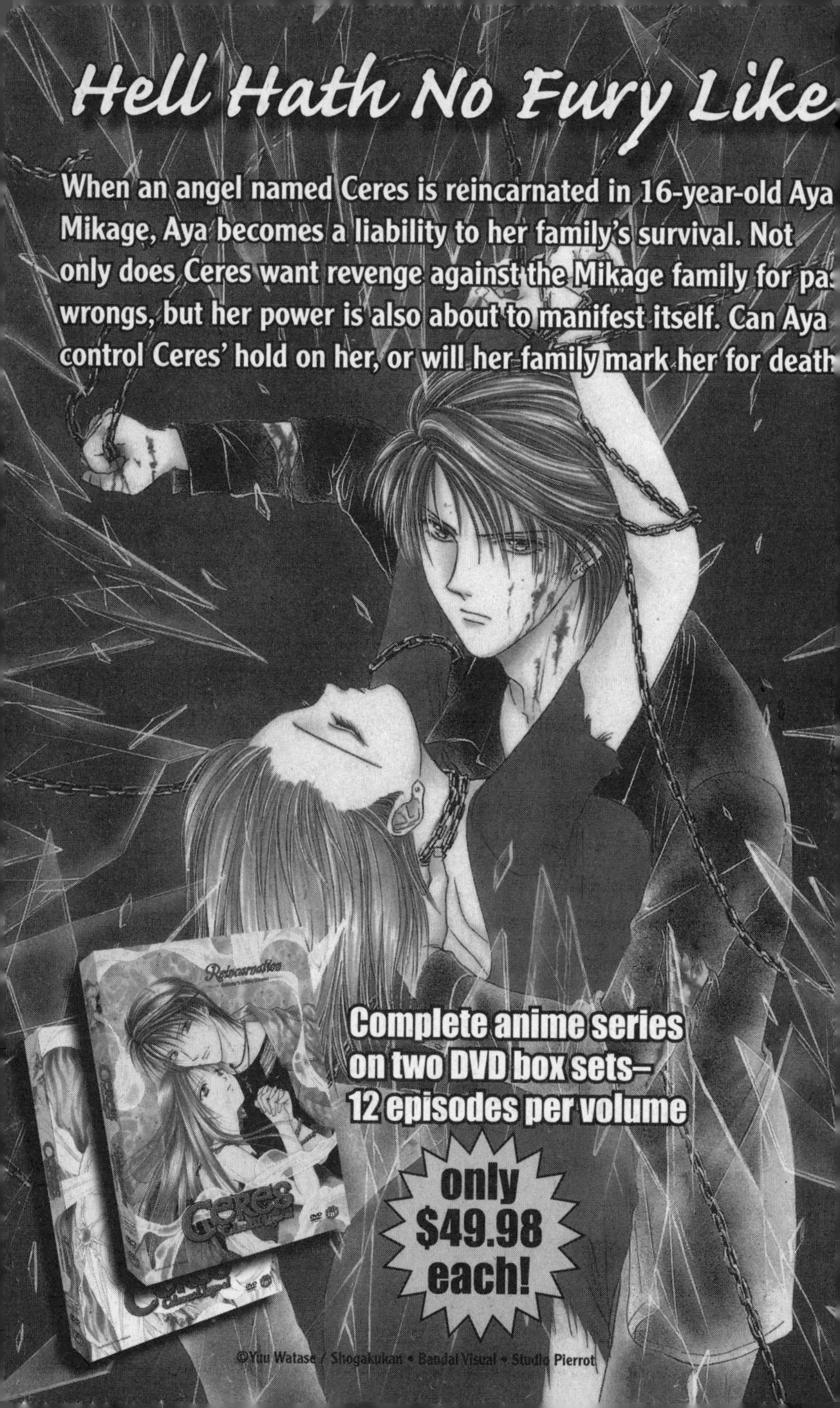

Hell Hath No Fury Like
When an angel named Ceres is reincarnated in 16-year-old Aya
Mikage, Aya becomes a liability to her family's survival. Not
only does Ceres want revenge against the Mikage family for pa
wrongs, but her power is also about to manifest itself. Can Aya
control Ceres' hold on her, or will her family mark her for death
Complete anime series
on two DVD box sets–
12 episodes per volume
only
$49.98
each!
©Yuu Watase / Shogakukan • Bandai Visual • Studio Pierrot

LOVE SHOJO? LET US KNOW!

☐ Please do NOT send me information about VIZ Media products, news and events, special offers, or other information.

☐ Please do NOT send me information from VIZ' trusted business partners.

Name: _____

Address: _____

City: _____ **State:** _____ **Zip:** _____

E-mail: _____

☐ Male ☐ Female **Date of Birth** (mm/dd/yyyy): ___ / ___ / ___ (Under 13? Parental consent required)

What race/ethnicity do you consider yourself? (check all that apply)

☐ White/Caucasian ☐ Black/African American ☐ Hispanic/Latino

☐ Asian/Pacific Islander ☐ Native American/Alaskan Native ☐ Other: _____

What VIZ shojo title(s) did you purchase? (indicate title(s) purchased)

_____

What other shojo titles from other publishers do you own? _____

_____

Reason for purchase: (check all that apply)

☐ Special offer ☐ Favorite title / author / artist / genre

☐ Gift ☐ Recommendation ☐ Collection

☐ Read excerpt in VIZ manga sampler ☐ Other _____

Where did you make your purchase? (please check one)

☐ Comic store ☐ Bookstore ☐ Mass/Grocery Store

☐ Newsstand ☐ Video/Video Game Store

☐ Online (site:_____) ☐ Other _____

How many shojo titles have you purchased in the last year? How many were VIZ shojo titles?
(please check one from each column)

SHOJO MANGA
- ☐ None
- ☐ 1 – 4
- ☐ 5 – 10
- ☐ 11+

VIZ SHOJO MANGA
- ☐ None
- ☐ 1 – 4
- ☐ 5 – 10
- ☐ 11+

What do you like most about shojo graphic novels? (check all that apply)

- ☐ Romance
- ☐ Comedy
- ☐ Other _____
- ☐ Drama / conflict
- ☐ Real-life storylines
- ☐ Fantasy
- ☐ Relatable characters

Do you purchase every volume of your favorite shojo series?

- ☐ Yes! Gotta have 'em as my own
- ☐ No. Please explain: _____

Who are your favorite shojo authors / artists? _____

_____

What shojo titles would like you translated and sold in English? _____

_____

THANK YOU! Please send the completed form to:

VIZ media

NJW Research
ATTN: VIZ Media Shojo Survey
42 Catharine Street
Poughkeepsie, NY 12601